永远的
尕布龙

（汉英对照）

辛 茜 著

青海师范大学外国语学院 译

青海人民出版社

图书在版编目（ＣＩＰ）数据

永远的尕布龙 : 汉英对照 / 辛茜著 ; 青海师范大
学外国语学院译 . -- 西宁 : 青海人民出版社 , 2024.
12. -- ISBN 978-7-225-06709-4

Ⅰ . I25

中国国家版本馆 CIP 数据核字第 2024RB9315 号

永远的尕布龙（汉英对照）

辛茜　著

青海师范大学外国语学院　译

出 版 人　樊原成

出版发行　青海人民出版社有限责任公司

　　　　　西宁市五四西路 71 号　邮政编码 : 810023　电话 : （0971）6143426（总编室）

发行热线　（0971）6143516/6137730

网　　址　http : //www.qhrmcbs.com

印　　刷　青海友谊彩色印刷有限责任公司

经　　销　新华书店

开　　本　787 mm × 1092 mm　1/16

印　　张　22.75

字　　数　550 千

版　　次　2024 年 12 月第 1 版　2024 年 12 月第 1 次印刷

书　　号　ISBN 978-7-225-06709-4

定　　价　118.00 元

《永远的尕布龙（汉英对照）》

青海师范大学外国语学院翻译团队

高原科学与可持续发展研究院高原外语教育与跨语言文化研究团队

共同翻译

策　　　划　李和成　马金芳　张胜鹏

翻译团队成员　李增垠　妥洪岩　张　卿　马吉德

　　　　　　　　吉先才让　籍天璐　刘　娇　才仁旺姆

校　　　译　Hastings Andrea Renee

目 录
Contents

引 子

尕布龙已经离开我们快十年了。

日子过得真快啊，想起他这一生对老百姓的情感，对老百姓的付出；想起他对青海省畜牧业的发展、对扶贫工作、对改善青海生态环境做出的贡献，没有人不感激在心，没有人不为之动容。

按常理，一位从政50年，在省级领导岗位上任职22年，担任过青海省委常委、副省长、省人大常委会副主任的高级领导干部，和我之间的距离应该是遥远的。我没有见过他，也没有在他活着的时候关注过他。但是，在他离开人世后的几年间，我却对他有了一种亲人般的爱戴和情感，有了书写他、记录他、赞美他的愿望。特别是，每当从书房向窗外遥望，看到那蓝色晴空、白云低垂的北山上，越来越深、越来越密集的一片片绿林，这种心情就越发强烈。

可是，讲述他的故事，写下他不同于寻常人的付出，一生的幸福与美好，需时光倒流60多年……我不敢确定，人们是否有耐心阅读，是否会真的相信，这个世界上，还会有这样的领导干部，这样的共产党员，这样善良忠厚、胸怀宽广的人。也同样不敢信任自己，是否有笔力能够把这样一位出生、生活、工作在青海大地，将自己一腔热血无私抛洒，为老百姓的疾苦、安危呕心沥血，为自己笃信的，为人民服务的郑重誓言鞠躬尽瘁、勤政廉明的当代英雄、时代楷模，真实而鲜活地呈现给大家。

The Author's Opening Words

How time flies! Gabulong has been away from us for almost ten years.

When thinking of his affection and dedication to the people of Qinghai throughout his life and his contribution to the development of animal husbandry, poverty alleviation, and improvement of the ecological environment of Qinghai Province, people are so grateful and moved.

Logically speaking, the distance between my life and someone of Gabulong's status should be considerable. He was a senior leading cadre who spent 50 years in politics, serving as a member of the Standing Committee of the Qinghai Provincial Party Committee and as the vice governor and deputy director of the Standing Committee of the Provincial People's Congress for 22 years. I never met Gabulong or followed his career when he was alive. Nevertheless, in the years that followed his passing, I developed an affection for him, coming to think of him as dearly as a family member. As I learned more about his life, a desire emerged to record and share it with others. I would often look out from the windows of my study at the green forests of Beishan Mountain under the blue sky and white clouds and think of Gabulong. As I took in this view, my desire to write about his life became deeper and deeper.

In order to tell his story, a life of happiness and beauty and extraordinary contribution, we'll need to turn the clock back more than 60 years. I am not sure whether people will be patient enough to read this story and whether they will really believe there was such an honest and open-minded leading cadre and CPC member in the world. I am also unsure of my ability to accurately and vividly convey his life to readers. He is a contemporary hero who was born, lived, and worked hard in Qinghai province to selflessly serve the common people.

鲜花盛开的哈勒景草原

尕布龙的家乡在青海省海北藏族自治州海晏县哈勒景蒙古族乡永丰村。村里有一条发源于肯特达坂山南麓的河，这是黄河上游一条重要的支流，汉语称湟水，蒙古语为博罗充克克。河水蜿蜒曲折，流过丰饶的金银滩草原，经湟水谷地汇入黄河。夏天的时候，湿润的河岸开满了金黄色的金露梅、白色的银露梅，一对对百灵鸟在草丛间耳鬓厮磨，欢唱鸣叫。

很早以前，在年钦夏格日山常年不化的积雪下，逐水草而居的羌人、

缓缓流淌的博罗充克克——湟水

The calmly flowing Boluochongkeke-the Huangshui River

The Flowery Halejing Prairie

Gabulong's hometown lies in Yongfeng Village that belongs to a Mongolian township—Halejing of Haiyan County of Haibei Tibetan Autonomous Prefecture of Qinghai Province. A river which originates from the southern foothill of the Kentedaban and consists of one of the most important branches of the upper reach of the Yellow River runs through the village. The river, being called Huangshui in Chinese and Boluochongkeke in Mongolian, winds its way on the Jinyintan Prairie to the Yellow River through the Huangshui Valley. In summer, yellow dasiphora fruticosa and white potentilla glabra line the wet banks of the river and pairs of larks hiding among grass, sing merrily.

Long ago, under the perennial snow of the Nianqin Xiageri Mountain, lived the nomadic ancestors of the Mongolian and Tibetan peoples who guarded the beautiful grasslands of Qinghai Lake.

In 1926, Gabulong was born to a nomadic Mongolian family of the Nanzuomo tribe. His ancestor Gushi Khan's 19th great-grandfather was Habutu Hasar, Ghengis Khan's younger brother; therefore, Gadeng, Gabulong's maternal grandfather, was a 9th generation descendant of Rob Zacha Khan.

In history, the Mongol nationality had east Mongolia and west Mongolia that had one ancestor—Genghis Khan. West Mongolia, referring to the □Weilate□Weitela Tribe of Moxi Mongol, mainly lived in Xinjiang, Gansu, Qinghai and Ningxia. It was called

蒙古族、藏族先民们守护着美丽的青海湖畔草原，过着逐水草而居的游牧生活。

尕布龙的母亲加合洛
Ms. Jiaheluo, Gabulong's Mother

1926 年，尕布龙出生在蒙古族南左末旗一户牧民人家，其祖先固始汗是成吉思汗二弟"一代神弓"哈布图·哈撒儿第十九代孙，尕布龙的外祖父尕登为罗布藏察汗第九代后裔。

历史上的蒙古族，分为东、西蒙古，成吉思汗是东、西蒙古各部共同的祖先。西蒙古，指漠西蒙古卫拉特部，主要生活在新疆、甘肃、青海、宁夏一带。元朝称西蒙古为"斡亦剌惕"；明朝称西蒙古为"瓦剌"，称东蒙古为"鞑靼"；清代时，西蒙古被称为"厄鲁特"。西蒙古内部又分为和硕特部、杜尔伯特部、土尔扈特部、准噶尔部，固始汗是西蒙古和硕特部的著名领袖，与西域历史的渊源关系甚密。

公元 1636 年，明崇祯九年，固始汗率领游牧于漠西阿尔泰山和天山一带的蒙古族和硕特部，来到青海湖沿岸、柴达木地区和祁连山皇城大草滩一带，定居于此，再没有返回原先的游牧地漠西草原。

据《青海蒙古族历史简编》记载，尕布龙家族群科札萨克旗原牧地从博罗充克克河源，即湟水西源起，东至囊吉立图巴尔布哈河，接丹噶尔城，北至大通河流域，南到图禄根河，西至恰克图北山木鲁。尕布龙的父亲索南木，是一位宽厚仁慈的蒙古族汉子，母亲加合洛美丽端庄、温和善良。他们育有三儿四女，尕布龙是三子，长子才布腾、次子拉哈措。

游牧民族的生活，像高山雪水，透彻明净；像一曲长歌，如泣如诉，更何况蒙古族意志顽强，骨子里流淌着祖先的血液，祖先的马蹄曾潮水般踏遍古老大陆，在辽阔无比的西域草原纵横驰骋，直到另一片海洋。他们的情感，他们的寄托，深邃凝重，永远充满着对祖先的追思；他们的生活，他们的期望，悠远绵长，永远伴随着马头琴的琴声，在月夜里与遥远沧桑的历史对话，在蓝天白云下，赶着羊群在草原上漫游……

"Woyilati" in the Yuan Dynasty, "Wala" in the Ming Dynasty and "E'lute" in the Qing Dynasty, while East Mongol was called "Dada". There were Heshuote Tribe, Duerbote Tribe, Tuergute Tribe and Zhungeer Tribe in West Mongol. Gushi Khan, the outstanding leader of Heshuote Tribe, was closely connected with the origin of the history of the Western Regions.

In 1636 (the 9th reign of the Emperor Chongzhen of the Ming Dynasty) Gushi Khan led his clansmen living in the Altai Mountains and Mount Tianshan to the areas along the Qinghai Lake, Chaidam district and Huangcheng prairie in the Qilian Mountain. Then they settled there and never went back to the place where they came from.

The Brief History of the Mongol Nationality in Qinghai Province records that the former pasture of Qunkezhasake Banner, to which Gabulong's family belonged, started from the origin of the Boluochongkeke River (the west branch of the Huangshui River), reaching the Nangjilitubaerbuha River in the east to connect Dange'r City, flowing through the Datong (Daitong) River drainage basin in the north, entering the Tulugen River in the South and the Beishan Mulu of Kyakhta in the west. Gabulong was lucky to have a lenient and kind father, Suonanmu and a great mother Jiaheluo who was a combination of beauty, mildness, and goodness. Gabulong also had two elder brothers, Caibuteng and Lahacuo.

The life of nomads is hard but simple. Mongolians are a strong-willed people, with the blood of their conquering ancestors flowing through their veins. Their emotions and sustenance are deep and solemn, always filled with the remembrance of their ancestors. Their lives and expectations follow the music of the horsehead fiddle (a traditional Mongolian bowed string instrument), in dialogue with the distance vicissitudes of history on moonlit nights. Under the blue sky and white clouds, they herd sheep roaming the grassland.

Gabulong's family was very poor; therefore, he herded sheep and cows when he was very young. He even worked as a horse-keeper to make a living, but he still couldn't make the ends meet. However, Gabulong was educated by his parents to believe that as long as he remained practical, modest, and down-to-earth, he would find his way no matter what unexpected difficulties he might encounter in life. They also instructed him to be kind to everything and everybody, as things also had lives and souls as human did.

尕布龙出生贫苦,从小放羊放牛。为了生活,他当过马夫,干过苦力,生活依然艰难。但是,尕布龙的父母亲从小就教育他,人生的道路上,将会遇到许多意想不到的挫折困难,只要能甩掉心高气傲的傲慢之气,脚踏实地,便能找到人生的方向。万物有灵、有性、有生命。不论对待人,还是对待万物,一定要有一颗慈悲之心、怜悯之心,要爱护草原上的一草一木,帮助身边的每一户乡民。

1949年,海晏县解放,人民政府很快撤旗建制,让生活在祁连山南麓和青海湖北岸之间的蒙古族分属于哈勒景、托勒、金滩、银滩、甘子河乡。从此,牧民们的生活如沐春风、如霖甘露,有了自己的天空和彩云,有了自己的草场和牛羊。

尕布龙和大哥才布腾、二哥拉哈措在一起

Gabulong and Caibuteng, Gabulong's eldest brother and Halacuo, Gabulong's second brother

绿色的山岭,流淌的小河,金银滩变成了花的海洋。那时,尕布龙已经是一位23岁的青年。固始汗后裔所拥有的健壮体魄、执拗性格,让他如勇士般矫健、刚强。他热爱草原生活,喜欢纵马、摔跤,更喜欢结交朋友,像父亲索南木一样生性豁达豪爽,像母亲加合洛一样乐善好施。

那时候,他单纯、年轻,心中无时无刻不梦想着自己能成为一名骑士,一个在草原上纵横铁马冰河的战士,让草原充满祥和、安宁与幸福。

解放军的到来,让他格外欣喜,也有些不安。一天,一早醒来,尕布龙就骑着马,跑到解放军驻地,悄悄观察。他睁着一双大大的眼睛,看解放军学习、练兵,看解放军像牧人一样帮着老人去放牧。他不明白,眼前身穿黄绿军服、头戴红五星军帽、脚打绑带的解放军战士,为什么每天脸上都挂着笑容、嘴里哼着歌,勤快地帮着村子里的牧民收青稞、捡牛粪、拾柴、打水、扫院子;为什么干完活了,不在牧人家吃饭、喝茶,还要赶回去自己做饭吃。渐渐地,他喜欢上了解放军,喜欢上了闪烁在他们军帽

He was taught to protect the grassland and to help his fellow villagers.

In 1949, Haiyan County was liberated by the People's Liberation Army, and soon the local people's government formed its organizational system in place of the former tribal systems. The Mongolian people who lived along the southern foothill of the Qilian Mountain and the north shore of the Qinghai Lake were designated to the villages of Halejing, Tuole, Jintan, Yintan, and Ganzihe. Since then, those herdsmen began to control their own fate and step on a road of pursuing happy life.

The change of the social system brought a fresh look on nature so Jinyintan Prairie looked even more beautiful with lush grass and colorful wild flowers. Gabulong, a 23-year-old young man who was as physically and mentally strong as his ancestors, enjoyed his life on the prairie by riding horses, practicing wrestling, and making friends. He was as generous as his father and as kind as his mother.

Being simple and young, his dream was to become a horseman who protected the peace and happiness of his fellowmen living on the grassland by patrolling on his horse.

The arrival of the PLA men gave him both joy and worry. One day, getting up very early, he rode his horse to the PLA garrison to observe them. He found that no matter what those soldiers did (learning, training, helping the local herdsmen with herding), they were always happy. He didn't understand why they would merrily help the villagers harvest barley crops, collect yak downs and firewood, fetch water and sweep courtyards; he didn't understand why they would go back to the garrison to cook by themselves instead of having a cup of tea or dinner at the villagers' home after their work. He gradually started to like the soldiers wearing army green military uniform and cap with a red star on it. He, a young man who had never left his hometown, was deeply attracted to them.

One day, he borrowed a soldier's military uniform and quietly went to a photo studio to capture a picture of a new dream for his life. He had come to the realization that there were soldiers in this world who were totally different from the ones employed by former herd owners and bandits. After being exposed to this new way of life, he developed a dream to become like the soldiers of the People's Liberation Army and devote himself to helping the poor.

In the early years after the liberation, Jintan villagers and Yintan villagers had disputes over the grassland. Among them, the conflict between the Tibetan Dayu tribe

上的那颗红五星。这对于一个从来没离开过草原的年轻人，有着多么大的吸引力啊！

有一天，他借战士的军装穿上，悄悄去照相馆留下了生平第一张照片。原来，这个世界上，还有与牧主头人、土匪不一样的兵，还有与自己的生活不那么像的另一种生活。他憧憬着、渴盼着，希望自己能像解放军一样，至少给身处黑暗的人们送去一丝光亮，给天下穷苦人给予星星点点的帮助。

解放初期，金滩乡与银滩乡长期以来因草场纠纷遗留下许多矛盾。特别是藏族达玉部落与群科札萨克蒙古族之间的草山纠纷，使双方关系发展到持械殴斗、纠葛连连的地步。蒙古族乡官府控告，要求驱逐达玉部落，达玉部落也有心返回黄河南岸的芒拉故地。由于解放军的进入，反动势力更是不甘心失败，借机散布谣言，制造纠纷，激化矛盾，强占了两个部落曾经为此争执不休的塔

尕布龙借了身军装，留下了平生第一张照片

Gabulong's first photo taken in a photo studio when he was in a borrowed set of PLA man's uniform.

勒滩草原，让不明真相的两个部落又一次上了敌人的当，以致剑拔弩张，互不相让。

尕布龙看在眼里，心中焦虑。他很愿意给解放军帮忙，因为他最清楚这里面的是是非非、恩恩怨怨，也只有他们自己才能化解心中的冰山。于是，他独自一人，骑马去金滩乡、银滩乡找到两个部落的千户和头人反复说明情况，等双方头人的态度有了转机，才带着解放军拿着哈达、茯茶，到头人家里做工作。用他坦诚直率、公平端正的良好人品，凭借他长期以来与头人们建立起来的朋友关系，帮助解放军和平解决了两个乡的草山纠纷，避免了不必要的争斗。

1950年，尕布龙被送到西北革命干部培训班学习。在这之前，他曾经在湟源县读过两年书，可这一次，他在学校学到的东西，让他刻骨铭心。

and the Mongolian Kozasack tribe had escalated to armed fights. The head of the Mongolian tribe made accusations against the leader of the Tibetan tribe, asking the Tibetan tribe to be expelled. The Tibetan tribe also wanted to leave and go back to their old home located in Mangla on the south bank of the Yellow River. Because of the entry of the People's Liberation Army, the reactionary forces were even more unwilling to accept defeat. They took the opportunity to spread rumors, create conflicts, intensify disputes, and forcibly occupy the disputed Taletan grassland. The two tribes of the land were not aware of the truth underneath the rumors, and their conflict continued to escalate.

Gabulong was anxious about this situation. Because he understood the cause of the dispute between the two tribes, he was willing to help the People's Liberation Army. He knew that only the tribal members themselves could dissolve the hatred between them; therefore, he rode alone to Jintan Village and Yintan Village on his horse to repeatedly explain the real situation to the tribal and military officials and tribal chiefs. When the attitude of the leaders of both sides began to turn around, he went to them again with members of People's Liberation Army to solve the problems, bringing gifts of hada and brick tea. Finally, with his wisdom, honesty, and integrity as well as his friendship with the officials and chiefs, he successfully solved the dispute between the two townships without unnecessary fights.

In 1950, Gabulong was dispatched to a training course for revolutionary cadres in Northwest China. Although he had previously studied in Huangyuan County for two years, he was deeply impressed by what he learned this time. He began to realize that only the Communist Party of China led by Chairman Mao at that time could save the life of herdsmen and make ordinary people control their own fates. He was also aware that the only way to develop the minority areas was to acquire knowledge.

In 1952, the PLA soldiers left for Xizang from Xining City via Haiyan County, which was a big event at the beginning of the founding of the People's Republic of China.

As Gabulong was burly and strong and an excellent speaker of Tibetan, Mongolian, and Chinese, he was recommended as an interpreter, going to Xizang with the soldiers. It was at this time that Gabulong acquired the name we know him by. He was originally named Gabuzang, which was also the name of another young villager. With his

他认识到，只有中国共产党才能领导劳动人民彻底翻身，只有毛主席领导的中国共产党才是牧人的救命恩人，只有掌握了知识，才能让落后的民族地区发展、腾飞。

1952年，中国人民解放军从西宁出发，途经海晏，进驻西藏。这在当时，是中华人民共和国成立初期的一件大事。

尕布龙身材魁梧结实，嗓音浑厚响亮，藏语、蒙古语极好，汉话讲得也不错，因此，他被推荐为"通司"（翻译），随解放军进藏。其实，尕布龙原名叫尕布藏，当时村子里还有一个年轻人也叫这个名字，解放军便征求他的意见，给他重新起了个名字——尕布龙。当然，这件事现已极少有人知道了。

到了西藏后，随同进藏的一部分人留在西藏参加了工作，可尕布龙牵挂家中父母妻儿，思念着哈勒景草原，执意要返回家乡。出发时，解放军给他发了30块白洋，返回途中，他一路住在解放军兵站。

那时候，慕生忠将军的探路大军还没有进藏，西藏通往青海的路途漫长而艰险。翻过唐古拉山后，苍茫无边的可可西里大草原寂寥无声，群山巍峨，静默不语，清澈的河水在空气稀薄的天界汩汩独行。

傍晚，骑着马的尕布龙和几个乡亲疲惫不堪地找到了可可西里兵站。此时，驻守兵站的干部和战士正忙作一团。一位初上高原的解放军某部团长，吃过饭后，不知是因为水土不服还是高原反应，腹泻不止，生命垂危。尕布龙见状，扯过马缰绳，疾驰如飞地进入深山，采回来一种不知名的草药，让这位团长嚼碎服下。围在一旁焦急等待的战士们眼睁睁看着，服过草药的团长很快止住腹泻，缓过神来。大家松了一口气，团长更是感激不尽，他便喜欢上了这位年轻、率真、朴实的蒙古族青年。晚上，他和尕布龙聊了很久，给他讲自己的战斗故事、革命经历，鼓励他回到家乡后，要继续努力工作，为新中国的成长、新牧区的建设出把力。

回到家乡后，尕布龙当上了民兵连连长。他白天背着枪骑着马，配合解放军在草原上宣传党的政策。晚上维护治安，保障牧民的财产和生命安全。

当时，草原上常有土匪出没，以马德山为首的残匪，给草原带来了很大威胁。为了剿灭这伙匪帮，从1950年起，解放军和民兵连整整战斗了两年，耗费了大量的人力、物力、财力。

permission, the PLA soldiers decided to rename him Gabulong.

After arriving in Xizang, some accompanying people chose to settle there, but Gabulong missed his family and hometown so much that he insisted on going back. He was given some money by the army and allowed to stay at PLA garrisons along the route.

At that time, General Mu Shengzhong had not yet arrived in Xizang with his troops. The journey between Xining and Xizang was far and difficult. Beyond the Tanggula Mountains, the endless Hoh Xil Prairie and the great mountains around it stood silently, but only the gurgle of the clear rivers that ran by themselves to the skyline could be heard.

One night, Gabulong along with several villagers arrived at the Hoh Xil garrison. The soldiers there were rushing everywhere for a regimental commander began to have severe diarrhea after supper and fell very ill. No one knew whether it was caused by non-acclimatization or high altitude. When Gabulong found out, he rushed to the forest and came back with an unknown herb. He instructed the patient to chew the herb, and soon the commander recovered. Everyone breathed a sigh of relief, and the commander was especially grateful to the young and simple Mongolian man who had come to his rescue. That evening, he talked with Gabulong for a long time, sharing his battle stories and revolutionary experiences. He also encouraged Gabulong to continue working hard after returning to his hometown to contribute to the development of this newly founded country.

After Gabulong returned home, he became commander of the militia company. Armed with a gun, he traveled by horse to help the PLA spread Party propaganda during the day and maintain public security at night.

At that time, there were still bandits on the prairie. Among them, tHebandits led by Ma Deshan caused a lot of trouble to people living on prairie. In order to eliminate this gang, The PLA and militia fought from 1950-1952, expending considerable manpower as well as material and financial resources.

As company commander, Gabulong took part in several battles against tHebandits. His right pinky finger was injured in one fight. The cashier of Yongfeng Village recollected that it was cut off by one of tHebandits, but no one could be sure about this. THebattles were a cruel experience. He once watched a young and handsome PLA

尕布龙作为民兵连连长，参加了数次剿灭匪徒的战斗，右手小拇指在一次战斗中受伤，据永丰村的会计金奎回忆说，隐约记得是被土匪砍掉的，但不确定。那是一段残酷的经历，尕布龙眼看着年轻英俊的解放军战士头一天还在高高兴兴地帮着牧民打水、扫院子，第二天却牺牲在他的身边。这位血气方刚、不善言辞，像爱自己兄弟一样热爱子弟兵的年轻牧人，忍受着难以言说的悲伤。他知道，这些来自远方的人，这些鲜活的生命，如此义无反顾地英勇战斗，付出年轻的生命，不是为了自己，是为了拯救草原，让草原人民过上平静安宁的生活。于是，他更加忘我地工作，心里深藏着对党、对人民的无限热爱和感激之情。他是草原的儿子，有着蒙古人实现英雄壮举的血性和永不屈服的性格，为了草原人民的幸福生活，为了让自己成为英雄，成为像他们那样的人，他用自己的方式努力着。

1952年6月，由海晏县武装部部长介绍，尕布龙加入了中国共产党，把自己完全交给了党，交给了他为之矢志不渝、奉献终身的事业。那时候，他为自己构想的远景，不是如何贪图安逸、享受权力带来的优越。他认为中国共产党的奋斗目标，就是一切为了人民，为着人民的幸福和安康。在那段时间，他先后担任了海晏县民政科副科长、县委统战部副部长。而被他救过的那位团长也一直关注着尕布龙的成长，为他的每一点进步高兴。

抗美援朝期间，团长向有关部门举荐，让刚刚入党的尕布龙参加了少数民族代表团赴朝鲜慰问。在朝鲜战场上，尕布龙被志愿军战士保家卫国、英勇作战的精神感动，把朝鲜人民送给他的礼物——一盒高丽参，悄悄塞给了一名志愿军战士。他说："我好得很，你们打仗辛苦，听说吃这个对身体好，请你收下我的心意。"

后来，我读了记者赵阳写的一篇文章才知道，这段意义非凡的慰问活动结束后，归国的慰问团还受到了周恩来总理的接见，让尕布龙感受到了周总理的亲切关怀，祖国大家庭的温暖。

曾在草原上意气风发、桀骜不驯、自由无羁的年轻牧人尕布龙，在经历了伟大的社会变革，中华人民共和国成立的辉煌与光荣后，体会到了什么是信仰、什么是奉献。明白了究竟应该怎样做，才能让自己成为一个对祖国、对人民有用的人，才能成为一名合格的共产党员。

1954年10月，尕布龙被派往黄南藏族自治州河南蒙古族自治县任县委书记处第一副书记、副县长，他即将离开无比热爱的家乡哈勒景乡永丰村。

soldier happily helping herdsman fetch water and sweep the yard one day only to lose his life next to Gabulong in battle the following day. He knew that these soldiers who came from distant places fought bravely and selflessly against tHebandits to give the people of the grassland an opportunity to live happy and peaceful lives. As a result, he worked even harder, with deep love and gratitude for the Party and the people. He made efforts in his own way to bring happiness to his people and to become as brave as the PLA soldiers.

In June of 1952, Gabulong was recommended by the director of the Department of Armed Forces of Haiyan County to join the Communist Party of China. He dedicated himself to the Party and to the a great cause for which he strove throughout his life. He set a rule for himself to never lead a life of luxury and to never take advantage of his power for personal gain. In his opinion, the goal of the Party must be for people's peace and prosperity. In those years, he took up several important positions including deputy chief of the Haiyan County Civil Affairs Office and deputy minister of the United Front Work Department of the Haiyan County Party Committee. The regimental commander who was once saved by Gabulong at Hoh Xil PLA garrison had been paying close attention to Gabulong's progress and applauded him for every achievement.

During the War to Resist U.S. Aggression and Aid Korea, Gabulong was recommended by the regimental commander to visit North Korea as one of the representatives of Chinese minority groups. On the North Korean battlefield, he was deeply moved by the spirit of the volunteer soldiers who fought bravely to defend their homes. He was presented a box of Korean ginseng by a Korean, but he gave it to a Chinese soldier fighting in the war and said "I am doing well, but you are fighting hard. I heard that eating this is good for your health, so please accept it."

Later, I read an article written by the reporter Zhao Yang which said that after the visit to North Korea, the delegation was received by Premier Zhou Enlai, which further infused Gabulong with the loving care of Premier Zhou and the warmth of his motherland.

Since Gabulong had experienced profound social changes and witnessed the people's pride in founding of People's Republic of China, he, who used to be a vigorous and free herdsman, began to realize the meaning of belief and dedication. He also started to contemplate how to be a good communist and contribute to his country and people.

草原生活

Life on grassland

　　10月的青海高原，草木见黄，秋风渐至。尕布龙年轻的妻子华毛，正赶着羊群在哈勒景草原上放牧。

　　草原是美丽的。

　　哈勒景草原的冷峻和神秘，就像一朵雪莲，绽放在明媚的草地上。男人们在向阳避风又临近水源的地方扎帐驻牧，女人们一年四季，挤牛奶、打酥油、晒牛粪，操持家务，乐此不疲。

　　藏族姑娘华毛，活泼美丽，性格爽朗。她原来生活在贡清部落，婚后与尕布龙一起来到了群科札萨克蒙古族部落，婚后两人感情深厚。1952年，上海电影制片厂的导演凌子风来到青海金银滩，拍摄了由休毅担任编剧的故事影片《金银滩》。影片反映的是中华人民共和国成立后，青海湖畔牧民们的生活情景，其中表现的青年牧民之间波澜起伏的爱恋之情，就取自蒙古族青年尕布龙和藏族姑娘华毛之间生动有趣的爱情故事。电影在国内播出后，反响强烈，人们第一次欣赏到了青海湖畔金银滩美丽的草原风光，感受到了牧区人民真实的生活状态，尕布龙和华毛也因此在草原上出了名。

　　就在这个时候，细心的华毛感觉到了丈夫的变化。刚结婚的时候，丈夫好结交朋友，性格倔强，天马行空，喜欢到各部落游走。可现在，秉性善良耿直的尕布龙，渐渐变了个样。

In October of 1954, Gabulong was sent to Henan Mongolian Autonomous County of the Huangnan Tibetan Autonomous Prefecture to be the first deputy secretary of the county party secretariat and deputy county chief. He was going to leave his dear hometown — Yongfeng Village of Halejing Township.

The picture of the Qinghai Plateau in October shows yellow trees and half withered grass drifting about in the chilly autumn wind. When he got the news of working in another place, his young wife Hua Mao was herding sheep on Halejin Grassland.

The grasslands are beautiful.

The coldness and mystery of the Halejing Grassland is like a snow lotus blooming on the bright grass. Men build tents in areas close to the water and sheltered from the sun and wind. Women enjoy milking cows, making butter, drying cow dung, and doing housework all year round.

Gabulong's wife Huamao was a vivacious, beautiful, and optimistic Tibetan girl from the Gong Qing tribe. After she married Gabulong, she came to live with him in Qunkezhasake, a Mongolian tribe on the Halejin prairie. They loved each other deeply since from the time they got married. In 1952, Ling Zifeng, director of Shanghai Film Studio, came to Jinyintan to shoot a film named Gold and Silver Beach written by Xiu Yi. The film portrayed the life of the herdsmen living along the Qinghai Lake after the founding of the People's Republic. The touching love scenario of the young herdsmen in the film was adapted from the love between Huamao and Gabulong. The response to the film was strong. People throughout China enjoyed the beautiful scenery of the the grasslands along Qinghai Lake for the first time and felt the real life of the people of the pastoral area. Furthermore, the film also made Gabulong and Huamao famous.

At this time, the attentive Huamao started to notice a change in her husband. When they first got married, he was very outgoing and open-minded. He loved traveling to various tribes and could easily make friends. But now, Gabulong's disposition was gradually changing.

He had become less talkative, and he seemed to have also grown out of the arrogance and vitality of his youth. He was maturing into a steady and prudent man, characteristics aligned with his identity as a Mongolian herdsman. However, he was already thinking of leaving his beloved wife, young son, and life on the grassland.

In late autumn, smoke rising from Halejing Prairie glistened in the sun. As

他有些不太爱说话了，少了血气方刚时的骄躁、年轻人的气盛，却拥有了作为一个蒙古族男人、草原牧人应该具有的持重、成熟。但是，这时候，他却要离开家，离开他热爱的哈勒景草原、妻子和年幼的儿子。

深秋，肥沃的哈勒景草原炊烟袅袅，琥珀般闪闪发亮。缠绵的小河弯弯曲曲，尕布龙心里充满了离别的惆怅之情。当初，自己没有留在西藏工作，就是因为思念家人、眷恋故土。可是现在，自己是一名共产党员、国家干部，怎么能再由着性子呢？

晨曦的微明中，他和自己的三妹夫存排出发了。

他边走边回头，内心滚动的情思，像飘动在村口敖包上的缕缕松香，绵长而忧伤。但，尕布龙是一位牧民之子、蒙古族汉子，骨子里的坚毅和顽强，牵着他往前走。

清风吹过，宽阔的草原显得异常优美典雅。这片盛开着金露梅和银露梅的广阔草原，留下过王洛宾与卓玛情意绵绵的故事，诞生过传遍世界的名曲《在那遥远的地方》，在中华人民共和国刚刚诞生的艰苦岁月里，又成功地研制出了我们自己的第一颗原子弹、氢弹。这里有相思之苦，有八月里红似珊瑚的篝火，有中国人的梦想，也留下了年轻的尕布龙深情回望的身影。

静静的草原

The peaceful grassland

Gabulong gazed at the river winding through the grassland, he was filled with the sadness of departing. It was his nostalgia that prevented him from settling in Xizang when he went there with the People's Liberation Army. But as a Party member and an official whose goal was to serve the people, how could he be controlled by his own emotions?

One dawn, in the first rays of the morning sunlight, Gabulong set out for Henan County with his brother-in-law Cunmai.

As he left the village, he looked back with reluctance, but he was led forward by the determination and tenaciousness of his masulinity.

The endless Jinyintan Prairie was graceful and magnificent in the breeze. It was the place that gave birth to the touching love story of Zhuoma and Wang Luobing and the melodic song "That Far Away Place." During the founding of New China, it was also the place where the Chinese successfully developed their own atomic and hydrogen bombs for the first time. It was the place that held people's nostalgia, burned open fire in August, set sail the Chinese dream, and marked Gabulong's yearning.

草原上的云

美丽的河南大草原

The beautiful Henan Prairie

骑着马走了整整五天，终于到了河南县。

黄南藏族自治州河南蒙古族自治县在青藏高原东部、青海省东南部。西倚青藏，东襟甘陇，北通宁海，南望川康，是青、甘、川三省津要之所在，是青海省唯一的蒙古族自治县，俗称"河南蒙旗"。

历史上的河南蒙旗早在新石器时代便有了人类活动，秦汉时这里为羌地，唐代为吐蕃属地，北宋时属于河州，南宋时为金属地，元朝时为甘肃

Clouds Floating on Prairie

After riding on their horses for five days, Gabulong and his brother-in-law finally arrived at Henan County.

Henan County lies in southeastern Qinghai, east of the Qinghai-Tibetan Plateau, bordering Gansu Province in the east and Zeku County in the north. The county is also close to Sichuan Province; therefore, it is a key point among Qinghai, Gansu, and Sichuan. It is the only Mongolian autonomous county known as the Mongolian Banner of Henan.

Human activity in the Mongolian Banner of Henan can be traced back to the Neolithic Age. It was a part of Qiang minority group in the Qin and Han Dynasties and of Tubo (Tibetan Regime in ancient China) in the Tang Dynasty. It was designated to Hezhou in the Northern Song Dynasty and the Jin State in the Southern Song Dynasty. It was called Hezhou Lu (a prefecture-level city) of the Gansu Executive Secretariat Jurisdiction in the Yuan Dynasty. It was governed by Wanhufu Army Office of Duogandusidasima in the Ming Dynasty and by Xining Executive Minister in the Qing Dynasty. It was nominally administrated by Tongde Prefecture Administrative Office of Qinghai Province in the Republic of China, but actually governed by Prince of Henan.

In 1952, Henan Mongolian Banner was peacefully liberated and taken over by the Henan Mongolian Working Committee of CPC. Then on October 16th, 1954 the government of Henan Mongolian Autonomous Region was founded.

恢复了生态的夏拉滩草原

The Xialatan Prairie with recovered ecology

行中书省河州路，明属朵甘都司答思麻万户府，清属西宁办事大臣统辖，民国时期属青海省同德专员公署，实际由"河南亲王"自行治理。

1952 年，河南县和平解放，中共河南蒙古族工作委员会进驻河南蒙旗。1954 年 10 月 16 日，河南蒙古族自治区人民政府成立。

建县初期，百废待兴，农牧民渴望新生活的愿望是那样的强烈。

身轻如燕的尕布龙，在秋景怡人的草原上扬鞭催马。

他知道旧社会人间的苦难，他知道人们心中的渴望，他恨不能长出一对翅膀，飞翔在草原上空，尽快为民众酿出生活的蜜汁。

离自己的家乡哈勒景越来越遥远，但是，一望无际的绿色草原、明净悠远的蓝色天空，让他忘却了离别之苦。

第二天一早，尕布龙就带着县上的同志策马扬鞭 20 多公里，来到了智后乡南旗大队，今天的优干宁镇南旗村。

极目天地，蒙古人的大帐似朵朵白云，飘荡在芬芳的草地上。当时正是牧人转场、准备迁往秋窝子的季节，各家的蒙古包从东面依次撤帐，牧人们准备整理帐篷、驮运物品。

按照规矩，蒙古部落以德高望重的长者为中心，坐北朝南，从右至左，围成一个大圈扎帐。各蒙古包周围用柳条交叉编织成 5 尺高、7 尺长的菱形网眼做内壁，蒙古族人称为"哈那"。普通蒙古包只有四扇哈那，最大

As Henan County was first set up, every aspect of life needed rebuilding. People there eagerly hoped for new life.

At this moment, Gabulong, a lad full of youth and strength, was appointed by the Party to help those people.

He knew what hardship those people had been through and what expectation they were holding for new days yet to come; therefore, he wished to help them as soon as possible.

Gabulong was getting father away from his hometown—Halejing Prairie, but the endless green grassland and hyaline sky before him eased his homesickness.

The next morning, he led several colleagues working in the county, riding their horses for more than 20 kilometers, to go to Nanqi Production Brigade of Zhihou Township (today's Nanqi Village of Youganning Town).

Big Mongolian tents, like white clouds, adorned the green grass. At that time, it was the season when herdsmen migrate to their autumn homes. The yurts of each family were being taken down and removed from the east one by one, and the people were busy packing up their things.

As a rule, the layout of Mongolian tents is that the tent of the most respectable elder is in the center and faces the south, then the other people's tents are set up around this centered one from the right to the left, making a big circle. Each Mongolian tent is fenced with diamond-shaped wicker grid of five-feet (165cm) high and seven-feet (231cm) long. Such a fence is called an inner wall and "Hana" in Mongolian. Ordinary tents can be surrounded by four "Hana," while the biggest one is surrounded by twelve Hana. When the time comes to migrate, tents will be withdrawn from the east, and the elder's tent in the center will be reserved as the last one to be removed.

When Gabulong arrived there, it was noon time with the sun beaming on the blue tassel of the biggest tent. An elder man who looked quiet and solemn walked out from a tent facing the north, holding a blue Hada.

Gabulong hurried forward and bowed deeply to accept the old man's blessing.

People followed the elder man then divided themselves into a passage.

Nice smelling milk tea welcomed Gabulong together with butter and roasted Qinke barley flour.

As Gabulong and his companions were honorable guests from the county

的蒙古包可搭 12 扇。撤帐时，又从右往左依次进行，留到最后拆的是长者的蒙古包。

尕布龙翻身下马。火红的太阳正照在蒙古包尖顶蓝色的流苏上，草原宁静安详。从正北面的蒙古包里走出一位面貌沉静、表情庄重的长者，双手捧着一条蓝色的哈达。

尕布龙紧走几步，深深弯腰，接受老人的祝福。

跟随其后的人，呼啦啦让出了一条道。

喷香的奶茶味飘了出来，长者的蒙古包里尚有未拆的灶台、红色的毡子。奶茶、酥油、炒面摆在长桌上。

县上来的贵客，一定要先请到大蒙古包里，与长者交谈。

可尕布龙说："还没到吃午饭的时候，让我们先来帮你们搬东西。"说着，便挽起袖子，把蒙古袍的长襟别在了腰带上。

尕布龙大步流星地向前走着，三妹夫存排跟在身后，心领神会。

他们来到一个蒙古包前。

周围忙碌的牧人放下手中的活，向他们聚拢。

有人想看看热闹，有人想验证一下，从县上下来的干部到底有没有两

美丽的河南蒙旗大草原

The beautiful prairie of the Henan Mongolian Banner

government, they must be invited to the elder's tent to chat.

However, Gabulong refused the treat and said, "It's not yet lunch time, so let me help you with moving." With that, he rolled up his sleeves and pinned the long skirt of his Mongolian robe to his belt.

He strode forward, followed by his brother-in-law Cunpai who knew what Gabulong was going to do.

Then they came to a tent.

The herdsmen who were busy with withdrawing and packing stopped to gather around them.

Some gathered as spectators, while other wanted to verify if the cadre from the county was capable enough for the work.

More people were gathering. Keeping cool, Gabulong made no great efforts to lift up one of the biggest "Jiamure," which is a sheep skin bag for butter weighing up to 100kg or more. Almost simultaneously, Cunpai lifted up the same size of "Jiamure". They calmly carried the butter bags toward a yak and loaded them on each side of the bearer, tightening the burden on the saddle with ox hair ropes.

The onlookers cheered for their mighty strength. If they hadn't witnessed the event themselves, they wouldn't have believed that the important cadres of the county level were so strong and efficient.

"Wow! Who sent this man with the strength of a yak?"

The old men twisted their beards and looked at him with approval.

The young men, standing on their tiptoes, rushed to greet him.

In times of peace, men who are strong, hard-workers, and good at wrestling are the heroes of the grasslands.

Therefore, Gabulong became a name known to every household on the very first day that he took office.

Since then, Gabulong was aware that without experience, he wouldn't understand the common people's hardship or requirements. He also realized that only when he kept the needs of the people in mind, he could serve them heartily and become a good party cadre. In his mind, a good cadre of the party must be a person who always remembers the place where he was born and raised and cares for the common people.

Gabulong's actions aligned with his principles. No matter what he did and how

下子。

围观的人越来越多。尕布龙沉住气，双手一用力，最大的一个"加木热"让他轻而易举地搬了起来。加木热是牧区装酥油的羊皮袋子，最大的超过200斤。几乎同时，存排也搬起一个同样大小的加木热，和尕布龙一左一右，神色泰然地走到一头大牦牛前。

没等大家回过神，尕布龙和存排一左一右，把两个沉重的加木热稳稳地架在牛鞍上，同时，飞快地扯过牛毛绳，结结实实地绑在了鞍子上。

在场的人尖叫起来。如果不是亲眼所见，怎么能相信，县里来的大干部会有这么大的力气，这么麻利的身手。

"哦呀呀，这是哪里来的大力士，像牦牛一样壮。"

老人们捻着胡须，赞许地望着他。

年轻人踮起脚尖，抢着跟他打招呼。

在没有战争的和平年代，力气大、能干活、会摔跤的男人就是草原上的英雄。

上任第一天，尕布龙的名字，就在河南大草原上传开了……

也就是从那时起，他就意识到，只有亲身经历了，才能真正体会到老百姓的甘苦；只有把老百姓的冷暖时时放在心坎上，才能全心全意为老百姓办事，成为老百姓信任的好干部。而共产党的好干部，什么时候都不能忘记养育自己的土地和人民。

尕布龙是这样想的，也是这样做的。从此，不论干什么工作，不论官职有多高，手中的权力有多大，他心中放在第一位的始终是百姓。关心百姓疾苦，为百姓排忧解难，惠民生，谋发展，竟成了他一生的追求与信念，南旗村也成了尕布龙情系一生、始终牵挂的地方，直到他去世。

尕布龙一行策马疾驰来到草原上。

由于海拔较高，地势复杂，地处三江源保护区的河南蒙古族自治县，水源丰富，洮河、泽曲河、尕玛日河流程长，流域大，落差大，水质好，拥有天然优质草场近千万亩。距离县城东南50公里处的李恰如山，奇峰耸立，是黄河上游重要支流洮河的发源地。洮河娇艳，在宽广无垠的草原上日夜兼程，两岸高山杜鹃满山满坡，似瀑布流泻，虽身处海拔3700米的高度，却是黄南州境内冬季唯一不结冰的河，每年有珍禽白鹤、鹭鸶等来此栖息。

powerful he became, what meant the most to him was always the common people. He cared for their hardships and difficulties so much that his lifelong pursuit and belief was always to favor people and promote development. The Nanqi Production Brigade (today's Nanqi Village) had been one of his beloved places till his death.

Gabulong rode his horse to the prairie with his companions.

Owing to high altitude and complex terrain, Henan Mongolian Autonomous County lying in the Sanjiangyuan Reserve enjoys rich water resources and high-quality natural meadow of nearly millions of hectares. The Tao River, Zequ River, and Gamari River in Henan County have long paths, a huge drainage basin, and good water quality. The towering Liqiaru Mountain, fifty kilometers away from the county, is the origin of the Tao River that is one of the most significant branches of the upper reach of the Yellow River. The Tao river meanders its way through the prairie, bounded by hills which are flamed by alpine rhododendron in spring. Although the river stands on an altitude of 3,700 meters, it is the only unfrozen river in Huangnan Tibetan Autonomous Prefecture and a habitat for white cranes and egrets every year.

However, when Gabulong arrived at Henan County, he saw Hequ Prairie plagued by rodent pest, rinderpest, pleuropneumonia, aftosa, and animal skin disease, which resulted in the struggling of livestock against death and desolated core area of the Sangjiangyuan Region.

According to the document, the rodent pest once affected the meadow in Henan County of more than 333333.33 hectares with more than 200 mouse holes per hectare. The pest rate reached 28.5% with the worst of 80% on Xialatan Prairie and the vegetation coverage fell from 94.44% to 76.66%, with high quality grass decreasing to 73.72% and weeds increasing to 35.64%.

Gabulong was tortured by the sight of meadow freckled with barren black soil. Every morning the presence of seven or eight big mice in his room worried him.

At that time, people generally did not have an awareness of rat extermination. They believed that it was wrong to kill rats, failing to recognize the fatal damage brought by rats to the herdsmen and grasslands. Gabulong immediately went to the countryside to conduct a field investigation. He also invited experts from the provincial level to work with the local vets and village cadres to discuss and study methods for killing rats as well as the cause of the desertification of the local grassland. He and his group travelled

可是想当年，意气风发的尕布龙来到河南县时，出现在他眼前的河曲大草原——三江源核心地带一片苍凉。鼠害严重，牛瘟、牛肺疫、口蹄疫、皮肤病蔓延，大量牲畜挣扎在死亡线上。

据史料记载，河南县鼠害面积曾经达 500 多万亩，每亩平均鼠洞 200 多个，平均鼠害破坏率 28.5%，鼠害最为严重的夏拉滩草原破坏率高达 80%，植被覆盖率由原来的 94.44% 下降到 76.66%，优良牧草产量下降到 73.72%，杂草产量增加到 35.64%。

看着大片大片裸露贫瘠的"黑土滩"，尕布龙心急如焚。

美丽的哈勒景草原

The beautiful Halejing Prairie

每天清晨，七八只大老鼠，在屋里窜来窜去的情景，让尕布龙揪心不已。

当时，人们普遍没有灭鼠意识，认为灭鼠就是杀生，根本认识不到鼠害带给牧民、带给草原的致命伤害。尕布龙立即下乡，实地调查，从省上请来专家，组织畜牧站工作人员、乡村干部讨论研究灭鼠的办法，总结草原沙化的根本原因。挨家挨户给大家做工作，讲解过度放牧、鼠类破坏、人为因素对草原生态产生的不利影响。

2019 年 8 月，我来到原河南县委书记韩华在湟中的老家。

to every household to explain the adverse effects on the ecology of grassland caused by overgrazing, rodent destruction, and other human factors.

In August of 2019, I came to visit Han Hua, the former Secretary of the Henan County Committee, in his hometown of Huangzhong County.

Han Hua's ninety-year-old father and mother were more than eighty years old, and his siblings lived with them. There was a harmonious picture in his home with his three sisters cooking, his brothers, brothers-in-law and himself chatting with their parents as the grandchildren played.

We enjoyed Lamian noodles made by Han's sisters, and I also enjoyed some old stories told by Han's father, Han Jiajing, who took a nap after lunch.

It was a sunny afternoon. Sitting in a yard with a garden full of a variety of flowers, Han Jiajing opened his memory with clear logic and smooth expression, recollecting those hard yet unforgettable days.

The official rat extermination began in 1955, and was led by Gabulong, who was serving as Deputy Secretary of the Henan County Committee at that time.

Han Jiajing was the director of the local vet station.

At the beginning of the work, the two vets from the provincial vet station led the team. However, when it was time for them to be taken by Han Jiajing to the villages for the field investigation, which was Gabulong's idea, they left without telling any local relative units. They could not handle the high altitude, cold weather, and scarce oxygen in Henan County.

The old Han understood how hard it was to live in the harsh environment of Henan County and never blamed the vets for leaving.

This episode made Gabulong aware that it was the local people who could solve their own difficulties; therefore, the rat extermination depended on the locals of Henan County. He invited technical staff from the provincial animal husbandry department to train the local people, making sure cadres from every village knew how to get rid of rats and mix the farm chemicals. Completing the training, all the trainees, especially those village cadres, were mainstays of the rat extermination team.

With this background, Gabulong was able to widely organize the whole area from the township level to county level to work on wiping out the rats. He made a rule for every unit to appoint 200 people to take part in the large-scale rat extermination. There

韩华书记 90 岁高龄的父亲，80 多岁的母亲都健在，兄弟姐妹们都生活在父母亲身边。韩华书记的三个姐姐负责做饭，他和哥哥、姐夫陪老人聊天，孙子孙女跑来跑去，一家人其乐融融。

吃过姐姐做的家常拉面，睡过午觉的老爷子韩嘉靖给我讲起了 60 多年前的往事。

午后的阳光洒在开满鲜花的院子里，老爷子的记忆力非常好，思路清晰，表达流畅。他说，那是一段极其艰苦而忙碌的日子，心酸而难忘。

正式灭鼠开始于 1955 年，时任河南县委副书记、副县长的尕布龙亲自担任总指挥。

老爷子韩嘉靖任河南县畜牧兽医站站长。

刚开始，省上派下来两位技术人员，指导河南县的灭鼠工作。可当兽医站站长韩嘉靖奉总指挥尕布龙书记之命，带着他们下乡调研普查时，因为受不了河南县高寒、缺氧之苦，他们悄悄离开了。

未等我开口，韩嘉靖老人笑了笑说："这不怪他们，可以理解。想当年河南县自然环境恶劣，条件艰苦，确实难熬。"

在这种情况下，尕布龙意识到，灭鼠还得靠当地群众干部，自己的问题，必须自己解决。于是他就把青海省畜牧厅的技术人员请到河南县委办，多次举办培训班，让各乡各村干部了解灭鼠知识，接受专业培训，学习如何配置农药、喷洒农药的灭鼠方法，学成后，这批乡村干部都成了当地灭鼠的带头人。

与尕布龙一起灭鼠的原河南县兽医站站长韩嘉靖

Han Jiajing, former director of the vet station of Henan County, who used to fight against the rodent damage with Gabulong

有了这个基础，尕布龙才开始广泛动员组织全县乡镇，每个单位出 200 人，开展大规模连片灭鼠。当时，各乡镇、村社都成立了灭鼠队，队

were rat killing teams in every village and town with members ranging from a group of dozens to several hundred, who were busy with the work like scouts patrolling the grassland. At that time life was tough, and traffic was not well established; therefore, camping on the prairie for one or two months was the routine for Gabulong and his team, which included Han Jiajing. At first, they killed rats with indigenous methods. For example, if there were two rat holes close together, they would put a rat-trap in front of one hole and then they would lay on the ground and blow into the second hole. The rats would soon run out into the trap. They also trapped rats by ambushing the rat holes with bows and arrows.

Although the indigenous ways worked, which made Gabulong and his men excited, they were in low proficiency. Later, they tried mixing oats with cooking oil and pesticides, and stuffing the poison into rat holes or spreading it around the entrances. As they accumulated more experience, they finally managed to kill rats with chemicals by mixing a saline solution. As they became more experienced, they even began to take out lymph from sheep and then mix it into a saline solution to produce a vaccine, which was delivered to every village to distribute to the herdsmen. All the measures proved to be more efficient than the indigenous ones, which satisfied Gabulong. However, he couldn't relax his efforts. When the extermination time came, Gabulong urged the personnel from every village involved to head for the targeted grassland with their rations. They stayed on the prairie for several months, digging holes, mixing chemicals, pouring chemicals in rat holes, mixing prescriptions for oxen and sheep, and injecting the vaccine into sick herds or treating them with medicine.

After the grandchildren went to take a nap, Han Jiajing's wife came to sit beside him, saying, "When the rat extermination work intensified, my husband would work with Gabulong for several months without returning home. He devoted himself to the work so much that he neglected his own family and didn't give thought to our survival. I was only able to feed the children with some wildflowers or wild spinach that I picked on the grassland. We were nearly poisoned by those wild plants one time."

Han Jiajing smiled and said, "No one cared about their own families at that critical time. Gabulong completely dedicated himself to the work without thinking of anything else. We just followed his example."

"I didn't blame you for not being at home, but you could have at least sent your

员多则数百人，少则几十人，犹如骑着战马的侦察兵奔波在每一片草原上。那年月，交通不便，生活艰苦。每到灭鼠季节，尕布龙就带着韩嘉靖站长和灭鼠队员把帐篷扎在草原上，一待就是两个月。刚开始，只能用些土办法，只要看见两个相距不远的鼠洞，便在一个洞口放好笼子，趴在草地上用嘴对着另一个鼠洞吹气，洞里的老鼠不一会就会跑出来，钻进笼子里。老鼠习惯用土丘堵住洞口，他们就将洞口打开，在上面支上弓箭，等老鼠跑来垒起土丘封堵洞口时，会触动弓箭，被箭射中。

土办法很奏效，尕布龙也很开心。但是，效率太低。他们又用食油与燕麦拌成毒饵，投进老鼠洞，或撒在洞口。再往后，他们开始大胆试用化学药物灭鼠，自己配制生理盐水，逼到最后，兽医站竟然想出办法，从羊身上取出淋巴，再配以自制的生理盐水，研制出疫苗，发放给各乡村。这个办法果然奏效，比土办法强多了，尕布龙暗自高兴，不敢松劲，一到灭鼠季节，就催促各乡、各村灭鼠队带着干粮出发，一连数月和大家一起在草原上挖坑、拌农药、放农药，按照牛羊体重配药，给牛羊打针、喂药、抹药。

小孙子睡着了，韩华书记的母亲坐到了老伴身边说：“最紧张的时候，我老伴一连几个月跟着尕布龙书记在草原上灭鼠，没在家住过。也不管我和孩子们吃什么，喝什么，我就到草原上给孩子们采马莲花、挖野菠菜，有一回还差点中了毒。”

韩嘉靖老人笑了笑说：“那时候，谁还管家里的事，尕布龙书记都在没命地干，我们还能打退堂鼓？”

“见不到你面，可是你总得把工资给我啊！”

韩华书记的母亲嗔怪地瞪了一眼老伴。

“一大家子人，要吃饭，我又没工作，只好到了夏天打土块，冬天漫山遍野地拾牛粪，用一袋子牛粪 5 角钱的收入，贴补家用。”

“你记不记得，”韩华书记的母亲抬起头想了想说：“有年春节，尕布龙书记来我们家，身上穿得特别朴素，看着一点儿也不像县委书记。孩子们正在吃酸奶，里面泡着翻跟头（青海人过年时常做的一种面食）。我说，尕书记，家里没啥吃的，你就将就吃点吧！尕布龙说，这个东西好啊，我就吃这个，别把官看得那么重，共产党的干部就是人民的公仆，是为大家服务的。”

salary back to me."

Han Hua's father grumbled at his wife.

"A whole family needed to be fed but I didn't get a job. So, what I could do is to make mud bricks in summer and pick yak dung to make the ends meet."

"How could I feed a whole family without a job? All I could do was make mud bricks in summer and pick up yak dung to make end meet."

Han Jiajing's wife recalled, "Do you remember that Gabulong came to our home one year during the Spring Festival? He wore such simple clothes that he didn't look like the secretary of the County Committee. Our children were eating yogurt mixed with Fangentou, a kind of deep-fried local food for the Spring Festival. I said to him there was no feed to be found in our home except for what the children were eating. I invited him to make himself do eating the simple food with the children. However, Gabulong disagreed with me and said the food was fine enough. He also told me that a CPC cadre whose motto is to work for the people and serve for the people did not need anything special.

Two years later, Gabulong's efforts in rat extermination and grassland recovery were rewarded. 70% of the local grassland turned green again, and many sick livestock had recovered.

Gabulong didn't take his achievements as a reason to relax but quickly moved on to the next project. The local grassland was so barren that it could not support the livestock. Gabulong started to work on the land by planting large areas of grass, Chinese rhubarb, and rhodiola rosea. He also led people to irrigate, causing the dry and infertile local prairie to come to life again.

After several years of Gabulong's efforts, the Hequ Prairie gradually revived. Furthermore, some competent barefoot vets were also produced for the local communities. They were responsible and devoted people who played a great role in the development of agriculture and animal husbandry on the prairie. At that time the economy of the grassland areas was less developed, and vets were very critical to the local economy. Every vet was responsible for 400-500 sheep or cattle when breeding season came. They worked on the inoculation of livestock to achieve a 100% rate of survival. No medicine was easily available at that time, so the vets shipped medicines from Lanzhou and Xiahe of Gansu Province by yak to make ointment for horses

两年后，灭鼠初见成效，70%的草场重现绿色，染病在身的牛羊，经过治疗好了一大半。

尕布龙丝毫不敢懈怠，接下来，又针对草场贫瘠，牛羊不够吃的情况，开始大范围治理黑土滩，大面积种草，种大黄、红景天，组织大家引水灌溉，使干旱枯寂的草场尽快得到修复。

经过几年的艰辛努力，河曲草原渐渐恢复了生机，也给当地县乡培养了不少称职的赤脚兽医。这些来自基层的赤脚兽医尽职尽责，在长期的草原农牧建设中，发挥了重要作用。想当年，这可是一件了不起的事情，曾经落后贫穷的草原牧区，兽医的作用不可替代，每年牛羊繁殖季节，每个兽医都要承包400—500头牛羊，负责疫苗接种工作，确保牛羊成活率达到百分之百。在缺医少药的情况下，他们从兰州、夏河用牦牛驮回草药，自制药膏给马治疗皮肤病，取得了非常好的疗效，为河南县的畜群恢复作出了突出贡献。

多年后，当草原鼠害影响到全国很多地区，使牧区的经济发展、自然生态受到严重影响，全国许多地方展开大规模灭鼠行动时，20世纪90年

1984年9月10日河南蒙古族自治县成立30周年（尕布龙在右三）

On September 10th, 1984 took place the 30th anniversary of the founding of Henan Mongolian Autonomous County

(Gabulong is the third from the right)

suffering from skin disease, which contributed to the recovery of the cattle in Henan County.

Several years later rodents became a common headache for many districts in China, hindering the economic development and damaging the ecology in pasturing areas. However, in the early 1990s, Henan County had become the second rodent-free prairie in China and the first such prairie in Qinghai Province. It was also the largest production base of organic animal husbandry and was boasted as the finest and fairest grassland in Qinghai alongside Tianjun County and Qilian County.

Gabulong liked to say, "Our beautiful home is our beautiful prairie, so we must protect our own home." Since then, although the secretary of the County Committee would shift, the impact of Gabulong's foresight in protecting the prairie environment, adhering to ecological development, and advancing local people's mindsets would never change. The work in Henan County focused on developing the animal-husbandry economy, controlling and treating livestock and poultry outbreaks, and promoting organic livestock products. As early as 2005, residents in Henan County stopped using plastic bags to reduce the "white pollution" caused by plastics on their prairie, which was another legacy left by Gabulong.

As time goes by, the trade and economy in Henan County is booming, and people there are leading a prosperous life. High-quality grassland is endless, on which live the Hequ horse, one of the three rare horse families, and the Oula sheep, a high-quality sheep family. A picturesque scenery is being unfolded there.

That was a really hard time!

Gabulong, secretary of the County Committee, rode a horse to catch mice during the day and at night squeezed himself with half a dozen of herdsmen into a tent pierced by cold wind from all sides. They used plastic sacks filled with hay as pillows and were covered with nothing but their own clothes. They drank water from the grassland ponds and ate fried barley flour mixed with water. No one knew how many such formidable days and nights they had endured.

However, it was during those difficult days that Gabulong transformed Henan County from a barren land dominated by rodents into a fertile grassland where people led a peaceful and promising lives.

Han Jailing closed his eyes gently. Today's conversation took him back to bitter

代初,河南蒙旗大草原已然骄傲地成为我国北方第二个草原无地面鼠害县,全省第一个草原无地面鼠害县,全省面积最大的有机畜牧业生产基地,和天峻县、祁连县一起被评为青海最好最美的草原。

尕布龙常说:"美丽的草原,就是我们美丽的家园,一定要保护好我们的家园。"此后,不管哪一届领导上任,哪一位县委书记到位,都一直秉承着时任书记尕布龙保护草原环境,坚持生态发展、生态治理,转变当地人观念的超前意识。主抓畜牧经济、畜禽疫病防治,发展有机畜产品。早在15年前,河南县牧民群众便克服生活中的种种不便,杜绝使用塑料袋,减少了塑料袋对草原的污染,这个习惯是尕布龙在河南县任职时留下来的,一直保持不变。

多年过去了,河南蒙旗大草原商贸经济繁荣,人民安居乐业;优良草场连片分布,三大名马之一河曲马,优良畜禽品种欧拉羊名噪全国,草原盛景美轮美奂。

那时候真不容易啊!

县委书记尕布龙白天和我们一起骑马抓老鼠。晚上,和五六个牧民挤在一顶窄小、四面透风的帐篷里,用装草料的袋子当枕头,用身上的衣服当被子,渴了喝草滩上的积水,饿了吃泽曲河水拌的炒面,多少个日日夜夜啊,数也数不清。

可就是在那样艰苦的条件下,贫寒萧瑟、生活无望的河南县硬是在尕布龙书记的带领下,消灭了鼠害,改造了黑土滩,让河南蒙旗大草原恢复了往日的生机,让老百姓过上了安宁有序、有盼头的好日子。

韩嘉靖老人微微闭上眼。今天的谈话,让他的思绪回到了那段苦涩又无比怀念的日子。90岁高龄的他,面容祥和平静,从来没有后悔过自己当初的选择,也从来没有因为受过的苦存有一丝怨言。尕布龙书记就是他的榜样,有尕布龙书记在,他就觉得苦得值得,苦得有意义。尕布龙书记离开河南县到省上工作后,他依然在畜牧兽医站工作,依然遵照尕布龙书记的教导,时时刻刻为河南蒙旗大草原的未来和生态环境着想,时时刻刻没放松过对自己的要求,也没有因为20世纪60年代三年困难时期,他把放在兽医站里、用来和六六六粉拌灭鼠药的清油给大家分了,被揪出来批斗、挨打觉得委屈。

他说:"黄河源头出了个尕布龙,黄河尽头出了个焦裕禄。"都是一样

but nostalgic days. At the age of 90, his face is peaceful and calm. He has never regretted his choice to participate in the work, nor has he ever complained about his suffering. He took Gabulong as his role model; therefore, as long as the secretary was there, he felt it was meaningful and worthwhile to experience all those hardships. After Gabulong left Henan County to work in the provincial government, Mr. Han still worked in the local vet station. He kept Gabulong's instruction in mind to strive for the future and ecological environment of the Mongolian Banner grassland—Henan County. He was always strict with himself and never felt wronged when he was criticized and denounced in public after he offered the hungry local people rapeseed oil that was planned to mix with rodent poison to kill rats during the "three-year natural disaster" in 1960s.

Han Jiajing said, "There was a Gabulong at the source of the Yellow River and a Jiao Yulu at the end." Both of them were equally great secretaries of the County Committee. It is true that without the foundation laid by Gabulong, Henan County wouldn't be so prosperous today. Gabulong's attitude toward life and work, his loyalty to the Party, and his love for the people and his hometown are qualities we must learn from forever.

In 2015 Han Hua, Han Jiajing's son, was appointed to the secretary of Henan County Committee, becoming the 13th successor to Gabulong.

Han Jiajing told his son that he didn't need to learn fancy things. As long as he followed in the footsteps of Gabulong, he would do his job well.

Keeping his father's words in mind, Han Hua traveled to every corner of the county to work on ecology, education, health care, and poverty alleviation. In order to further promote the welfare of the local people, he sought to work with Tsinghua University and Northwest University for Nationalities to set up scientific experimental farmlands on the Mongolian Banner grassland. They were determined to carry out the strategy of regional cooperation, market pollution-free local animal products, promote sustainable development of the local grassland, and further increase the income of the local herdsmen. He also followed Gabulong's practice of training minority cadres and selecting local talents to cultivate, pushing the educational equilibrium of the whole county forward. Similar to Gabulong, he attached great importance to environmental protection by Gabulong's campaign of "Protecting the Ecological Environment and Beautifying Our Home."

的好县委书记。没有尕布龙书记打下的坚实基础，就没有河南县的今天。尕布龙书记对工作、对生活的态度，对党、对事业的忠诚，对家乡、对人民的热爱，值得我们永远学习。

2015 年，韩华被任命为河南县委书记，是继尕布龙后的第 13 任县委书记。

韩嘉靖老人对儿子说："你啥都不用学，就学尕布龙书记。学好尕布龙，你这个县委书记就能当好。"

韩华书记牢牢记着父亲的话，像尕布龙书记一样走遍了河南县的山山水水、沟沟坎坎，抓生态、抓教育、抓卫生，重扶贫工作、重民族团结，为了老百姓的长远利益，和清华大学、西北民族大学联合，在河南县蒙旗草原搞科学试验责任田，下决心搞区域合作，向市场推广草原上的无污染畜产品，

20 世纪 50 年代，尕布龙任黄南州委副书记、河南县委第一书记时作报告

In 1950s, Gabulong, Vice Secretary of Huangnan Tibetan Autonomous Prefecture Committee and the first Secretary of Henan County Committee, is making a report at a meeting.

尕布龙和河南县的牧民在一起交流

Gabulong is communicating with herdsmen from Henan County

提高草原优胜劣汰、可持续发展，进一步提高牧民收入；和尕布龙书记一样注重培养当地民族干部，选拔培养当地优秀人才，为全县的教育均衡发展起到了积极推动作用；和尕布龙一样重视生态环境保护，率先发起了领导干部生态责任田，开展"保护生态环境，美丽我的家园"的行动。

不同的是，当年的尕布龙书记骑马下乡，今天的韩华书记乘的是四驱越野车。然而，他们全心全意为人民服务的信念是一致的。

Although the way of reaching the people is different between Gabulong, who rode horses, and Han Hua, who took a four-wheel drive off-road vehicle, they both shared the same value of wholeheartedly serving the people.

殚精竭虑为人民

　　尕布龙是一位头脑清晰、聪明睿智的人，他的目光总能透过眼前的尘雾，看到光明和远方。他不忍看到牧人的孩子们当"睁眼瞎"，他希望草原上的孩子能和城里人的孩子一样尽早学习文化，掌握知识。来到河南县后，在他的努力下，中共河南工委在卡松木部落，试办了全区第一所帐房小学。之后，又办起了28所初级小学、5所完全小学，使1249名学龄儿童进入学校。

　　不仅如此，他还在当地基层干部和牧人中选出适龄青年，分期分批地在县上办速成识字班和文化短训班，在基层搞扫盲活动，对成年人进行识字教育，使他们脱离文盲状态。

　　同时，他创造条件，选拔出130名优秀青年，送往青海民族学院和西北民族学院学习。由于家境贫困，很多人无法坚持学习，他又将自己节省下来的工资按期捐给他们当中的33名牧人子弟，让他们安心学习，完成学业。回来后即刻分配工作，交付担子，将他们培养成了河南大草原上第一代有文化、有能力的年轻干部。

在河南县担任县委书记的尕布龙

Gabulong as the secretary of Henan County Party Committee

Serving the People with Utmost and Unflinching Dedication

Gabulong was widely revered as a sober-minded and wise man, always seeing the brightness from afar through a shroud of mist and fog. He could not bear to sit by idly and watch the herdsmen's children become completely illiterate. He hoped that the children on the grasslands could explore a diverse cultures and acquire knowledge as early as their peers in the city. After coming to the Henan Mongol Autonomous County, he lead the Working Committee of the Communist Party of China in Henan County to establish the first primary school of the Kasongmu tribe. This school was followed by the founding of 28 primary schools and 5 complete primary schools in which 1,249 school-age children had access to education. On top of that, he also selected young people of school age from among local grassroots cadres and herdsmen and organized crash literacy classes and short-term cultural training courses in the county. This allowed the campaign of wiping out illiteracy to be conducted at grass-roots level, thereby empowering adults to throw off the shackles of illiteracy by virtue of education.

At the same time, he created conditions to select 130 young people with outstanding performance to study at Qinghai Nationalities University and Northwest University for Nationalities. Many of these students found themselves unable to persist in learning due to their poverty-stricken families. In the face of such predicaments, Gabulong donated his salary to 33 of the herdsmen's children on a regular basis, thus enabling them to pursue

送去学习的年轻干部回到了草原

Young cadres who were dispatched to study returned to the grasslands

　　玛久是河南县宁木特乡的一位民办女教师。1964 年，她从河南县黄茂乡完小毕业。毕业后，被河南县文卫科送到青海民族学院集中培训了一年。回来后，尕布龙把她安排到河南县宁木特乡两个大队任帐篷民办教师，同时教语文、数学、藏语文。所谓帐篷教室，是尕布龙书记从县上解决的一顶蒙古包，里面只有 20 个小凳子，没有课桌。学生是村干部们挨家挨户动员牧民送来的，课本、铅笔、书包是尕布龙书记自己买的。玛久从小生活在河南蒙旗大草原，怎么能不理解尕布龙书记的一片苦心，尽心尽力，几十年如一日，任劳任怨地完成了一至三年级的教学任务，将学生送到县上继续就读。

　　丹培老人回忆道，1964 年，河南县召开庆祝大会，他的父亲去县上参加大会。回来后，父亲执意让儿子丹培去县上上学，丹培不愿去，父亲硬是把他拉到了县招待所。进了尕布龙的办公室，丹培见还有几个年轻人也在里面，尕布龙正在给他们讲读书的重要性，可他一句话也听不进去，还是不想去。尕布龙就给他们每人给了 20 元钱，安排好他们的食宿，让他们去学校上学。后来，他们一起上学的 20 名蒙古族学生，毕业后都回乡

their education without financial stress After completing their studies, the young graduates were immediately assigned to jobs with major responsibilities. With education and work experience, they became the first generation of cultured and competent young cadres on the grasslands of Henan County.

Majiu was a private female teacher in Ningmute Township, Henan County. Upon her graduation from Huangmao Township Complete Primary School in Henan County in 1964, she was sent to Qinghai Nationalities University for a one-year intensive training program by the Department of Culture and Health of Henan County. After returning, Gabulong arranged for her to work for two brigades of Ningmute Township, as a private tent teacher, teaching Chinese, mathematics, and Tibetan. The so-called tent classroom took the form of a yurt, which wouldn't had been built but for the request from Gabulong to the county government. It contained only 20 small chairs and no desks. The village cadres carried out a myriad of door-to-door visits, mobilizing herdsmen to send their children to school. Each and every textbook, pencil, and school bag was purchased by Secretary Gabulong himself. Born and raised on the grasslands of the Henan Mongol Autonomous County, there was not even the slightest possibility that Majiu could not be cognizant of Secretary Gabulong's meticulous care. As a result, she worked hard to teach students from grades one to three and send them to the county for further education.

Danpei, a senior citizen, thought back to the year 1964 when his father attended a celebration conference in Henan County. After returning home, his father insisted that he go to school in the county. Danwei didn't want to go, so his father dragged him to the county hostel. Stepping into Gabulong's office, they spotted several young people listening to the instructions of the Secretary on the significance of studying, whereas little Danpei still paid no heed at all and felt reluctant to attend school. Gabulong then gave those young men 20 yuan each, arranged their accommodations, and sent them to school. After graduation, twenty Mongolian students who went to school together returned to the township as cadres to work in the pastoral areas.

Xueribu, a cattle herder and orphan who grew up on the grasslands of Henan County, was selected by Gabulong to study at Northwest University for Nationalities. After returning from his studies, he served as a leader of the county and became an ethnic minority cadre who was loyal to the party and diligent and enthusiastic about his work.

At the home of Nima, former Vice Chairman of the Chinese People's Political

尕布龙在河南县检查牧业工作

Gabulong was inspecting the pastoral work in Henan County

当了干部，在草原牧区工作。

血日布是河南县草原上长大的放牛娃、孤儿，被尕布龙选送到西北民族学院学习。学成归来后，担任了县上的领导，成了一名对党忠诚，对工作勤勉热心的少数民族干部。

在担任过海南州政协副主席的尼玛家中，我见到了血日布。他是一位工作能力很强，且健谈爽快的人。尽管过去多年，当年尕布龙在河南县工作时的情景仍历历在目。

"我在县上工作多年，没见过哪位干部像尕布龙那样，身为县委书记，一大早起来为村里的奶牛组捡拾湿牛粪，还要背着木桶，走很远的路，为年纪大的牧民家里取水。有空闲时间了，就到食堂帮忙，做馒头、包包子。"

血日布有些激动："这样的事，做一次两次，我也能做到，但是经常这样做，我可能做不到！"

2017年7月，我去河南县寻找与尕布龙一起工作过的人，时任县委书记的韩华同志，专门为我的到来邀请当年和尕布龙书记一起共事过的老领

Consultative Conference in Tibetan Autonomous Prefecture of Hainan, I met Xueribu, a talkative, forthright sort of person well versed in work. Despite the many years that had passed, the scenes of Gabulong when he was working in Henan County still lingered deeply in the heart and mind of Xueribu.

"I have worked in the county for many years, and I have never seen a cadre like Gabulong. As the county Party secretary, he got up early in the morning to pick up wet cow dung and trudged a long distance with a wooden barrel on his back to fetch water for the elderly herders. He would also spend his spare time helping at the canteen by making steamed buns or wrapping dumplings."

Xueribu seemed a tad excited and said, "I can do such a thing every once in a while, but I could not make it a regular part of my schedule!"

In July 2017, I went to Henan County to look for people who had worked with Gabulong, and Comrade Han Hua, then secretary of the county Party committee, invited former leaders and colleagues as well as old friends who were all Gabulong's co-workers to gather at a symposium at the county Party committee's publicity department, in an effort to conjure up the memories of the good old days as he worked in Henan County.

That day, I once again met Xueribu, who was only in his 20s when he worked with Gabulong. Speaking with him in his 90s, he was still exhilarated when talking about Gabulong. In fact, back in the early days of the post-liberation period, Gabulong worked as an interpreter in Henan Mongol Autonomous County, therefore he was no stranger to the grassland. Xueribu recalled that when the secretary first came, he bitterly criticized him: "What on earth are you doing to turn such a fertile grassland into a barren black soil area?" Xueribu shed tears of guilt.

"Bearing in mind the harsh conditions of Henan County, Gabulong showed concern for the lives of the cadres. In 1961, a young commando was set up in Henan County, and people from the county organs also got equipped and stood ready to go to the countryside with bedding on their backs. Early that morning, Gabulong led a squad of people to the ditch. As soon as he saw us walking with luggage on our backs, he got down from his horse and instructed everyone to dismount. Just then, twelve police officers arrived on horseback, who were also asked to dismount. All the luggage of the young commandos was put on these horses. Gabulong trekked a whole six kilometers with everyone else before reaching the Xiawu ditch."

下乡时的尕布龙

Gabulong was in the countryside

导、老同事、老朋友在县委宣传部开了一个座谈会，讲述尕布龙在河南县工作生活的往事。

那天，我再次见到了当年只有20多岁，现已90多岁的血日布老人。说起尕布龙，他还是那样激动。其实，早在解放初期，尕布龙作为翻译就来过河南蒙旗，他对这片草原是了解的。他记得，尕书记刚来时，曾经狠狠地批评过他："把这么好的草场变成了黑土滩，你们这些人是干什么的？"说得血日布直流眼泪。

"尕布龙心里明白河南县的艰苦，时时刻刻关心着干部的生活。1961年，河南县成立了青年突击队，县机关的人也整装待发，背着被褥下乡。那天一早，尕布龙就带着一个班的人到了沟口，一看到背着行李走路的我们，立即下了马，命令大家一起下马。正在这时，过来了12位骑马的民警，他又让民警下马，把青年突击队员背在身上的行李全部放在马背上，和大家一起徒步走了16公里，才到达夏吾沟口。"

尕布龙常年下乡了解情况。下乡时，总要吃住在条件最差、生活最困难的人家。有一次，他和通讯员郭多到宁木特乡卫拉大队下乡，到一户叫华义的残疾人帐篷里了解情况。华义双腿瘫痪，常年卧病在床，和妹妹生

Gabulong paid year-round visits to the countryside to get informed of the situation. When he was there, he always ate and lived in the most destitute homes with the worst conditions. On one occasion, he and his correspondent Guo Duo went to Weila Brigade, Ningmute Township, where they resided in the tent of a disabled man called Huayi, who was bedridden with paralyzed legs and dragged out his existence with his younger sister. In a small and broken tent with leaks in the window, the sister cooked for her disabled brother.

The situation tugged at the heart of Gabulong, who immediately ordered Guo Duo to notify the people in charge at the brigade and township to meet right in front of the tent.

The next morning, more than ten people, including the Party committee secretary of Ningmute Township, the township chief, and branch secretaries of various brigades as well as captains, congregated in front of Huayi's tent. Gabulong asked them to take a closer look inside one by one and asked, "Comrades, you see it! The weather is getting increasingly cold, and our herdsmen still live in a dilapidated tent. How can we sleep at night? We have not fulfilled our responsibilities!"

Therefore, it was decided at the meeting that the township committee and the brigade would be held accountable for solving the difficulties of Huayi's family within a month. Then the masses were mobilized to contribute their money and labor, hence the emergence of a brand-new, cow hair-textured woven tent for his family in less than twenty days.

When Huayi and his sister saw the new tent, their eyes welled up with tears of gratitude and excitement, "Many thanks to the Communist Party of China and Secretary Gabulong!"

Subsequently, Gabulong requested that all the homes of the county's 3000-plus herdsmen be visited to have their living conditions checked. All the tents of impoverished households must be solved on the spot. In just two years, all the rain-leaking cow-hair tents were replaced with warm and sturdy yurts.

Gabulong didn't merely make brief visits to the countryside to dictate work. On the contrary, he worked, ate, and slept together in the same tent with the farmers and herdsmen, during which he carefully observed and experienced their real living conditions and engaged in heart-to-heart exchanges of views. On a scorching hot summer day when the grassland was tumbling with heat waves, Gabulong, who was working with farmers and herdsmen in the field, took off his clothes and threw them in the nearby grass. Upon seeing this, an old woman rushed over to hold Gabulong's clothes tightly in her arms.

At the symposium that day, I also had the opportunity to meet Guo Duo, a

活在一起，帐篷又小又破，里外透风，妹妹正在狭小的帐篷里给残疾哥哥做饭。

看到这种情况，尕布龙心里非常难受，立即安排郭多通知乡上和大队的负责人，到华义的帐篷前开现场会。

第二天早上，华义的帐篷前聚集了宁木特乡党委书记、乡长，各大队支部书记、队长 10 余人。尕布龙依次让乡党委书记、乡长及各支部书记、队长到华义的帐篷里看后，对大家说："同志们，大家看到了吧！天气越来越冷，我们的牧民还住在这么破旧的帐房里，我们能看得过去吗？能睡安稳觉吗？是我们的干部没有尽到责任啊！"

于是，会议决定由乡委和大队负责，一个月内解决华义家中的困难。随之发动群众，出钱出物出劳力，不到 20 天，就给华义家织了一顶新帐篷。

20 天后，一顶崭新的牛毛帐房搭起来了，华义兄妹看到新帐房的那一刻，眼里噙满了泪水："还是共产党好，尕书记好啊！"

随后，尕布龙又要求把全县 3000 多户牧民的居住条件全部排查了一遍，就地解决贫困户的所有帐篷问题。在短短两年时间内，把过去牧民住的夏天漏雨水、冬天不抵寒的牛毛帐篷全部换成了暖和结实的蒙古包。

尕布龙下乡到基层，绝不指手画脚，也不走马观花，而是与农牧民一起劳动，一起吃饭，睡在同一个帐篷里，心贴心地交流，细细地观察和体会农牧民真实的生活状况。有一年夏天，艳阳高照，草原上翻滚着阵阵热浪。正在地里和农牧民一起干活的尕布龙把衣服脱下，随手扔在旁边的草丛里，一位老奶奶见了，急忙跑过来，把尕布龙的外衣紧紧地抱在怀里。

在那天的座谈会上，我还有幸见到了给尕布龙当过四年警卫的通讯员郭多。郭多是河南县优干宁镇阿木乎村人，蒙古族，1948 年 11 月 1 日出生。1965 年，不满 17 岁的郭多参加了工作。第二天，时任河南县委副书记、组织部部长的张赞庭同志找他谈话，经组织研究决定，派他担任尕布龙书记的警卫员，负责书记的安全保卫工作，并特别交代，尕书记下乡前需提前侦查清楚地方情况，了解下乡点的安全，郭多欣然接受了这一特殊任务。

郭多体格健壮，脸庞宽大，浓眉大眼，提起尕布龙，还未开口，眼里已盈满了泪水。

"我跟尕书记在一起工作了四年，几乎形影不离。尕书记很少在办公室待着，经常下乡一住就一个多月。我给尕布龙书记当了四年警卫，几乎

correspondent who served as Gabulong's guard for four years. Guo Duo, a Mongolian native of Amuhu Village, was born on November 1st, 1948. He started to work in 1965 when he was less than 17 years old. The next day, Comrade Zhang Zanting, then deputy secretary of the Henan County Party Committee and chief of the Organization Division, told Guo Duo that the organization decided to appoint him as Gabulong's security guard. Zhang Zanting specifically clarified that the local situation must be investigated and scouted out before the Secretary went to the countryside. Guo Duo readily accepted this mission of special significance.

Guo Duo had a robust physique, a broad face, bushy eyebrows, and big eyes that brimmed with tears before he could even speak the name of Gabulong.

"I worked almost inseparably with Secretary Gabulong for four years and found that he rarely stayed in the office and often lived in the countryside for more than a month at a time. My four years as his security guard was tantamount to spending four years on horsebacks together with Secretary Gabulong, who held meetings, conducted research, and publicized the Party's policies. He learned about people's lives in the daytime, and personally looked after the production team's flocks of sheep and collected firewood and cow dung for the herders at night."

Gabulong was held in high esteem and sorely missed by Guo Duo. At that time, Guo Duo was young, and Gabulong cared for him like a child, yet he was also very strict with him. Once, he followed Gabulong to the countryside, where the Secretary discussed with the village cadres about running an elementary school in the village. Twiddling his thumbs, Guo Duo began to dig out a bird's nest and killed a dozen small birds. After finding out about it, Gabulong was infuriated. "You might as well learn more Chinese characters rather than using your spare time to do awful things. Birds are also living creatures and should be loved and cared for. You may realize it once you are educated." Since then, Guo Duo seized each and every moment to pick up Chinese characters and read books. Afterwards, he not only knew the Tibetan language, but was also well versed in Chinese. In his old age, he started collecting and collating the annals of Henan County.

In the eyes of Guo Duo, Gabulong was an approachable person who led a simple existence. He was also a good cadre who kept close contact with the general public. He was broad-minded, modest, prudent, and upright. He placed group interests above personal gains, treated everyone with equality, and dedicated himself to service without asking anything in

跟尕布龙书记在马背上度过了四年。白天开会、调研，宣传党的政策，了解民情；晚上他还亲自看护生产队的羊群，替牧民拾柴火、捡牛粪。"

郭多敬重尕布龙，对尕布龙充满怀念之情。那时候，郭多年龄小，尕布龙像照顾孩子一样关心他，但是对他要求很严。有一回，郭多跟随尕布龙下乡，尕布龙和村干部商量村里办小学的事。郭多没事可干，去村边掏鸟窝，弄死了十几只小鸟。尕布龙知道后很生气："你有闲工夫干坏事，还不如多认几个字。鸟也是有生命的，应该爱护，有了文化你就懂道理了。"从此，郭多一有时间就认汉字，读书，此后不但识藏语，还能熟练地运用汉语，晚年一直从事搜集整理河南县县志的文字工作。

在郭多眼里，尕布龙书记是一个平易近人、生活简朴的人，是一位同人民群众保持密切联系的好干部。他顾全大局、胸怀坦荡、严于律己、谦虚谨慎、待人忠厚，对所有人一视同仁。他这一辈子只知奉献，不求索取。是一位同牧民群众同吃同住同劳动，关心群众疾苦，坚持为群众办实事办好事的好干部。

南旗村的老社长尕角回忆道：1963年，尕布龙书记来南旗村下乡住在他们家，每天都要把周茂村和南旗村的干部叫到一起，商量如何在南旗村成立制造毡房的加工厂，修筑畜圈，发展畜牧经济。他用自己的工资给家中无劳力的贫困户买粮食，还手把手地教大家使用牛奶分离器打酥油。1964年，尕布龙书记组织牧民劳务输出，搞分红，增加了牧民的收入，改善了大家的生活，让村民们住上了温暖的蒙古包。

宁木特镇的旦增老人过去当过民兵，之后成了村里的会计，尕布龙下乡到他们村就住在他家。一大早，尕布龙就把他叫起来，不让睡懒觉。冬天，地冻得生硬，冷风刺骨。上午，尕布龙带着村干部到牧民家了解情况，谁家最穷，他就去谁家，谁家有难，他就帮谁，每到一户人家，都要留下午饭钱。下午，一个村挨一个村开会，告诉村干部，村子是个集体，应该有集体精神，干部要关心群众，不要只顾自己。

尕布龙请来畜牧专家改良河曲马，鼓励黄河沿岸的村民种菜，种粮食，挖药材，增加收入。哪个村有了好的经验，他马上在别的村推广，谁家酸奶做得好，他就请到村子里来向大家传授技艺，千方百计想办法提高牧民的生活水平。

1963年，河南县下了一场很大的雪，车辆根本无法行驶，尕布龙心中

return. He was a good cadre who ate, lived, and worked with the herdsmen, caring deeply about the sufferings of the people and never wavering in his commitment to serve the masses.

Gajiao, a former communal chief of Nanqi Village, recalled that in 1963, Secretary Gabulong dwelled at his home in Nanqi Village. He would summon the cadres of Zhoumao Village and Nanqi Village together on a daily basis to discuss how to establish a processing plant in Nanqi Village to manufacture yurts, build animal pens, and develop the livestock economy. He spent his own salary on buying food for the poor households without labor at home and also taught people how to use the milk-cream separator to make butter. In 1964, Secretary Gabulong organized the herdsmen to export their pastoral services and earn dividends on their work, leading to the improvement in their incomes. As the villagers improved their standard of living, they were able to reside in warm Mongolian yurts.

Danzeng, an elderly man in Ningmute Township, used to be a militiaman before he became a village accountant. Gabulong lived in his house after coming to the countryside. Early in the morning, Gabulong woke him up to prevent him from sleeping in. In winter, braving biting wind and frozen ground, the secretary led a group of village cadres to the herdsmen's homes to check on their living conditions, leaving lunch money with each family he visited. His assistance invariably went to the poorest families who suffered the most.

In the afternoons, he held meetings with one village after another, during which he told the cadres that they should possess a collective spirit since each village is a community. Cadres should care about the masses regardless of their own profits.

Gabulong did his utmost to improve the herdsmen's livelihoods. For example, he invited animal husbandry experts to improve the breed of Hequ horses, and he encouraged villagers along the Yellow River to plant vegetables, grow grain, and dig medicinal herbs for more income. Whenever a village had good experience, he immediately popularized it in other villages, inviting those who produced the best yogurt to the village to teach others their skills.

In 1963, a heavy snowfall hit Henan County, making the paths utterly impassable to vehicles. Overwhelmed with anxiety, Gabulong was eager to learn about the situation in the countryside.

Gabulong said to Douhela, director of the Bureau of Animal Husbandry, "Let's go! We have to get down there. If we can walk, we'll walk. If we can't walk, we'll crawl til we get

着急，迫切地想了解乡下的情况。

尕布龙对畜牧局局长斗合拉说："走，我们得下去，能走就走，不能走就是爬也要去。不然，会让群众失望的。"

斗合拉劝不住，只好把食物驮在马背上，和尕布龙一起出发了。

那一天，雪下个不停，乌青的天空铅云笼罩，白茫茫的世界，刺得人睁不开眼睛。气温降到了零下30多摄氏度，冷得人连腮帮子都动不了。积雪深厚，一脚踩下去，半天抽不

尕布龙和扎喜旺徐参加黄南州三十周年州庆
Gabulong and Zhaxiwangxu were attending the 30th anniversary of
Huangnan Tibetan Autonomous Prefecture

出脚。尕布龙走在前面，其他人跟在后面，一步一喘地在茫茫雪野中走了整整一天，才走到村子里。当天夜里，他进到一户叫拉玛杰的牧民家，看到拉玛杰上身只穿着一件光板皮袄，什么也没说，脱下自己的干净衬衣就让拉玛杰穿上了。拉玛杰感动得流下了眼泪，跟在身边的智后茂乡南旗大队队长、支部书记尕角，看在眼里，记在了心上。

当天夜里，尕布龙顾不上休息，饿着肚子，带着干部挨家挨户去每一个帐房看望牧民，把食物分给大家后，才安心地吃了顿简单的晚饭。

夜里，他住在一户贫困的牧民家里。老人的家里除了一块毡子，一个烧奶茶的炉子和几样简单的日用品，什么也没有。他注视着老人，关心地询问老人，生活上有没有困难。

老人连连摇头："没有，没有！帐房是县上刚解决的，送来的炒面就放在屋子里。"尕布龙没有说什么，等老人睡着后，他躺了一会儿，睡不着，起身想喝口水。突然发现老人放在屋角的靴子已经烂得没法穿了。他想了想，从自己大衣的下摆上剪了一块皮子，找出随身携带的针线，用一双粗大而又不十分灵巧的手一针一针地缝了起来。

天快亮了，两只靴子缝好了，虽然不好看，但在寒冷的冬天，总算可

there. Otherwise, we will let the people down."

Douhela could not persuade the secretary to stay, so he had to put the food on tHeback of the horse and set off with Gabulong.

That day, snow fell incessantly, the dark sky was shrouded by thick clouds, and people could barely keep their eyes open amid the blinding whiteout. The temperature plummeted to less than negative 30 degrees Celsius, making it difficult for people to even move their cheeks. The snow was so deep that people could not pull their feet out. Gabulong, walking ahead of everyone else, panted as he trudged through the vast expanse of the snow all day before finally reaching the village. That night, he went into the home of a herdsman named Lamajie and saw him wearing only a bare leather jacket. Without saying a word, the secretary took off his own clean shirt and let Lamajie put it on. This deed not only moved Lamajie to tears, but it was also engraved in the mind of Gajiao, captain of Nanqi Brigade, Zhihoumao Township who followed the secretary.

That night, Gabulong, who was running on no sleep and an empty stomach, took the cadres to visit the herdsmen at each tent and distribute food to them before having their own simple dinner.

At night, he stayed in a poor herdsman's house, where there was nothing but a single piece of furniture, a stove for boiling milk tea, and a few simple daily necessities. He gazed at the old man and asked whether he had any difficulties in life.

The old man shook his head repeatedly and replied, "No, no! The tent was just provided by the county, as well as the fried noodles." Gabulong didn't say anything. After the old man fell asleep, he laid down for a while. Struggling to sleep, he got up for a drink of water and suddenly he noticed the man's shabby and worn-out shoes in the corner of the house. He thought for a moment and then cut a piece of leather from the hem of his own coat. Taking out the needle and thread he carried with him, he started to sew the shoes stitch-by-stitch with his rough and not-so-nimble fingers.

It was almost dawn when the two boots were sewn up. Despite their homely appearance, they could provide an effective shield against the cold of winter. Gabulong heaved a sigh of relief and went to sleep.

His security guard Guo Duo told me the whole story. Gabuke, chief of the second production team of Zuomao Team (Brigade), Ningmute Township, also knew about this, yet I didn't see him. Beyond that, no one else witnessed the event or knew what happened.

以御寒，他这才放心地睡了。

这件事是他的警卫员郭多讲给我听的。当时，知道这件事的还有一人，当年宁木特乡作毛大队第二生产队队长尕布科，只可惜我没有见到他，此外，没有第二个人亲眼看到，没有第二个人知道这件事。

当天晚上，又下了一场大雪。

赛马会上尕布龙为骑手颁奖
Gabulong was presenting an award to a rider at a horse race

第二天，尕布科早早来到尕书记的帐篷里，给他送糌粑和奶茶，发现尕布龙脸色发青，不停地咳嗽，便心疼地说："尕书记，你跟我走，到我家的帐篷去住，你是县委书记，如果你冻病了，我这个生产队队长是有责任的。"

尕布龙却松开尕布科硬拉着他的手："尕布科，没关系，我们都是草原上的牧民，住在这样的帐篷里虽然有一点冷，但只有这样才能了解到老百姓的疾苦，才能体会到群众的冷暖呀！"

那个时候，他的工资只有24.5元，每月工资都由警卫员郭多代领。其中5元交党费，剩下的要付下乡到牧民家中吃饭的钱，住一宿交1斤粮票6角钱。尕书记说，吃一顿饭虽然吃不穷一家人，老百姓还乐意给你。但如果我们干部下乡吃饭都不给钱，那风气就会变坏，久而久之就成了大问题。

平时，尕布龙的大多数工资也都用于救济穷苦的农牧民，只要碰到贫困的老人，身上装着多少钱，多少粮票，都要拿出来给人。遇到贫困牧民向他借钱，他从不过问对方的用途，只问清还钱的时间。每当牧人按约定时间还钱时，他才详细地询问。如果钱用到了正路上，他会把钱再交给还钱的牧人，让他们好好劳动、好好生活、好好学习。

南旗村一个叫多洛的牧民得了眼病，在去省城看病的路上和妻子遭遇

That night, there was another heavy snow.

The next day, Gabuke came to Secretary Gabulong's tent early to give him tsampa and milk tea, only to find him looking pale and coughing. Gabuke said sadly, "Secretary, please come with me to live in my tent. You are the county party secretary, and I, as a production team leader, would be responsible if you fall ill."

However, Gabulong let go of the hands of Gabuke clutching at him and replied, "It doesn't matter. We are all herdsmen on the grassland. Although it's a little cold to live in such a tent, only in this way can we truly understand the suffering of the people!"

His salary back then was only 24.5 yuan per month, which was collected by his security guard Guo Duo. Five yuan went to pay his party membership dues and the rest was used to eat at herdsmen's homes— 60 jiao for a half-kilogram food voucher and an overnight stay. Secretary Ga said that although people were happy to offer food and one single meal would not cause a family to become impoverished, if thousands of cadres went to the countryside to eat without giving money, then the atmosphere would deteriorate and it would become a big problem over time.

Normally, most of Gabulong's salary was also used for helping needy farmers and herdsmen. Whenever he encountered poor old people, he would give them all the money and food coupons he had on him. If a poor herdsman borrowed money from him, he always asked when it would be returned rather than what it was for, and he only asked in detail about the purpose of the money after the herdsman paid it back. If it was used for rightful purposes, he would give the money back to the man and tell him to work hard, study well, and live a better life.

A herdsman named Duoluo in Nanqi Village, who suffered from an eye disease, died in a car accident with his wife on the way to the provincial hospital. When Gabulong learned of this, he entrusted another herdsman to take care of the three bereaved children. The oldest child was just ten years old and the youngest five. Gabulong himself paid for their living expenses until they became adults.

At that time, Luogai, then Party branch secretary of Amuhu Village, saw that Gabulong did this on a regular basis and asked with surprise, "Secretary Ga, do you have enough money left over for yourself?" Gabulong said with a smile, "Lack of money is only a trivial matter. What I am really in want of are food stamps."

Jiaye, another party branch secretary standing next to him, said with emotion, "I have

车祸双双离世。尕布龙知道后，把失去父母、孤苦无依的三个孩子，最大的十岁、最小的五岁，安顿给一户牧民照顾，承担了三个孩子的生活费用，一直到他们长大成人。

当时，担任阿木呼村党支部书记的洛改，见尕布龙经常这样，有些诧异地说："尕书记，你这样做，自己的钱够用吗？"尕布龙微微一笑说："钱不够用还好说，主要是缺粮票。"

一旁的支部书记加叶则感慨地说："像尕布龙这样的人，这样的共产党员干部，我从没见过，以后，也不会有了。"

半年后，2017年的深秋，郭多来西宁看病，找到了我，和我再次谈起他尊敬的尕布龙书记。2018年春天，他又来了一次，这一次来主要是看病，顺便再来看看我。两次来，都要和我合张影，还要求我洗出来给他寄去。第一次照的，我洗了给他寄过去了，第二次的照片我没有寄，准备来年夏天去河南县亲自交给他。不想，等我去时，他已经过世，给我留下了无法弥补的遗憾。

2019年夏天，河南县正举办那达慕大会。彩旗飘动，气氛热烈。歌舞声中，白色的蒙古包像成熟的蘑菇，欢快地点缀在碧绿的草地上。年轻女人着盛装亭亭玉立，骑着骏马的小伙子在赛马场上扬鞭飞腾。蒙古包里，摆满了香喷喷的牛羊肉、奶茶、包子、熬饭。我坐在观礼台上，眼前总是浮现出尕布龙纵马在前，郭多紧随其后的身影，那是艰苦的岁月，难忘的岁月，尕布龙和郭多不知吃了多少苦，如果他们能活到今天，看到河南蒙旗大草原的富庶安康，看到牧民们一张张喜悦的笑脸，该有多么欣慰啊！

never seen a Communist Party cadre like Gabulong. Nor will I come upon another like him in the future."

Half a year later, in the late autumn of 2017, Guo Duo dropped in on me after he came to see a doctor in Xining, and he talked again about his esteemed Secretary Gabulong. In the spring of 2018, he visited while in Xining for the same reason. During both visits, he requested that we take photos together and that I send them to him. I developed the film from our first visit and sent the photo to him, planning to give him the second photo in person when I went to Henan County the following summer. By the time I got there, he had passed away, leaving me with irreparable regret.

Nadamu Fair was in full swing in the summer of 2019 in Henan County, which was permeated with fluttering colorful flags and a festive atmosphere. Amidst singing and dancing, white yurts buoyantly dotted the vast expanse of the turquoise grasslands like ripe mushrooms. Young women dressed up in their finest attire, while young lads whipped their fiery steeds to gallop around at full tilt on the racecourse. Yurts were filled with the aroma of beef, lamb, milk tea, steamed buns, and cooked rice. When I sat on the viewing platform, scenes of the past glory unfolded before my eyes: Gabulong burned down the roads on a horseback at full pelt whilst Guo Duo followed him closely. Those good old days were also days of bitterness. While both men had endured untold sufferings, if they were still alive today, surely they would feel gratified to see the beaming smiles of the herdsmen on the fertile and affluent grasslands of the Mongolian Autonomous County of Henan.

痴心不改

还是 2017 年 7 月，河南县委书记韩华带着我来到拉毛才让的家。进入院门，一株茂盛的大黄像小树紧紧依偎在院墙上，客厅里没有别的摆设，长长的条桌上只有拉毛才让获得的各种奖状、优秀共产党员证书。

拉毛才让是尕布龙在河南县工作时，发展的第一个女共产党员，优干宁镇多特村第一任支部书记。多年来，她为自己的家乡、村民，为这片辽阔的草原做了自己力所能及的事。

落座后，韩华书记和河南县党校的两位副校长才项南加和周毛措，用藏语和拉毛才让愉快地攀谈起来，间或发出朗朗笑声，又不时回过头给我翻译。虽然无法与拉毛才让直接交流，但正好，可以让我从容体会、细细观察她宁静的表情和庄重的仪态，感受她不平凡的人生经历，以及她奋斗的足迹、执着的信仰。

和牧区的藏族老人一样，拉毛才让穿着红缎绳边，黑布质地的长袍，腰带紧束，长辫披肩，看起来精神矍铄，不像是一位 80 多岁的老人。有点特别的是，她的胸前没有任何配饰，只有一枚毛主席像章。像章是银色的，大小适中，清洁素雅。1976 年，毛主席逝世，拉毛才让去兰州开会时得到了这枚像章。她很珍惜，很喜欢。回来的路上，她揣在怀里，如同把恩人请回了家。从此以后，她就再也没有与这枚像章分离片刻，一直佩戴在自己胸前，从不离身。串像章的带子稍有磨损，她便用红黄相间的毛线再编根新的，这一戴竟是 45 年。

Remain True to the Original Aspiration

In July 2017, Han Hua, Party Secretary of Henan County, took me to Lamao Tsering's home. At the gate of the courtyard, a lush rhubarb was clinging to the wall like a small tree. The living room was bedecked with no other furnishings than a myriad of awards that she had won and her certificate of Outstanding Communist Party Member lying on the long table.

Lamao Tsering was the first female Party member trained by Gabulong when he worked in Henan County. She was also the first branch secretary of Duote Village, Youganning Township. Over the years, she has made her own contribution to her hometown and villagers, as well as to this vast grassland.

After taking their seats, Secretary Han Hua and Cai Xiang Nanjia and Zhou Maocuo, the two vice principals of Henan County Party School, chatted happily in Tibetan, laughing together, and occasionally turning to me to translate the conversation. Although I was not able to communicate directly with Lamao Tsering, I took this opportunity to scrutinize her quiet expression and solemn demeanor, thinking about her extraordinary life experience, as well as her determined spirit.

Like the other elderly Tibetan people in the pastoral area, Lamao Tsering wore a robe made of black cloth with red satin and drew her belt tightly with long braids covering her shoulders. For a senior citizen, she seemed quite cheerful and full of life. Characteristically, there were no accessories on her chest except for a silver, medium-sized Chairman Mao badge yielding a simple and elegant look. In 1976, when Chairman Mao passed away, Lamao Tsering

河南县委书记韩华看望拉毛才让

Han Hua, secretary of the Henan Party Committee, was visiting Lamao Cairang

　　小时候，拉毛才让的日子过得很苦。2 岁时父亲去世，10 岁时患了感冒的哥哥因没钱医治也离开了人世，只留下她和母亲相依为命。那时候，没有人能帮助她们母女，周围的人、亲戚都太穷，她们只能挖地里的蕨麻为生。饿得睡不着觉时，拉毛才让就想，为什么不让自己和哥哥一起死掉，为什么要留下她和母亲在人世间受罪。

got this badge when she went to Lanzhou for a meeting. She cherished it dearly and clutched it near to her heart on her way home, as if cordially inviting her benefactor back home. Since then, she has been wearing tHebadge on her chest and has never separated from it for a moment for 45 years. Once tHeband is slightly worn, she will use red and yellow wool to knit a new one.

Lamao Tsering's childhood was difficult and unstable. Her father died when she was two years old, and her brother, who suffered from a cold, stopped breathing at the age of ten because he could not afford medical treatment, leaving her and her mother alone to make ends meet. No relatives or people around could help them at that time since they were all pauperized. They had to dig ferns in the ground to eke out their livelihoods. When Lamao Tsering was too hungry to sleep, she wondered why she and her mother were left to suffer in this mortal world, instead of departing this life with her brother.

Her mother found a job working for a family, and secretly saved some food which she couldn't bear to eat to bring back to her daughter every night. But Lamao Tsering still felt hungry, pining away every single day with the torment of starvation during the years of physical growth. In winter, the wind howled around the grasslands along with large swaths of snow falling on the run-down tent where the mother and the daughter lived, striking a chill even colder than the snow to the heart of Lamao Tsering.

Gabulong's arrival to the remote and impoverished Henan County was like a fire in the winter and a rain in spring. At that time, Gabulong often took the county cadres to Lamao Tsering's hometown of Duote Village, now Youganning Township. He worked with the villagers to educate everyone that it was Chairman Mao, the Communist Party, and the People's Liberation Army that rescued the grasslands of the Mongolian Autonomous County of Henan so that the herdsmen could have ample food to eat and lead a comfortable life. In the future, everyone can work hard to get rich and live a happy life.

A cooperative was soon established in the village, and 16-year-old Lamao Tsering voluntarily took on the task of carrying water with 100 buckets on 50 round trips per day. Although the skin on her shoulders had been rubbed raw, she felt elated and energized. Located in Youganning Beach in the north of Henan County, Duote Village is blessed with rich high-altitude meadow pastures, enabling it to develop an animal husbandry economy. Grateful villagers knew how to improve their lives and reverse the fate of poverty. On a quiet and auspicious day, Gabulong established the first Party branch in Duote Village, developing seven

母亲在一户人家找了活干，每天晚上，偷偷省下自己舍不得吃的口粮，带回来给拉毛才让吃。但是拉毛才让还是觉得饿，长身体的她没有一天不是在忍受饥饿的痛苦与辛酸中度过的。到了冬天，草原上的卷毛风裹着大片大片的雪，落在母女俩栖身的破帐房上，拉毛才让的心比雪还要冰冷。

　　尕布龙的到来对于寂寞、贫穷的河南县来说，就像冬天里的一把火，

拉毛才让在讲述过去的故事
Lamao Tsering was telling the story of the past

春天里的一场雨。那时，尕布龙常常带着县上的干部到拉毛才让的老家多特村，现在的优干宁镇驻村，跟村民拉家常，教育大家，是毛主席、共产党、解放军拯救了河南蒙旗草原，让牧民们吃饱肚子，过上了好日子。今后，大家完全可以用勤劳的双手劳动致富，过上幸福的生活。

　　村子里很快成立了合作社，16岁的拉毛才让主动承担起挑水的任务，一天100桶，往返50趟。虽然肩膀磨破了，可心里是甜的。多特村在河南县北边的优干宁滩，拥有丰美的高寒草甸牧场，具有发展畜牧经济的优

members and personally assuming the position of acting branch secretary.

That was a period greatly charged with passion and ambition, a captivating tale of blazing trails with lofty aspirations to achieve prosperity in the village under the leadership of Secretary Gabulong. How could Lamao Tsering not feel electrified with her morale being boosted to maximum? In 1957, at the age of twenty, she was asked to hand in an application form to join the Party. In 1960, when she turned twenty-three, she joined the Communist Party of China.

Secretary Gabulong told her, "Communist Party members exist to serve the people of their hometowns. Party members should never degenerate into mere talkers." Over the years, she has always kept the secretary's words in mind.

Together with Secretary Gabulong on the grasslands, Lamao Tsering exterminated rats, collected firewood, picked up cow dung, dug ditches, repaired roads, ran tent schools, and went from door to door to get informed of the actual situations and address issues, which allowed her to gain a true awareness of the value of life. Two years later, Lamao Tsering was elected by the party branch of Duote Village as the branch secretary, becoming the first female party member to serve as the branch secretary on the grasslands of the Henan Mongol Autonomous County.

"Villages see other villages as their yardsticks, and so do households; people regard party members as role models, and party members model themselves after cadres. Excellent party members and cadres exert a tremendous influence on the general public who keep a close eye on whether they always take the needs of the people into consideration and lead them to develop production." This was what Gabulong often said to her.

Under the leadership of Secretary Gabulong, Lamao Tsering ran around in the villagers' tents and toiled away on the endless stretch of grasslands. Because she was illiterate, she used the methods taught by Secretary Gabulong to tally up the number of sheep with sheep dung and the number of cattle with small stones. Gabulong would translate and explain important documents to her, and she would memorize them word by word to explain them to the villagers. Some herdsmen abstained from killing animals and did not cooperate with the rat extermination. She, like Secretary Gabulong, patiently explained to the villagers the adverse effects of rodent damage on the grasslands and the animal husbandry economy. On one occasion, when members of the production team were killing rats, the containing rat poison in the warehouse was damaged, leaving the rat poison containing highly toxic ingredients floating in the air. Lamao Tsering knew the toxicity of rat poison well. Without thinking, she ran into the warehouse and moved the rat poison to a safe place. As a result, she was seriously poisoned

势。村子里的人懂得感恩，知道该怎样改善生活，改变贫穷的面貌。在一个宁静、吉祥的日子里，尕布龙在多特村成立了第一个党支部，发展了7名党员，自己亲自代理支部书记。

那是一段充满激情与希望的年代，那是一段在尕布龙书记领导下为家乡富饶、艰苦创业、豪情万丈的时光，怎能不叫拉毛才让感慨万千、热血沸腾呢？1957年，20岁的拉毛才让递交了入党申请书。1960年，23岁的她加入了中国共产党。

尕布龙书记对她说："共产党员就是为家乡人民服务的，绝不能做徒有虚名的党员。"多年来，她一直牢记着尕布龙书记的话。

同尕布龙书记一起在草原上灭鼠、拾柴火、捡牛粪、挖水渠、修路、办帐篷学校、走村串户、了解实情、解决困难的工作实践，让朴实的拉毛才让意识到了一个人活着的价值。两年后，拉毛才让被多特村党支部推选为支部书记，成了河南蒙旗大草原上，担任支部书记的第一位女性共产党员。

"村看村，户看户，群众看党员，党员看干部。优秀的党员干部对群众的影响很大，群众看党员干部看的是党员干部能不能处处为百姓着想，能不能带领群众发展生产。"这是尕布龙常对她说的话。

在尕布龙书记的带领下，拉毛才让奔波在村民的帐房里，劳作在茫茫草原上。不识字就用尕布龙书记教给她的方法，用羊粪蛋统计羊的数量，用小石头计算牛的数量。必须领会学习的材料，经过尕布龙书记翻译讲解后，一字不落地背下来，讲给村民听。有些牧民忌讳杀生，不配合灭鼠，她就像尕布龙书记那样，耐心地给村民讲解鼠害对草原、对畜牧经济带来的不利影响。有一次，生产队队员正在灭鼠，仓库中装着老鼠药的包装袋破损，含有剧毒成分的老鼠药在空气中弥漫开来。拉毛才让深知老鼠药的毒性，顾不得多想，一个人跑进仓库，将老鼠药搬到了安全的地方，结果自己中毒严重险些丧命，抢救了三天才慢慢苏醒过来。

拉毛才让说："山有自己的斜坡，人有自己的个性，我就是这样一个人。"

岁月的磨砺，尕布龙的言传身教，把拉毛才让锻炼成了一名忠诚于党，忠诚于脚下这片土地，全心全意为人民服务的优秀基层干部。她说，她从来没有忘记过，年轻时在党旗前举起右手庄严宣誓的情景，她一直珍藏着早已发黄的那张批准她入党的文件。

and it took her three days to recover, narrowly escaping death.

Lamao Tsering said, "Each mountain has its own slope, and people their distinct personality. I am a person with my own personality."

The passage of the years, coupled with Gabulong's mentorship transformed Lamao Tsering into an outstanding grass-roots cadre who was loyal to the party and to the land under her feet and served the people wholeheartedly. She said that she had never forgotten the moment she raised her right hand in front of the party flag and swore solemnly as a young girl. She still treasured the yellowed document approving her party membership.

In March 1997, Lamao Tsering took out her only savings and went to Beijing to realize her last wish. During her five days in Beijing, she watched the hoist of the national flag every morning and paid tribute to Chairman Mao's Memorial Hall during the day. Whenever she saw the red flag with five stars rising, tears flowed from her eyes. Silently she blessed the policies of the Communist Party to shine forever and the people's lives to get better and better.

Whenever someone complained in front of her, she would stand up and sternly tell everyone that she could not forget the suffering and sins of the old society; and that she must not forget the turbulence and heavy price caused by lack of ideological unity.

She had once come up with an idea to take her treasured party flag to each and every village to tell everyone about the great changes that had taken place in the grassland of Henan Mongol Autonomous County under the leadership of the Communist Party of China. Secretary Han Hua thought she was too old for this and talked her out of it. Moved by her enthusiasm, Secretary Han Hua took leaders of the county party committee to visit her, wishing her health and happiness.

"We never dared to dream of such prosperous days!" said Lamao Tsering, affectionately holding my hand.

In her youth, she was a beautiful girl with an oval face, thin eyebrows, narrow eyes, and a straight nose, features typical of any Tibetan beauty. One year, Lamao Tsering got really sick. On a day that felt heavy and oppressive, she could not open her eyes or speak.

Feeling weak all over, she seemed to have come to another world. In her hallucination, she heard someone talking a lot in front of her bed. She was a little confused, but she heard one sentence very clearly.

"Lamao Tsering is childless and unencumbered, to whom shall we give the things she leaves behind? Let's just donate them to the monastery!"

1997 年 3 月，拉毛才让拿出仅有的一点积蓄去了趟北京，实现了最后的心愿。在北京的五天里，她每天早晨观看升国旗，白天瞻仰毛主席纪念堂。每当看到五星红旗冉冉升起，她的眼泪就止不住地往下流，心里在默默祝福，中国共产党金子般的政策永放光芒，人民生活一天更比一天好！

每当有人在她面前有所抱怨、不满，她总是挺起身子，义正词严地告诉大家，不能忘记旧社会受的苦、遭的罪；更不能忘记当年由于人们不团结、思想不统一造成的动荡不安和付出的惨重代价。

她曾经有过这样一个想法，带着她珍藏的一面党旗，到各个村子里，以自己的亲身经历，讲述在中国共产党的领导下，河南蒙旗草原发生的巨大变化，老百姓稳定安逸的生活是怎么得来的。终因她年龄太大，被韩华书记劝住了。感动之余，韩华书记带着县委领导去她家中看望，希望她身体健康，快乐幸福。

"现在的日子是我们做梦也想不到的啊！"拉毛才让拉着我的手动情地说。

年轻时的拉毛才让是一位美丽俊俏的藏族姑娘，有着藏族美女标准的鹅蛋形脸，细长的眉眼，挺拔的鼻梁。有一年，拉毛才让生了一场大病。那天，天色阴沉得可怕，她睁不开眼睛，说不出话。浑身无力，轻飘飘地，仿佛来到了另一个世界。幻觉中，她听到有人在她床前说话，说了很多话。她有些迷糊，但是，有一句话她却听得非常清楚。

"拉毛才让是个无儿无女无牵挂的人，她家里留下的东西该给谁呢，就捐给寺院吧！"

没想到，就在这时，拉毛才让突然惊醒了。

她睁开双眼吃力地说，"我死后，不要为我浪费钱。家里的东西，哪怕有一针一线，也要留给村子那些生活比我困难的乡亲们。"

我和拉毛才让共进了一顿午餐，可是她却吃得很少，完全是因为礼貌才来的。我深深地体会到，她愿意和我坐在一起，是因为她对尕布龙书记深切的感情，出于我们之间相互的尊重与默契。她是一位性格倔强、信念执着，不受任何人摆布，有着自己独立精神和意志的女共产党员，是一位心地善良、桀骜不驯的藏族女人。

由于语言的障碍，我们无法进行深层次的交流。可我相信，如果可以，我们两个人一定能敞开心扉，说些女人之间的心里话。

Unexpectedly, Lamao Tsering returned to consciousness abruptly.

She opened her eyes and said with an effort: "Don't waste money on me after my death. I want to give everything in my house, either a single needle or a single thread, to those who are in need in our village."

Having lunch together with Lamao Tsering, I found that she ate very little and seemed to have come entirely out of politeness. I realized that it was out of her deep affection for Secretary Gabulong and our mutual respect and tacit understanding that she agreed to sit next to me. As a female communist, she is stubborn and persistent, with an independent spirit and will, not living at the mercy of anyone. As a Tibetan woman, she is kind-hearted, yet unyielding.

Due to the language barrier, we did not have a deep conversation. But I believe the two of us would have certainly opened our hearts to each other, if possible.

How time flies! Secretary Han Hua said with emotion: "Gabulong had worked in Henan County for ten years without everyone even realizing it. In those ten years, where there was an epidemic, snow disaster, or famine among farmers and herdsmen, there would be his figure. In those ten years, the county had built schools as well as a 137-kilometer-long road, ending the history of no roads in Henan County. In those ten years, he seldom returned to his home in Haiyan County, but regarded the shepherds in Henan County as his family and the Henan Prairie as the Halejing Prairie in his hometown. He also seldom went to the provincial capital. If there was a meeting in the mainland, he would send other leaders to attend. He never regarded being an official as a means to find satisfaction in others' toil."

In November 1959, Gabulong was appointed as secretary of the Henan County Party Committee. In June 1960, he was promoted further to deputy secretary of the Huangnan Prefecture Committee, and he served concurrently as secretary of Party Committee, chairman of CPPCC Committee, and political commissar of the People's Armed Forces Department of Henan County. In 1963, Gabulong was elected as an alternate member of Qinghai Provincial Party Committee. On December 24, 1965, he was elected vice-chairman of Qinghai Poor and Lower-Middle Peasants' Association.

Because of his hard work, Gabulong was recognized and affirmed by the party and accepted by the masses. He then became more assertive in his outlook on the world and in his values, which in turn made for his pure, transparent heart and lofty ambition. Working for the welfare of the people became his lifelong pursuit.

There is also another story about Gabulong that lingers in the minds of the retired cadres.

日子过得真快啊！韩华书记感慨地说："不经意间，尕布龙在河南县干了十年。十年间，哪里出现疫情、雪灾，哪里的农牧民闹了饥荒，他的身影就会立刻出现在哪里。十年间，县上盖了学校，修通了全长137公里的路，结束了河南县没有公路的历史。十年间，他很少回海晏老家，他把河南县的牧人当作了自己最亲的人，把河南大草原当成了家乡的哈勒景。他也很少去省城，内地有会议也尽可能让其他领导去，他不认为到一个地方任职是去当官和享福的。"

1959年11月，尕布龙被任命为河南县委书记。1960年6月，组织上又提拔他担任黄南州委副书记，兼任河南县委书记，县政协主席、县人民武装部政委等要职。1963年，尕布龙当选为青海省委候补委员。1965年12月24日，他被选为青海贫下中农协会副主席。

在勤奋努力的工作中，在不断被党认可、肯定，被群众接受的过程中，尕布龙更加坚定了自己的人生观、世界观、价值观，这些经历造就了他纯洁的心灵、高远的志向，一心只求为人民谋福利，成了他终身努力的方向。

还有一件让河南县的老干部们铭记在心的事，"三年困难时期"，河南草原一片萧瑟，干部群众吃不饱肚子，农牧民生活面临危机。尕布龙却笃定自若，顶着重重压力，采取紧急措施，组织男人狩猎，女人挖野菜、蕨麻、捡地皮菜，摘野蘑菇；动员乡村干部，走乡串户，解决农牧民困难，用草原上的红景天、秦艽换粮食。河南县不但无一人因饥饿致死，还竟然在生活异常艰苦的困难时期，积极倡导、实施文化基础建设，成立了河南县新华书店支店、电影放映队。两年之后，又成立了县电影发行管理站，定期为农牧民举办运动会，让各县、乡农牧民到县上参加赛马、射箭、摔跤、拔河比赛，改善全县农牧民群众的精神面貌。

他还特别关心照顾外地来的干部，鼓励和赞扬他们的奉献精神，向上级领导汇报，给予他们生活、政治上的优待。有一位来自上海的干部，讲一口上海话，面对牧民群众束手无策。他就经常带着他下乡，给他当翻译，教他说藏话，让他学会在高原生存的本领，教他如何完成工作任务。后来，那位上海干部竟然能讲一口流利的当地话，由于深受尕布龙影响，他成了一位优秀的基层干部，为河南县成为民族团结县打下了坚实的基础。

尕布龙认为，发展地方经济，从根本上解决农牧民的生活问题，关键是抓教育，关键是改变人们根深蒂固的陈旧观念，要让当地干部出去交流

During the "three-year natural disaster", the grasslands in Henan were bleak. Neither the cadres nor the masses had enough to eat, and the farmers and herdsmen were facing a crisis. Under heavy pressure, Gabulong, however, kept his countenance and took some emergency measures in an orderly manner. He organized men to go hunting and women to dig for wild herbs and pick wild vegetables and mushrooms. He mobilized rural cadres to go from village to village to solve the difficulties of farmers and herdsmen by trading Rhodiola rosea and Gentiana macrophylla on the grassland for grain. Thanks to his measures, not a single person in Henan County died of hunger. Moreover, a branch of Xinhua Bookstore and a film screening team were set up in Henan County amid the extremely difficult period of time under his advocacy of cultural infrastructure construction. Two years later, the Henan County Film Distribution Management Station was founded, and sports games were held on a regular basis for farmers and herdsmen from all townships, allowing them to take part in horse racing, archery, wrestling, and tug-of-war competitions in the county, so as to improve their spiritual outlook.

He paid special attention to cadres from other places. Speaking highly of their dedication, he praised them to his superiors, advocating for them to receive privileges in life and politics. There was a cadre from Shanghai who spoke Shanghainese and was always helpless in the face of the herdsmen. To help him survive on the plateau and fulfill his tasks, Gabulong often took him to the countryside, served as his interpreter, and eventually taught him Tibetan. Later, the Shanghai cadre was able to speak fluently in the local dialect. Influenced by Gabulong, he also became an excellent grass-roots cadre, laying a solid foundation for Henan County to become a national unity county.

In Gabulong's mind, education was the key to developing local economy and meeting tHebasic needs of farmers and herdsmen. To be specific, changing people's deep-rooted ideas. One approach was to send local cadres to other places for exchange and have them contribute their share in building their hometown after they come back.

This simple cadre understood the true meaning of poverty alleviation long ago. He often said to his colleagues: "We should be brave enough to admit poverty, yet not willing to be poor; to admit backwardness, but not reconciled to it; to be careful to understand the people's feelings, yet still uphold justice and dare to tell the truth." His remarks, which inspired countless grass-roots cadres, remained fresh in the memories of the old cadres who had worked with him.

Gabulong worked in Henan County for ten years and dedicated his youth to the people there. The moment he set foot on this ancient land, full of expectations, he decided to exert all

学习，再返回来建设家乡。

这位朴实的领导干部，很早以前就懂得了扶贫工作的真实含义。他常对身边一起工作的同事说："要有承认贫穷，但不甘心贫穷的热心；要有承认落后，但不甘落后的雄心；要有深入底层，体察民情的细心；要有主持正义，敢讲实话的真心。"这句话，不知激励过多少基层干部，也让曾经和他一起共事的老干部记忆犹新。

尕布龙在河南县工作了十年，把他最美好的青春年华献给了河南县人民。自从他满怀期望踏上这片古老的土地，他便用自己的全部精力，让河南县的人民过上了由开创到发展的新生活。

十年间，一排排明亮整洁的房子出现在人们面前；学校、商店、医院、公路，方便了农牧民的生活；1953年，中国人民银行河南蒙旗支行正式成立；1954年，河南县有了第一个邮电所；1957年，全县牲畜达到约32万头，比起1952年增长了50.52%；1958年，河南县成立了县工业交通局、奶粉厂、面粉厂、被服厂、制鞋厂、造纸厂、皮毛加工厂、水力发电厂……

历史不会因时间的久远而被遗忘。

多年过去了，河南县人民从未忘记过尕布龙。

老人们说：草原上的蓝天认识尕书记；草原上的白云认识尕书记；草原上的每匹马认识尕书记；草原上的每头牛认识尕书记；草原上的每只羊认识尕书记；草原上的每根草认识尕书记。

哪里风大，尕书记就出现在哪里；哪里雪大，尕书记就出现在哪里；哪里灾大，尕书记就出现在哪里；哪里难大，尕书记就出现在哪里；哪里苦大，尕书记就出现在哪里……

1998年，扶贫工作开始，现任领导带着进村的干部到达尕雄滩，当地的老百姓一见到背着被褥的干部们，便高兴地奔走相告："快去看看吧，尕布龙书记的队伍来了！"

尕布龙离开老家去河南县工作的日子里，妻子华毛在山坡上放牧，在山下种地，有了空闲就给村里人缝缝补补做衣服贴补家用，不给当官的丈夫增添丝毫负担，成了村子里的劳动模范。有一次，她在生产队挤牛奶，一头受惊的牦牛一脚踢在华毛的腰上，华毛的腰被踢伤了。当时她自己太大意，远在河南县的尕布龙又毫不知情，因此错过了治疗的最佳时机。

然而，在河南工作的后期阶段，偏僻的草原腹地，依然没有避免"文革"

his energies to bring a new life to the people of Henan County.

During the ten years, row-upon-row of bright and tidy houses came into people's view; schools, shops, hospitals, and roads facilitated the lives of farmers and herdsmen. In 1953, Henan Mengqi Sub-branch of the People's Bank of China was formally established. In 1954, Henan County had its first post office. In 1957, the number of livestock in the county reached 320,000, an increase of 50.52% over 1952. In 1958, Henan County set up its industrial traffic bureau and hydropower plant, with factories of milk powder, flour, clothing, shoes, paper and fur processing continually springing up...

History will not fade away because of the passage of time.

Years after year, the people of Henan County have never forgotten Gabulong.

Just like the seniors said: The blue sky on the grassland knows Secretary Ga; The white clouds on the grassland know Secretary Ga; Every horse, cow and even sheep on the grassland know Secretary Ga; Every blade of grass on the grassland knows Secretary Ga.

Where there is a strong wind, there is Secretary Ga; Where there is heavy snow, there is Secretary Ga; Where there is a disaster, there is Secretary Ga; Where there is suffering, there is Secretary Ga; Where there is pain, there is Secretary Ga...

Just as poverty alleviation work began in 1998, when Secretary Gabulong and his party arrived at Gaxiongtan, the locals, seeing them carrying their bedding, ran around the village telling everyone: "Let's go and have a look. Secretary Ga and his party are coming!"

In the days when Gabulong left his hometown to work in Henan County, his wife Huamao grazed on the hillside and farmed at the foot of the mountain. In her spare time, she would sew and mend clothes for the villagers to help with the family expenses, adding no burden to her husband. She even became a model worker in the village later. Once, when she was milking the cow in the production team, a frightened yak kicked Huamao's waist. She was severely injured, but she did not take the injury seriously. Her husband, Gabulong, who was far away in Henan County, did not know anything about it, so she missed the best time for treatment.

However, in the later stage of his work in Henan, the remote grassland hinterland was unable to escape the difficulties of the "Cultural Revolution". In the years when happiness and sorrow were intertwined and reality was chaotic, Gabulong was severely criticized and all his posts were removed because he was immersed in economic and cultural construction and demanded justice for Trashi Tséring, the first female county magistrate in Henan County.

带来的灾难。喜忧无界，现实混乱的年月里，由于尕布龙埋头抓经济文化建设，又为担任过河南县第一任女县长的扎西才让主持公道，受到了严厉批判，职务全被免了。

扎西才让是曾经名震草原的河南蒙古女亲王。1940 年，她继承了青海河南厄鲁特蒙古和硕特前首领旗九世和硕亲王更噶环觉亲王的爵位，为蒙古人尊敬爱戴。1949 年 8 月，甘肃省省会兰州解放，扎西才让派额附黄文源为代表，同甘南地区民族上层致敬团一道赴兰州向人民解放军表达致意。夏河解放后，她又亲自率河南蒙旗部分扎萨克和部落首领赴夏河欢迎人民解放军。1950 年，扎西才让亲赴西宁拜会赵寿山主席，表达对人民解放军和人民政府的真诚拥护。1952 年 8 月 6 日，中共河南蒙旗工委进驻河南蒙旗，扎西才让欣喜万分，率全旗头人和上千群众到纳木罕嘉赛斯呼兰热烈欢迎，并在纳木罕杜里奥东举行了隆重的欢迎仪式，结束了河南蒙旗延续数百年的封建王公制度，河南蒙旗得以和平解放。

1953 年，扎西才让应邀赴西安向西北军政委员会汇报工作，受到了时任西北军政委员会副主席习仲勋、民族委员会主任汪锋等领导同志的接见。1954 年 6 月 16 日，河南蒙古族自治区一届一次人民代表大会召开，扎西才让被选为自治区人民政府主席。1955 年，河南蒙古族自治区改为自治县，扎西才让改任县长。1963 年她调至省政协担任省政协常委、副秘书长、省妇联副主任，由一位曾经闻名青、甘、川、藏广大地区的蒙古亲王，蜕变成了一名优秀的少数民族女干部。"文革"开始后，尕布龙认为扎西才让对党忠诚、待人诚恳，是一心为河南蒙旗人民政权建立、人民幸福生活日夜操劳，受到群众拥护、与党合作共事的优秀民主人士，不可能反党反社会主义。但是，在那个特殊的历史时期，不但没有人理会尕布龙的意见，还因为此事影响到了尕布龙本人。

1966 年，扎西才让被押回河南县批斗，在离县城 5 公里的荷日恒大队，遭到了曾经爱戴过她的牧民们的无情批斗。这是她做梦也没想到的事，她很绝望，即使小女儿昂毛暖暖的小手温柔的抚摸和轻声的呼唤也没能把她拉回到充满希望的世界里来。高贵的女亲王扎西才让竟于当晚，于气病交叠中含冤离世。

草原黑沉沉的，像无极的暗夜，每个人的心都坚固而冰冷。不知什么缘故，许多朋友、亲属，甚至夫妻都成了互相伤害的对象。更让人想不到

Trashi Tséring was the Mongolian princess of Henan whose fame spread all over the grassland. In 1940, she inherited the title of "Prince of the First Rank" from Künga Weljor, the ninth Prince of Uuld Mongolia and Khoshut in Henan, Qinghai Province, and was respected and loved by the Mongolians. In August 1949, as Lanzhou, capital of Gansu Province, was liberated, Trashi Tséring sent Huangwenyuan, her son-in-law, to Lanzhou to pay tribute to the People's Liberation Army together with the upper-class ethnic salute group in Gannan region. After the liberation of Xiahe, she personally led some Zasak and tribal leaders of Henan Mongol Autonomous County to Xiahe to welcome the People's Liberation Army. In 1950, Trashi Tséring visited Chairman Zhao Shoushan in Xining to express her sincere support for the People's Liberation Army and the People's Government. On August 6, 1952, when the CPC Henan Mongol Autonomous County Working Committee arrived in the Henan Mongol Autonomous County, Trashi Tséring was overjoyed. She led all the tribal leaders and thousands of people to Namhan Jiaseshulan to greet them, and held a grand welcoming ceremony in East Namhan Dorio, liberating Henan Mongol Autonomous County peacefully and ending the feudal maharaja system that lasted for hundreds of years there.

In 1953, Trashi Tséring was invited to Xi'an to report her work to the Northwest Military and Political Committee, and there, she met with Xi Zhongxun, then vice chairman of the Northwest Military and Political Committee, Wang Feng, director of the Ethnic Affairs Committee, and other comrades. On June 16, 1954, the First People's Congress of Henan Mongol Autonomous Region was held, on which Trashi Tséring was elected chairman of the people's government of the region. In 1955, the Henan Mongol Autonomous Region was changed into an autonomous county, and Trashi Tséring was appointed as the county magistrate. In 1963, she was transferred to the Provincial CPPCC as a member and deputy secretary-general of the Provincial CPPCC Standing Committee, as well as the deputy director of the Provincial Women's Federation, turning from a Mongolian princess who enjoyed a wide reputation in the vast areas of Qinghai, Gansu, Sichuan and Xizang to an outstanding female minority cadre. After the "Cultural Revolution" began, Gabulong believed that Trashi Tséring was loyal to the party and sincere to the people, working day and night for the establishment of the people's regime in the Henan Mongol Autonomous County and for the improvement of people's wellbeing. She had the support of the local populace and cooperated with the party, and she was by no means an anti-socialist who opposed the party. However, in that special historical period, no one listened to him, but even directed their anger at Gabulong.

的是，批斗尕布龙的大会上，一位叫那阔的牧民，这个被他热心帮助过的牧民打他打得最凶。就是这个人，曾经因生活困难，穿着一双露出脚趾的靴子，尕布龙见后，马上把自己的靴子脱下来给了他，自己则打着赤脚回去找了双布鞋穿。可是，就是这个人，不但用皮鞭狠狠地抽打他，还用穿过尕布龙靴子的那双脚，狠狠地踢打着他。就这样，尕布龙的腿被那阔无情地踢断了。

那是他远离亲人，遭受非人待遇的日子。他不能够解释什么，只能默默地承受着、忍耐着。更为残酷的是，就在这时，又传来了他13岁的儿子得急病去世的消息。这突然而至的悲伤在沉静的夜空，像一把刀刺入他的骨髓，成了他心头永远不敢触碰的伤痛，难以愈合，却又无从发泄，他只能吞咽着苦水，隐忍着，从不表达。

以后的日子里，他从不向人提起他曾经有过亲儿子这件令他心如刀绞的往事。以致很多人，包括他的亲属、身边的秘书、司机都忘记了，抑或根本就不知道这件事。

幸好，很早的时候，尕布龙的堂妹就把自己的孩子留在了他家，给了他和华毛一个懂事孝顺的女儿。他和妻子像对待亲生孩子一样疼爱着她，从没有对人说过，她是抱来的孩子。

尕布龙是一个坚强的人，可是，再强大的人也会有儿女情长；再有毅力的人，也放不下失子的痛楚。在后来的日子里，他内心的伤，内心的痛，只有他自己知道，谁也无法想象。

带着深重的打击和痛苦，他整日忍着疼痛，拖着伤腿，跪在地里收割青稞、燕麦。晚上还要接受批斗，腿疼得实在站不住，有人不忍心，给了他一个板凳，可那是瘸了一条腿的板凳，不知是谁，什么缘故，还没等他坐稳，上前使劲一推，让他重重地摔在地上，再也爬不起来了。

尕布龙被送往医院。

提起那段时光，和尕布龙一起工作过的老干部们心里都很难受。

斗吾说，那时，有人给尕布龙书记贴了大字报，我们就在大字报上写上："尕布龙是我们的好书记。"

我们从来没有觉得他有什么不好，更不忍心看他跪在地上被人打，他拖着病身子打扫厕所，我们就偷偷地帮他打扫。这么好的人、这么好的县委书记，对党忠贞不渝，怎么会是反革命啊！

In 1966, Trashi Tséring was escorted back to Henan County for public criticism. In the Heriheng Brigade, five kilometers away from the county seat, she was mercilessly criticized by the herdsmen who once loved her. This was something she never dreamed of. She was desperate. Even her little daughter's gentle touch and soft call failed to pull her back to the world full of hope. The noble princess died of unbearable humiliation and illness that night.

The bleak grassland seemed to have turned everyone's heart into a cold stone. For some reason, former friends, relatives, and even spouses began to tear each other down. Even more unexpected was that at the public criticism of Gabulong, he was beaten most severely by a herdsman named Nakuo, who once received help from him. It was this man who once wore a pair of boots with exposed toes. When Gabulong saw him, he immediately took off his boots and gave them to Nakuo, while he himself went back barefoot. However, it was this man who not only relentlessly beat Gabulong with a whip, but also brutally kicked him with the feet that once wore Gabulong's boots. Consequently, Gabulong's leg was mercilessly broken by Nakuo.

In those days, being far away from his family, he suffered a lot of inhumane treatment. With no one to turn to, he could only suffer in silence. To add insult to injury, news came that his 13-year-old son had died of an acute illness. The news was like a knife to the heart, leaving a lasting scar. Yet he had no way to vent, but choked down his tears in silence.

He never again talked about his son or his tragic death. As a result, many people, including his relatives, secretaries, and drivers, either forgot his son's existence or were unaware that he ever had one.

Fortunately, Gabulong's cousin left her daughter at his home at an early age, giving him and Huamao a sensible and filial daughter. He and his wife brought her up as their own child, never telling anyone about her origin.

Gabulong was a powerful man, yet that did not stop him from being sentimental. After all, no matter how strong he was, he could not let go of the pain of losing his child. In the days that followed, he kept this unimaginable pain to himself.

With grievous hurts and heavy blows, he dragged his injured legs and knelt to the ground to harvest highland barley and oats. At night, he had to be present for public criticism. His legs hurt so much that he could hardly stand. A kind man showed mercy and gave him a bench, but before he sat firmly, someone stepped forward and pushed him hard, causing him to fall heavily to the ground, unable to get up. Gabulong was taken to the hospital.

Each time those days were brought up, the senior cadres who once worked with

多年后，回到黄南州河南县的尕布龙受到群众欢迎

Several years later, Gabulong returned to Henan County, Huangnan Prefecture, and was welcomed by the masses

　　冰雪纷飞的早晨，有个年轻人带头捆绑尕布龙，把他押到会场批判，还抡起棍棒打了尕布龙。年轻人的父亲知道后，气得用绳子绑了自己的儿子，狠狠揍了儿子一顿。

　　"你个没良心的逆子。你忘了，是尕书记在我们家最困难的时候，自己省吃俭用，用工资给我们家买了青稞、酥油。你爷爷生病，又是尕书记把你爷爷送进医院，缴了医药费。没有尕书记，就没有我们家的今天，你这个浑小子，你给我滚出去。"

　　朴实的人说着朴实的话，没有一句不是他们的肺腑之言。

　　洛改老人还记得，他怀里揣着一块煮熟的牛肉，偷偷去医院看望尕布龙的那一天。尕布龙面容憔悴，整个脸浮肿着。即使这样，临走时，他还送给了洛改一本藏文版的《雷锋》。

　　他告诉洛改，别失望，好好学习，好好工作，为群众办事，为人民服务，

Gabulong felt uncomfortable.

Douwu told us that when anyone hung a poster about Secretary Gabulong, they would add the line "Gabulong is our good secretary."

He had always been a good man in their hearts, and they couldn't bear to watch him kneel on the ground and be beaten or see him drag his sick body to clean the toilet, so they often helped him secretly. How could such a good man, a conscientious party secretary, be counter-revolutionary when he is faithful to the party?

On a snowy morning, a young man took the lead in tying Gabulong up, escorting him to the venue for criticism, and beating him with a stick. When the young man's father learned of this, he was so angry that he tied his son up with a rope and beat him severely.

"You ungrateful bastard! You really don't remember who bought highland barley and ghee for our family with his own salary in our toughest times? And who took your grandfather to the hospital and paid the medical expenses when he was seriously ill? It was Secretary Ga that made us who we are today. Now get out, you heartless boy!"

These were simple words from a simple man, but they all came straight from his heart.

The old man Luogai still remembers the day when he secretly went to the hospital to visit Gabulong with a piece of cooked beef in his arms. Gabulong's face was haggard and swollen. Even so, when he left, Gabulong gave him a Tibetan version of Lei Feng.

He told Luogai not to be disappointed, but to study and work hard to serve the people. Everything would pass.

In his eyes, all the pain he had endured was nothing compared with the suffering and sorrow of farmers and herdsmen. Gabulong calmed down, buried the pain in his heart and endured it alone, never expressing his fear to another person.

After staying in the Henan County Hospital for a while, his legs did not get better. Though physically and mentally exhausted, he believed in the Communist Party as he believed in himself, and he kept the sobriety and purity of his soul.

The county hospital, running out of options, withdrew his treatment. Gabulong, therefore, was sent back to his hometown—Yongfeng Village in Haiyan County.

At that time, his wife Huamao was in poor health and could not do heavy work, while his daughter Zhao Geli, who had to work in the production team, herd sheep, and take care of her mother, was too busy to look after him. Gabulong was thus taken to his eldest brother Caibuteng's home.

一切都会过去的。

和农牧民的悲苦忧伤相比，自己的坎坷艰难算得了什么呢？尕布龙的心平静了下来，他把痛苦埋在心里，独自忍受从不表达。

住了一段时间后，河南县医院没有让他的双腿站起来，尕布龙身心有些疲惫、焦虑，但他依然如故，像相信自己一样相信共产党，保持着灵魂的清醒与纯洁。

没有别的办法了，县医院放弃了治疗，尕布龙被送回了老家海晏县永丰村。

那时候，妻子华毛的身体已经很差，干不了重活，女儿召格力要在生产队劳动、放羊，还要照顾妈妈，身心俱疲的尕布龙被大哥才布腾接到了自己家。

尕布龙的父母，有位多年来往的朋友王安，他是湟源县卫生院的院长，医术高超。大哥才布腾和二哥拉哈措把尕布龙送到了王安家。治疗期间，大哥和二哥每周轮流去湟源照顾弟弟尕布龙，每次去时，善良的大嫂都要磨好足够的青稞炒面，做几个大锅盔——青海人吃的家常馍馍，给他们带上。

一年多后，尕布龙的腿病竟然被治好，重新站了起来。

河南县的乡亲们高兴地奔走相告，是泽曲河的水保佑了尕书记，是草原人的诚心感动了苍天。

Hearing that Wang An, a friend of Gabulong's parents and the president of Huangyuan County Health Center, had excellent medical skills, his eldest brother Caibuten and second brother Lahacuo sent Gabulong to Wang An's house. During the treatment, his two brothers took turns going to Huangyuan every week to take care of their younger brother Gabulong. Each time, his kind-hearted eldest sister-in-law would grind enough highland barley powder to make several big homemade steamed buns commonly seen in Qinghai and send them to Gabulong with his brothers.

Amazingly, more than a year later, Gabulong's legs were cured, and he could stand up again.

When this good news reached the villagers in Henan County, they rushed about telling each other that it was the water of Zequ River that blessed Secretary Ga and the sincerity of people in grassland that moved the heavens.

牧人之家

1968 年 2 月，病愈后的尕布龙回到河南县，在黄南州革委会生产指挥部工作。1970 年 7 月，尕布龙担任了青海省畜牧兽医总站革委会主任一职。1971 年 2 月，尕布龙当选青海省委常委兼畜牧局局长。1979 年 8 月，尕布龙任青海省委常委、省政府副省长。

省政府办公厅给他分了一套省长住宅楼，可他迟迟不搬，依旧住在畜牧厅家属院只有 80 平方米，没有自来水、卫生间、暖气的平房里。

办公厅的人去看望他，不禁大吃一惊。四间潮湿阴冷的平房，被他用土坯简单地隔成了 5 间半，半间当自己的卧室，里面只有一张床、一个书桌，其余 5 间搭了 11 张床，接待从牧区来西宁看病、办事的农牧民。他不仅给他们管吃管住，还为他们联系医院，解决生活上的困难。

4 年前，尕布龙遇到了从黄南州河南县来西宁看病的一位牧民，因为打听不到医院，满面愁容地在马路边徘徊。问清缘由后，他马上把他带到自己家，随后联系医院，送医院治疗。之后，家乡永丰村的人来了，玉树草原上的人来了，都住在他家里。有时候住不下，他还给畜牧局的年轻人做工作，把病人安排在他们的宿舍里。再后来，他的小家就变成了现在这个样子的大家，变成了一个让农牧民免费吃住的"牧人之家"。

他是这样考虑的，住在省政府院子里固然方便，而且显得很体面，可是省政府的住宅区设有警卫，搬过去后，那些不会说汉语，找他求医、办事的农牧民群众不敢进门，怕是再也不会找他了。

Home for Herders

In February 1968, after recovering from illness, Gabulong returned to Henan County to work in the production headquarters of the Revolutionary Committee of Huangnan Prefecture. In July 1970, Gabulong assumed the post of director of the Revolutionary Committee of Qinghai Provincial Animal Husbandry and Veterinary General Station. In February 1971, Gabulong was elected as a member of the Standing Committee of the Qinghai Provincial Party Committee and director of the Animal Husbandry Bureau. In August 1979, Gabulong served as a member of the Standing Committee of the Qinghai Provincial Party Committee and Vice Governor of the Provincial Government.

The General Office of the Provincial Government assigned him a governor's residential building, but he didn't move in, choosing instead to stay in a bungalow with only 80 m2 in the residential area of the Animal Husbandry Department without running water, toilets, or heating.

His office colleagues couldn't help but be surprised by the simplicity of his home when they went to visit him. The cold, damp four-room bungalow had been simply divided with mud bricks into five and a half rooms, with the half-room serving as his bedroom. His bedroom was furnished with a single bed and desk, while the other five rooms were equipped with eleven beds to receive farmers and herders from pastoral areas, who came to Xining to see doctors or handle other affairs. He not only provided them food and board, but also contacted the hospital for them and eased their difficulties in life.

Four years earlier, Gabulong met a herder from Henan County, Huangnan Prefecture, who came to Xining to see a doctor. He was wandering along the road gloomily because he could not find the hospital. After talking with the man, he immediately took him to his home, and then contacted the

牧人之家

Home for Herders

hospital and sent him to the hospital for treatment. Since then, people from Yongfeng Village, his hometown, and from the Yushu grasslands would stay at his home whenever they came to Xining. Sometimes when there weren't enough beds for the herders in his home, he even persuaded his young colleagues in the Animal Husbandry Bureau to make room for the patients in their dormitories. Later, his small home became what is now called "Home for Herders," where farmers and herders can eat and live for free.

He thought about it this way. Although it was convenient and decent to live in the residential area of the provincial government, there were guards stationed at the gate. If he moved there, the farmers and herdsmen who sought him for help wouldn't dare approach the gate if they couldn't speak Chinese. Therefore, he chose not to live there out of fear that they would never seek him for help again.

Whenever he was at home, Gabulong would cook and eat together with the herders. Whenever he was away on business trips, he would leave meal tickets for the herders to eat at the cafeteria of the Animal Husbandry Bureau. In those years, he had no housekeeper, so he had to do everything himself. If there were patients staying at his home, he would get up early in the morning to make a fire and boil water.

Whenever there were a lot of people at his home, he would run out of food stamps. During the Spring Festival, when his close friends came to pay him New Year greetings, he told them, "Don't bring me anything. If you have extra food stamps, I'll appreciate if you give me some."

Colleagues from the Provincial Government Office repeatedly mentioned that he should move home, but each time he explained to them, "I've been a leader in the pastoral area for nearly twenty years. Many herders come to me seeking help. I can speak Tibetan and Mongolian, so I can serve as an interpreter for the Tibetan and Mongolian herders who come to the provincial capital city to seek medical treatment and to handle other affairs. They need me!"

In 1982, the provincial government's residential and office areas were managed separately, so there were no more guard posts in the residential area. Only then did Gabulong decide to move into the residential area of the provincial government. Although he lived in a two-story building which was allocated only to governors, the upper and lower rooms were converted into a "herders' home" to receive farmers and herdsmen.

Gabulong's home was still very special. The scene that Qinghai Daily reporter Gu Yue saw was like this: a unit building of about 150 square meters, with an empty hall and no decoration. The large living room on the first floor was spacious and bright, but there was no sofa, coffee table, calligraphy, paintings, or decoration. There were just two large dining tables made up of old square tables whose

在家时，他和大家一起做饭吃，下乡或者开会回不来，就把饭票留下，交代好，让农牧民到畜牧局的食堂打饭吃。那几年，家里没有保姆，什么事情都得自己干，来看病的人住在家里，他一早就起来生火、烧开水。

家里来的人多了，最缺的是粮票，春节和他非常熟悉的人去他家里给他拜年，他说："什么也不要给我送，有多余的粮票给我几张最好。"

省政府办公厅的人一再向他提起搬家的事，他每次都这样解释："我在牧区当县委、州委领导近20年，找我的牧民很多，我会藏语和蒙古语，可以给来省城求医、办事的藏族、蒙古族牧民当翻译，他们需要我！"

1982年，省政府住宅区和办公区分开管理，住宅区不设岗哨，尕布龙这才搬进了省政府。虽然他住的是省长住的二层楼，不过，上下几间房，又被他改造成了接待农牧民群众的"牧人之家"。

可是他的家还是很特别，这是青海日报社记者古岳见过的一幕：一套约150平方米的单元楼房，过道里空荡荡的，没什么摆设。一楼的大客厅宽敞明亮，却没有沙发、茶几，没有字画、装饰，只有两张油漆已经脱落的旧方桌拼就的大餐桌，六七把旧靠背椅子。门口一角是个旧方桌，桌上有一台20英寸的旧彩电。窗台上有一部电话机，两盆花草，对面墙上拉着深色的布帘子。

掀开帘子的人很好奇，他对好奇的人风趣地说："可不要小看，这可是我自己搞的室内装潢哦！"

靠窗户的一头，是张简易的单人床，床下到另一头，沿墙根儿铺着一长溜红色的腈纶地毯，地毯上，卷着十几块草垫子，草垫子里露着不同颜色的花被褥。

尕布龙很认真地说："这里能住一个班，床上睡的是班长，床下睡的是士兵。"

可不要以为，二楼的5间卧室是留给自己享用的。走上楼梯，拐弯处是第二个卫生间，阳面角落的一间才是尕布龙自己的卧室兼工作室，里面一张单人床，一个书桌。其余4间，每间都支着4张小单人床，和小旅店的摆设一样。即使这样，来的人多了，还是不够住，单人床只好当双人床用。

每天都有从海北、海南、黄南、果洛、玉树来的藏族、蒙古族同胞，海东地区来的回族同胞投奔他，有看病、办事的，甚至旅游的。有住两三天的，也有住一年半载的。

paint had fallen off, and six or seven old back chairs. In the corner of the doorway there was an old square table with a 20-inch color TV. There was a telephone on the windowsill, two pots of flowers and plants, and a dark curtain on the opposite wall.

One person drew back the curtain with curiosity. He said tastily to the curious person, "Don't underestimate it. I did the decoration myself!"

At one end of the window, there was a simple single bed, from the bottom of the bed to the top, a red acrylic carpet was spread along the wall. On the carpet, there were more than a dozen straw mats, and beddings of different colors wrapped by the mats.

Gabulong said seriously, "It's spacious enough to accommodate a squad here. The squad leader sleeps on the bed, and the soldiers sleep under the bed."

Don't imagine that the five bedrooms on the second floor were reserved for Gabulong himself. Up the stairs and around the corner was the second bathroom. The room in the corner of the sunward side was Gabulong's bedroom and study room, with a single bed and a desk inside. Each of the other four rooms was equipped with four single beds, the same as that of a small hotel room. Even so, with more and more lodgers coming, there was still not enough accommodation, so the single beds had to be used as a double beds.

Each day, Tibetans and Mongolians from Haibei, Hainan, Huangnan, Guoluo and Yushu prefectures, and Hui people from Haidong district came to him seeking help. Some were seeking medical treatment, some handling business affairs, and even some came to tour Xining. Some stayed for two or three days, and some lived there for several months or even a year.

A few years later, more and more people knew about the "herders' home," and his house was often full of people. These people were also relying on Gabulong's personal salary to feed them during their stay. He had to buy at least six or seven tons of coal and up to 250 kilograms of flour a year. In winter, he would pickle a few large jars of sauerkraut. Whenever vegetables, oil, or tea were used up, he would buy more. He couldn't keep track of how much he was buying, he just made sure not to buy anything too expensive. At that time, the homes in the residential area of the provincial government were equipped with electric stoves, but Gabulong kept burning briquettes in order to allow patients living at his home to boil Chinese medicine, because farmers and herdsmen in rural and pastoral areas did not dare to use electricity. In order to save electricity, he did not allow anyone to use the washing machine to wash bedding and sheets. In order to provide fresh milk for the seriously ill herders and more importantly to save money, he even hired people to raise sheep and cows in the yard of the provincial government.

几年后，知道"牧人之家"的人越来越多，他家里常常住满了人。这么多人要吃要喝，用的都是尕布龙自己的工资，一年至少得买六七吨煤、四五百斤面粉，冬天要腌几大缸酸菜，蔬菜、油料、茶叶，用完了就买，买了多少，他说也说不清，只是不敢买太好的。那时候，省政府家属院用上了电灶，可尕布龙家为了让住在家里的病人熬中药，一直烧煤球，因为乡下牧区的农牧民不敢用电。为了节省电，洗被褥、床单时他不让家里帮忙的人用洗衣机；为了让重病的牧民喝上新鲜的牛奶，更为了省钱，他还雇人在省政府院子里养过羊、养过牛。

有一回，竟然一下子来了将近 50 位农牧民，要住六七天，实在没办法，尕布龙经办公室允许，在家门前的一棵大杨树下搭了顶白色的帐篷，盘了个大锅灶，做熬饭、煮面条。很多人经过时，看到来自牧区的人，蹲在台阶上端着大碗吃饭，报以惊诧的眼神，或者摇摇头："这么多人来吃饭，尕省长挣多少钱也不够啊。"那时候，他的工资还不到 300 元。

那时，家里住着小外孙女，侄子们也常来。夏天，如果不是遇到刮风下雨的天气，尕布龙从不让家里人关大门。

他对侄子、外孙女说："不要每天都把门关得那么严实。门关着，谁还敢进省长家的门？"

家里来的人多，最辛苦的要数做饭的人。通常，一顿饭要煮四五锅面条才够大家吃。有时，突然来了人，或者有疾病患者，还需要厨师半夜起来擀面条、烧茶。一位厨子忙不过来，就叫来两位，说是照顾省长的起居，其实是照顾来看病、办事的人。

家里先后换过 30 多个厨子，有些人实在干不下去跑了。干得最久的人是何巴和严婶夫妇。何巴叫何胜章，来家里的人都亲切地把他们两口子当作自己的叔叔、婶婶，按照青海人的习惯，称他们为何爸、严婶。时间长了，别人都以为何胜章的名字叫何巴。当然，叫什么并不重要，重要的是，何巴和严婶不但尽心尽力在尕布龙家里洗衣、做饭、打扫卫生，还成了这个世界上离他最近，用心照顾他、爱他的人。

何巴和严婶正式来尕布龙家帮忙是 1985 年。5 年后他们回了海晏老家。可是，没过多久，由于顶替他们的人还是待不下去，加上他们俩日夜惦念着尕布龙，就又回来了。一直到 1998 年，何巴生了重病，2002 年，何巴去世。

好在严婶健在，让我得以与她交谈，倾听她的诉说。

Once, nearly fifty farmers and herdsmen came to him for board and lodging for six or seven days. Gabulong had no option but set up a white tent under a large poplar tree in front of the residential building after getting permission of the provincial government office. He set up a big stove to cook rice and noodles. When people passed by and saw those people from the pastoral area squatting on the steps eating meals from big bowls, many people were very surprised, some of them shook their heads and said, "With so many people coming to eat, Governor Ga's income is far from enough." At that time, his salary was less than 300 Yuan.

At that time, his granddaughter lived with him, and his nephews often visited him. In summer, as long as the weather wasn't too windy or rainy, Gabulong would never let them close the door.

He said to his nephews and nieces, "Keep the door open! With the door closed, who would dare to enter the governor's home?"

When there were many people living at home, the hardest worker was the cook. Usually, four or five pots of noodles were cooked to feed everyone for one meal. Sometimes, when unexpected visitors came, or if there were patients living at home, the chef had to get up in the middle of the night to make noodles and tea. The work proved too much for a single cook, so he hired a second. The cooks were indeed looking after the patients and other people who lived at home in the name of taking care of the governor's daily life.

More than thirty cooks worked at Gabulong's home over the years, and some of them just couldn't bear the heavy workload and left. The couple, Heba and Aunt Yan, were the cooks who worked there the longest. Heba's name is He Shengzhang. People who came to the Governor's home kindly regard them as their uncle and aunt. According to the habits of people in Qinghai, they called them Uncle He (same pronunciation with Heba in Qinghai dialect) and Aunt Yan. After a long time, people supposed He Shengzhang's name was Heba. Of course, it doesn't matter what his name was. What's important is that Heba and Aunt Yan not only did their best to wash, cook, and clean at Gabulong's house, but they also became the closest to him in the world, caring and loving him from the bottom of their hearts.

It was in 1985 that Heba and Aunt Yan officially came to Gabulong's house to be helpers. They returned to their hometown in Haiyan County five years later. However, it wasn't long before they returned because the person who replaced them was unwilling to stay, and they were missing Gabulong day and night. They served until 1998 when Heba got a serious disease. He later died in 2002.

Fortunately, Aunt Yan is still alive, allowing me to talk to her and listen to her stories.

After the death of Heba, Aunt Yan lived in Huangyuan County with her sister. She was ill on my

老伴去世后，严婶住在湟源县城，与自己的妹妹做伴。我去时，她正生着病，见了我，像见了多年不见的老朋友，握住我的双手，眼睛一红，落下泪来。

"那是一个多么好的人啊！"严婶说，能够在他家待那么多年，关心他、照顾他，完全是因为他对天下人好。

这个对天下人好的人，给他们留下的记忆是如此深刻，以至于一提起尕布龙，眼泪就夺眶而出。

何巴爱哭。每逢尕布龙身体不适，或者劳累过度，何巴总想劝他几句，可他死活不听，何巴就会暗自垂泪。

为了能常常见到儿子，同时，又能照顾尕布龙，长期待在他身边，何巴夫妇还把自己的儿子送到大寺沟，帮尕布龙植树多年。

在山上植树时，尕布龙肺病发作，止不住地咳嗽，咳得上气不接下气，怕别人看着难受，躲到厨房里咳时，一时窒息，晕倒在地。何巴吓得扑在尕布龙身上号啕大哭："你这是为啥呀，为啥呀？把自己累成这样……"

后来，何巴生了重病，不得已回到老家，可一想起尕布龙，看见院子里种的树就又会伤心落泪。

尕布龙对何巴说："找到我这里来的大部分人都是农牧区的贫困群众，城里没有别的什么人可以投靠，语言又不通，没人管怎么能行？"可惜两年后，我想去湟源再看看严婶，听她讲讲尕布龙的故事时，她已不在人世了。

20 世纪 70 年代末，那位在河南县和尕布龙一起工作过的洛改老人，带着生了病的女儿和另外一个老人到西宁看病，住在河南县办事处。在楼道里，他遇到在河南县工作过的熟人老王，聊了几句后，老王走了。可没过一会，老王又回来了，说尕布龙让老王把他们三人接到尕布龙家里去住。

来到尕布龙家里，看到屋子里都是地铺，能住十几个人。

尕布龙对他们说："以后不要去旅馆住，今天刚走了几个宁塔乡的人，地铺空着，你们就住在我家里，可以省些钱。明天上午我有事，中午我送你们去医院，你们听不懂汉话，没法跟医生交流。"

尕布龙还吩咐家里人，把他们带来的酥油处理好，放在一个小盆里，熟肉也晾在饭桌上。他说："这些东西都要吃掉，不要放坏了，不要浪费。"

海南州一个藏族牧民的孩子患了急性脑膜炎，情急之中，这位牧民首先想到的是在省上当领导的尕布龙。他觉得，只有尕布龙才能救他的儿子。

visit. At the moment of seeing me, she was so excited as if we were old friends who hadn't seen each other for many years. She held my hands, her eyes turned red, and tears came down.

"What a good person he was!" Aunt Yan said. They stayed with him for so many years, caring for him and taking care of him wholeheartedly because he had been kind to the people of the world.

Gabulong left them with such a deep impression that tears burst into their eyes whenever his name was mentioned.

Heba was easily moved to tears. Whenever Gabulong was unwell or overworked, Heba always wanted to persuade him to rest, but if he refused to listen, Heba would weep secretly.

In order to see their son often while they are taking care of Gabulong, they sent their son to Daisigou to help Gabulong plant trees for many years.

When planting trees on the mountain, Gabulong developed lung disease and could't stop coughing, often to the point that he couldn't catch his breath. He didn't want anyone to worry about his health, so he would hide himself in the kitchen whenever he had a coughing attack. Once when he was hiding in the kitchen, he collapsed on the ground. Heba was so frightened that he rushed to his side and cried loudly, "Why are you doing this to yourself? You are working yourself to death!"

Later, Heba became seriously ill and had to return to his hometown, but when he thought of Gabulong, he would be moved to tears again when he saw the trees planted in the yard.

Gabulong said to Heba, "Most of the people who came to me are poor people from the farming and pastoral areas. They have no other people in the city to rely on, and communication is another problem because of the language barrier. How can we put them aside?" Two years later, I intended to go to Huangyuan County to see Aunt Yan again and listen to her stories of Gabulong. Unfortunately, she had already passed away.

In the late 1970s, an old man called Luogai, who had worked with Gabulong in Henan County, took his sick daughter and another old man to Xining for treatment and lived at the Henan County Office. In the corridor, he met Wang, an acquaintance who had also worked in Henan County. After a few conversations, Wang left. But after a while, he came back, saying that Gabulong asked him to take the three of them to Gabulong's home.

When they came to Gabulong's home, they saw the place was full of sleeping mats on the floor, which could accommodate more than a dozen people.

Gabulong said to them, "Don't go to the hotel any more. A few people from Ningta town just left today and those sleeping mats are available now, so you can live in my home to save some money. You don't understand Chinese, it's hard for you to communicate with the doctor, so I will accompany you to

孩子送到尕布龙家时是晚上9点，9点10分孩子就被送到了医院。在抢救孩子的10个小时里，尕布龙一直焦急地守候在抢救室外，直到孩子完全脱离危险。

天峻县天棚乡的藏族牧民旦增夫妇患肺病，想到西宁治疗，可是家中困难，害怕付不起住宿费，不敢来西宁。打听到尕布龙家能住，春节后住了进来，一住就是8个月，8个月的治疗时间里，尕布龙亲自给他们联系医院，找医生、付药费，有空了还去医院看望他们。

夫妻俩肺病痊愈返回草原时，泪眼婆娑地对尕布龙说："我们一辈子都忘不了您的恩情。"

尕布龙摇摇头："我本来就是一个放羊娃，是共产党培养了我。你们就是我的生身父母，我为你们做点事，是对养育之恩的报答，是尽了自己的一点责任和义务。"

尕布龙还是一个非常细心的人，发现来看病的人身上穿的衣服破旧，担心他们去医院看病被医生嫌弃。个子高点的，就把自己身上的衣服脱下来让人家穿上；个子矮小的，就拿出自己的钱，打发何巴去商店买身新衣服。只要别人需要，什么都舍得。

有的人即使不提困难，他也要硬塞上几十元钱。他觉得，三四十元钱对于城里人不算什么，可是给了生活困难的乡下人，有时能派上大用场。

尕布龙家乡永丰村的卓玛一家，永远铭记着他的恩情。1975年，卓玛还没有出生，她的奶奶发现自己上腹部有一个肿块，经常咳嗽、呕吐、腹痛，经诊断她得了肝包虫病，当时牧区医疗条件有限，无法治疗。看着卓玛深受病痛折磨的奶奶，家人心急如焚，当时，他们想到了在省里当副省长的尕布龙，知道村里人有大病大灾的都会去找他。可平时，与尕布龙家没有什么交往，他会不会管我们呢？怀着这样的疑虑，他们忐忑不安地找到了尕布龙。

尕布龙说："什么也不要多说，看病要紧！马上把病人接到西宁来，不敢耽搁。"

卓玛的奶奶被送到医院，须立即做手术。

家里人一筹莫展。既担心做手术会有风险丢了性命，又担心手术费用。

尕布龙一边给卓玛的奶奶做思想工作、安慰她，一边对医生说："大夫，他们从牧区来，手头不宽裕，手术费我会想办法，你们一定不要耽误治病。"

the hospital at the noon time tomorrow since I am busy in the morning."

Gabulong also asked the family to put the ghee they brought in a small basin, and to put some cooked meat on the dinner table. He said, "Eat all these things up soon, and don't let any food go to waste."

A child of a Tibetan herder from Hainan Prefecture was suffering from acute meningitis. In an emergency, the herder immediately thought of Gabulong, who was at the time the provincial leader. He felt that only Gabulong could save his son. The child arrived at Gabulong's home at 9:00 P.M, and the child was taken to the hospital at 9:10. During the ten hours of treatment, Gabulong waited anxiously outside the emergency room until the child was completely out of danger.

The Tibetan herder Danzeng and his wife from Tianpeng Town, Tianjun County, suffered from lung disease. They wanted to receive medical treatment in Xining, but they lived in poverty and were afraid of not being able to pay for their accommodation, so they dared not come to Xining. When they found out that Gabulong provided accommodations for herders for free, they came and lived at Gabulong's home after Spring Festival. They lived there for eight months and during the treatment, Gabulong contacted the hospital and doctors in person, paid for their medicine, and visited them in the hospital when he was free.

When the couple recovered from their lung disease and returned to the grassland, they said to Gabulong with tears in their eyes, "We will never forget your kindness for the rest of our lives."

Gabulong shook his head and said, "I was a shepherd in my childhood; it's the Communist Party of China that nurtured and cultivated me. You are just like my parents. It's my duty and obligation to repay your upbringing."

Gabulong is also a very attentive person. He found that the clothes of the people who came to see a doctor were worn out and worried that they would be looked down on by doctors when they went to the hospital. He often gave his own clothes to the tall herders; for the shorter herders, he took out his own money and sent Heba to buy new clothes from the store. He was willing to give everything he had to those who were in need.

Even if some people didn't mention their difficulties, he would voluntarily give them some money. He felt that thirty or forty yuan was not a big deal for the city people, but it could sometimes come in handy for the villagers who lived in poverty.

The Zhuoma family from Yongfeng Village, Gabulong's hometown, would always remember his kindness. In 1975, before Zhuoma was born, her grandma found a lump in her upper abdomen. She was often coughing, vomiting, and suffering abdominal pain, and was diagnosed with a parasitic disease in

尔布龙和治愈返乡的牧民合影

Gabulong and the herdsmen returning home after recovering

her liver. At that time, medical conditions in the pastoral areas were very limited, so Zhuoma's grandma couldn't get medical treatment. Seeing Zhuoma's grandma suffering from illness, the family was anxious. They thought of Gabulong, who was the vice governor of the province then, and they knew people in the village would resort to him if they were seriously ill. But they didn't have any connection to Gabulong. Would he care about them? With such concerns, they anxiously tried to contact Gabulong.

Gabulong replied, "It's urgent to save the patient's life! Take the patient to Xining immediately. Don't delay."

Zhuoma's grandma was sent to the hospital and needed an immediate operation.

The family was helpless. They worried not only about the risk of death during the operation, but also the cost of the operation.

After persuading and comforting Zhuoma's grandma, Gabulong said to the doctors, "They are from the pastoral area and don't have enough money for the operation, but don't worry about the operation fee. I will take care of it. Please do not delay the treatment." He also mention to the doctor, "They don't speak Chinese; please be patient and help them." Then he went back to prepare the operation fee.

After the operation, Gabulong went to the hospital to visit Zhuoma's grandmother every day. Sometimes he was busy at work, but he still went to the hospital, without even having time for a meal. Zhuoma's grandma told him not to come again, but he said he had nothing to do after work. In fact, he was worried that his fellow villagers had no relatives in Xining and had no one to turn to when facing difficulties. Zhuoma's grandmother stayed in the hospital for more than a week. After being discharged from the hospital, Gabulong took her to his home and had her stay for more than three months, only letting her return home after she had recovered completely.

In Zhuoma's second year of junior high, her mother got sick. She often felt pain in her abdomen and became thinner. She went to the county hospital for a checkup but got no results. Whenever she had an attack, she gritted her teeth and took some painkillers for temporary relief. Zhuoma's mother had another serious attack when Spring Festival was just around the corner. She didn't feel better after several days of anti-inflammatory and painkilling injections. Somehow Gabulong heard about this during his stay in the village for the Spring Festival and went to Zhuoma's home to discuss the treatment of Zhuoma's mother. He said, "Her treatment can't be delayed any longer. We have to go to the provincial hospital. After the Chinese New Year, I will return to Xining to help you contact the hospital."

Zhuoma's father was very conflicted after Gabulong left. Although it was a great blessing to be

他又央求医生，"他们不会讲汉话，请多多费心照顾。"随即回去准备手术费用。

手术后，尕布龙天天去医院看望卓玛的奶奶，有时候工作忙，连饭都顾不上吃就来到医院。卓玛的奶奶让他不要再来了，他却说，下班没事。其实，他是担心同村乡亲在西宁无亲无故，遇到困难没法解决。卓玛的奶奶在医院住了一个多星期，出院后，尕布龙又把她接到自己家里休养了三个多月，等完全康复了，才让她回去。

卓玛上初二那年，她阿妈又生了病，经常感到腹部疼痛难耐，人也日渐消瘦。到县医院检查后，没查出原因，每次病情发作，她都咬牙坚持，吃点止痛药，暂时缓解病痛。春节快到了，她阿妈的病再次发作，打了几天的消炎、止痛针都没有得到控制。这事不知道怎么让回家过年的尕布龙知道了，主动到卓玛家商量给卓玛阿妈治病的事情。他说："这病不能再拖了，得到省上大医院看看，过完年我就回西宁帮你们联系医院。"

送走了尕布龙，卓玛的阿爸心里很矛盾。到省城去看病，住到尕布龙家里，对于寻医无门的卓玛家来说是天大的福音，不仅能够找到省里的好医院、好医生，而且住在他的家里，可以节省一大笔花销。但尽管这样，医药费仍然是个大问题，省里的医院进得去，住不起，家里13口人吃饭，根本没有多余的钱。况且，尕布龙的妻子也身患重病，怎么好意思再给他添麻烦。春节后，卓玛的阿爸一直没主动跟尕布龙联系。

可是没过多久，卓玛阿妈的病情越来越严重。尕布龙知道后，不由分说，直接派车接走了她。把她安排在青海大学附属医院接受治疗。经诊断，她得的是腹腔囊肿，医生建议立即做手术。一听要做手术，得花大钱，卓玛的阿妈就不想治了。

尕布龙当时就急了，他说："有什么困难跟我说，我们大家一起想办法，病必须得治，医药费不够了，我来想办法。"

在卓玛的母亲手术治疗期间，只要一有空尕布龙就亲自到医院看望她，并嘱咐她一定要吃好、喝好、休息好。病愈返回草原时，卓玛的阿妈紧握着尕布龙的手，对他说："我们家一辈子忘不了您的大恩情。"

卓玛长大了，考上了西宁卫校，每逢周末，尕布龙都要打电话叫她来家里吃饭。

第一次去尕布龙家时，一进门，卓玛就被眼前的场景惊呆了。这哪里

able to stay with Gabulong and have his help to find a good doctor, the medical expenses would still be a big problem for them. They didn't have extra money and couldn't afford the medication fee because there were thirteen people in the family to feed. Besides, Gabulong's wife was also seriously ill, how could they impose on him at such a time? Zhuoma's father didn't take the initiative to contact Gabulong after the Spring Festival.

However, it didn't take long for Zhuoma's mother's condition to get worse. After Gabulong learned this, he sent a car to pick her up and arranged for her to receive treatment at the Affiliated Hospital of Qinghai University. She was diagnosed with an abdominal cyst, and the doctor recommended immediate surgery. Hearing that the surgery would cost a lot of money, Zhuoma's mother decided against treatment.

Gabulong was anxious at the time and said to her, "If you have any difficulties, tell me, we all work together to find a solution. But you must accept the treatment. If medical expenses are a problem, I will take care of it."

During Zhuoma's mother's surgical treatment, as long as he was free, Gabulong would visit her in person in the hospital and tell her to eat, drink, and rest well. When returning to the grassland after her recovery, Zhuoma's mother held Gabulong's hand tightly and said to him, "Our family will never forget your great kindness."

Zhuoma grew up and was admitted to Xining Health School. Every weekend, Gabulong would call and invite her to his home for dinner.

When seeing Gabulong's home for the first time, Zhuoma was stunned by the scene before her as soon as she entered the door. It was hard to believe it was the home of a provincial leader, and the meals were so simple. Only on weekends, daughters and nieces would bring mutton from their hometown to cook a pot of meat and make dumplings for the farmers and herdsmen who lived at his home.

Perhaps people think that provincial leaders like Gabulong must have their own meal standards and enjoy special meals, but this was not the case for Gabulong. Except for work, meetings, and inspecting work in the rural areas, he had the same meals as the herders living at his home every day, and he never got separate meals. While eating, he would watch quietly from the side and made it sure that everyone got to eat, and those who had a big appetite got a second bowl of food, and only then would he fill a bowl for himself before going to his small room to eat quietly.

One day, the curious Zhuoma saw him take the bowl to the small room again, and ran to him and asked, "Grandpa, Grandpa, why are you always the last one to eat? Aren't you hungry? Aren't you bored eating here alone?"

卓玛和她的奶奶

Zhuoma and Her Grandma

Gabulong said, "If the bowl is too hot, Grandpa can't hold it. Grandpa is used to eating alone."

In fact, the naive Zhuoma didn't know at all that Gabulong was worried that if he ate with the herders, they would be restrained and couldn't eat well. In addition, he only ate when everyone was almost full. If there was no more food in the pot, he would eat some steamed buns, never bothering the chef to cook more. Only when many people hadn't had a chance to eat, or when someone showed up at meal time, he would let the chef cook one more pot of noodles. In his heart, farmers and herdsmen were always more important than himself.

When I wrote this, I couldn't help but be moved to tears. How can there be such a kind person in this world? This is what biological parents are willing to do for their children!

Over the years, there had been too many people living at Gabulong's home. He himself couldn't remember how many people had stayed there, and he didn't know the names of most. Some people came abruptly and didn't even share their names. They simply asked Gabulong to take them to the hospital for treatment. After the treatment, they left without even saying goodbye, so Gabulong had to pay their medical bills. No one can remember how many times this happened. I only know that the bills signed by the driver Cui Shengman at the provincial hospital and paid by Gabulong with his salary are more than 400,000 yuan.

In order to thank the doctors and nurses in the hospital, he presented more than a dozen sheep from the sheep pens of his niece Huamaocuo and his daughter Zhao Geli to the doctors and nurses every year.

Cui Shengman told me, "Director Ga has never asked anyone for anything in his life, and he has never once burdened someone else for his own affairs or family. The only times he ever asked for favors was when he was asking doctors and nurses for help on behalf of villagers. He was willing to do anything to help the poor. Even so, Gabulong's kindness sometimes brought about misunderstandings. Once, he was sued by a family."

"What? Sued?"

"Yes!"

It was a winter when Director Ga passed by a herdsman's house and heard the sound of chanting in the courtyard during an inspection in the countryside with Cui Shengman. When entering the door, he saw an old man with a sallow face and his eyes closed, lying unconsciously on a brick-made bed. His family knelt on the ground, shaking the sutra cylinder.

On seeing the scene, anxiously, Gabulong promptly ordered the family to move the patient into the car and let Cui Shengman drive him to the provincial hospital overnight. Unexpectedly, the doctors failed to rescue the old man because of his serious illness, and the man died in the hospital. As a result,

像省城大干部的家，而且吃得也很简单，只有到了周末，女儿、侄女从老家拿来羊肉，才能给住在家里的农牧民煮一锅肉，包一顿饺子改善伙食。

也许人们认为，像尕布龙这样的省级领导干部，一定有自己的伙食标准和小灶，可在尕布龙这里却不是这样。除了工作、开会、下乡，他每天和住在家里的牧人吃一样的饭，从不另外开灶。吃饭的时候，他在一旁悄悄地观察，见大家都端着碗吃了，饭量大的盛了第二碗饭，他才盛上一碗，独自到小屋子里静静地吃。

有一天，好奇的卓玛看见他又把碗端到了小屋子，就跑过去问他："爷爷，爷爷，你为什么总是最后一个吃饭，你不饿吗？为什么自己一个人在这里吃，多没意思？"

尕布龙说："碗太烫了，爷爷端不住，爷爷一个人吃饭习惯了。"

其实，天真的卓玛哪里知道，尕布龙是担心自己和牧民在一起吃，牧民们会拘束、吃不饱。另外，他是要看着大家都快吃饱了，他才吃。如果锅里的饭没有了，他就吃点馍馍，不给厨师添麻烦。吃不上的人多，或者正在这时又来了人，他才会让厨师再做一锅饭。在他心里，农牧民群众永远比他自己更重要。

写到这里时，我的眼泪禁不住掉了下来。这个世界上，怎么会有这样善良的人呢？这是亲生父母为自己的孩子才肯做的事啊！

多年来，尕布龙家里来的人太多了，他自己也记不清究竟住过多少人，而且大部分叫不上名字。也有人突然来了，连名字都不愿说，只是让尕布龙把他带到医院看病治疗，看完病连招呼不打就走，花费的医疗费不管多少只能由尕布龙出。像这样的事谁也记不清有多少件，我只知道，仅经驾驶员崔生满在省医院签过的单子，尕布龙用自己工资付清的就有40多万元。

为了答谢医院的医生护士，他每年都要从自己侄女华毛措、女儿召格力的羊圈里拉十几只羊给医生护士送去。

崔生满对我说："尕主任这一辈子没求过人，没为自己的事、家人的事求过谁，只求过医生，求过护士。为了他心心念念的乡亲们，为了那些生活贫困的老百姓，他啥事都能做，啥都舍得。即使这样，尕布龙的好心有时候还能生出些误会。有一次，一家人还把他给告了。"

"什么，还告他？"

"是啊！"

the family insisted that Gabulong should take the responsibilities of the old man's death and sued him to the court.

"Then what happened in the end?" I asked anxiously.

"I forgot the rest of the story. Anyway, Director Ga encountered a lot of troubles in helping others get medical treatment, and it was common for him to be wronged by others."

According to the rough estimates of the people worked with him, in the thirty years before 2001 alone, Gabulong brought over 7,000 poor farmers and herdsmen who needed medical treatment to the Affiliated Hospital of Qinghai University. He personally visited the bedside of many of those who were hospitalized. In order to get the exact number, I asked Gabulong's nephew Xiao Eli to help me calculate the following statistics: From 1975 to 1981, during the seven years Gabulong lived at the residential unit of the Animal Husbandry Bureau, it was up to 2,555 people if counted as one person each day; it was up to 21,900 people if counted as three persons each day. During the twenty years from 1982 to 2001 when he lived at the provincial government residential building; and during the four years from 2002 to 2005, when he lived at the residential unit of the National People's Congress, if counted as one person per day, it was 1,460 people, totaling 25,915 people. That is to say, over the course of thirty-one years, Gabulong received at least 25,000 farmers and herdsmen from pastoral regions for free in his home.

This kind of life had never stopped for more than 30 years, over 10,000 days and nights.

Such perseverance and repetition seem ordinary and simple, but it is difficult for ordinary people to endure.

Whenever asked why he was so kind to those herders and farmers, he always responded, "Most of the people who come to me are poor people from pastoral areas. They have nobody to rely on in the city, and they don't speak Chinese. If I don't care for them, who will?"

His heart is shining like gold and transparent like crystal. For him, the sorrows of others were his own, but he also shared their joys. Relieving the worries of the farmers and herdsmen and helping them overcome difficulties brought him great happiness and was an important part of his life. His heart was always connected to the hearts of the people. He never saw this as a hindrance or a bother. The purity and authenticity of human nature, the calmness and kindness without pretense, are innate in him, full and strong.

As a provincial leader, his life seemed too simple.

In the morning, he ate a bowl of tsampa, drank a cup of tea, and turned on the small semi-conductor to listen to the news. For lunch, he ate a bowl of mixed vegetables or rice, or a plate of fried potatoes and cabbages. In the evening, he usually ate a bowl of noodles, and then watched the news.

那是一年的冬天，尕主任带着崔生满下乡检查工作，经过一户牧民家，听见院子里传出念经的声音。进门看时，一位老人双目紧闭，脸色蜡黄，毫无知觉地躺在炕上，一家人跪在地上，摇着经筒。

尕布龙一看急了，连忙吩咐他们一家把病人抬到车上，让崔生满连夜开车到省医院看病。谁能想到，那个老人病情太重，医院没抢救过来死了。结果，那家人非说是尕布龙把他们的病人给治死了，一直告到了法院。

"那最后咋办了？"我焦急地问。

"后来咋办了，我也忘了，反正尕主任为了帮别人看病遇到了很多麻烦，被人冤枉是常有的事。"

根据他身边工作过的有心人粗略统计，仅2001年之前的30年间，他带到青海大学附属医院就诊的贫困农牧民患者，就达7000多人。有很多患重病的人，他都亲自在病床前守护过。为了了解得更加准确，我询问了尕布龙的侄子肖俄力，和他一起认真地统计了一下。1975年至1981年，尕布龙在畜牧局家属院居住7年，每天按1个人算，共是2555人次；1982年至2001年搬到省政府院子后20年，一天按3个人算，共是21900人次；2002年至2005年在人大居住4年，每天按1个人算，共是1460人次，总共25915人次。就是说，31年来，尕布龙在自己家，共免费接待来自基层看病办事的农牧民至少达到25000多人次。

这样的生活，30余年，一万多个日夜，从未间断。

这样的坚守，这样的重复，看似平凡、简单，常人却难以做到。

他却这样说道："到我这里来的大部分人是农牧区的贫困群众，城里没有可以依靠的人又不会说汉话，我不管谁管？"

他的心像金子一样闪亮，像水晶一样透明。对他来说，百姓的悲苦是自己的，百姓的快乐也是自己的。为农牧民群众解忧，帮助他们渡过难关就是他最大的幸福和心愿，也是他生活的一部分。他的心和老百姓的心始终是相通的，他不觉得这是一件拖累他、烦扰他的事，他的心中一片晴朗。人性中的纯粹、本真，绝无矫饰伪装的平静和善意在他身上与生俱来，饱满而结实。

作为一名省级干部，他的生活显得过于简单。

早上，吃一碗糌粑，喝一碗茶，扭开小半导体听新闻。中午吃一碗熬饭或者米饭，炒一盘土豆、白菜。晚上回来，吃一碗等到他吃时已经煮成

He watched the news on a very old and small Panasonic color TV. He always turned off the TV immediately after watching the news and took time to chat with the farmers and herdsmen who stayed at his home, inquiring about their livelihoods and listening to them, or he would read the newspaper to familiarize himself with the materials for the next day's meeting. Because people from the farming and pastoral areas constantly came to him asking for help in medical treatment and other affairs, he knew the information from the grassroots very quickly, allowing him to solve problems in the shortest time.

Gabulong's salary was often not enough, because it was used not only to feed those who came to live with him, to buy medicine for his wife Huamao's illness, but also often to pay for the hospitalization fees for farmers and herdsmen. When he returned home during the Spring Festival, the villagers waited eagerly for him as the vice governor. He could not go back empty-handed, so he usually bought some vermicelli, tea, soy sauce, and vinegar to the villagers as New Year's presents. Sometimes he would bring some rice, and occasionally a handful of leeks to the villagers for making dumplings on the eve of the New Year. He never gave cigarettes and alcohol, nor did he accept them as gifts. Even if he paid New Year greetings to the leaders of the provincial government, old friends, or colleagues, he still took tea, soy sauce or vinegar as presents.

He believed that "tobacco and alcohol are not good for health, while tea, soy sauce, and vinegar are used every day, which are economical and practical!" The bed he slept on had to be repaired several times because he had moved so many times. He had only two or three suits of faded Chinese tunic clothes, the collars and cuffs of which were worn out, but he was still reluctant to throw them away. Instead, he asked his daughter to replace those worn collars and sleeves with new ones and wore them for long time. He always said that as long as the clothes were clean, there was no need to buy new ones, and it's just wasting money. He loved to eat meat, but he seldom had a full stomach just because he had no extra money to buy meat. Only when his daughter Zhaogelli and niece Huamaocuo brought their own beef or mutton from his hometown Haiyan County, he would let the chef cook a big pot or make dumplings to share with everyone. Occasionally he asked his nephew or granddaughter to buy a few fried dough sticks at the breakfast stall for a change. Even for the New Year's Eve dinner, the only extra dishes were only a bowl of dumplings and a plate of mutton. The vegetables he usually ate were limited to cabbage, potato, radish, and green onions, and he never ate expensive vegetables.

When Ma Fenglan, who had been the cook for three years at Gabulong's home, cooked meal for the first time, she thought that the vice governor's lunch should not be so simple, so she fried him a small plate of scrambled eggs with tomatoes and cooked a bowl of noodles. Gabulong looked at the meal that was served, and asked her, "What's on this plate?"

糊糊的汤面饭，然后看新闻。

电视是一台很旧的小松下彩电，看完新闻就立即把电视关掉。抓紧时间和来家里投宿的农牧民聊天、唠家常，询问最基层的事情，倾听他们的心里话，或者看看报纸，熟悉一下第二天开会的材料。因为不断有农牧区的人找他看病、办事，来自基层的信息他知道得最快，能够让他有的放矢，在最短的时间里解决问题。

尕布龙的工资，要让来家住的所有人吃饱，保证妻子华毛的用药，还要经常替农牧民交住院费，常常是不够用的。春节回家，村里人眼巴巴地等着当副省长的他，他又总不能空手回去，只好买一些粉条、茶叶、酱油、醋，给村民拜年。有时会带些大米，偶尔会送一小把韭黄，让村民年三十包顿饺子。他从不送烟酒，也不收烟酒，即使给省政府的领导、老朋友、同事拜年，拿的也是茶叶、酱油和湟源陈醋。

他认为，"送烟酒对身体不好，茶叶、酱油和醋每天都要用，经济实用！"他睡的床，因为搬家多次，修了好几回。两三套洗得发白的中山装，领子、袖口磨烂了也舍不得扔，让女儿换上领口、袖子接着穿。给他买件新的，他也不要。总是说，衣服干净就行了，没必要浪费买新的，不该花的钱一分也不能随便花。他爱吃肉，可他却很少放开肚子吃，他没有多余的钱买肉。只有女儿召格力、侄女华毛措从海晏拿来自己家的牛羊肉，才让厨子煮一大锅，或者包一顿饺子，和大家共享。有时候，会偶尔让侄子、外孙女到早餐摊上买几根油条，换换口味。即便是年夜饭，也只是增加一碗饺子，一盘手抓羊肉。平时吃的蔬菜也仅限于白菜、洋芋、萝卜和大葱，从不舍得吃细菜。

在尕布龙家做过三年饭的马凤兰刚来时，以为副省长的午餐不应该这么简单，就给他炒了一小盘西红柿炒鸡蛋，下了一碗面条。尕布龙看了看端上来的饭，问她："这盘子里的是什么？"

马凤兰说："西红柿炒鸡蛋，拌面条吃。"

"可这是什么菜啊？"

尕布龙继续追问，脸色变得很不好看。

马凤兰不解："不就是一盘西红柿炒鸡蛋吗？"

"那你就自己吃吧，我不吃。"

马凤兰这才反应过来，他这是在怪她炒菜浪费。

Ma Fenglan said, "Scrambled eggs with tomatoes, you can eat it with noodles."

"But what kind of dish is this?"

Gabulong continued to ask, his face turned stern.

Ma Fenglan puzzled, "Isn't it just a plate of scrambled eggs with tomatoes?"

"Then eat it yourself; I won't eat it."

Ma Fenglan realized that he was criticizing her for being too wasteful and extravagant in her cooking.

What made her even more puzzled was that the electric switch at home was always hung at mid-position. She thought the switch was loose, and as soon as she saw it, would push it up, muttering that she had to find an electrician to repair it.

But one day, she saw in the kitchen that Gabulong carefully restored the switch she had pushed up to the middle position. She couldn't help but blurt out, "Oh, it's you who pulled it down. Why?"

Gabulong smiled mysteriously and said, "Because by doing this, we can save electricity."

There was another thing that impressed Ma Fenglan. Once, she bought a bar of good-smelling soap from a store. Gabulong saw it and asked her how much the soap cost. Upon hearing it was seven yuan, Gabulong said to her, "I don't like the smell, go back and exchange it."

When Ma Fenglan came back with the replaced soap, Gabulong took a look and asked the price. Then he said to her that he still didn't like the smell. He asked her to exchange it for another one. Ma Fenglan went to get another one, but he was still not satisfied. It wasn't until Ma Fenglan had made seven trips back to the store and brought back a bar costing three yuan that Gabulong finally smiled with satisfaction and said to her, "This is what I want; I like the smell."

Ma Fenglan finally figured out what Gabulong meant, and said with a little bit of anger, "You are so cheap; what are you going to do with the money saved?"

"My money is for my own use," Gabulong replied with an equally cold tone.

After a long time, Ma Fenglan realized that his money was spent on "irrelevant" people, and he was also very generous to her. Every time she went home, he would send her with enough money for travel expenses, as well as some food. When Ma Fenglan was getting married in Xining, Gabulong personally arranged her wedding ceremony. But he himself led a very simple life not only in his diet, but also in his clothing. He had only three suits of dark colored clothes. He would ask Ma Fenglan to buy a custom-made one only when the color of the old ones had faded away and they were too worn out to wear. The clothes he wore were nothing but dark colored Chinese tunic suits and white shirts. He never liked colored ones.

更让她觉得纳闷的是，家里的电闸总是挂在半中腰。她以为是电闸松了，只要看见了，就连忙推上去，嘴里还嘀咕着，啥时候得找电工修修。

可有一天，她在厨房里瞅见尕布龙把她推上去的电闸又小心地恢复到了中间位置，忍不住脱口而出："哎哟，原来是你拉下来的，这是为啥呀？"

尕布龙有些神秘地笑了笑说："你不知道，这样可以省电。"

还有一件让马凤兰记在心里的事。有一次，她去商店买回一块好闻的香皂，尕布龙看见了，问她香皂多少钱？马凤兰说7元钱。尕布龙就对她说，我不喜欢这个味道，你拿去换一块吧。

回来后，尕布龙看了看，一问价格，还是说不喜欢这个味道，让她再去换一块，马凤兰又去换了一块，直到耐着性子的马凤兰折腾了7趟，买了块3块钱的香皂，才让尕布龙满意地露出了笑容，笑着对她说："我要的就是这块，我喜欢这个味道。"

这下，马凤兰终于明白了尕布龙的意思，有些生气地说："你这么节省，省下的钱要干什么？"

"我的钱自有我的用处。"尕布龙的口气也很冷淡。

时间长了，马凤兰才知，他的钱都用在"不相干"的人身上了，对她也很大方，每次回家，都要给她足够的路费，给她带一些吃的东西。马凤兰结婚，是在西宁办的婚礼，由尕布龙亲自操持。可他自己，不光饮食简单，里里外外就三身黑乎乎的衣服。颜色掉了，破得没法穿了，才叫马凤兰给她定做一套，无非是深色的中山装，白布的衬衣，带颜色的从来不喜欢。

有一年冬天，黄南州一位牧民治好了病准备回家，和尕布龙告辞。他看着大病初愈的牧民，心中不忍，吩咐马凤兰把女儿召格力刚给他做的一条棉裤拿出来给那个牧民带上。马凤兰一听，扭身进了自己的屋子，说什么也不吭气，就是不出来。

牧民走后，她对尕布龙说："这次说啥也不听你的，你自己就这一条棉裤，还要穿着它下乡，给了别人，你怎么过冬？"

离开尕布龙家后，马凤兰一直牵挂着他。有一年过端午节，马凤兰给他送去自己包的粽子，剥了粽叶蘸上蜂蜜让他吃，尕布龙很喜欢，说自己还是头一次吃。尕布龙生病后，躺在病床上，吃不下去东西，马凤兰哭着说："这么好的人，为什么要得这样的病，受这样的罪啊！"

一天傍晚，司机崔生满拿来了几张葱花饼。

One winter, a herder in Huangnan Prefecture was cured and came to say goodbye to Gabulong as he prepared to return home. Gabulong looked at the herdsman who was recovering from a serious illness and felt pity on him. He asked Ma Fenglan to take out a pair of cotton trousers that his daughter Zhao Geli had just made for him, so that he could give it to the herder. When Ma Fenglan heard this, she turned and walked into her room, saying nothing.

After the herdsman left, she said to Gabulong, "I won't listen to you this time. You have no extra cotton trousers, and you have to wear them when working in the countryside. If you give them away, how will you get through the winter?"

Even after leaving Gabulong's home, Ma Fenglan still cared about him. On the occasion of the Dragon Boat Festival one year, Ma Fenglan visited him with some zongzi (a kind of food) she had wrapped. She peeled the leaves and dipped the zongzi in honey for him to eat. Gabulong liked it very much and said that was the first time he ate it. After Gabulong fell ill, lying on the hospital bed, unable to eat anything, Ma Fenglan cried and said, "Why does such a good person suffer from such a disease?"

One evening, Cui Shengman, Gabulong's driver, brought scallion cakes.

Cui took the cakes to the kitchen, cut them into small pieces with a knife, put them on a plate, and placed it on the dinner table. The scallion cake was yellow and crisp, with a strong fragrance. Gabulong picked up a small piece and ate it, repeatedly saying that it was delicious. At this time, Cui was about to leave, and Gabulong accompanied him to the gate. But when he came back, he found that the cakes on the plate were eaten up. Gabulong looked at the empty plate and smiled softly, with slight regret in his eyes.

Thinking of this, Gabulong's granddaughter Dashijieli always had tears in her eyes. She said, "Poor grandpa, he hadn't even tasted scallion pancakes! But at that time, we ate all of them, and there was nothing left for Grandpa."

The scallion cake incident has always been in Dashijieli's heart, and it is also heavily pressed on my heart. Many people today can't even remember how many times they've eaten rare delicacies, let alone a few slices of scallion cakes. But there were few decent meals on the dinner table at Gabulon's home. Even a plate of scrambled eggs and fried peppers would have been rare. It's hard for us to find a leader like Gabulong in today's society. No wonder some people say that I am making up stories.

There are even more incredible things about Gabulong. As a provincial leader, Gabulong had never entered a big hotel, let alone a magnificent high-end hotel. If he had entered one, he might have been frightened. Because of his consistent attitude and temperament, no one would dare to invite him to such a restaurant for dinner. Even if someone invited him, he would not go. He was busy caring about

小崔拿到厨房，用刀切成小块装在盘子里放到饭桌上。葱花饼又黄又脆，散发出浓浓的香味。尕布龙拿起一小块吃了，连连说香。这时，小崔要走，尕布龙送出了门。可等他回来时，盘子里的葱花饼一块也不剩了。当时，尕布龙定定地看着吃空的盘子，轻轻地笑了笑，眼里竟然流露出难得的遗憾。

想起这件事，尕布龙的孙女达什姐莉眼里总是充满了泪水。她说："可怜的爷爷，连葱花饼都没吃过！可当时我们怎么就全吃完了，一点也没给爷爷留下呢。"

葱花饼的事，一直放在达什姐莉的心里，也沉甸甸地压在我的心上。现在，对很多人来说，别说是几张葱花饼，就是稀世佳肴，也不知吃过了多少回。可尕布龙家里的饭桌上，很少有像样的饭菜，一盘炒鸡蛋、炒辣椒，都很难得。这样的人，这样的领导，在现在这样的社会里是稀缺的，难怪有人说我是在瞎编故事。

还有更加令人难以置信的事，作为一名省级领导干部，尕布龙从没有进过大饭店，更别说富丽堂皇的高级酒店。他要真进去了，可能会把他吓坏的。因为他一贯的态度，脾气性格，没人敢请他到这样的饭店去吃饭，即使请了，他也不去，他一心想着的是家里生病的老百姓，下班了他们会等着他。

平常，他连茶叶都舍不得喝，喝山上的黑刺叶，还说很养生。

可是，这都什么年代了，为官多年的尕布龙为什么过着这样简朴的生活，为什么把钱舍得用在不认识的人身上，而自己却过着如此清苦的生活呢？我心里一阵难过。好东西谁不喜欢吃，好衣服谁不喜欢穿啊。可是，他就是这样一个严格要求自己、规范自己，竭尽全力帮助别人的人。那时候，大吃大喝的风气开始盛行，而且越来越严重，他制止不了，只能约束自己，严格要求身边的人。

有些人对他的做法不以为意，说吃一顿饭算什么，能有多大的事？

他说："一顿饭确实不算什么，但是，吃惯了，就止不住了，就会把风气带坏了。"对于人们的不理解，他从来不解释，也没有解释的必要。他觉得，这个社会上，还有那么多温饱无着的贫困户，还有那么多需要帮助的人，自己吃得饱、穿整洁就可以了。担任省级领导干部，外表高大健壮的他，感情是细腻、柔软的，内心是干净、透明的。他认为，无论如何

the sick people at home, and they would be waiting for him when he got off work.

He even seldom drank tea to save money, and he usually put the black stalk leaves he had picked from the mountain in his cups, saying they were very healthy.

But in what age we are living? Why did Gabulong, who had been a government leader for many years, lead such a simple life? Why did he spend his money on people he didn't know, while he himself lived such a miserable life? I felt so grieved for him. Who doesn't like to eat delicious foods and to wear nice clothes? However, he was such a person who was strict with himself, very disciplined, and did his best to help others. At his time, the habit of eating and drinking extravagantly began to prevail, and it became more and more serious. He couldn't stop it. He could only restrain himself and strictly regulate the people around him.

Some people were dissatisfied with his practices, saying that enjoying a meal is not a big deal. How bad can it be?

He said, "A meal is really nothing, but if you get used to it, you can't stop it, and it will eventually spoil social morality." When people misunderstood, he never explained, and there was no need to explain. He felt that in this society, there are still so many poor households without food and clothing, and so many people in need. He is satisfied to have enough food to eat and have clean clothes to wear. As a provincial leader, he looked tall and strong, but his feelings were delicate and tender, and his heart was clean and transparent. He believed that in any case, he was not worthy of wearing extravagant clothes while standing on tHebarren land, unless the land became fertile.

Later, I met the driver Cui Shengman in an office of the Provincial People's Congress, and I couldn't wait to ask him about the scallion pancakes. Cui Shengman waved his hand and said, "They were not scallion cakes, but the fried leek dumplings we eat in Qinghai. Director Gabulong hadn't even eaten a fried leek dumpling, and his granddaughter Dashijieli also rarely ate it. She misremembered it."

Cui Shengman hadn't seen him eat anything good while he served as a driver for Gabulong. He always led a simple life, and his life and diet were even simpler once he got diabetes. He mostly ate fried noodles mixed with barley, beans, and soybean flour. Even when he returned to his hometown, he just watched other people eating nice food, and he himself ate a bowl of fried noodles.

Cui Shengman had been with Gabulong for thirteen years. He told me that every time he drove Gabulong to a county for a meeting, other leaders usually accepted receptions arranged by the local government, and on their leaving, they had expensive cigarettes and wine in the trunks of their cars. However, the vice governor whom he served for always ate simple meals, stayed in the cheapest hotels, and paid the bills himself. Even if when they felt thirsty and ate a watermelon on the way, he would

自己都不配穿着华贵的衣裳站在贫瘠的土地上，除非，把它们变得肥沃起来。

后来，我在省人大的一间办公室见到了驾驶员崔生满，我迫不及待地问他葱花饼的事。崔生满摆摆手说："那不是葱花饼，是我们青海人吃的韭菜盒子。尕主任连个韭菜盒子都好好没吃过，她的孙女达什姐莉也很少吃，记错了。"

自从给尕布龙开车后，崔生满就没见他吃过什么好饭。本来就节省，得了糖尿病后，吃得就更简单了，大部分是青稞、豆面、黄豆混合的炒面。就是回到老家，也是看着别人吃好的，自己端着碗在一旁吃炒面。

崔生满在尕布龙身边待了13年。每一次去州县开会，别人吃饭、喝酒、唱歌，走的时候，还要往后备厢里塞进去好烟好酒，好不舒心。可自己服务的副省长，却总是吃简单的饭，住最便宜的旅馆，还要他们自掏腰包，就是路上渴了吃个西瓜，也要严肃地一再追问，是不是自己买的，让他不要做白吃白拿的事情。

20世纪90年代末，省上在北山召开林业工作会议。中午吃饭时，上了一盘草莓。尕布龙没吃过，以为是摆设，只是静静地欣赏着。有人硬是让他吃了几颗，他慢慢吃着，细细品尝着，禁不住说："这个小东西味道还不错！"

一桌人心酸得低下了头。

省政府曾经多次给尕布龙调配过小轿车，但是他根本就不要，他只用能跑农牧区的越野车，而且一用好多年。

1996年全省房改，他的小妹夫赵庆玺动员他参加房改。说了两三次，他都不吭气。赵庆玺是山东人，参军来到青海。当年，尕布龙的小妹妹嫁给这位解放军的时候，尕布龙很高兴，很喜欢，也很尊重这位当解放军的小妹夫。平常家里人有事不敢跟他说话时，只有这个小妹夫的话他还能听几句。最后，小妹夫问急了，他才说："我手里没有钱，拿啥房改？"

赵庆玺感叹着，回忆着尕布龙留在他心中的印象："他是一位了不起的人，没有人能做到他所做的。他的思想、品德、为人如此高贵，是我们这些凡人无法企及的。"

我不禁有些伤感，想起中华人民共和国成立初期，被毛主席下令处决的贪污犯张子善、刘青山，在国家经济最困难的时候，大吃大喝、铺张浪费，

seriously ask him whether or not it was bought with his own money and warned him not to accept any presents for doing nothing.

In the 1990s, the provincial government held a Forestry Work Conference on the North Mountain. At lunch, a plate of strawberries was served. Gabulong had never tasted strawberries before. Thinking it was a display, he just looked at it quietly. Someone persuaded him to eat a few. He tasted them slowly and carefully, and couldn't help saying, "This little thing really tastes good!"

People at the table lowered their heads sympathetically.

The provincial government allocated sedan cars to Gabulong many times, but he refused. He only needed off-road vehicles that could run in farming and pastoral areas, and he used one vehicle for many years.

Housing reform policy was implemented in Qinghai province in 1996, so his younger brother-in-law Zhao Qingxi mobilized him to enroll in the housing reform. He suggested this to him two or three times, but Gabulong did not say anything. Zhao Qingxi was from Shandong and came to Qinghai because of joining the army. When Gabulong's youngest sister married this PLA soldier, Gabulong was very happy and respected his brother-in-law. Gabulong was willing to listen a few words from this younger brother-in-law when other family members dared not persuade him. Finally, the younger brother-in-law asked anxiously, and Gabulong responded, "I don't have any savings; how can I enroll in housing reform?"

Zhao Qingxi sighed and recalled the impression that Gabulong left in his heart, "He was an amazing person; no one can do what he did. His thoughts, morals, and behavior were so noble that we ordinary people can never become like him."

I can't help feeling a little sad. I think of the corrupt criminals Zhang Zishan and Liu Qingshan who led extravagant lives and were finally executed under Chairman Mao's orders in the early days of the founding of the People's Republic of China when the country was experiencing economic hardships. How did Gabulong, who served as a high-rank official for several decades,

maintain such an arduous and simple style and remain unmoved in this secular world? Didn't he know that the world was undergoing wonderful changes, and people nowadays don't advocate simple lifestyles like his anymore? Could it be that he closed himself in his own world and knew nothing? Or did he know everything but just didn't want to do that? While rejecting the erosion and pollution of secular utilitarianism himself, he always took a sober and introspective posture to care about all living beings in real life with as much dedication and emotion as possible.

What a noble mind!

为什么时隔几十年后，身居要职的尕布龙还能够保持如此艰苦朴素的作风，不为世俗所动呢？难道他就不知道，世界正在发生奇妙的变化，现在的人早就不崇尚他这样简单的生活方式了？难道是他把自己封闭在自己的世界里，什么也不知道？还是他什么都知道，只是不愿意那样做？他在拒斥世俗功利对自身侵蚀污染的同时，始终以清醒自省的姿态，用尽可能多的投入和情感去关心现实生活中的芸芸众生。

这究竟是怎样的一种思想境界呢？

我们又该怎样度过自己的一生？

面对这样一位好书记、好领导，那些手握重权，家中藏有上亿发霉钞票、无数古玩珍宝，天天享受锦衣玉食的人，又会做何感想呢？

他们一定会在心里偷偷发笑。笑尕布龙的愚钝、痴迷，笑他的落伍、不洒脱。他们怎么也不会想到，他之所以这样做，是因为他的心里始终以人民为上、以人民为天。他爱民如子，视民为亲，心里时刻装着老百姓的安危、疾苦。他始终无法忘记自己是草原上长大的牧羊人，不能因为当了官，就忘了过去。他认为，精神的快乐，远远高于物质的快乐、身体的快乐。关心他人，以人为本，就是共产党员不忘老百姓，不脱离群众，百分之百为人民服务的初心。贫困的牧民能住在他的家里，是对他的信任，也是对党的信任，不仅让他有机会倾其所有帮助他们，同时，也可以帮助他了解牧民最真实的生活状况，掌握平时难以了解的情况。这是尕布龙深入生活、深入基层、了解民情、解决问题，最接地气的工作方法，是尕布龙的发明创造，也是只有他才能够长期实践和坚持的工作方法。

How should we spend our lives?

In the face of such a good secretary and leader, how will those with great power, who own hundreds of millions of moldy banknotes and countless antique treasures in their homes, and lead extravagant lives, feel?

They must laugh secretly in their hearts, laughing at Gabulong's stupidity and obsession, laughing at his outdated ideas and formalism. They would never have thought that the reason he did this was that he always had people in his heart and met people's needs first. He loved his folk people like his children, regarded them as relatives, and was always concerned with their safety and suffering. He could never forget that he was a shepherd who grew up on the grassland, and he could not forget the past just because he became a leader. He believed that spiritual happiness was far superior to material happiness. Caring for others and putting people first was the original aspiration of Communist Party members. Poor herders could live in his home because of their trust in him and in the party. It not only gave him the opportunity to devote all his resources to help them, but it also helped him understand the actual living conditions and situations of the herders, which he had no other way of knowing. This was the most grassroots and down-to-earth working method for Gabulong to go deep into life, understand the people's conditions, and solve problems. It was Gabulong's invention and creation. It was also a working method that only he could practice and persist in for a long time.

温　情

　　夏日的午后，金银滩草原雨雾蒙蒙，哈勒景的河水在缓缓流淌。穿过野花点缀的小路，尕布龙的老家在离村口不远的地方，门庭洁净，静穆安宁。

　　见我进门，正在厨房和面的召格力急急忙忙擦了擦手上的面粉，握住了我的手。

永丰村老家

The childhood home at Yongfeng village

Warmth

In the summer afternoon, the Jinyintan grassland was rainy and foggy, and the river of Halejing was flowing slowly and quietly. Across the footpath dotted with wild flowers, not far from the entrance of the village, was Gabulong's childhood home, the courtyard of which was clean, quiet, and peaceful.

Seeing me entering the door, Zhao Geli, who was kneading dough in the kitchen, hurriedly wiped the flour from her hands to hold my hand.

Zhao Geli, the daughter of Gabulong, is sixty-two years old. Her face was ruddy, her swarthy hair fluttered neatly behind her head, without a trace of gray. It was just the years of herding and overwork that caused her to suffer from severe rheumatoid arthritis, and her bent legs made her walk a little shaky.

A craftsman, requested by Zhao Geli, was repairing the roof of the house, which was leaking.

In the yard, dahlias and peony, holding the umbrella-like green leaves, looked vigorous, and a rhubarb tree that should have grown on the grassland grew new leaves and shimmered. The lush lilac canopy covered most of the leaves and had already bloomed.

Zhao Geli took my hand and walked into Gabulong's bedroom.

A large bed covered with a red blanket occupied half of the house. This was the bed that Gabulong slept on with his secretary and his driver when he visited home. The

召格力今年 62 岁，是尕布龙的女儿。她脸色红润，黑黝黝的头发利利索索地绾在脑后，不见一丝白发。只是长年累月的放牧生涯和过度劳累，让她得了严重的风湿性关节炎，弯曲的双腿，使她走起路来有些摇晃。

家里的顶棚漏雨，召格力请了匠人正在修补。

院子里，大丽花和牡丹撑着伞一样的绿叶显得生机勃勃，一棵本应长在草原上的大黄却长出了簇新的叶子，泛着微光。树冠茂盛的丁香遮住了大半个房檐，已经开过了花。

召格力牵着我的手，走进尕布龙的卧室。

一张铺着红色毯子，干干净净的大炕，占据了房屋的一半。这是尕布龙回家时，和秘书、司机睡的炕，炕柜上面整齐地叠放着他盖过的被褥，简单的陈设和尕布龙生前时一样。堂屋的正面墙上挂着他年轻时的照片，照片上的他，神情俊逸、眼睛透亮。

我坐在炕头，喝着一杯热茶，禁不住问："你的父亲，是省上的领导，怎么会让你一辈子待在偏远的草原上放牧为生？"

召格力的眼睛一红，泪如泉涌。她在这个院子里长大，幼小的心里，一直觉得父亲就是一座山，一个飘浮的梦，一颗需要永远追逐的亮闪闪的星星。年少时的她知道，父亲是公家的人，父亲在外面做的

这是一张挂在尕布龙老家屋子墙上的照片

This is a photo hanging on the wall of

Gabulong's childhood home

尕布龙用过的被褥还整整齐齐地放在炕柜里

The beddings used by Gabulong is still neatly

placed in the kang cabinet

bed was neatly made. The simple furnishings were the same as when Gabulong was alive. On the front wall of the main room was a picture of him when he was young, handsome, and spirited.

Sitting on the bed, sipping a cup of hot tea, I couldn't help but ask, "Your father is the leader of the province. How can you graze on the remote grassland all your life?"

Zhao Geli's eyes reddened and tears surged like a spring. She grew up in this yard. In her young heart, she always felt that her father was like a mountain, a floating dream, a shining star to be chased forever. When she was young, she knew that her father worked for government, that what her father did outside was more important than anything at home, and that whatever her father said was correct and unquestionable.

When her father went to work in Henan County, her mother followed and lived with him in Henan County for a period of time. Unfortunately, we don't know anything else about that period of the couple's life. Maybe the husband was busy with work all day and had no time to consider his wife's feelings, or maybe the wife was really concerned about everything at home. What is even more unknowable is whether or not their son accompanied his mother to visit the father he rarely saw. In short, Huamao returned without hesitation. In the year when Huamao's waist was kicked by a yak, Zhao Geli was only eight years old to take on the load of housework. As a major laborer in the family, she participated in the collective work in the village to earn work points to support the family when she was only eleven years old. At that time, Zhao Geli was very short and had very little strength. She couldn't even reach the lock of the gate, so she put her back basket on the ground, stepped on it, and stretched out her hand to lock the door. At the age of seventeen or eighteen, Zhao Geli could do the same heavy work as the men in the village.

During that period of time, after finishing the work assigned to her by the village committee, she took her mother outside, letting her sit on the grassy ground covered with blankets in the sun, and gave her a massage. This kind of persistence was effective, and after five years, her mother was able to walk slowly on her own with crutches, which made the family very happy.

The sun rose, and a white horse, stepping on a patch of white clouds, floated down from the horizon and fell on the grassland. One day, Zhao Geli suddenly wanted to ride a horse to find her father far away. She wanted to have a deep talk with him, but where

事情，重于家里所有的事，父亲说的话，也是最正确的，不容置疑。

父亲去河南县工作后，母亲曾经去河南县和父亲生活过一段时间，只可惜再也没办法知晓那段对他们夫妻来说非常重要的经历。也许是丈夫整日忙于工作，无暇顾及妻子的感受，也许是妻子实在惦记家里的一切，更不可知的是，他们的儿子有没有跟随母亲一起去看望他很少见到的父亲。总之，华毛义无反顾地回来了。华毛的腰被牦牛踢伤的那一年，召格力才8岁，不得已承担起了繁重的家务。11岁时，她已经作为家庭的一个主要劳力，参加大队的劳动挣工分养家了。那时候，召格力个子很小，力气也

尕布龙的妻子华毛和女儿召格力在一起

Gabulong's wife Huamao with her daughter Zhao Geli

很小，连大门的锁子都够不着，她就把背篼扣在地上，踩在背篼上，使劲伸出手把门锁上。到了十七八岁，召格力已经和村里的男人们一样干背灰、上肥的重活儿了。

那段时间，忙完大队分配给她的活，她就把母亲抱到院子外面，让母亲坐在铺着毡子的草滩上晒太阳，给母亲按摩。这样的坚持是有效的，五年后，母亲能拄着拐棍自己慢慢走路了，一家人很高兴。

太阳升起来了，白马踏着一朵白云，自天边而下，落在草原上。有一天，召格力忽然间想骑着马去遥远的地方寻找自己的父亲，和父亲说说心里的话，可到哪儿才能找到父亲呢？父亲很少回家，即使在家，也有忙不完的事。

could she find him? Her father seldom came back home, and even during his stay at home, he was always busy with other things.

The longest time her father stayed at home was during the Spring Festival. During Spring Festival, he would go from house to house to give New Year's greetings to the villagers, summon the elderly and the folks in the village to drink New Year's tea at home, teach the villagers about party policies, and educate the young people in the village to be diligent, frugal, and filial to the elderly. On the second day of the Lunar New Year, committee members of the village were invited to come to the family home, and Gabulong would discuss the major events of the village with them and give them advice.

Gabulong often said to the people in the village, "When encountering illness and disaster, you should extend warm hands to one another; when there are happy events in any family, you should give your blessings. But a happy life requires your own efforts and struggle. I will not provide you with any convenience in other things."

At the age of seventeen, Zhao Geli attended tHebarefoot doctor's class and learned the skills of injection, replacing medication, and delivering babies. She began to fantasize that one day she could go to Xining Health School and work in the capital city of Xining after graduation like her classmates. Even if she couldn't stay in Xining, she would be satisfied with working at a hospital as a nurse in a county or township.

At night, the quiet grassland was connected with the night sky, and the breeze was blowing on Zhao Geli's young and beautiful face. With her thoughts, Zhao Geli stared at the stars, unable to sleep. She was eager for her father to help her realize her dream.

That year, she finally looked forward to the arrival of the Spring Festival. On the day before the new year, her father returned home with a tired body. At that time, her father was already a member of the provincial standing committee and head of the Animal Husbandry Bureau of Qinghai Province.

In the evening, the family happily shared the New Year's Eve dinner together.

Zhao Geli was busy with preparing the dinner, and she didn't dare disturb her father's high spirits.

But the next morning, Zhao Geli could not find her father.

"Where is Dad?" she asked her mother.

Her mother replied, "Your dad went herding sheep early in the morning. Did you

父亲在家待得最长的时间是春节。每逢春节，父亲都要挨家挨户给乡亲们拜年，召集村里的老人和群众到家里喝年茶，给村民讲党的政策，教育村里的年轻人，勤俭持家、孝顺老人。大年初二，还要请村里的干部来家里，商议和指导村子里的大事。

尕布龙常对村里的人说："遇到病痛灾难时，要对乡亲伸出一双温暖的手；在父老乡亲喜庆的日子里，一定要把祝福送给他们；但是幸福的生活需要自己努力奋斗，其他的事，我是不会给你们提供任何便利条件的。"

17岁时，召格力参加了赤脚医生学习班，学会了打针、换药，学会了接生孩子。她开始幻想，有一天能像学习班上的同学一样去西宁的卫校上学，和同学一样留在省城西宁，哪怕是县上、乡上的医院，穿上白大褂在正规的医院工作。

年轻时的召格力
Zhao Geli in her youth

去牧民家接生归来的召格力
Zhao Geli returning home after delivering a herder's baby

forget? Every Spring Festival, your dad will spend three days feeding the sheep for you and the villagers when he comes back."

Zhao Geli got on a horse and went to look for her father.

As soon as she saw her father, Zhao Geli shouted.

It was the morning of New Year's Day, and it was so cold that the breath coming out of her mouth could be frozen into ice. In the morning mist, Gabulong was riding a horse, herding a group of sheep to the depths of the grassland.

Zhao Geli saw that he was wearing an old leather jacket, and his body was not as flexible and light as before. Time flew so quickly, and the middle-aged father was not so vigorous as before and had a touch of melancholy. His back was still broad and strong, but Zhao Geli could sense the heavy responsibility he carried. Seeing his daughter coming toward him on horseback, Gabulong looked at her affectionately and asked, "What are you doing here? You should be sleeping in."

Zhao Geli blushed, and summoned up the courage to say what she had been holding back from her father, "Dad, I am now a barefoot doctor in the village. People in the village say that I have been doing excellently as a doctor, especially in delivering babies, which I've done better than others."

"That's great, my daughter is capable!"

"But, dad, all my classmates have gone to Xining for further study. May I also go to the Provincial Health School and work in the hospital in the future?" Zhao Geli pulled her father's sleeve affectionately. "Dad, I want to be a doctor. I will definitely become a good doctor that you can be proud of."

Gabulong didn't speak, and a swell of sad emotion rose in his heart.

During the "Cultural Revolution", his thirteen-year-old son had died of a sudden illness.

At that time, he was far from home and was dismissed from his work in Henan County. His fate, his misfortune, the pain of his loneliness, and the hatred of guilt all fell on his suffering heart.

It was a painful period of time that he couldn't bear to look back on. Gabulong's hard-battered heart had solidified and closed from then on, not easily opened or called to reflection.

Since then, being childless, he had regarded Zhao Geli as his biological daughter

夜晚，静谧的草原与夜空相连，清风吹拂着召格力年轻美丽的脸庞。有了心事的召格力凝望着星星，难以入眠。她多么渴望父亲能帮她实现心愿。

那年，终于盼到了春节。年三十，父亲风尘仆仆地回到了家，那时的父亲已经是青海省常委兼任畜牧局局长。

晚上，大家在一起快快乐乐地吃了一顿年夜饭。

召格力忙前忙后，不敢打扰父亲的兴致。

第二天早上，召格力找不到父亲了。

"阿爸去哪儿啦？"她问母亲。

母亲说："你阿爸一大早就去放羊了。你忘了，每年春节，你阿爸回来都要替你、替村里的乡亲们放三天羊。"

召格力拽过一匹马，飞奔着去寻找父亲。

一看见父亲的身影，召格力就喊了起来。

那是大年初一的早上，天冷得能把嘴里呼出的哈气冻成冰。晨雾中，尕布龙骑在马上，正赶着一群羊往草原深处走。

召格力见他穿着一件陈旧的皮袄，身子已不如从前那么灵活轻盈。时间过得很快，步入中年的父亲，少了往日的矫健，多了一缕淡淡的惆怅。他的背影还是那么宽厚结实有力，可召格力能感觉到他肩负的重任。见女儿骑马跑来，尕布龙疼爱地望着女儿问："你又跑过来干啥，今天可以睡个懒觉嘛。"

召格力红着脸，鼓起勇气对父亲说出了憋在心头的话："阿爸，我现在是村里的赤脚医生了。村里的人都说我看病看得好，特别是接生的活比别人干得都好。"

"那好啊，我的女儿能干哟！"

"可是，阿爸，一起学习过的同学都去西宁上学了，我能不能也到省卫校上学，以后到医院工作？"召格力动情地拽着父亲的衣袖。"阿爸，我喜欢当医生呢，我一定会成为值得你骄傲的好医生。"

尕布龙没有说话，心里一阵酸楚。

"文革"期间，他年仅13岁的儿子突发急病夭折。

那时，正是他远离家乡，在河南县工作被革职批斗的日子。他的命运、他的不幸，他孤独罹罪的锥心之痛、愧疚之恨，一齐降临在他正在遭受屈

and loved her together with his wife. At this moment, he raised his head, looking at the glow of sunlight on the horizon, his face slightly melancholy. Through his gaze, his daughter Zhao Geli saw how difficult and long-lasting the vicissitudes of life had been on her father's trembling heart.

Zhao Geli looked at her father without blinking.

Dad's heart was soft but also hard.

After a while, Gabulong stared into his daughter's dark eyes intently, touched her head, and said softly, "Zhao Geli, you are a sensible child. Your mother is not in good health and needs care. Dad is too busy to take care of her, so you'd better stay at home to be a herder. Be a barefoot doctor, take good care of your mother, and depend on yourself for a living. Besides, I can't take advantage of my power to arrange work for you in the city. Dad's power is given by the people and should be used on the people!"

"Dad!" Sobs choked her voice.

She felt extremely desperate. That year, Zhao Geli was already a grown-up girl. She would not act like a baby or lose her temper with her father, but she did not understand why he would be so cold to his daughter.

But how could she know the contradiction in her father's heart? At that time, the words "Serving for the People", which were easier said than done, weighed on her father's heart, and they had already surpassed his family relationships, joys, and sorrows...

White snow covered the rugged peaks of the red-mouthed mountain. In the silence, cold snowflakes fell on Zhao Geli's hair and face. Zhao Geli wiped away the tears, endured the grievance in her heart, and gathered the sheep in the wind and snow with her father.

After the Spring Festival, her father returned to Xining to work. Zhao Geli herded on the grasslands, got married, and gave birth to children in her hometown. She delivered babies, served as a doctor to support herself, and lived with her mother in the village.

A few years later, the competitive mother fell off a horse again and broke her lumbar spine. Since then, Zhao Geli's mother had been paralyzed in bed, unable to take care of herself. Gabulong didn't bring her to Xining, the provincial city, to live with him. Only Zhao Geli and her mother could understand the sadness. From then on, Gabulong

辱的心上……

那是一段痛入骨髓、不忍回首的日子，尕布龙受到重创的心从此凝固，从此封闭，不轻易打开，不轻易回想。

从那之后，膝下无子的他，早已把召格力当作亲生女儿，和妻子一起疼爱着她。此刻，他抬起头，望着地平线上越来越宽阔的一抹霞光，神情略显忧郁。透过这目光，女儿召格力看到了父亲颤抖的心走过了一段多么艰难持久，痛不欲生的沧桑路程。

召格力眼睛一眨不眨地望着阿爸。

阿爸的心柔软又坚硬。

过了好一阵，尕布龙专注地凝视着女儿那双黑黝黝的眼睛，摸着她的头轻轻地说："召格力，你是一个懂事的孩子，你阿妈身体不好，需要人照顾。阿爸工作太忙顾不上，你就留在家里安心放牧，当赤脚医生，好好照顾你的阿妈，靠自己的能力生活吧！再说，阿爸也不能搞特殊，把你安排在城里工作。阿爸的权力是人民给的，应该用在老百姓身上啊！"

"阿爸！"召格力泣不成声。

她感到无比绝望。那年，召格力已经是一个大姑娘了。她不会给阿爸撒娇，不会给阿爸发脾气，可是她不理解，阿爸为什么会对女儿这样冷酷无情。

可她哪里知道父亲内心的矛盾。那时候，"为人民服务"这几个说起来容易做起来难的大字，在父亲心头的分量，早已超越了人间亲情、悲欢离合……

白色的雪洋洋洒洒，覆盖住了大菊红口嵯峨嶙峋的山峰。沉默中，冰凉的雪片落在召格力的头发上、脸上。召格力擦干泪水，忍着心中的委屈，和父亲在风雪中收拢羊群。

春节过后，父亲回西宁工作了。召格力在草原上放牧，在家乡结婚、生子，为村里的乡亲看病、接生，自食其力，

尕布龙卧病在床的妻子华毛

Gabulong's wife Huamao, who is ill in bed

seemed to put all his affections and love on the people.

In order to let her father work at ease and to take care of her paralyzed mother, Zhao Geli never mentioned her concerns to her father again, and she never left the grassland.

Her girlhood dream went with the wind, and her father's glorious mission seemed to have become hers. Zhao Geli became his her father's helper, and the flock behind her was like her father's logistical support, continuously available to her father so that he could help others.

Gabulong in old age often took Zhao Geli's hand and said, "Fate will not treat you badly, as long as you are honest and work hard!" Zhao Geli burst into tears and remembered it in her heart.

The memories of more than forty years ago seemed to have happened yesterday. Zhao Geli, who was fast approaching old age, was struggling with tears, surging with unspeakable pains and sadness. She had been wiping the tears that flowed down with tHeback of her hand, but after all, she understood and appreciated her father. It was her father who gave her the courage and hope to live, and it was her father who left her with his innocence and a precious spiritual wealth. Her father was the pride and glory of her life, and she was proud to be Gabulong's daughter.

In the small room on the side, there was a small fire-heated bed, which was the same bed where her mom Huamao had been lying for half a lifetime. I walked over and gently stroked the sheets on the bed, thinking of this amazing woman.

After her mother was paralyzed, Zhao Geli was always attending to her, serving her food, pouring water, and washing her body.

Her mother had been lying on the bed for twenty-five years, and she changed her diapers for twenty-five years without letting her mother have any bedsores or sufferings. Her mother had a cheerful personality and a pleasant laugh. When she was happy, she would invite folks in the village to come and play cards.

The villagers asked her why she didn't move to the provincial capital city of Xining?

She smiled and said, "I can do nothing but encumber him if I live with him."

However, in the difficult nights, pains, irritability, and loneliness sometimes made the mother unable to sleep. Zhao Geli would get up several times a night, turn her body

和母亲一起生活。

几年后，争强好胜的阿妈又从马上跌下来，摔坏了腰椎。之后，阿妈瘫在炕上，生活不能自理。父亲也没有把阿妈接到省城西宁和他一起生活，其中的悲伤，只有她们才能够体会，从此，尕布龙似乎把自己的情与爱全部放在了老百姓身上。

为了让父亲安心工作，为了照顾躺在炕上的母亲，召格力再也没向父亲提过自己的心事，再也没有离开过草原。

少女的梦想随风而去，父亲光荣的使命仿佛也成了她的。召格力成了父亲的帮手，身后的羊群像是父亲的后勤保障，被源源不断地提供给父亲，让父亲再去帮助别人。

老年后的父亲，经常拉着召格力的手说："命运是不会亏待你的，只要你诚实做人、踏踏实实劳动！"召格力泪流满面，铭记在心。

40多年前的往事仿佛就发生在昨天，快进入老

海北藏族自治州第七次妇女代表大会
The Seventh Women's Congress of Haibei Tibetan Autonomous Prefecture

年的召格力，心事重重，泪水涟涟，涌动着难以言说的伤痛和心酸。她一直在用手背擦着不断流淌下来的泪水，可她终究是理解父亲、感激父亲的。是父亲给了她生活的勇气和希望，是父亲给她留下了他一世的清白，留下了一笔珍贵的精神财富。父亲是她一生的骄傲、一生的荣耀，她为自己能成为尕布龙的女儿感到骄傲。

侧面的小屋子里，有一个小火炕，是阿妈华毛躺了半辈子的炕。我走过去，轻轻抚摸着炕上的床单，想着这位了不起的女人。

阿妈瘫痪后，召格力一直守候在身边，给阿妈端饭、倒水、洗身子。

阿妈躺了25年，她给阿妈换了25年的尿布，没有让她生过一点褥疮、受过一点罪。阿妈性格开朗，笑声动听。开心的时候，还会请村子里的乡亲来家里打打纸牌。

over, speak with her, and help her get through the long night.

In 1992, Zhao Geli's 8-year-old daughter Dashijieli went to live with Gabulong, her grandfather. Gabulong loved his little granddaughter very much, and he would occasionally wait to pick her up at the gate of Jiefang Road Primary School when he was free. But he was still strict with this second-grade little granddaughter. Dashijieli wore the simplest clothes in the primary school. Until she was in middle school, she wore clothes handmade by her mother. She never told her classmates that her grandfather was the governor, not because her grandfather told her not to, but because she felt that her grandfather was too ordinary and plain, and she was afraid that her classmates would laugh at her.

One evening after school, Dashijieli entered the gate of her home and saw her grandpa sitting under a lilac tree chopping wood. As she approached, she saw he was struggling to pick up something with his thick hand.

On seeing his granddaughter, Gabulong waved to her, "Dashijieli, come and help Grandpa!"

Dashijieli ran over and saw that a small piece of wood had fallen into the cracks in of the bricks.

"Grandpa, it's just a small piece of wood; you are too stingy."

Grandpa said, "It's not stingy; it's a waste. Just take it out for me."

Dashijieli had to squat down to pull out the small wooden block from the crack in the bricks.

There were many rooms in the house, but Dashijieli never had her own separate bedroom. She always shared the room with the patients from pastoral areas. Sometimes when there were too many people, she had to spare her bed for others and slept on a mattress on the floor of her grandpa's bedroom.

Before the college entrance examination, Dashijieli needed to review her homework at night, but Gabulong was afraid that she would disturb the patients' rest. She had to pretend to sleep and wait until the others fell asleep, and then she quietly went to the dining hall to study and finish her homework.

In the eyes of Dashijieli, Grandpa was not a high-rank provincial leader at all. He was more like a shepherd, a good man who was dedicated to others. Grandpa had lived a tiring and difficult life. He had no rest days, no holidays, and he never traveled. He was

乡亲们问她，为什么不搬到省城西宁去住？

她笑着说："我到他那里去能干什么，只能拖累他！"

但是，到了难挨的晚上，痛苦、烦躁、孤独，有时会让阿妈无法入眠，召格力便不辞辛苦地一夜起来数次，给阿妈翻身，陪阿妈说话，帮助阿妈熬过漫漫长夜。

1992年，召格力8岁的小女儿达什姐莉来到尕布龙身边，和爷爷一起生活。尕布龙很疼爱小外孙女，偶然得了空，还会等在解放路小学门口接外孙女回家。但是对这个才上小学二年级的小外孙女，他仍然要求严格。上小学的时候，达什姐莉的穿着是最朴素的，直到上中学的时候还穿着妈妈亲手纳的布鞋。达什姐莉没有告诉过同学自己的爷爷是省长，不是因为爷爷的嘱咐，而是觉得自己的爷爷太不像个领导，太平凡、太朴素，怕说出来会惹同学笑话。

有一天晚上放学回家，一进大门，达什姐莉就看见爷爷坐在一棵丁香树下劈柴火。走近时，爷爷正吃力地用粗大的手抠东西。

尕布龙一见外孙女就朝她招手："达什姐莉，快来给爷爷帮忙！"

达什姐莉跑过去一看，原来是一小片木块掉进了砖缝里。

"爷爷，这么点小木片就算了，你也太小气了！"

爷爷说："这不是小气，这是浪费，你快给我取出来。"

达什姐莉只好蹲下身子，从砖缝里把小木块抠了出来。

家里房间很多，但是达什姐莉从来没有自己单独的卧室，一直和牧区来的病人们住在一间屋子里。有时候，人太多，还得把自己的床让出来，到爷爷的卧室打地铺。

高考前，达什姐莉晚上要复习功课，尕布龙怕她影响病人休息，她只好先假装睡觉，等大家都睡着了才悄悄到餐厅看书、写作业。

在达什姐莉的眼里，爷爷根本不是一位当大官的省级领导，他就是一个牧人，一个一心为他人着想的好人。爷爷这一生很累、很苦，没有休息日，没有节假日，从来没有旅行过。他总是担心自己外出，家里住的牧民遇到困难没人帮忙。爷爷一辈子为百姓操劳、为百姓着想，唯独没有为自己和自己的幸福着想。留在达什姐莉心里的爷爷孤独、寂寞，没有享受过多少天伦之乐，没有吃过、用过好东西。

爷爷好可怜！达什姐莉的眼睛湿润了。

always worried that if he went out, the herdsmen at home would have no help when they ran into trouble. Grandpa worked for the people all his life, but he didn't think about his own happiness. The grandfather in Dashijieli's heart was lonely and solitary. He hadn't enjoyed much happiness with his family, and he hadn't eaten or used good things.

Grandpa was so pitiful! Daishijieli's eyes were moist with tears.

It wasn't until many years later that Dashijieli, who served as the deputy head of the Publicity Department of Haiyan County, realized the reason why her grandfather lived in this way. She felt that it was because Grandpa never forgot that he was a poor herder, and that it was the party who made the pastoral people live a happy life. It was the party who cultivated him into a provincial-level cadre.

Dashijieli remembered that her eldest brother, Dongzhurenqing, had been a top-level student. When graduating from junior high school, he was admitted to a key high school in Xining, but Gabulong didn't let him go and instead sent him to a vocational school.

When Dashijieli graduated from junior high school, her grandpa again advocated for going to a vocational school. This time, Dashijieli was disobedient and secretly applied for the No. 5 High School. After Gabulong found out about it, he didn't talk to her for three days.

He wished that Dashijieli could graduate early and go back to her hometown to work and stay with her mother. However, when his granddaughter was admitted to the No. 5 High School, his heart softened again. He specifically took a day off and accompanied her to the school for registration. When someone saw him, he took the initiative to run over and tell Gabulong that he could tell the principal to assign Dashijieli to a top-level class, but he refused by saying, "As long as she works hard, it makes no difference which class she studies in. Don't make any special arrangements because I'm a governor."

In 2006, Dashijieli graduated from Qinghai University with honors.

That year, Gabulong was getting very old and he was not as healthy as before. His colleagues and friends advised him to arrange Dashijieli to work in Xining so that she could take care of him, but he did not follow their advice.

He said to his granddaughter, "You'd better go back to your hometown Haiyan, find a job there, and support yourself with your own hands! By working in Haiyan, it's

直到好多年过去后，担任了海晏县委宣传部副部长的达什姐莉才体会到了爷爷为什么会这样过一辈子的原因。她觉得，是爷爷从未忘记过自己是一个贫苦的牧民，从未忘记是党让草原人过上了幸福的生活，是党把他培养成了一名省级领导干部。

达什姐莉记得，她的大哥东主仁青学习成绩一直很好，初中毕业后考上了西宁的重点中学，可尕布龙没让上，让大外孙只读了中专卫校。

达什姐莉读完了初中，爷爷还是主张上中专。这一次，达什姐莉没听话，偷偷报考了五中，尕布龙知道后，三天没和孙女说话。

他想让达什姐莉早点毕业回家乡工作，陪在妈妈身边。不过，等孙女真的考进五中时，他的心又软了，专门请了假，陪孙女去学校报到。有人见了，主动跑过来对他说，可以给学校领导说说，把达什姐莉分到一个好班，又让他给阻止了："上哪个班都一样，只要好好学习就行，不要什么事都搞特殊。"

2006 年，达什姐莉以优异的成绩从青海大学毕业。

那一年，尕布龙年事已高，身体大不如从前，周围的领导和朋友们都劝他把达什姐莉安排在西宁工作，对他有个照应，可他还是没有这样做。

他对孙女说："你还是回到家乡海晏，到最基层的地方工作，靠自己的本事吃饭吧！还可以守在妈妈身边，照顾妈妈。"

国庆长假后的第一天早晨，草原上寂静无声，达什姐莉独自

尕布龙的外孙女达什姐莉

Gabulong's granddaughter Dashijieli

尕布龙大哥、大嫂、二哥及侄子侄女们

Gabulong''s eldest brother, sister-in-law,

second brother and nephews and nieces

convenient for you to take care of your mother."

On the first morning after the National Day holiday, it was very quiet on the grassland, and Dashijieli came to register and work at the Cultural Station by herself. She got turned around several times at the township government building with now fences or gates before eventually finding the door of the "Halejing Township Cultural Station" written in a line of small characters on the very edge of a row of dilapidated bungalows. Apart from the building, there were only boundless grasslands, stiff cold winds, and the sound of a dog barking.

Dashijieli couldn't help shedding tears. She grew up with her grandfather and had become accustomed to city life. Like other classmates, she dreamed of working in a bright office building in the city. At this time, she was at a loss and disappointed, as if she could not accept the arrangements of fate, and did not know how to open a new chapter in her life.

That winter, Gabulong, who had always been thrifty, personally bought a down jacket for Dashijielii from the Wangfujing shopping center.

He had never bought clothes in a mall; it was the first but also the last time.

Back home, Gabulong took out the down jacket from the beautiful bag and said to his granddaughter, "It's cold in winter; keep warm."

Dashijieli wept for a long time with the down jacket her grandfather had bought for her as an exception, and the grievances of her grandfather insisting on letting her work in the township suddenly disappeared!

Two years later, Dashijieli had a boyfriend. She took him to visit her grandfather, and she asked for his opinion on his future grandson-in-law.

On entering the door, Dashijieli held out tHebag in her hand and said, "Grandpa, I made you a suit..." Her words were still in the air when tears came to his eyes, his mouth started to tremble, and he said, "Good, Good, Good!" He then turned around and went into the bedroom.

Dashijieli also started to cry. She knew in her heart that Grandpa loved her deeply.

At Dashijieli's wedding ceremony, he told his granddaughter that she should go home often to spent more time with her mother.

Being strict with his family members did not mean Gabulong had no emotions or affections for them. As a father, his feelings for his daughter were complicated, and he

来到文化站报到。她在没有围墙、没有大门的乡政府转了好几圈，才在一排破旧平房的最边上，找到了写着一行小字的"哈勒景乡文化站"的房门。除此之外，只有无边的草原、生硬的冷风和隐约传来的狗吠。

达什姐莉忍不住掉下了眼泪。她在爷爷身边长大，已经习惯了城市生活，和其他同学一样也曾怀揣过在城市明亮的写字楼里上班的梦。此时，她很茫然，也很失望，似乎无法接受命运的安排，不知该怎样开启人生的新篇章。

那年冬天，一向节俭的尕布龙亲自从王府井商场给达什姐莉买了一件羽绒服。

他从来没有在商场买过衣服，那是第一次，也是最后一次。

回到老家，尕布龙把装在漂亮袋子里的羽绒服拿出来，对孙女说："冬天冷，别冻着。"

达什姐莉哭了。她抱着爷爷破例给她买的这件羽绒服哭了很久，因为爷爷坚持让她在乡镇工作的怨气一下子消失了！

两年后，达什姐莉有了男朋友。达什姐莉带着他来看望爷爷，让爷爷把把关，看看他未来的准外孙女婿。

一进门，达什姐莉就捧着手中的袋子："爷爷，我给您做了一套衣服……"话音还没落，他的眼圈就先红了，嘴角颤抖着说："好，好，好！"转身进到卧室去了。

达什姐莉也哭了，她心里明白。爷爷对她有多么疼爱、多么不舍。

结婚时，他又嘱咐孙女，要经常回家，多陪陪阿妈。

对家人严格要求，并不等于他没有感情、不爱她们。作为父亲，他对女儿的感情是复杂的，他无法用语言表达自己的愧疚。每年春节回乡，他都会对村子里的年轻人说："我的女儿召格力很了不起，一辈子照顾老人，你们要像她这样孝顺自己家的老人。"

那一年，怀孕9个月的召格力从马上摔了下来，给父亲打完电话后，就被送往西宁。但是来不及了，召格力途中分娩，没办法，又返回了县医院。当时通讯不便，尕布龙在西宁左等右等等不到，以为女儿出了意外，发了疯似的连夜往回赶。从西宁到海晏110多公里，他一家家医院挨着找，越找越心慌，越找越害怕，等找遍了沿途的医院，终于见到女儿时，他眼圈红着，脸上的泪痕还没有擦干。

could not express his sense of guilt in words. Every year when he returned home during the Spring Festival, he would say to the young people in the village, "My daughter, Zhao Geli, is great, taking care of the elderly throughout her life. You should be filial to the elderly in your own family like her."

One year, Zhao Geli, who had been pregnant for nine months, fell off a horse. After calling her father, she was sent to Xining. But it was too late, Zhao Geli started labor on the way, and there was no choice but to return to the county hospital. At that time, tele-communication was inconvenient, and Gabulong waited for a long time in Xining and before he started to worry about his daughter, thinking that she might have had an accident. He hurried back to Haiyan that night. Along the way of more than 110 kilometers from Xining to Haiyan, he searched all the hospitals for his daughter. The more he searched, the more he became flustered and scared. When he finally saw his daughter, his eyes were red, and the tears on his face had not yet dried.

Another year, Zhao Geli became very ill, and the hospital issued a critical illness notice. After her operation, Gabulong had been waiting at the corridor outside the ward. It was late at night when Zhao Geli woke up from the anesthesia. When she opened her eyes, she saw that her father, who was standing by the bed and wiping his tears, looked obviously older. His back was a little hunched, his hair was white, his face was haggard, and he looked so sad and hopeless.

Zhao Geli cried bitterly, the grievances and regrets suppressed in her heart, the respect, love, and sympathy for her father, all came to her heart.

When Zhao Geli was forty years old, Gabulong, who had never spent money casually, bought a Shanghai brand watch for his daughter. That day, when her father put the shiny watch on his daughter's hand, Zhao Geli smiled and shed tears of joy.

On that day, she was convinced that her father loved her, and she was content.

In the past few years, Zhao Geli's legs hurt so badly that she couldn't herd the sheep, so she left the work of the family to her youngest son and daughter-in-law, and she opened a steamed bun shop with others in the town. Since she was a child, the most important thing her father said to her was to be self-reliant, and she didn't want to burden her children. She got up at 6 o'clock every morning and rushed to the shop to be busy, but it didn't take long before she had to close it. Acute rheumatoid arthritis prevented her from standing and working for a long time, so she couldn't continue to

还有一年，召格力病得很严重，医院下了病危通知书。做完手术后，尕布龙一直在病房外的走廊守着。召格力从麻醉中醒来时，已是下半夜。她一睁眼，见正站在床边抹眼泪的父亲明显衰老了许多，背有点驼，头发也白了，面容憔悴，显得那么伤心、绝望。

召格力失声痛哭，压抑在她心头的委屈、遗憾，对父亲的尊敬、爱戴、心疼，一齐涌上心头。

召格力40岁那年，不舍得随便花钱的尕布龙给自己的女儿买了一块上海牌手表。那一天，当父亲把亮晶晶的手表放在女儿手上时，召格力一边笑着，一边流下了欢喜的眼泪。

那一天，她确信，父亲是爱她疼她的，她知足了。

这几年，召格力的腿疼得厉害，放不了羊，就把家里的活都交给了小儿子和儿媳，自己在镇上和别人搭伙开了一家馍馍店。从小，父亲对她说的最多的一句话就是自食其力，她不想给孩子们添麻烦。她每天早上6点起床赶到店里忙碌，可没开多久，严重的类风湿性关节炎使她无法长时间站着干活，故而也就没法继续经营馍馍店了。

因为尕布龙的儿子幼年夭折，他的大哥才布腾把自己的小儿子尼玛才仁过继给尕布龙当了义子。小时候，尼玛才仁和父母姐姐住在海晏县牧区，到了入学年龄，他被接到西宁，在尕布龙身边生活、学习。中学毕业后，尼玛才仁在省政府车队待业，后在海南州、黄南州参军服役。复员后，本来可以被安置到西宁市防暴队工作，但是尕布龙不同意，把他安排到了省牧科院工作，还特意给院领导交代，让他到基层牧科所锻炼。

尼玛才仁结婚时，尕布龙坚持不请客，不摆宴席，也没有像别人的孩子结婚那样，小车迎送，朋友欢聚。

曾经在海晏县当过兵的左德明先生，1976年转业后回到了河北省黄骅市，一直无法忘怀他在海晏县服役时，尕布龙亲自给他们修营房，给他们讲战斗故事的难忘岁月。2016年1月28日，左德明先生终于和召格力取得了联系。2017年，他再次来到永丰村，在22哨所依稀可见的残垣断壁前，在尕布龙广场的塑像前，深深地追思着尕布龙。之后，又和我有了联系，从他那里收到了这样一段文字：

　　45年前，我在青海海晏县当兵，召格力是永丰村的赤脚医生，

operate the steamed bun store.

Because Gabulong's son died at a young age, so his elder brother Caibuteng gave his youngest son Nimacairen to be adopted by Gabulong. When he was a child, Nimacairen lived with his parents and sister in the pastoral area of Haiyan County. When he reached school age, he was taken to Xining to live and study at Gabulong's home. After graduating from high school, Nimacairen was waiting for work in the provincial government motorcade, and later served in the army in Hainan and Huangnan Prefectures. After he was demobilized, he could have been placed in the Xining City Anti-riot Team, but Gabulong disagreed and assigned him to work at the Provincial Academy of Animal Husbandry. He specifically had the leaders of the Academy to arrange for him to work at the grassroots unit of the Animal Husbandry Institute.

On arranging Nimacairen's wedding ceremony, Gabulong insisted that they not invite guests or hold a banquet. Unlike the wedding ceremony of other families, he did not arrange cars to serve and hold any parties.

Mr. Zuo Deming, who once served as a soldier in Haiyan County, returned to Huanghua City, Hebei Province after being demobilized in 1976. He has never forgotten those unforgettable years when he served in Haiyan County, Gabulong personally repaired their outpost rooms and told them battle stories. On January 28th, 2016, Mr. Zuo Deming finally got in touch with Zhao Geli. In 2017, he came to Yongfeng Village again, and in front of the faintly visible ruins of 22nd sentry posts in front of the statue at Gabulong Square, he deeply thought about Gabulong. After that, I got in touch with him and received the following text from him:

Forty-five years ago, I was a soldier in Haiyan County, Qinghai province, and Zhao Geli was a barefoot doctor in Yongfeng Village. Our outpost was stationed at an ordinary private house in the east of Yongfeng Village. Whenever we got ill and needed to see a doctor, we went to Zhao Geli. Gabulong's home was not far from the entrance of Yongfeng Village. It was an adobe-built house but was clean and tidy. The only difference in his home from other homes was that they had a sewing machine and a medicine box. At that time, Zhao Geli's mother, Huamao, supported the family by herding on the hillside, farming under the hill and making clothes for the villagers, never adding the slightest burden to her husband who was a government leader in the

我们的哨所就在永丰村东头三间普通的民房里，有个头疼脑热的，免不了去找召格力。尕布龙的家在刚进永丰村不远处，是干打垒的土房，干净、整齐，家里唯一和别人不同的是多了一台缝纫机、一个药箱。那时，召格力的妈妈华毛在山坡放牧、山下种地，闲来给乡亲们做衣服，贴补家用，不给在省城当官的丈夫增添丝毫负担。我还记得，当时，家里还有个叫蒙生的小男孩，让尕布龙带到西宁上学了。逢年过节，尕布龙就坐一辆吉普车给家里带来点米面，夏天回来还到哨所给我们修营房、讲战斗故事。那时候，我特别崇拜尕布龙，但我也有不明白的一点，就是觉得他为什么要把老婆、女儿扔在家里受苦。我感到不公平，认为他重男轻女，直到尕布龙去世，才知道那个被他带到西宁上学的男孩蒙生是他在大街上捡回来的，当时那个男孩才 3 岁，感动得我当时就哭了，可是后来不知为什么，那个男孩长大后，竟离开了他。

多年来，尕省长的亲属一直在乡下放牧、耕作，没有沾上"大官"的光。前年，我特意吩咐我的儿子到永丰村去一趟，找到了金奎，从那里得到了一些老朋友的消息，知道召格力与别人合伙开了一个馍馍铺，让我心里发酸。一个副省长的女儿，60 多岁了，已经到了享受天伦之乐的岁数，可还在为衣食奔波，又忽然觉得，尕布龙有些不近人情了，不但没给孩子们留下财富，还让她们继续放牧，过着辛辛苦苦的日子。

笔者在召格力的新居

The writer is at the new apartment of Zhao Geli

春节前，儿子容丞从学校回来，我带着他，来到了召格力在县上的新居。屋子虽然不大，但收拾得非常干净整洁。

召格力找出父亲生前得过的奖状，朋友送来的两幅画，"时代楷模"的证书和奖章，还让我看了尕布龙年轻时骑在马上的照片。我很想看看她

provincial capital city. I still remember that at that time, there was a little boy named Mengsheng in the family, who was taken to Xining for schooling by Gabulong. During the holidays, Gabulong would bring some rice and flour to the family by jeep, and he would come to our outpost to repair our rooms and telling battle stories when he returned home in the summer. At that time, I admired Gabulong, but one thing I didn't understand was why he left his wife and daughter at his village home to suffer. I felt it was unfair and thought he was gender-biased against woman. It was not until the death of Gabulong that I knew that the boy Mengsheng he brought to Xining for schooling was an abandoned child who had been picked up by him on street. The child was only three years old at the time. I was moved to tears when I heard this. However, for some reason, the boy left him when he grew up.

For many years, the relatives of Governor Gabulong had been herding and farming in the countryside, without the glory of being related to this "high-rank official". The year before last, I specially asked my son to go to Yongfeng Village and found Jin Kui. From him, I got some news of some old friends, and I felt really upset when I heard that Zhao Geli operated a steamed bun store with others. As the daughter of a vice-governor, in her 60s, she should enjoy family happiness, but she is still struggling for livelihood. I suddenly feel that Gabulong is a little merciless, not only because he didn't leave any wealth to his children, but also because he let them continue to herd and live hard lives.

Before the Spring Festival, my son Rong Cheng returned from school. I took him to Zhao Geli's new apartment in the county.

Although the apartment was not big, it was very clean and tidy.

Zhao Geli took out the awards her father had won in his life, two paintings presented by his friends, and the certificate and medal of "Model of the Times." She also showed me photos of Gabulong riding a horse when he was young. I wanted to see the photos of her mother Huamao, but she didn't find any.

I said to Zhao Geli, "These photos are very precious. Keep them safe!"

Zhao Geli's face suddenly turned red. She smiled and said, "I know, I know!" She carefully wrapped them up and put them in the cabinet.

At noon, Zhao Geli made tsampa (a highland food made with fried barley flour) for me, which was delicious and not greasy at all. The yak meat was very tasty, and

母亲华毛的照片，但是，翻了好久也没找到。

我对召格力说："这些照片很珍贵，你要好好保管啊！"

召格力的脸一下子泛出了红光。她笑着说："我知道的，知道的！"便细心地把它们全都包好放在了柜子里。

中午，召格力为我拌了青稞炒面糌粑，好吃极了，一点也不油腻。牦牛肉很香，我一连吃了几小块。让我惊讶的是，召格力右手握住小刀，灵巧地飞舞着，把一个牛骨头吃得干干净净，连一点渣子都没留下。召格力自豪地说："这也是父亲从小教育的结果。"

我接过那根漂亮的牛骨头，仔细看着，召格力说："小时候吃肉，骨头啃不干净，父亲会让我第二天热了，重新再吃一遍。现在，我可是吃肉的高手，还会做水油饼。你吃过吗？"

我摇摇头："听都没听说过。"

召格力开心地笑了："那就再来，我给你做水油饼！"

达什姐莉也笑了。

I ate several small pieces in a row. To my surprise, Zhao Geli, holding a knife in her right hand, skillfully ate a cow bone clean without leaving any residue. Zhao Geli said proudly, "I learned the skill from my father when I was a kid."

I took the beautiful bone and gave it a closer look. Zhao Geli said, "In my childhood, whenever I didn't finish eating the meat off the bones, my father would have me eat from them again the next day. Now I am an expert on eating the bone clean, and I can also make water-oil pancakes. Have you ever tasted them?"

I shook my head, "I've never heard of it."

Zhao Geli smiled merrily, "Then come again, I will make water-oil pancakes!"

Dashijieli also smiled.

忠　诚

尕布龙对待牧区来的陌生人像亲人一样，有的老人病严重了，身边又没有人，他连尿盆都要给人家端过去。谁家孩子的学习、生活、工作遇到了困难，他总要想办法解决。可平时，他不但对自己要求严格，对自己的儿女、孙子、侄子和身边的工作人员要求也很严格，教育他们要自食其力。

20 世纪 70 年代，尕布龙大年初一与海晏县永丰村生产队队长刘索南一起放牧

Gabulong was herding with Liu Sonam, on the New Year's day in 1970s, the production team leader of

Yongfeng village, Haiyan County

Loyalty

Gabulong treated strangers from the nomadic area like his relatives. When the elderly were ill and had no one to take care of them, he would help with their bedpans. When children encountered difficulties in their studies, life, or work, he would look for ways to solve their problems. On the contrary, he was very strict not only with himself, but also with his children, grandchildren, nephew, and the staff around him, educating them to support themselves. He never used his authority to do anything for his own family. His wife, daughter, and grandchildren lived in the nomadic area for their whole lives herding cattle. The only way that his family took advantage of his power was that the three children of his daughter, Zhao Geli, were sent to study in Xining for better education. Nevertheless, his three considerate grandchildren followed their grandfather's instruction and returned home to work at the grassroots level. His grandson, Dongzhu Renqing, studied medicine and was assigned to work as a repairman in a sand and gravel factory after graduation. Zhao Geli summoned up the courage to ask her father for a job transfer but was refused. Gabulong said, "Work wherever you are assigned by the organization, as we are all the same serving the people."

He always encouraged children: "We should love grassland and develop the pastoral regions. Although the natural conditions of pastoral regions are difficult, someone must be in charge of developing the regions. If all nomads resettle in cities, who will develop the grassland and livestock production?"

他从不利用手中的权力为家人办事。妻子、女儿、孙子、孙女，一辈子生活在牧区，靠放牧为生，唯一受到照顾的就是把女儿召格力的三个孩子都接到西宁上学，接受了比牧区好一些的教育。但是，三个懂事的孩子，又都听从爷爷的教诲，回到家乡，在最基层工作。学医的大外孙东珠仁青毕业后被分配到砂石厂当修理工，女儿召格力鼓起勇气给父亲说了一下调动的事，尕布龙没有答应。他说："组织分配到哪里就到哪里工作，都是一样为人民服务嘛！"

他经常勉励子女："要热爱草原，建设牧区。虽然牧区自然条件艰苦，总要有人来建设。如果牧民都进城，草原建设、畜牧业生产由谁来发展？"

时间长了，家里的人都习惯了他的作风，也不再提要求，过着和其他老百姓一样平平淡淡的生活。

以前，家乡永丰村附近有一块解放军种的农田，每年春耕秋收，有不少解放军官兵在地里劳作。尕布龙的侄子肖俄力，是他大哥才布腾的儿子，从小机灵好动。有一次放羊时，肖俄力看见地头放着一大堆解放军官兵留下的书，就从这堆书里挑了几本，用皮袍子包着带回了家。

那天，尕布龙正巧回家探亲，他拿起书问肖俄力："书是从哪来的？"

肖俄力回答："是解放军叔叔丢在地头的。"

尕布龙听后很不高兴。他说："别人的东西你怎么能随便往家拿？"

肖俄力当时很委屈，对叔叔说："这些书都是好书，能从中学到不少东西。"

可是尕布龙却说："就算是这样，你也不能拿，诚实是做人的根本。"

有一年，尕布龙去海北视察调研，路过老家时顺便看望母亲，那时肖俄力还小，对叔叔坐的北京吉普车很好奇，就赖在副驾驶位置上不下来，还让司机开车往前走了一段距离。

尕布龙看到后，招招手让肖俄力下车，然后摸着肖俄力的头说："汽车是国家配给叔叔，让叔叔为老百姓服务的，你怎么可以随便坐？你要好好上学，考上大学，认真工作，有一天，老百姓需要你坐小车了，你才有资格坐，坐上小车后，你还要好好为老百姓服务。"

20世纪70年代，尕布龙住在畜牧局家属院平房里的时候，肖俄力每逢星期天都要来叔叔家里。来了，就得帮着干活，洗衣服、洗被子。冬天，冷水刺骨，肖俄力提出让叔叔买一台洗衣机，尕布龙不答应，他说，洗衣

Over time, his family members got used to his working style, no longer asked for anything, and lived simple lives like other ordinary people.

There used to be a farm near Yongfeng village for the Liberation Army. When the fields were ploughed in the spring and the crops were harvested in autumn, there would be many soldiers working in the field. Gabulong's nephew, Xiao Eli, the son of his elder brother, had been smart and active since he was young. Once when he was herding sheep, Xiao Eli saw a pile of books left on the ground by the soldiers so he picked up a few and wrapped them in his sheepskin robes to take home.

That day, Gabulong happened to visit his family. He picked up a book and asked Xiao Eli, "Where did you get the book?"

"They were left on the ground by the Liberation Army."

Gabulong got very unhappy and asked, "How can you bring others' belongings home?"

Xiao Eli was offended and said to his uncle "These are all good books, and we can learn many things from them."

But Gabulong replied, "Even so, you can't take them. Honesty is the foundation of being a man."

Once when Gabulong went to Haibei for field research, he stopped for visit his mother when he passed by his hometown. Xiao Eli was young at that time, and he was very curious about his uncle's Jeep. He didn't want to get out of the passenger seat and asked the driver to give him a ride for some distance.

Seeing Xiao Eli, Gabulong waved for him to get out of the car, and told him with a stroke on his head, "The car has been allocated to your uncle by our country to serve the people. How can you play in the car? You need to study hard, go to college, and work hard. One day, the people will need you to take a car, and you must be qualified to take it first. You must make use of the car to serve the people well."

In the 1970s, when Gabulong lived in a single-story house on the residential grounds of the Animal Husbandry Bureau, Xiao Eli would come to visit every Sunday. He had to help with the housework and laundry. During winter, the water was too cold, and Xiao Eli asked his uncle to buy washing machine but was rejected. Gabulong said that washing machines not only tore clothes, but also wasted electricity, so it was better to wash by hand. Gabulong patiently taught Xiao Eli how to sweep the floor without

机会把衣服洗坏的，还浪费电，用手洗最好。他还耐心地教肖俄力怎样扫地才不会扬起尘土，不许他穿订有鞋钉的皮鞋，不让他赶时髦，教育他要做一个朴实无华的人。

尕布龙与侄子肖俄力

Gabulong and his nephew Xiao Eli

肖俄力在湟源牧校上学，毕业后分配到农牧厅工作。几年后，尕布龙去农牧厅检查工作，厅里的一位领导请示尕布龙，准备提拔肖俄力，尕布龙严肃地说："你现在把你领导的位子让给他，我也不感谢你，你现在让他在单位烧锅炉，我也不生你的气。他是学业务的，就让他好好干工作。"

后来，肖俄力当上了贵南牧场的场长。有一年临近过年时，肖俄力买了两条中华烟，打算给叔叔拜早年。

那天，肖俄力让自己乘坐的小轿车停在省政府大院内尕布龙家门口，兴冲冲地进了门。可是一进门，就见叔叔的脸色阴沉，看都不看他一眼。肖俄力心里一惊。

"你这是干什么来了？"尕布龙头也不抬地问他。

肖俄力低着头说："拜年来了。"

说完，恭恭敬敬地把事先准备好的中华烟放在了尕布龙面前。

kicking up dust, forbade him to wear shoes with spikes, didn't allow him to dress fashionably, and educated him to be a man of unpretentiousness.

Xiao Eli attended the Animal Husbandry School in Huangyuan, and was assigned to work at the Qinghai Agriculture and Animal Husbandry Bureau after graduation. Years later, Gabulong went to the Bureau to inspect the work, and he was consulted by a leader from the Bureau about promoting Xiao Eli. Gabulong answered seriously, "I will not be grateful even if you let him take your leadership position now, and I will not be mad if you let him fire the boiler for the Bureau. He is a professional, so let him work hard."

Later, Xiao Eli became farm director of the Guinan Ranch. One year, shortly before the Spring Festival, Xiao Eli bought two cartons of cigarettes, planning to pay his uncle an early New Year's greeting.

That day, Xiao Eli parked his car in front of Gabulong's house in the provincial government compound and rushed in excitedly. But as soon as he entered the door, he was shocked by the gloomy look on his uncle's face, who did not even look at him.

"Why are you here?" Gabulong asked without looking at him.

Keeping his head down, he answered, "To pay a New Year visit." Then he respectfully placed the prepared cigarettes in front of Gabulong, who usually smoked cheap cigarettes costing 0.45yuan for a packet. Gabulong glanced at Xiao Eli and said, "I can't afford to smoke such expensive cigarettes. Take them back, and bring no such gifts later."

Xiao Eli was very embarrassed and stood still.

"What car did you take here? Where did you park your car?" asked Gabulong again.

"By sedan; I parked it in the government compound," Xiao Eli answered.

Gabulong's face got even worse. "Oh, so you're a big shot now? I am the provincial governor, but you drive a better car than mine. Have you ever thought about what people would think to see such a nice car parked in front of my house? What are you trying to show? Are you implying that since you got promoted, you are now more powerful or better than others? What are you flaunting? Don't use official cars for personal affairs in the future!"

The more he spoke, the angrier he became. "Your government official position

平时，尕布龙抽的烟是四角五分钱一包的。

尕布龙瞥了肖俄力一眼说："这么金贵的烟我抽不起，你拿回去，以后也别送。"

肖俄力很尴尬，呆呆地站着。

尕布龙又问："你是坐什么车来的，把车停在哪里了？"

肖俄力说："小轿车，停在政府院子里了。"

尕布龙的脸色更难看了："你现在有本事了，比我这个省长坐的车都好啊。你也不想想，这么好的车停在我家门口，群众会咋想？你想告诉大家什么，是你肖俄力当了官，有本事了，还是你比别人强？你炫耀的又是什么？以后办私事不要用公车！"

尕布龙越说越生气："你头顶上的乌纱帽，不是牛头上长出的犄角，是人民给你的。你要一心一意为人民服务，你要是犯了错误，人民随时会把你的乌纱帽拿掉。"

从这以后，肖俄力即使下乡工作，也乘坐吉普车，不敢再摆谱了。

肖俄力的二姐华毛措长得秀丽端庄，性格温婉贤淑，还上过学，又一直陪伴在尕布龙母亲身边，尕布龙很喜欢这个侄女。华毛措出嫁的时候，他亲自为侄女做了上马席。这个手艺还是他在河南县任县委书记时，在食堂学会的。不过正如熟悉他的曾任海北州委组织部部长的马丽雯所说，他会做的上马席，不过是煮一锅羊肉，炒个土豆丝，烧一大碗烩菜。当时，尕布龙的车就停在家门口，即使这样，他也没有用公车送华毛措上门，而是一直目送着送亲的亲戚陪着侄女步行去了

20 世纪 70 年代，尕布龙在海西州调研

In 1970s, Gabulong was on field research in Haixi

尕布龙和河南县的干部在一起

Gabulong was with some officials in Henan County

is not by chance; it has been given by the people, you must therefore serve the people intently. If you make mistakes, the people will remove your position at any time."

From that day on, Xiao Eli took a Jeep to work, even if he was going to the countryside. He dared not show off by driving a sedan.

Hua Maocuo, Xiao Eli's second elder sister, was a beautiful and dignified woman with a gentle and virtuous character, and had also received education at school. She lived with Gabulong's mother, and Gabulong loves this niece very much. When Hua Maocuo was getting married, he prepared tHebanquet himself. He learned his cooking skills in the canteen when he was the secretary of the party committee of Henan County. However, according to Ma Liwen, the head of Organization Department of Haibei Prefecture, who knew more about Gabulong, he would have made boiled mutton, fried potato slices, and a big bowl for stew for tHebanquet. During tHebanquet, Gabulong's car was parked at the door, but he did not use the car to deliver his niece to her husband's home. Instead, he, with the other relatives, accompanied the bride to the groom's home on foot. Unfortunately, his beautiful and virtuous niece, Hua Maocuo, couldn't be saved from a serious illness, and died when she was young, which made Gabulong heartbroken.

Nima, who was once the vice chairman of the Committee of Gonghe County, Hainan Prefecture, was in constant contact with Gabulong in the 1970s and 1980s. Nima is a Tibetan who engaged in accounting work at the grassroots level for a long time. He first met Gabulong in 1971 when he was the accountant of a commune in Dao Tanghe Township. Gabulong brought ten students from the School of Finance to work in the commune for an internship. The commune sent six carriages to pick the students up, one of which was driven by Nima himself.

Upon arrival at the town, Nima bought 100 kilos of barley and 25 kilos of flour. But Gabulong noticed this when he was loading the carriage.

Gabulong had a look and said: "What are these? Have you bought them for the commune?"

"I am the accountant of the commune, and I bought some things for my family since it was convenient" answered Nima.

Gabulong said seriously, "Are you here for public or personal business? Leave your own business for tomorrow and unload the things!

男方家。可惜的是，美丽、贤惠的侄女华毛措生了一场大病，没能抢救过来，很年轻时就去世了，令尕布龙心痛不已。

20 世纪 70 年代到 80 年代，曾经在海南州共和县担任过政协副主席的尼玛，和尕布龙接触较多。尼玛是一位在基层长期从事财会工作的藏族干部。1971 年，他第一次见到尕布龙，那时，他还是倒淌河乡一个公社的会计，尕布龙带了 10 名财校的实习生到公社，公社派了六辆马车去接，尼玛赶着其中一辆。

到了乡上，尼玛给自己家买了 200 斤青稞、50 斤面粉。正在往马车上装时，被尕布龙看见了。

尕布龙走过来看了看他，问："这些是什么东西，给乡里买的吗？"

尼玛说："我是公社的会计，顺便给自己家买了点东西。"

尕布龙严肃地说："你是来办公事接工作人员的还是办私事的？你自

20 世纪 80 年代初，尕布龙在海北下乡时与秘书、司机及基层干部合影留念

Gabulong with his secretary, driver, and an official at grassroots level when he went to the countryside in Haibei

in the earry 1980s

Nima's face turned totally red, and he removed the packages from the cart carriage and left them at the town. He first drove the workers home, and then returned to the town with his family carriage for tHebarley and flour he had bought.

The next day, Gabulong went to Nima's for lunch. There was nothing delicious to serve. Nima asked his wife to make some wheat-flour bread and boiled mutton for Gabulong, served with a bottle of alcohol he had brewed himself.

When being served, Gabulong said, "There are four people in your family. You'll need the wheat flour for the elderly and for Spring Festival. I will definitely not eat the bread. I also won't drink. Take them back, and I can eat what your family usually eats." After lunch, Gabulong said to Nima, "It was my fault to criticize you in front of everyone yesterday. I apologize. You are young, and you were selected as the accountant because the commune members trust you. What you did yesterday obviously reveals your tendency to merge personal business into public affairs. Although it was a smaller matter, it is the start of taking advantages. The more advantages you take, the bolder you become, and this will gradually lead you to corruption and crime." Nima lowered his head with embarrassment. Gabulong continued, "You need to remember that people cannot be greedy for wealth. Be strict with yourself, even in the small things. Be an honest person, work conscientiously, and do everything for the people and for our work."

Nima had been working as an accountant for fifteen years before he engaged in other financing works later. Gabulong's words to him not only benefited him for a lifetime, but also influenced his next generation. His son and daughter were also engaged in accounting and never had any financing problems.

Tian Zhongyu, who worked in Hainan, was promoted in the late 1980s by the Provincial Agricultural Office. He was recommended by Jian Shunsheng to be the secretary of Gabulong. Tian Zhongyu was nearly fifty years old and was no longer suitable for secretarial work, but he had been working in rural places for many years and thus familiar with the situations in agricultural and pastoral areas. Although he was introverted and didn't talk much, he was honest and quite proficient in writing any documents. Jian Shunsheng insisted that he be the secretary of Gabulong.

After working together for some time, Gabulong was very satisfied with Tian Zhongyu, who was deeply impressed by Gabulong. Tian Zhongyu often told his family,

尕布龙的秘书田种玉

Tian Zhongyu, Gabulong's secretary

己的事明天办，把东西卸下来！"

尼玛的脸一下红到了耳朵根。没办法，他只好把粮食先卸到乡上，把工作人员送到家里后，又赶着自己家的毛驴车来乡上把粮食拉回了家。

第二天，尕布龙去尼玛家吃午饭。当时，也没有什么好吃的，尼玛让自己的媳妇给尕布龙做了点白面饼子，煮了点羊肉，拿出了一瓶湖东种羊场自己烧的白酒。

吃饭时尕布龙说："你们家里四口人，逢年过节要用白面，老人吃饭要用白面，今天的这个白面饼子我是坚决不吃，把你们家平常吃的杂粮拿出来就可以了。我也不喝酒，都拿下去。"吃完饭，尕布龙对尼玛说："昨天，当着大家的面批评你，是我不对，我向你检讨。"又说："你还年轻，公社和社员对你很信任，让你当会计。可你昨天的行为明摆着是公私兼顾，虽然是小事，但也是占便宜的开始，慢慢地，占的便宜多了，你的胆子就大了，就会贪污，就会犯罪。"说得尼玛羞愧地低下了头。"你要记住，人一辈子万万不能贪财，要从一点一滴严格要求自己，老老实实做人，认认真真工作，一切为人民、一切为工作。"

尼玛在会计岗位上干了15年，后来从事的也是与财务打交道的工作。尕布龙的这番话，不仅使尼玛受益一生，还影响了他的下一代。尼玛的儿子、

"If I hadn't worked with him and seen with my own eyes, I wouldn't have believed there is such a person in the world, such a provincial leader."

After some time, Tian Zhongyu's wife said to him, "You are now the secretary to the vice governor of Qinghai Province. Can you ask for the governor's help to transfer our two daughters' jobs from Hainan to Xining?"

Tian Zhongyu, a man of good temper, replied with a sudden burst of anger. "How is it possible? His own daughter is also herding on grassland. How can I possibly mention such a matter to the governor?"

Tian Xin, the eldest daughter of Tian Zhongyu, remembered clearly that her father rarely got off work at a normal time while he was working for the governor. He not only had to work overtime, but he also had to go to the countryside for field research during holidays. After returning, he had to finish writing the research materials that night, so as to report to the Provincial Party Committee the next day. Nevertheless, Gabulong never gave orders to his secretary, whenever there was something to do, he always, with a friendly request, asked, "Mr. Tian, how about making some more efforts working overtime tonight?" As secretary, what else could be done but to accept the request? Tian Xin also remembered that once she had left Hainan for Xining with her younger sister, they went to Animal husbandry Bureau to see their father as he was not at home. They met Gabulong who commented, "Mr. Tian, how blessed you are to have such beautiful daughters. They don't look like you." Tian Zhongyu, who was dark and skinny, smiled while urging his daughters to return home quickly.

When Tian Zhongyu returned home at that night, he told his two daughter, "The governor is very impatient. He has to report materials as soon as he comes back from his investigation in the countryside. In the future, don't come to visit me at the office."

He continued with a deep breath, moving his tired armed, "For the governor, the most unbearable thing is to see people suffer. Whenever he sees people suffering, he feels uncomfortable and can't sleep. He tries with any means to solve problems and never makes empty promises."

Tian Xin later became the dean of Xining Painting Academy. She did traditional Chinese painting, and she became my good friend as well. She recalled that her father had worked as the secretary for the governor for some time, and he hadn't done anything for the family. However, the whole family admired and respected him. Years later, Tian

女儿至今从事会计工作，没有出过任何经济问题。

田种玉是 20 世纪 80 年代末省农办从海南州调上来的干部，由简顺生介绍给尕布龙当了一段时间的秘书。当时，田秘书的年龄接近 50 岁，已经不适合当秘书，但田种玉在基层工作多年，了解农牧区情况。虽然不爱多说话、性格内向，可为人诚实，材料写得很好。简顺生便给田种玉做工作，坚持让他给尕布龙当秘书。

工作了一段时间后，尕布龙对田种玉很满意，田种玉更是感慨良多。田种玉常对自己的家人说："如果不是在他身边工作、亲眼见到，真的不敢相信，世界上还会有这样的人，这样的省级领导干部。"

又过了一段时间，田种玉的妻子对他说："你现在是副省长的秘书，能不能给省长说说，把两个还在海南州工作的女儿调到西宁？"

不爱发脾气的田种玉忽然就生气了："这怎么可能，省长自己的女儿还在草原上放羊呢，我有什么脸给省长提这个事。"

田种玉的大女儿田昕记得很清楚，父亲自从当了尕布龙的秘书，很少能正常时间下班。常常加班加点不说，节假日还要下乡调研。回来后，又急着写调研材料，第二天就向省委汇报。不过，尕布龙从来不给秘书打官腔、下命令，有了事情，总是和颜悦色地对父亲说："老田啊，怎么样，今天晚上你就加个班吧！辛苦一点好吗？这个材料明天就要用。"听了这话，当秘书的还能说什么，只好连夜把材料赶出来。田昕还记得，周末她和妹妹从海南州回到西宁，见不到父亲就去了畜牧局。尕布龙见了，慈爱地望着她们姐妹说："老田啊，你咋这么有福气，生了这么漂亮的两个女儿，一点也不像你！"又黑又瘦的父亲一边讪讪地微笑着，一边催促两个女儿赶快回家。

晚上，田种玉回到家，嘱咐两个女儿："尕布龙省长性子特别急，下乡调研一回来，就要急着报材料。以后，别再到单位来添乱。"

他活动着困乏的胳膊长叹一声："尕省长这个人，最受不了的就是看见老百姓受苦，见了就难受，就睡不着觉，就要想尽办法解决问题，绝不说虚话！"

田昕后来成了西宁市画院的院长，画国画，成了我的好朋友。她印象中，父亲给尕布龙副省长当了一段时间的秘书，给家里没办过一件事情。但是，全家人都佩服他、敬重他。多年后，退休在家的田种玉在报上看到尕布龙

Zhongyu, who was living at home after retirement, saw the news of Gabulong's death in the newspaper. He sat on the sofa squeezing the paper in his hand and couldn't stop his tears from flowing.

It was not easy to be the secretary and driver for Gabulong. Not only were there no holidays, but also we couldn't have a good meal.

In 1980, Yang Jie, a young driver, worked for the deputy director of the Standing Committee of the Provincial People's Congress.

Gabulong put forward three conditions when Li Zhigang, the former director of Water Resources Bureau, recommended Yang Jie.

First, the driver must be a party member; second, no transferring work at will; third, no arrangements for his spouse and children. Li Zhigang said seriously, "Governor, Yang Jie meets the three conditions. I will be responsible for any problems."

Sitting in Yang Jie's tidy office, I asked him with a smile if he had fulfilled the last two conditions.

He couldn't help smiling and said, "I had to fulfill them; there was no other choice."

At first, Yang Jie couldn't stand for the way Gabulong worked. Once they went to the countryside, but returned without eating enough. Yang Jie was so hungry and had to drive a long distance.

Yang Jie couldn't help getting angry. "Why are you doing this? You are the vice governor. The county has already arranged a meal for us. We can eat first, we could eat , why driving away secretly!"

Gabulong kept silent instead of answering. After reaching in the city, he had Yang Jie stop the car, and he bought a sheep leg for Yang Jie. Gabulong also teased, "You have really been wronged this time. Go home and have some mutton. Don't be angry with me. We are even now."

Later, Yang Jie got used to this. As long as he got full, it didn't matter how tasty the food was.

In the 1980s, people needed a ticket to buy a TV due to a supply shortage. Yang Jie together with Yuan Zhaosheng, Gabulong's secretary, called, in the name of Gabulong, the director of Commercial Department and asked for three TV tickets, but unexpectedly, the tickets were sent directly to the governor's office.

去世的消息，手里紧紧捏着报纸，一下子跌坐在沙发上，眼泪止不住地往下淌。

给尕布龙当秘书、当驾驶员可不是一件容易的事，不但没有节假日，连一顿像样的饭都吃不上。

1980年，年轻的司机杨杰，来到担任省人大常委会副主任的尕布龙身边，给尕布龙当驾驶员。

尕布龙对推荐他的原省水利局局长李志刚提出了三个条件。

第一，必须是党员；第二，不准随意调动工作；第三，不准安排配偶、子女的事。李志刚严肃地说："省长，这三个条件杨杰完全能符合，出了问题我负责。"

坐在杨杰窗明几净的办公室，我笑着问杨杰，后面这两条你做到了吗？

杨杰不由得一笑："做不到，也得做！"

刚开始，杨杰实在受不了他的这种工作方式。有一回下乡，连肚子都没吃饱就往回走，饿得实在发慌，还得开长途。

杨杰忍不住发了火："您这是为什么，您再怎么着也是堂堂副省长，人家县上把饭已经安排好了，咱们吃了饭再回呗，还让我开着车悄悄跑了。"

尕布龙沉默着不回答。进了城，他让杨杰把车停在路边，亲自下车给杨杰买了一个羊腿。坐在车上，尕布龙还逗他开心："这次确实让你受委屈了，回家吃顿羊肉，别再生我气了，现在咱俩扯平了啊。"

以后，杨杰也习惯了，不图好吃好喝，只要能把肚子填饱就行。

20世纪80年代，物资供应紧张，买电视要用票，杨杰和尕布龙的秘书袁兆盛，借尕布龙的名义给商业厅厅长打电话，要了三张买电视机的票，可谁想得到，人家把票直接送到了省长办公室。

下午，尕布龙叫来秘书袁兆盛，让杨杰开着车一路飞驰，来到青海湖东岸，离一个小村子不远的野草滩上。

下乡是常有的事，杨杰没觉得有什么特别。车停稳了，尕布龙没有像往常一样带着他们去村子里，而是让他们俩就地扎好牛毛帐房，给了他们两个纤维袋，去捡牛粪，这让杨杰和袁兆盛感到此次出行有点不同寻常。

天色已暗，茫茫草原空阔寂寥。他俩怕遇到狼或野狗，带上车上的摇把，挽起袖子，低着头耷拉着脑袋去捡牛粪。

牛粪捡来了，茶烧好了，炒面也吃过了。尕布龙对一脸惶惑的杨杰和

In the afternoon, Gabulong called his secretary Yuan Zhaosheng and had Yang Jie drive them to a grassland on the east bank of Qinghai Lake, near a small village.

Going to the countryside wasn't abnormal, and Yang Jie noticed nothing unusual. After stopping the car, Gabulong did not take them to the village as he did before. Instead, he asked the two of them to pitch a tent and gave them two fiber bags to collect cow dung. At that point, the two realized there was something a little unusual about this trip.

It was already dark, and the grassland was extensive and quite lonely. They were both afraid of encountering wolves or wild dogs, so they took the crank handle of the car, rolled up their sleeves, and lowered their heads to collect the dung.

After returning from collecting the cow dung, they had tea and barley flour. Gabulong told Yang Jie and Yuan Zhaosheng, who looked confused, that they would need to sleep there and couldn't go anywhere else.

Yang Jie and secretary Yuan were dumbfounded.

At that time, it was already late in autumn, the frost and dew were gone, the grass had turned yellow, and the river was covered with a thick layer of ice. At night, the temperature continued to drop, and the piercing cold wind blew the tent like a shaking leaf. Gabulong always had his luggage ready and went to sleep with ease in his fur coat. Yang Jie and secretary Yuan kept switched between the car and tent until morning when their faces were covered with frozen snot and tears.

Gabulong woke up in the morning.

Looking at the frozen men, he said stiffly, "How was it? Did you have a good sleep last night? I have brought you here to experience the life of nomads. Just think; the nomads herding animals on the grassland live in such tents without electricity or water. Can they watch TV? You live in houses with electricity and heating but are not satisfied and tried to use a back door to buy a TV for your own enjoyment. Do you think you have done the right thing?"

Looking at the rock-like wrinkles on Gabulong's forehead, they lowered their heads in silence.

Using such a method to educate on a trivial matter may look extreme in the eyes of most people, but Galong was always strict with himself and the staff around him.

Yang Jie said, "I gave eight years of my life to Gabulong as a driver, and I received

袁兆盛说："今晚就睡在这里吧，哪儿也不许去。"

杨杰和袁秘书傻眼了。

那时，已是深秋季节，霜露已过，草已见黄，河面上结着厚厚的一层冰。夜里，气温越来越低，刺骨的寒风把帐房吹得像一片抖动的树叶。尕布龙随时带着下乡用的行李、皮大衣，款款入睡。杨杰和袁秘书，一会儿钻进车里，一会儿在帐房里躺着，挨到天亮时，鼻涕、眼泪冻了满脸。

清晨，尕布龙醒来了。

看着冻得缩成一团的杨杰和袁秘书，他板起脸说："怎么样，昨天晚上睡得好不好？带你们来，就是要让你们好好体验一下牧人的生活。你们想想，草原上放牧的牧民，就住在这样的帐房里。帐房里没有电、没有水，能看上电视吗？你们住在有电、有暖气的房子里还不满足，还要千方百计地走后门买电视、图享受，你们做的对吗？"

1986 年尕布龙在海东地区检查农业生产

Gabulong was inspecting agricultural production in Haidong area in 1986

看着尕布龙前额上如岩石般蹙成一团的皱纹，他俩默默地低下了头。

为这样一件小事，用这样的方法教育，在一般人眼里想必有些过分了，但是，尕布龙就是这样严格要求身边的工作人员和自己的。

杨杰说："给尕省长当了8年的司机，受了8年的教育。尕省长的品格和

尕布龙深入基层调查农民粮食产量

Gabulong was investigating farmers' grain productivity

eight years of education in return. Governor Gabulong's personality and spirit have been profoundly engraved on my heart."

Gabulong believed that power comes from the people, and it can only be used for serving the people, not for personal benefits. From that moment on, no secretary or driver around him dared to take advantage of his name for personal gain.

In July 1972, Gabulong's mother passed away. Even in the time of grieving, he didn't forget his principles. He told Gaba, the committee secretary of Yongfeng Village to not accept any gifts from the guests. He said, "The family only has the right to receive the guests' condolences, but not their gifts." He also advocated practicing cremation for his mother's funeral, which was the first case of omitting funeral traditions on Qinghai Plateau.

Each of Gabulong's drivers (Hu Guanrong, Yang Jie, Zhao Zhonghai, and Cui Shengman) and secretaries (Kang Jianwu, Tian Zhongyu, Yuan Zhaosheng, and Yang Mufei) adapted over time to his working style, manner of handling things, and demeanor. They also developed the good manners of being honest, not wasteful, conscientious, and self-demanding.

Zhang Kui, the director of the Reforesting Office for North and South Mountains of Xining, was the same; he always refused when being invited by other institutes for meals.

He was sometimes joked, "Don't learn from Gabulong. Simply having a meal can corrupt you."

Zhang Kui said, "To be honest, I will not be corrupted by eating a meal. However, the meals are paid for at public expense. In other words, they are paid for with the hard-earned money of the people. I feel uncomfortable with such meals."

Gabulong was loyal to the party, and he absolutely respected and obeyed superior leadership. Whenever work was arranged for him by leaders at higher levels, he would promise to implement it unconditionally. He would never leave work without authorization, unless he believed that the work was contrary to the laws of nature or the interests of the people. He even asked the Provincial Party Secretary for official leave when going home to Haibei for the New Year. His principle of party spirit is was particularly strong, and he would always defend the party, never allowing anyone to slander the Communist Party.

As remained fresh in Yang Jie's memory, on the way back from a trip in Haibei

精神，早已深深地印在了我的心坎上。"

尕布龙认为，权力来自百姓，只能服务于百姓，而不能以权谋私。从那以后，他身边的秘书、司机再没有人敢借他的名义谋取任何私利。

1972年7月，尕布龙的老母亲去世。悲痛的同时，他仍然没有忘记嘱咐永丰村的村支书尕巴。祭奠时只接受来宾的祭拜，不收任何祭礼。他说："家人只有招待的权力，没有收礼的权力。"母亲的葬礼由他主张实行了火葬，这是青海高原上第一例移风易俗的葬礼。

从驾驶员胡光荣、杨杰、赵忠海到崔生满，从秘书康建武、田种玉、袁兆盛到杨牧飞，在尕布龙身边工作过一段时间后，每一个人都适应了他工作的方式、处事的风格、为人的态度，也养成了诚实做人，不铺张浪费，兢兢业业，严格要求自己的良好习惯。

西宁市南北山绿化办公室的副主任张奎也是这样，遇到兄弟单位请吃饭，他会通通拒绝。

有时，对方开玩笑地说："别学尕布龙那一套，吃顿饭还能把你给腐蚀了。"

张奎说："说实话，吃顿饭并不会把我腐蚀了，但这顿饭花的是公家的钱，说白了就是老百姓的血汗钱，这种饭，我吃不惯！"

尕布龙对党忠诚，对上一级领导绝对尊敬和服从，只要是上级领导安排的工作，他保证无条件地贯彻落实，绝不擅自离守。除非他认为，有悖于自然规律，有悖于人民利益。就连每一年春节回家乡海晏，都要向省委书记正式请假。尕布龙的党性原则特别强，什么时候都要维护党的利益，绝不允许别人诋毁共产党。

那是让杨杰记忆犹新的一件事。1986年，去海北解决草场纠纷，回来的路上，车上坐着一位同单位的女处长，这位女处长嫌转业的丈夫没有得到及时安置，说了几句牢骚话，惹得尕布龙勃然大怒。

他涨红了脸对那位女处长说："对军队干部转业，国家是有保障的，可安置需要一个过程，你着什么急！你的职务是谁给的？你入党的时候是怎么宣誓的？遇到这么点事，就对党有埋怨情绪，你是不称职的。回去后，我要撤你的职！你的家境这么好，还要埋怨，那些条件比你差的人，该怎么办？"

当时，车里的气氛很尴尬，尕布龙气得脸色通红，两眼瞪得铜铃一般。

for solving a pasture dispute in 1986, a female director of the same institute was also in the car. The woman made a few complaints that her husband, who had just transfered to civilian work, had not been resettled in time, for which Gabulong burst into anger.

He turned red and said to the woman, "The state has a guarantee for the job transfer of military cadres, but it has to go through the transferring process. Why are you in a hurry? Who assigned you to your position, and didn't you take an oath when you joined the party? If such a small matter causes you to complain about the party, you are unqualified for your position. I will remove you from your position when we get back. Your family is already in a pretty good position, but you have still found a reason to complain! What should those who are living in worse conditions than you do?"

The atmosphere in the car was very awkward. Gabulong's face turned red with anger, and he stared at the female director with a fierce look. She was so frightened that she didn't dare say a word. It was the other staff in the car who persuaded Gabulong to calm down.

Hualin Township of Datong County was assessed as an impoverished town by the State Council. Once at 8 o'clock in the morning, Gabulong, with his secretary and Yang Jie, rushed to the township government.

The office was filled with smell of alcohol, and the township party secretary and the township head were still drunk.

"You have arrived so early, Governor," said the township head as he rubbed his eyes.

"I was afraid you would go to the countryside, and I wouldn't be able to find you if I was too late," said Gabulong.

Gabulong asked the secretary of the township in surprise, "Why hasn't the loudspeaker in the village started playing yet? You don't listen to the news, do you?"

The secretary answered proudly, "Oh, we have a rule that the loudspeaker can't be turned on before the township head gets up."

"Oh, so what did you do yesterday?" asked Gabulong.

"We had an activity."

"Get up, let's go to the village together."

Gabulong's voice turned rather harsh.

The township head winked at those behind him.

"What are you doing? What is this for?"

女处长吓得不敢吭气，还是尕布龙身边的工作人员好说歹说，才让尕布龙消了气。

大通县桦林乡，是国务院评定的贫困乡。一天早上8点钟，尕布龙就带着秘书和杨杰赶到了乡政府。

办公室里，酒气冲天，书记和乡长还醉着。

"省长，你怎么这么早来了？"

乡长揉着眼睛。

尕布龙说："我怕来晚了，你们下了乡找不着。"

尕布龙诧异地问乡政府秘书："都这时候了，村子里的喇叭也不响，你们新闻也不听？"

乡政府秘书得意地说："哎，我们村里的乡规民约有一条，乡长不起床，喇叭不能响。"

"哦，那你们昨天都干什么了？"尕布龙问。

"我们活动了一下。"

"起来，我们一起到村子里走走。"

尕布龙的口气有些生硬。

乡长给身后的人挤了挤眼。

"干什么呢，你这是？"

"我让人给您宰一只羊。"

"这也是你们的乡规民约？你这样挤眉弄眼的，一年要挤掉多少只羊？"

尕布龙压着心头的火说："以后不许这样。"

走进村里，醉眼蒙眬的书记和乡长跟踉跄跄地跟在尕布龙身后。风卷着黄土四处飞扬，一只褐色的小鸡被惊吓得跳了起来，乡长伸手去抓，鸡挣扎着叫着跑了。

尕布龙再也忍不住了，他一把扯住乡长的胳膊，大声说："是鬼子进村了吗？你看看你像什么样子！"

糊里糊涂的乡长，借着酒劲也发了火："你还是个当省长的呢，吃个羊也怕，抓个鸡你也不敢，你到底是不是省长？"

尕布龙满脸通红，停住脚步，大吼一声："别再说了，到此为止！"

随后，便招呼秘书杨牧飞和杨杰上车，飞速返回县上。

"I had a sheep slaughtered for you."

"Is this another one of the township's rules? How many sheep a year do you slaughter with your winks?"

Gabulong suppressed his anger and said, "You can't do this next time."

In the village, the township party secretary and the township head, who were still drunken and bleary-eyed, staggering along behind Gabulong. The wind swept the soil about, and a brown chicken jumped out in front of them in fear. The township head tried to catch the chicken, but it ran away.

Gabulong couldn't stand it anymore. He grabbed the township head's arm and shouted, "Are you a Japanese invader entering the village? Look at the state you are in!"

Not really recovered from the alcohol the night before, the muddle-headed township head lost his temper, "You neither dare to eat some mutton nor catch a chicken. Are you really a provincial governor?"

Gabulong turned red, stopped, and shouted: "Don't say anything more; we are done here."

Then he called his secretary Yang Mufei and Yang Jie to get in the car, and they quickly returned to the town.

How could this man, who showed deep love for the people and tried his best to help them, tolerate such arrogant behaviors among the party cadres. He angrily pushed open the office door of the county party secretary and complained, "How do you select your staff? How do you appoint your party cadres? Hualin Township was assessed as an impoverished town by the State Council. How can you let such people work as the township party secretary and the township head? When will our people be lifted out of poverty and become wealthy? When will they be able to live a better life?" His eyes were filled tears and anger as he was speaking.

The next day, Gabulong, accompanied by the secretary of the Xining Municipal Party Committee, the secretary of the Datong County Party Committee, and the county governor, went to Hualin Township. They held a mass meeting for the whole township, and the leaders of Datong County announced the dismissal of the party secretary and the head of Hualin Township from their positions.

Gabulong said with passion at the meeting, "It is our fault that you have not been lifted out of poverty yet. We failed to appoint the right leaders and educate them well. I

这个一心热爱群众，为群众做尽了好事的人，怎么能容忍党的干部如此嚣张。他愤怒地推开县委书记的门，严厉地呵斥："你们是怎么选拔干部的?！又是怎么任用干部的?！桦林乡是国务院评定的贫困乡，你们让这样的人当书记、当乡长，我们的老百姓什么时候能脱贫致富，什么时候能

20 世纪 90 年代，尕布龙副省长与基层干部群众一起研究草原喷灌设计工作

In 1990s, Gabulong was with the workers at the grassroot level discussing about designing grassland

sprinkler system

初夏时节，尕布龙和乡亲们在金银滩

Gabulong was with the folks at Jinyintan at the beginning summer

apologize on behalf of the organization."

In the spring of 1984, Gabulong went to Sujitan Township in Haibei Prefecture to resolve a pasture dispute. It was already noon time when he arrived at the town. A nearby hill caught on fire, and all the township cadres went to put out the fire. Only one cook was at home, and a freshly slaughtered sheep was hanging in the yard.

Gabulong went to the cook and asked with a smile, "Can you give me something to eat?"

Having a looked at his farmer-like appearance wearing a ragged furry jacket and a pair of cotton-shoes, the cook said in cold voice, "There is nothing to eat. I am waiting for the provincial governor."

"Can we cook for ourselves before the governor comes? We began our trip early in the morning and are very hungry now," replied Gabulong, handing over a cigarette to the cook.

The cook accepted the cigarette, thought for a moment, and said, "Ok, but hurry up, or there will be trouble when the governor arrives."

His secretary Yang Mufei and Yang Jie rushed to make the fire, and Gabulong made dough for squared noodles.

Having prepared the dough, Gabulong came out to the yard looking at the slaughtered sheep and said, "Can we have a piece of meat to be fried for the noodles? The governor can't eat up the whole sheep." He smiled at the cook and gave another cigarette.

The cook reluctantly cut a small piece from the sheep and handed it to Gabulong, urging them, "Hurry up and leave when you finish the meal; the governor is about to arrive."

The cadres returned when the food was ready.

They were dumbfounded when they saw the governor holding a bowl of noodles while the sheep was still hanging in the yard, and they rushed to apologize.

Knowing that the man holding the bowl was the governor for whom he had been waiting, the cook stood frozen in the courtyard for a while.

Then he was next to Gabulong apologizing again and again.

Gabulong chuckled, "It doesn't matter."

But the cook was still in doubt and called his old mother to apologize on his behalf. They didn't know that Gabulong was used to such situations as he had encountered many.

One summer, a sick nomad came to Gabulong in the city for help. Unfortunately,

过上好日子？"说着，尕布龙气愤得眼里充满了泪水。

第二天，西宁市委书记和大通县委书记、县长，陪着尕省长一起来到桦林乡，召开全乡群众大会，由大通县领导当场宣布，撤销桦林乡书记、乡长的职务。

会上，尕省长动情地向群众说："你们没有脱贫，是我们把干部没有派好、没有教育好。我代表组织向你们道歉！"说着，他向群众深深地鞠了一躬。

1984年春天，尕布龙去海北州苏吉滩乡解决草场纠纷。到乡上时，已是中午，附近草山着了火，乡干部们都去山上救火了，只有一个炊事员在家，院子里挂着一只刚宰的羊。

尕布龙找到炊事员，和颜悦色地说："你能不能给我们弄点饭吃？"

炊事员看他穿一件光板皮袄、一双棉布鞋，像个农民，冷淡地说："没吃的，在等省长。"

尕布龙说："能不能在省长来之前，让我们自己做点饭吃，我们一早赶到这里，实在饿了。"

说着话，省长给炊事员让了一支烟。

炊事员接过烟，想了想说："行吧，可是得快点，不然省长来了麻烦可就大了。"

秘书杨牧飞和杨杰赶紧烧火，尕布龙亲自到厨房和面，打算做顿面片。

面和好了，尕布龙走出来，看了看挂在院子里的羊说："能不能给我少割一点肉，炒一下，放到面片里？反正省长一个人也吃不完。"他又笑眯眯地给炊事员递了一支烟。

炊事员很不情愿，但还是勉勉强强地割了一点点肉递给尕布龙。还一个劲地催："要快啊，吃完了就走，省长马上要来了。"

饭做好了，就在这时，乡上的干部回来了。

他们见尕省长正端着一碗面片，羊还挂在院子里，都傻眼了，忙不迭地向省长道歉。

知道端着碗吃饭的人就是自己要等的省长，炊事员像泥塑一般僵住了，立在院子里老半天回不过神来。

接着，就一直跟在尕布龙身后说对不起。

尕布龙乐呵呵地说："没事，没事。"

his car was away, but he immediately rented a van, sent the nomad to the hospital, and helped with the registration process. When he was done, he tried to take a taxi to his workplace but failed. He had no choice but to walk for three kilometers to return home.

After arriving home, he told his family members what had happened. They laughed, "Please have a look at yourself in the mirror."

He looked in the mirror and laughed at himself. He had just returned from north and south forestry farm that day. The weather was hot, and he was wearing rubber shoes with a straw hat. He was covered in dust, and his face looked black and chapped, like an old farmer who had just returned from the field. No wonder the taxi drivers refused to give him a ride.

Gabulong was always very strict with the staff around him, but he was also very considerate towards them at work. One summer he went to Haibei for an on-site meeting. After driving for a long time, Yang Jie got out of the car and lied down on the grass to rest. When Gabulong found that the leaders had not arrived yet, he retrieved some water from the river and washed the car for Yang Jie. The other leaders found it unbelievable and kicked Yang Jie's fee, "Get up! How can you let the governor wash the car? You have been spoiled by his kindness." Yang Jie didn't see anything abnormal about the situation, and neither did the governor. After such a long drive, the driver deserved to rest. Whenever Gabulong had extra time, he would help his driver with cleaning the car. Having worked together for so long, he built close relationships with his secretary and driver. When Gabulong was very seriously ill, he could only recognize Yang Jie and Cui Shengman.

Yang Jie is now the director of Administrative Department of the Provincial People's Congress Office. He is still fighting for the reforesting project implemented by Gabulong himself, always running to the hills to ensure that the Provincial People's Congress maintains he honor of being an advanced institution in reforesting work. If only Gabulong could see it now, he would be so pleased.

After Yang Jie's promotion, it was Cui Shengman who became the driver for Gabulong, then serving as the deputy director of the Standing Committee of the Provincial People's Congress. He was lively by nature, liked singing, had good handwriting, and spoke with loud and forthright voice. In the beginning, Cui Shengman could not get used to Gabulong's way of working. He was especially disgruntled that

可炊事员不相信，又把自己白发苍苍的父母双亲叫来，给尕省长赔礼。他们哪里知道，像这样的事，尕省长遇得多了，他一点也不在乎。

有一年夏天，有个生病的牧民来省城找尕布龙，不巧，他的车出去了，他就立刻雇了辆面包车，把病人送到医院，又跑前跑后地挂号、办住院手续。办妥了，他想打出租车回单位，站在路边前后拦了4辆车，都没停，无奈，只好走了3公里路回到了家。

到家后，给家人一说，家里的人都哈哈大笑起来："您对着镜子看看自己吧！"

他照了照镜子，自己也笑了。那天，他刚从南北山林场回来，大热天穿着胶鞋，戴着草帽，一身灰土，脸又黑又皱，像刚下田归来的老农，难怪出租车司机不愿意拉。

尕布龙对身边的工作人员要求严格，可在工作时很体贴他们。去海北州开现场会那年是个夏天。跑了半天路，杨杰下了车躺在草地上休息，尕布龙见领导还没来齐，就到小河沟里提了桶水替杨杰洗车。其他领导看见了，觉得不可思议，踢踢杨杰的脚："快起来，怎么能让省长给你洗车，不像话！尕省长把你们都惯坏了！"可杨杰不觉得有什么，尕布龙也觉得没什么，驾驶员开长途累了，歇歇是应该的。平时，只要他有空，就会帮驾驶员洗车。在一起工作时间长了，他和秘书、驾驶员感情很深，尕布龙病情最严重的时候，谁也不认识，就能认出杨杰、崔生满。

如今，在省人大办公室担任行政处处长的杨杰，依然战斗在尕布龙生前亲手栽植出来的人大绿化区，奔波在北山上，让省人大连续保持着绿化先进单位的荣誉，假如尕布龙地下有知，不知该有多么欣慰。

继杨杰之后，给时任省人大常委会副主任尕布龙当驾驶员的是崔生满师傅。崔师傅生性活泼，喜欢唱歌，写一手好字，就是嗓门大，直来直去。一开始他根本受不了，直闹情绪，特别是对于没有假期，没有休息日这一点尤其受不了，后来慢慢习惯了，也没有了怨言。可是，尕布龙心里却记着这些事，觉得自己的事占用了崔生满太多的时间，怕他与家里的兄弟姐妹们生疏了，心中过意不去，每逢春节，还要去崔生满老家，给他的兄弟姐妹拜年。

"你说说，我们家的亲戚跟他有啥关系呢？可他就是要去，挡都挡不住。其实，我心里明白，他是哄着我高高兴兴地跟他一年到头地往乡下、农村跑。

his weekends and holidays were occupied. However, he became accustomed to this over time and had no more complaints. Gabulong knew that he was excessively using Cui Shengman's time, and he worried that Cui Shengman's relationship with his siblings and other family members would suffer. Therefore, he visited Cui Shengman's siblings every New Year.

"Even though my family had no relation with him, he still insisted on visiting them. Actually, I know in my heart that he was really just trying to coax me to run around the countryside with him all year round. When we were planting trees, I had to carry things up the hills several times a day, from early in the morning to late in the evening. Fortunately, I was young and strong at that time, otherwise I could have never done it."

One afternoon while working, Gabulong told Cui Shengman with a smile,"There will be an important provincial meeting tomorrow. Secretary Yin Kesheng asked me to attend the meeting as the head of the delegation from Xining. You should dress up tomorrow, clean our car, wash the towels in car, and repair the parts that are worn. We will attend the meeting impressively."

Cui Shengman was happy upon hearing about the meeting. Following orders, he got a bucket of water, ran to logistics to pick up two semi-new towels, washed the car, used a hairdryer to dry it halfway, fixed the seat with a pin, parked the car in the garage, and went home.

To his surprise, as soon as he arrived home, he got a call from Gabulong, "Come over. Let's go up the mountain to Dasi Ravine. I have something important to tell you."

Cui Shengman was confused when he heard this, as he knew the road to Dasi Ravine was bumpy with muddy pits, and he would have to wash the car again after returning.

When Gabulong got in car, he had a look and said, "Well, you got the car very clean today."

Cui Shengman kept silent.

Arriving at Dasi Ravine, Gabulong tried to get out of the car but was stopped by Cui Shengman.

"You can tell me what needs to be done. I can run faster, and you can wait in the car."

But when Gabulong insisted on getting out of the car, Cui Shengman got so angry that he started the engine and drove over the muddy pits. The windshield was covered with mud.

It was a short drive, and they arrived after around ten minutes. Gabulong got

特别是在山上种树的时候，我每天都要往山上拉几趟东西，两头不见太阳，好在我那时候年轻，身体也壮实，不然早趴下了。"

有一天下午上班，尕布龙笑眯眯地对崔生满说："明天，省上有个重要会议，尹克升书记特意交代，让我作为西宁代表团团长出席。小崔，你明天上午把新衣服穿上，把车擦干净，车上铺的毛巾洗一洗，烂的地方补一补，明天，咱们干干散散去开会。"

崔生满一听，蛮高兴，提了桶水把车洗了，又跑到单位后勤，挑了两条半新的浴巾洗干净，用吹风机吹得半干，再用别针细细固定在车座上，把车停在车库里，打量了一番回了家。

想不到的是，刚进门就接到尕布龙的电话："你过来，咱们上山，去趟大寺沟，我有点重要的事交代。"

崔生满一听，头都蒙了。大寺沟沟底就是个烂泥滩，还是碱水，这一个来回，还得重新洗车。

上了车，尕布龙扭过头看了看："嗯，今天的车就收拾得干净啊！"

崔生满一言不发。

到了大寺沟，尕布龙要下车走进沟里去，崔生满不让。

"有啥事你给我说，我跑得快，你在车上等着。"

可尕布龙不听，执意要下车，气得崔生满一脚油门，腾的一声钻进烂泥滩，挡风玻璃上溅满了泥点子。

路程不长，十几分钟就到了，尕布龙下车叮嘱民工："这两天我和崔师傅要出去开会，你们先不要急着栽树，主要是浇水，把新栽的树浇透，我回来后要挨个检查。"

崔生满更生气了，没多大事，就这几句话，我就不能替你转达吗？非得亲自跑一趟。返回时，气鼓鼓的崔生满又是一脚刹车，挡风玻璃上的黄泥更多了。

走到公路上，崔生满停车，拿了条毛巾把自己前面的挡风玻璃擦了一个大大的圆，然后上车往回赶。

尕布龙一直沉默，这时，才小心翼翼地说："我这边也看不清。"

崔生满没好气地顶了一句："你看清楚干吗，车我开着呢。"

尕布龙又不吭声了。

回到家，尕布龙提高嗓门："何巴，赶快给小崔倒杯茶，今天小崔累了！"

off out of the car and told the workers, "I have to go to meetings these days with Cui Shengman. You don't need to plant trees while I am away. Just water the newly planted trees, and I will check them one by one when we get back."

Cui Shengman got even more angry, thinking that it this was not a big matter, and he could have gone to tell the workers instead. On their way back, Cui Shengman drove fast with anger, and the car got even dirtier.

Cui Shengman stopped the car on the way back, got out a towel, wiped the driver's side of the windshield, and then continued driving.

Gabulong kept silent for a while, and then said politely, "I can't see through the windshield on my side."

"Why do you need to see? I'm the one driving," said Cui Shengman angrily.

Gabulong didn't say anything in return.

Having arrived home, Gabulong asked loudly, "Heba, please get a cup of tea for Mr. Cui. He is tired from a long day."

Cui Shengman knew that he meant it, so he took his time drinking the tea at home. Gabulong asked Heba to get some water so that he could wash the car.

As other leaders of the provincial government got off work and passed Gabulong on their way home, they laughed and stopped to ask, "Are you washing the car by yourself. Where is your driver Cui?"

"He is tired today and having some tea. My driver is different from yours," said Gabulong.

Cui Shengman understood that the words were for him. He finished drinking the tea, walked out, took out a long leather pipe from the trunk, connected it to the kitchen faucet, and started spraying down the car.

Gabulong stopped him immediately and said, "This wastes too much water."

Cui Shengman tried to get water from the boiler room.

"That is public water; people will complain." said Gabulong.

"Don't worry about it; it has to be done this way. We can't just clean the car with a towel when it is covered with mud; it will leave scratches," replied Cui Shengman.

Gabulong couldn't say anything, so he just painfully watched him spray down the car until it was finally clean.

As Gabulong watched him nearby, he couldn't help smiling, "It's still our capable

崔生满知道他是故意的，就坐在家里慢条斯理地喝茶。尕布龙则吩咐何巴打水，去外面洗车。

正是下班的时候，省政府的领导们路过，见尕布龙在洗车，都过来笑哈哈地跟他打招呼。

"哟，尕省长，你亲自洗车啊，小崔呢？"

尕布龙笑着说："我们小崔今天累了，喝茶呢，我的师傅跟你们的可不一样。"

崔生满知道，尕布龙是说给他听的。他把一大杯茶喝完，放下茶杯走出门，从后备厢拿出长长的一节皮管子接在厨房的水龙头上，对着车就冲洗。

尕布龙连忙拦住："这么洗太浪费水了。"

崔生满又接到锅炉房里。

"这是公家的水，人家不说吗！"

"你不要管了，不这么洗没办法，黄泥汤粘在车上不能擦，会把车擦坏。"

这下，尕布龙不言语了，只好忍着痛让崔生满可劲冲，终于把车洗干净了。

尕布龙一直在旁边看着，不由得露出了笑容："还是我们小崔能干，我让何巴给你煮了饺子，吃过饭再回吧！"

"不吃！"说着，崔生满头也不抬地走了。

"哎！尕省长平易近人，对我们就像对待亲人一样，我也是从心里疼他才这样，搁到现在，哪个司机敢对领导这样。他这一辈子做的事情，不是惊天动地的大事，但每一件小事，一般人都做不到。"

那时候，尕布龙经常下乡，没进乡里村里之前，要先和司机、秘书在街边的小饭馆里吃一碗炒面片、喝碗面汤，填饱肚子，然后直接到村民家去了解情况。即使经过县上或者乡上，也不事先通知。如果太晚了，就索性住在农牧民家的土炕上，一大早再去县政府或者乡政府和干部们讨论村子里的实际情况，商议脱贫致富的办法。

如果县乡政府提前知道了，安排好了饭，他也不吃，有时，盛情难却非吃不可，要求把烟酒撤掉，多余的菜也撤了，只让上四菜一汤。吃完饭，就把自己、秘书、司机三个人的饭钱悄悄放在碗底下才离开。

出去开会、下乡，安排好的饭店，尕布龙是不住的，尽量找便宜的旅

Xiao Cui! I'll have Heba make dumplings for you. You shouldn't leave without eating."

"I don't want to eat." With that, Cui Shengman left without looking up.

"Ah, Gabulong always got along well with others, and he treated us like his relatives. I did so because I love him. What kind of driver would dare to do that? Although what he did in his life time was not earth-shattering, all the little things he did couldn't be achieved by others to the same standard."

At that time, Gabulong often went to the countryside. Before going into the towns or villages, he would first stop at a small restaurant with his driver and secretary to eat a bowl of noodles and drink some soup. Once their stomachs were filled, he would go straight to the villagers' homes to learn about their lives, without informing the local leaders in advance. If it was too late, he would stay the night at the villagers' homes and go to the local leaders the next morning to discuss the actual situations of the village and how they could overcome poverty.

Sometimes the local government knew about his trip ahead of time and prepared meals, but they were mostly refused. When they insisted until he couldn't refuse, he requested that they remove the cigarettes, alcohol, and extra dishes from the table. Only four dishes with a bowl of soup were accepted. After finishing the meal, he always left, secretly under a plate, the payment shared for his secretary, driver, and himself.

Gabulong didn't like staying in hotels arranged during meetings and visiting the countryside. Instead, he stayed in cheap hotels and shared a room with his driver and secretary. This was his way of investigating the situations in the farming and pastoral areas at the grassroots level. It was the same for years, even in the 1990s when living conditions were better.

On a business trip, Zhang Kui, the head of the North-South Mountain Reforesting Headquarters, said to Gabulong, "I don't feel comfortable sharing a room with you. I can't sleep; let's book separate rooms."

"I am afraid of sleeping alone; I would rather share a room with you," replied Gabulong in a serious manner. At 10:00 p.m., he urged Zhang Kui to turn off the TV and sleep so that they would be able to get up early the next morning. Zhang Kui couldn't sleep, but Gabulong fell asleep as soon as his head hit the pillow.

When Gabulong worked as the deputy commander-in-chief of the North-South Mountain Reforesting Headquarters of Xining, each year the headquarters office

馆住,和秘书、司机睡一间房,这是尕布龙下基层调查农牧区情况的一贯方式。多年来,从未改变过,条件稍好一点的90年代也是如此,在县上开会,也是一样。

出差在外,南北山绿化指挥部的张奎主任说:"省长,我和你睡一间房睡不着,咱们一人一间吧!"他就很认真地对张奎说:"我一个人睡害怕,你还是跟我住一个屋吧。"晚上一到10点,他就催张奎:"把电视关了,早点睡,明天早起。"张奎睡不着,尕布龙头一挨枕头就睡着了。

尕布龙在西宁市南北山绿化指挥部当专职副总指挥时,指挥部办公室每年要接待一次来自各厅局观摩各绿化区的领导。中午一时回不了,必须要在山上吃顿饭。

尕布龙每次都生怕办公室胡乱花钱,头一天,他就认认真真地交代办公室,只买二两香菜、二斤粉条、一斤葱、三斤凉粉、十斤羊肉,绝不能买多了。第二天做饭时,还要到厨房检查,也不管大家说他抠门。

他自己生病了,就悄悄跑到省医院挂号、拿药、付药钱,或者到卫生所打针、吃药。

小崔问他:"你都是这么大的领导了,干吗自己花钱看病?"

他说:"共产党给我发的工资够花了,能为国家节约一分是一分。"

"我看这个世界上,只有老天爷和医生能管住他,其他人的话,他都听不进去。老天爷下雨了,他上不了山。病情严重了,他得听医生的。"浓眉大眼的崔师傅,说起话来,不拐弯。

他的糖尿病是这样发现的,崔师傅一板一眼地说:"有一次尕省长带着我参加人防工程的一个竣工典礼,服务生给我和尕省长一人让了一只香蕉。下午3点,尕省长突然感到头晕目眩,我赶快把他拉到省医院,一检查,原来是血糖太高,需马上住院,从那天起,他才知道自己得了糖尿病。"

"多亏了那只香蕉,让他发现了自己的病,可尕省长一直觉得是因为那只香蕉才让他得了这个病。从此,一看见卖香蕉的,他就皱着眉头绕着走,听从医生的嘱咐,注意饮食,改吃粗粮。"

"谁能相信,一个副省级干部,自己一分钱舍不得花,可给别人花钱却舍得,要身上的肉,也舍得割下来。没钱了,还问我们借。"

我看看杨杰,杨杰点点头说:"跟我,跟秘书牧飞都借。"

"他还不还?"

received leaders from various departments and bureaus to observe the reforesting areas. Lunch had to be prepared when they could not return before noon.

Every time, Gabulong was afraid of his staff misusing money. On the first day, he strictly arranged for his office workers to purchase 100 grams of cilantro, one kilo of vermicelli, half a kilo of onion, a kilo and a half of grass jelly, five kilos of mutton, and nothing more. He would go to the kitchen to check that they had followed his orders when they were cooking the next day, and he didn't care if anyone called him stingy.

Whenever he was sick, he would quietly go to the provincial hospital himself to register and get treatment or medicine, always paying with his own money.

Cui Shengman asked him, "You are such a big leader, why do you spend your own money for medical services?"

"My salary from the Communist Party is enough for me. If I can save the country even a penny, I will." replied Gabulong.

"I think only God and doctors could keep him under control. He wouldn't listen to others. When God sent rain, he couldn't go up the mountains. When he was seriously ill, he would listen to doctors," said Cui Shengman, who talked straightforwardly.

Mr. Cui shared about how Gabulong was diagnosed with diabetes. "Once Gabulong and I participated in a completion ceremony of a civil air defense project, and a waiter gave each of us a banana. At three in the afternoon, he suddenly felt dizzy. I quickly took him to Qinghai Hospital for an examination. His blood sugar was too high, and immediate medical treatment was needed. From that day on, he knew that he had diabetes."

"Although he should have been thankful that tHebanana helped him discover his illness, he always thought that it was tHebanana that gave him diabetes. From then on, whenever he saw a banana seller, he just walked around frowning. He followed the doctor's advice, paid attention to his diet, and had coarse grain food instead."

"Who can believe that a provincial leader would not want to spend his money on himself but would be willing to spend it on others? It seemed that he was willing to give away anything, even his own flesh. He would borrow from us when he ran out of money."

I had a look at Yang Jie who nodded, "He always borrowed from Secretary Mufei and me as well."

"Did he pay you back?"

"Yes, he would pay us back after receiving his monthly salary. He borrowed more

"还，发了工资就还，没钱了再借。有一年，省上还给他发了困难补贴呢。"

省上安排在海南州贵德县召开全省州地市人大工作联席会。会议期间，尕布龙一再要求饭菜越简单越好，而且一律不准上烟酒饮料。会议结束时，按惯例总会有一场宴会，酒是少不了的，饭菜也得上点档次。

晚上，他走进餐厅，看见所有的桌子上都摆满了盘子，还放了烟酒，脸色顿时变得铁青。饭前讲话时，他气愤地说："同志们呐，就在此刻，因为发大水，南方一些地方，有上亿人正在遭受灾难，他们都是我们的骨肉同胞，我们还在这里大吃大喝，能吃得心安吗？请马上从所有的饭桌上撤下烟酒和饮料，并请会务组的同志负责清点折算，把这点钱捐给南方灾区。"

讲完话，他一屁股坐在那里。餐厅里则安静得能听见他呼哧呼哧喘粗气的声音。他平生最厌恶的，就是一些干部慷国家人民之慨，行铺张奢侈之能。

到刚察县开会那次，给大家留下的印象更深。会议结束后，大家在饭堂坐好了等他吃饭，等了好久不见他来。桌上摆了一桌子菜，大家也不敢动筷子，让人出去找才知道，他一开完会就径直到厨房向厨师要了一碗菜、两个馒头。这会儿已经吃完饭，去村子里转了，搞得一桌人颇为尴尬。

为吃饭，他得罪了很多人。他敢当面呵斥，甚至愤然离席，让人下不了台。有些人不理解，觉得他这是在作秀、给别人看。可是在他身边工作过的人都知道，他就是这么个人。他觉得，农村牧区还有很多人，吃得不好，穿得不好，他没有资格浪费、享受。

1990年7月的一个周末，尕布龙带领有关厅局领导和东部贫困县领导到海西州进行实地考察。一大早，从都兰出发，准备夜宿格尔木。身边的人问他，要不要给格尔木那边打个招呼，他不让。等他们赶到格尔木时，招待所的餐厅里已经没有饭了。

登记住宿时，尕布龙说："咱们这么多人，住便宜点好，一律住四人一间的房间吧。"

一些厅局领导不太高兴了，在格尔木有自己农垦宾馆和招待所的领导，私下给尕布龙做工作："到我们那儿住吧，条件比这里好，免费吃住"。

尕布龙坚决不去，对身边的秘书杨牧飞说："我们没钱，我们不去。

when he ran out of money again. One year, the province even gave him a hardship allowance.

The provincial government once organized a joint working conference of the Provincial People's Congress County of Hainan Prefecture. During the conference, Gabulong repeatedly requested the meals be as simple as possible, with no cigarettes, alcohol, or beverages included. It was customary to have a banquet at the end of the conference with drinks and high-quality food.

When Gabulong walked into the dining hall that evening and saw the tables full of dishes, cigarettes, and alcoholic drinks, he became livid. When he spoke before the meal, he said angrily, "Comrades, at this moment, hundreds of millions of people in some parts of the south are suffering from floods. They are our fellow citizens. Do you feel comfortable enjoying this lavish dinner? Please remove all drinks and cigarettes from the dinner tables immediately, and tHebanquet organizers will count and change them to cash, and the money will be donated to the victims in the south."

He sat down after his speech. The room was so quiet that his rapid breathing could be heard. What he hated most in life was that some cadres were generous at the expense of the country and the people and indulged in extravagance and luxury.

The meeting in Gangcha County left an even deeper impression on everyone. After the meeting, everyone sat down in the dining hall and waited for him to arrive. No one had seen him for a long time. The tables were full of dishes, but no one dared to move their chopsticks. Finally, they went to look for him and found that as soon as the meeting finished, he had gone to the kitchen and asked the chef for a bowl of vegetables and a steamed bun. When he finished eating, he went to the village. This made everyone at the tables feel awkward.

He offended a lot of people when it came to meals. He often berated people to their face, even angrily leaving banquets. Some misunderstood that he was making a show in front of people, but those who worked with him knew that he was a such a man. He thought that as long as people in the rural pastoral areas were living poor lives with limited food and clothing, he had no right to indulge himself or be wasteful.

On a weekend in July 1990, Gabulong led the leaders of relevant departments and bureaus and leaders of the eastern poverty-stricken counties to conduct a field investigation in Haixi Prefecture. They left from Dulan early in the morning and

如果嫌这里条件差，那你们去吧，我们三人就住在这里，按照标准住，我住惯了这样的房间，条件太好了睡不着。"

结果，那一晚，尕布龙和杨牧飞、崔生满住了一间房子，每人吃了一碗炒面片。

吃的时候，尕布龙看着一声不吭的崔生满："你今天开了一天的车，一碗面片吃不饱吧？来，给这个小伙子再来一个大饼。"

第二天中午，行至大柴旦，当地政府见来了这么多省上的领导，餐桌上摆上了中华烟、五粮液、饮料。

尕布龙站起身说："路过吃个便饭，难道这就是便饭吗？行了，把这些烟酒撤下去。"

随后，上了四个菜，一碗面片，还让每个人交了15元饭钱。

在山上植树那几年，崔师傅跟着尕布龙起早贪黑地干活，搬树苗、挖坑、浇水，吃了不少苦。

崔师傅说："不干能咋办，尕主任那么大岁数了还在山上干活，我能眼睁睁看着不干吗？"

和其他驾驶员比起来，崔师傅开的车是最破的。小轿车，尕布龙根本就不要，一辆淘汰下来的越野车每天上上下下往山上跑好几趟，不光拉人，还要拉肥料、活羊、树苗、工具。

一年夏天，天闷热，崔师傅拉了几只从大通脑山地区买来的野鸡。

一路上，捆住双脚的野鸡暴躁不堪，鸡毛乱飞，鸡粪臭得崔生满喘不上气，又不敢开车窗，怕鸡飞了，到大通县城时，戴着口罩的崔生满，头上的汗像淋了雨一样一个劲地往下淌，可一进城崔生满就被交警扣住了，原因是他戴着口罩，交警以为他有什么传染病。回去给尕布龙一说，尕布龙还乐了。说到这，还得交代几句，山上绿了，尕布龙寻思着，还应该有小动物陪伴这些好不容易长起来的树苗，就自己花钱和崔生满买来野兔、野鸡放到北山上。这是尕布龙自己的土办法，但确实起到了涵养山林的作用。如果遇到有人扣兔子、打野鸡，尕布龙会连忙上前劝说，告诉他们，这是他们买来放到山上的，是树苗最好的伙伴，为的是保护生态可持续发展。以后，就没人再来山上打扰它们了，山上的野兔、野鸡也越来越多了。

崔生满给尕布龙开了13年的车，最大的感受是，尕布龙的思想和作风能改变一个人，他觉得自己的思想和境界都发生了很大的变化，和以前

planned to stay the night in Ge'ermu. Others asked him if they should notify the leaders in Ge'ermu, but he didn't agree. By the time they arrived, the hostel was out of food.

When checking into the hostel, he requested, "We have many people. We would like to stay in the cheaper rooms with four people to a room."

Some leaders were not happy. Some even offered for Gabulong to stay with them at the other hotels. They said privately to Gabulong, "Come and stay with us. The conditions are better, and you can have free room and board."

Gabulong refused, and he said to Secretary Yang Mufei, "We don't have money; we won't go. If you think the rooms here are not good enough, then please go ahead. The three of us will stay here according to the standard. I am used to such a room, I can't sleep if it is too comfortable."

That night he shared a room with Yang Mufei and Cui Shengman, and each of them ate a bowl of fried noodles.

He looked over at Cui Shengman who was quietly eating the noodles and said, "You have been driving the whole day. One bowl of noodles is not enough." He called out to the waiter to bring for Cui Shengman.

They arrived at Dachaidan at noon the next day. Seeing many provincial leaders, the local government arranged a big meal with expensive cigarettes, alcohol, and other drinks.

Gabulong stood up and said, "I only asked for a simple meal, as we are just passing through. Is this a simple meal? Please remove the alcohol and cigarettes."

Then four dishes and a bowl of squared noodles were served, and it was also requested that everyone pay fifteen yuan for the meal.

In those years of planting trees, Mr. Cui always worked hard with Gabulong, carrying saplings, digging pits, and watering.

Mr. Cui said, "What can I do but to work? Gabulong was old, but he also worked planting on the hills. How could I just stand by and do nothing?"

Compared with other drivers, Mr. Cui had the most beat up car. Gabulong didn't want a small car but an SUV which he could use to go up and down the hills several times a day, carrying not only people, but also sheep, fertilizer, saplings, and other equipments.

Once on a hot summer day, Mr. Cui carried some pheasants in the car that he

不一样了。有一次下乡，吃早饭时，同桌的一位司机剥了三个鸡蛋，把鸡蛋黄放在烟灰缸里，拿着三个鸡蛋清到另一桌给了他服务的某厅长。回来后，崔生满问那个司机："你干啥去了？"

司机说："给我们厅长送鸡蛋去了，他只吃蛋清。"

"那这三个蛋黄咋办？你想巴结领导我不反对，但这三个蛋黄你必须自己吃掉，不许浪费！"

那个司机听说过尕布龙的为人处世，可没想到他的司机也是这样。他瞧着崔生满怒气冲冲，瞪圆了眼睛，一句话也没敢多说，把三个蛋黄吃了。

尕布龙刚刚去世的那段日子，崔生满经常梦见他，没有尕布龙的日子，少了许多麻烦，可又感到有些不习惯。尕布龙早都把崔生满当作了自己的家人，崔生满又何尝不是。

崔生满生病在省医院做了个手术，尕布龙只要没有大事，不开会，天天往医院跑，每天换着花样让何巴给崔生满做好吃的。病房里的人不相信给他送饭的是副省长："这哪是当省长的，一看就是你父亲嘛！"说的多了，崔生满也不再解释。

这就不说了，最头疼的是半夜三更地往医院送病人，有时候，困得迷迷糊糊的，不知道车往哪儿开。

在尕布龙身边工作确实不容易，能在他身边坚持工作多年，更是不容易。和杨杰一起工作过的秘书杨牧飞，也是一位谦虚、能干、爱学习的少数民族干部，被派到北京人大挂职学习去了，很多故事中，都有杨牧飞的影子。

到了 10 月，等我真的见到杨牧飞时，就像当时见到杨杰一样，有着同样的感觉，没有一点儿陌生感。那一天，尕布龙的外孙女达什姐莉也在，她悄悄对我说，见到杨杰叔叔和杨牧飞叔叔，觉得很亲切，仿佛又见到了爷爷，他们身上好像有很多相似的地方。

杨牧飞担任秘书以后，尕布龙和杨牧飞谈了一次话，他说："当我的秘书是很辛苦的，你一定要做好思想准备。你不能打着我的旗号办事，一切事情都要按照制度办。"其实，对于这一点，杨牧飞是有心理准备的。以前的秘书曾经说过，当尕省长的秘书要苦得起、累得起，没有节假日，还要什么都会干。

这么多年来，尕布龙从不利用职权给自己的家人搞特殊，也不给身边

bought from Datong.

The tied-up pheasants struggled on the way. Feathers were flying everywhere, and the smell of the pheasant poop was so strong that Cui Shengman could hardly breathe. He dared not open the car window for fear of the pheasants flying out. He arrived at the town drenched in sweat and wearing a face mask. When the traffic police saw his mask, they were suspicious that he had an infections disease and detained him. When he was finally able to get to Gabulong and tell him about what had happened, Gabulong was delighted at the news. He imagined that since the hills had greened, it would be good to arrange for some small animals to be transported to the hills. Gabulong and Cui Shengman bought rabbits and pheasants with their own money and freed them on the hills. This idea functioned as expected for the trees to grow faster. When people tried to catch the animals, Gabulong persuaded them that he had bought these animals in order to protect sustainable ecological development. The animals were later safe and increased in number.

Cui Shengman was the driver for Gabulong for thirteen years. What impressed him most was how Gabulong's ideology and style of work could influence others. There were great changes in his own thinking and behavior, quite different from before. During a breakfast on trip to the countryside, another driver at the same table peeled three eggs, giving the egg-whites to his leader sitting at another table, and throwing the yolks into an ashtray. When he came back, Cui Shengman asked the driver, "What did you do?"

"I offered the eggs to my leader; he only eats the whites," said the driver.

"What about the three yolks? I don't mind your currying favor with your leader, but these three yolks can't be wasted! You have to eat them," said Cui Shengman.

The driver heard about Gabulong's way of life, but he didn't expect his driver to be the same. He stared at Cui Shengman with an angry look, but ate the egg yolks without saying anything in return.

In the days following Gabulong's death, Cui Shengman often dreamed about him. There were fewer troubles in the life without Gabulong, but he felt a little unaccustomed to it. Gabulong regarded him as his family, and Cui Shengman did the same.

Once Cui Shengman had a medical operation. As long as he had no other business matters, he would visit him in the hospital, bringing along delicious foods that he had Heba make. Other patients at the hospital could not believe the man who delivered the food was the vice provincial governor. Many said, "How can he be the vice governor?

工作人员的职务晋升打招呼，经常叮嘱工作人员一切服从组织安排，要遵纪守法，踏踏实实做人做事。那时候，杨牧飞刚刚结婚，可尕布龙却要经常下乡，一去好多天回不来。给尕布龙做饭的何婶给达什姐莉说："你看看，尕主任天天拉着牧飞转，剩下牧飞的媳妇一个人在院子里走来走去多可怜！"

但是，杨牧飞非常尊重尕布龙，也很理解他，没有一丝抱怨。

每年召开两会期间，尕布龙安排好会议中的工作后，凌晨5点就赶到代表委员住宿的宾馆，早餐时，亲自给代表委员送茶端饭。有些人觉得不可思议，省人大常委会副主任是管大事的，坐在主席台上开会发言就行了，实在没必要给代表们端茶送水，不然要服务员干啥？实际上，没有几个人能理解尕布龙的想法。他认为，人大代表有很多来自基层，胆子小，不敢说真话，他主动亲近代表委员，给他们倒水，和他们打招呼聊天，可以让他们放松心情。因为人大代表在密切党和国家机关同人民群众的联系上，肩负着重要职责，起着重要作用，不仅要代表社会各界参与管理国家和社会事务，讨论决定重大社会事项，又是党同人民群众联系的纽带和桥梁。如果没有这种联系，人大及其常委的工作将失去根基和依托。而事实是，很多代表委员都被他这种热情周到的服务、务实严谨的作风感动而积极建

尕布龙出席牧民群众举行的"重建家园纪念碑"立碑仪式

Gabulong attended the ceremony held by the local herdsmen for the monument of "Rebuilding the Homeland"

He must be your father." Cui Shengman didn't bother to explain.

One of Cui Shengman's biggest headaches was taking patients to the hospital in the middle of the night. Sometimes he was so sleepy that he could barely drive.

Working with Gabulong was not easy, and it was even more difficult to work with him for many years. His secretary, Yang Mufei, who worked with Yang Jie, a was modest, capable, studious minority official. He was sent to the Beijing People's Congress for temporary study. In many stories of Gabulong, there is Yang Mufei's shadow.

When I first met Yang Mufei in October, I felt the same when I had first met Yang Jie; it was special closeness. Gabulong's granddaughter Dashijieli was also there that day. She quietly told me that when she saw Uncle Yang Jie and Yang Mufei, she was happy and felt close to them, as if she was seeing her own grandfather. They seemed to have a lot of similarities with him.

After Yang Mufei had started working as his secretary, Gabulong had a talk with him, "It is hard to be my secretary. You must be prepared. You can't do things by using my positional title. Everything should be done in accordance with the system." In fact, Yang Mufei had already prepared for this. He heard from the former secretaries that being Gabulong's secretary meant to endure the hardship, tiredness, no holidays, and to be able to do anything.

Over the years, he never used his position to make special arrangements for his family, nor did he give promotions those around him. He often told the staff to steadfastly obey the organizational arrangements and to abide by the law. At that time, Yang Mufei was newly married, but he needed to accompany Gabulong to the countryside for days at a time. Aunt He, who cooked for him, said to Dashijieli, "You see, Gabulong takes Mufei away with him every day, leaving Mufei's wife home alone."

But Yang Mufei had no complaints at all as he respected and understood Gabulong.

During the annual two-session conference of the National People's Congress and the Chinese Political Consultive Conference, Gabulong, after arranging the work of the meeting, would go to the hotel where the delegates were staying at 5 a.m. to serve them tea and breakfast. Some thought it was unbelievable. The deputy director of the Standing Committee is in charge of major affairs and giving speeches from the podium. Was it really necessary for him to deliver tea to the delegates? Couldn't waiters take care of that? What was in his mind was that most delegates were from

言献策。会后，他又会根据群众意见，有针对性地下乡调研，对青海林业、畜牧、水利、高原农业等方面提出很多有益的建议。其中，他提出的建设东大滩、黑泉水库、种畜改良、草原保护的建议，均来自两会，也得到了省委、省政府的高度重视。

　　几年后，杨牧飞不再担任尕布龙的秘书，可是在人们的印象中，杨牧飞和杨杰、崔生满一样，似乎一直没离开过尕布龙。只要遇到需要帮忙的事，不论白天还是黑夜，只要他们知道了，总会第一时间出现在尕布龙面前，就像家里人一样。同时，他对身边的工作人员也很尊重，凡事都商量，没有红过脸，没有过不愉快。尕布龙一辈子不轻易批评人，看到的大多是别人的长处，对待所有的事，都从工作、从党的事业出发，一心为民，一心为公，没半点私心，也从不为自己着想，也不搞小圈子、小感情。

rural areas and not courageous to tell the truth, so he voluntarily served and talked to them to help them relax. The delegates shoulder important responsibilities and play an important role in maintaining close ties between the party and state organs and the people. They not only represent all public sectors to participate in the management of the State and social affairs, discuss and decide major social issues, but also serve as a bridge between the party and the people. Without this connection, the work of the National People's Congress and its Standing Committee will lose its support. However, the fact was that many delegates were moved by his warm service and pragmatic and rigorous working style, and they actively gave speech and suggested strategies. After the conference, he went, according to the people's opinions, to the countryside for research, and put forward many useful suggestions on forestry, animal husbandry, water conservancy, plateau agriculture, and other aspects in Qinghai, from which his proposals on the construction of Dongdatan reservoir, Heiquan reservoir, breeding livestock improvement, and grassland protection came from the conference, and were highly valued by the Provincial Party Committee and the Provincial Government.

A few years later, Yang Mufei no longer served as a secretary. However, people had the impression that Yang Mufei, like Yang Jie and Cui Shengman, never left Gabulong. Day or night, as soon as they heard he needed help, they would appear in front of him as soon as possible, just like his family. At the same time, Gabulong also had great respect for those around him. He discussed everything, never blushed, and never had an unpleasant time. Gabulong never easily criticized people all his life. What he saw was mostly the merits of others. He dealt with things in the perspectives of work and the party, and he was dedicated to the people and the public. He was not selfish at all. He never thought about himself, and he never engaged in building small circles of relationships in his working circle.

日月星辰

　　窗外，下着绵绵细雨，西宁的夏天格外凉爽。简顺生为我泡了一杯龙井茶，任思绪飘向窗外，飘向让他铭记在心的 30 多年前，和尕布龙一起工作的日日夜夜。

　　20 世纪 80 年代初，简顺生在青海省农办工作，担任青海省副省长职务的尕布龙分管农牧，一到节假日，就带着简顺生下乡，深入基层。那几年，

韩华与召格力、达什姐莉在尕布龙雕像前

Han Hua, Zhao Geli, and Dashijieli stand in front of the Gabulong statue

Day and Night

With the drizzle outside the window, the summer in Xining gave one a feeling of exceptional coolness and comfort. Jian Shunsheng made me a cup of Longjin tea and then his mind slowly drifted away, wandering to memories of his days working with Gabulong more than thirty years ago.

In the early 1980s, Jian Shunsheng worked in the Agricultural Office of Qinghai Province. Gabulong, who served as the vice governor of Qinghai was in charge of agriculture and animal husbandry. Gabulong took Jian Shunsheng to the rural areas and grassroots communities every holiday. In those years, a "cruiser" (a battered old car) carried them across a lot of long and arduous journeys.

The sun was shining gloriously in July. With enough food, that is, some guokui (a kind of large round baked wheat cake), several pots of boiled water, and some cooked mutton, Gabulong, Jian Shunsheng, and the secretary drove to Haixi prefecture.

In those years, the road conditions were not as good as they are now, and there were few places to take a rest and have a meal. When they were tired of walking, they sat on the grass, made a cup of tea, gnawed on a piece of meat, ate a piece of guokui, and then moved on.

It was a hot summer, and after a night's rest in Golmud, Gabulong and Jian Shunsheng drove towards Mahai.

Along the way, the vegetation became increasingly dense, especially the reeds,

一辆淘汰下来的"巡洋舰"，载着他们，走遍了青海的山山水水。

正是艳阳高照的 7 月，尕布龙和简顺生、秘书带足干粮，也就是几块锅盔、几壶开水和煮好的羊肉，驶向了海西州。

那几年，路况没有现在好，能吃饭的地方也少。走累了，他们就在草滩上席地而坐，泡一杯茯茶，啃一块肉，吃一块锅盔，接着再走。

夏天天热，尕布龙带着简顺生在格尔木休息了一夜后，又往马海方向驶去。

一路上，但见草木越来越密，一人多高的芦苇浩浩荡荡，自天边而来。车无法行驶，他们下了车，钻进芦苇丛往深处走。黑压压的蚊子跟在身后，不一会儿，胳膊上、脸上就起了好几个大红包。

正在迟疑是否继续朝前走，不远处竟传来说话的声音。

尕布龙去海西调研时和当地干部谈心
Gabulong was talking with local officials when he investigated in Haixi

他们紧忙走了几步，见两位赤着上身的人忽地从芦苇丛中站了起来，警觉而担心地望着他们。

尕布龙和简顺生被吓了一跳。

定了定神，尕布龙才上前，和蔼地向他们询问。

原来，他们是两位来自海东地区民和县西沟乡的庄稼人，家里连续几年收成不好，结伴来这里种植小麦的。

尕布龙对此很感兴趣。这里原本是 20 世纪 50 年代山东知青开垦的一大片农场，已经闲置多年，无人耕种。

两位庄稼汉带着尕布龙和简顺生又往里走了一里多路后，只见芦苇消隐，一大片深绿的麦田，像潮水一样漫延，在猛烈的日光下，泛着微波，漾着绿浪。尕布龙的眼睛里顿时放着光芒，仿佛闻到了秋后的麦香。这个把老百姓的疾苦始终放在心上，把老百姓能否过上好日子视为己任、视为天职的共产党员，心里激荡着无法抑制的波澜，他想到了什么呢？他想到的不是远在西边的格尔木能有这样一片广阔的、可供人欣赏的自然美景，

which reached the height of humans and were spread across the vast horizon. When they couldn't drive any further, they got out of the car and walked into the deep reeds. A mass of mosquitoes followed behind them, and after a while several mosquito bites showed up on their arms and faces.

When they were hesitating over whether to move on or not, they heard someone's voice.

After a few quick steps, they saw two men with no tops suddenly standing up from the reeds, staring at them in alarm.

Gabulong and Jian Shunsheng were taken aback.

Gabulong composed himself for a second and then stepped forward and kindly asked about them.

It turned out that they were two farmers from Xigou Township, Minhe County, Haidong District. They had come to grow wheat together because of several years of poor harvest.

Gabulong was very interested. This was originally a large farm reclaimed by educated youth from Shandong Province in the 1950s, but it had been idle for many years and not cultivated.

After the two farmers had walked with Gabulong and Jian Shunsheng for more than 500 meters, the reeds faded away, and a large area of dark green wheat fields spread out like a tide, surging forward with great momentum rippling and sparkling in the strong sunlight. Gabulong's eyes lit up with expectation, as if he could smell the wheat after autumn. As a communist who was always concerned with people's hardship and regarded their well-being as his responsibility and first duty, the scene stirred up a surge of emotion in his heart. What was he thinking? How could such a vast natural beauty exist far away in the west in Golmud? Of course not. What he thought of was his recent investigation in Haidong and how he had witnessed the reality of impoverished families and villages so harsh that it made his heart ache.

Gabulong held the hands of the two farmers excitedly and looked at Jian Shunsheng with trembling lips. At this time, Jian Shunsheng realized his thoughts immediately, and they shouted out simultaneously, "Relocate the villages! Relocate the villages!" They realized that they could move people, who lived in the lack of arable land in Haidong Area and were swamped with financial difficulties, to this place

他想到的是，他刚刚在海东调研时，在许多乡村、许多人家看到的贫困状况，那窘迫无情的现实，令他心颤。

他兴奋地握住这两位庄稼汉的双手，激动地望着简顺生，双唇颤抖着，而此时的简顺生，跟他想到了一起，他们不约而同地说出了声："调庄、

尕布龙赴基层调研

Gabulong was investigating in grassroots communities

调庄！"把海东地区缺少土地，靠天吃饭，家境困难的人迁到这里来。这里有大片的良田，这里有空置的房子，更重要的是这里大有作为。

他们立即调转车头，赶回西宁，心中像揣着一团火，一团熊熊燃烧的希望之火。之前，堵在尕布龙心头，让他焦虑不安的正是前一段时间他去海东基层调研后，需要急需解决又无法解决的大问题。目前，国家的经济条件还不甚富裕，只能靠本地力量解决一些地区的贫困问题，但一时又无法从根本上改变现状，如今，他看到这一切怎么能不让他心潮澎湃，怎么能不让他激动不已。海西州有大量闲置的农场，还有知青们留下的空房子，这不正好是现成的办法吗？

回到西宁，尕布龙立即向当时担任省委书记的尹克升做了汇报，尹书记非常支持，并作出了具体批示。

where there were vast tracts of fertile land, vacant houses, and more opportunities for achievements.

They immediately turned around and drove back to Xining at full speed with a burning fire of hope in their hearts. Before, his time researching in Haidong had oppressed his mind as he struggled to come up with a solution to meet the urgent needs there. At that time, the country suffered from poor economic conditions, and they could only rely on local forces to alleviate poverty. However, they were unable to get to the root of the problem.

Now, his heart swelled with excitement as he thought of the potential for the idle land and vacant houses. Isn't this just the solution they had been looking for?

Back in Xining, Gabulong immediately reported to Yin Kesheng, the secretary of the provincial party committee at that time, and he was very supportive and gave specific instructions.

In the same year, He Kang, the Minister of Agriculture of China, came to Qinghai for inspection. Gabulong made a detailed report on the fact that Haidong had a large population living in poverty and that they needed to be lifted out of poverty as soon as possible. He also put forward the proposal of "taking advantage of resources in Haixi to alleviate the poverty in Haidong", which was approved by Minister He Kang.

As a result, the "Relocating Villages" campaign was launched in an effort to lift the people of Haidong out of poverty and help them embark on a journey to create happier lives.

However, nothing is simple. Just as Gabulong was confidently running around counties in Haidong and coordinating with the Golmud municipal government, the difficulties of "Relocating Villages" followed one after another until the local people of Haidong were full of worries.

It is no wonder that the "Relocating Villages" campaign was a major event that would require people to leave their hometowns and uproot their lives, families, and properties. At the beginning, people in counties like Ledu, Huangzhong, and Huangyuan could not understand the good intentions of the provincial party committee and the provincial government. Although their hometowns were impoverished with little land and many people, it was hard for villagers to leave behind their native lands. Encouraging the conservative villagers to let go of their deep-rooted traditional ideas

同年，又正逢农业部部长何康来青海视察，尕布龙就海东地区贫困人口众多，需要尽快改变贫困面貌一事做了详尽汇报，提出了"借海西之资源，济海东之贫困"的建议。这个建议，同样得到了何康部长的赞同。

于是，帮助海东人民脱离贫困，走上幸福生活的"调庄"之举，拉开了帷幕。

但是，做任何事情都不是那么简单的。就在尕布龙信心十足地奔走在海东各县，和格尔木市政府做大量协调工作时，"调庄"面临的困难接踵而至，海东当地的群众顾虑重重。

这也难怪，"调庄"是一件需要离开故土，连根拔起，连家产带人迁走的大事。一开始，乐都、湟中、湟源等县的人，无法理解省委省政府的良苦用心。家乡尽管贫苦，地少人多，但故土难离，根深蒂固的传统观念、保守思想，对村民来说，的确是个不易接受、很难迈过去的坎，而想走的人也无时不在踌躇疑虑，迁徙后的前景又会如何呢？生活会得到改善吗？会有好日子过吗？

放羊娃出身的尕布龙，家里住着那么多贫困的农牧民，他怎能不理解村民的心思呢？

可是，他并没有放弃，没有气馁，也没有因一时的困难妥协。他了解到，在格尔木，不仅仅是他们看到的那片农场，还有闲置的其他农场，都兰、香日德还有大片可以开垦的土地。农民，只要有了土地，就能够通过辛勤的劳动，过上好日子。

他开始不厌其烦地走乡串户，坐在农家的炕头上与村民促膝交谈，向他们讲述国家的政策，描述海西的面貌，展望海西的未来，并和大家一起商议出各种办法。

第一种办法是投亲靠友，让在海西有亲戚朋友的人，帮助他们；第二种办法是让国家给予少量的经济补贴；第三种是让每一户人家先出一个劳动力，种上一年庄稼，待来年有了收成，有了信心，再把家中的其他人接过去，一直到有人完全在海西定居下来，生活得到改善，之后，由政府派人带领同村的人去海西参观，实地感受。

就这样，经过三四年的努力，很多人在海西的辛勤耕耘获得了回报，人们这才开始慢慢地、自觉自愿地往海西搬迁。

1987年，本来要被派去其他地方任职的简顺生，在尕布龙动员做思想

and embrace the campaign was indeed an obstacle to overcome. Even those who wanted to leave were hesitant about the move. What would their future be after migration? Would life be improved? Would there be a good life for them?

Gabulong grew up herding goats and lived with so many poor farmers and herdsmen in his house. How could he not understand the misgivings of the villagers?

However, he was not discouraged and did not give up, nor did he compromise due to the temporary difficulties. He found out that in Golmud, not only the farm they visited, but also other large tracts of idle land in Dulan and Xiangri De could be reclaimed and cultivated. As long as farmers had land, they could live a good life through hard work.

He began to visit households tirelessly. He sat on brick beds in villagers' houses and talked with them patiently, telling them about the national policies, describing the situation of Haixi, casting vision for the future of Haixi, and discussing possible solutions with them.

The first solution was to look for help from relatives and friends who lived in Haixi. The second solution was to allow for a small amount of subsidies from the central government. The third solution was that each household would send a worker to plant crops for a year. After the first successful harvest, the workers would be more confident in convincing other family members to join them in the new land. Once some families had settled completely in Haixi and improved their lives, the government would bring more people from the same village to visit Haixi and experience it on-site.

In this way, many people were rewarded for their hard work in Haixi after three or four years. Consequently, more and more people began to gradually and voluntarily relocate to Haixi.

In 1987, Jian Shunsheng, who was supposed to be sent to other places, was transferred to be the administrative commissioner in Haidong after Gabulong persuaded him. His work was to focus on the implementation of "Transferring Villages" because it was Jian Shunsheng who understood Gabulong's ideas best and was most familiar with this work.

After several years of hard work, "Relocating Villages" achieved initial success. People had gradually accepted it and tasted the sweetness of harvest, and Gabulong's heart was at ease. Some time later, farmers came to his home to express their gratitude,

工作后，调往海东地区任行署专员，具体抓落实，抓"调庄"工作，因为只有简顺生最理解尕布龙的想法，也最熟悉这项工作。

又经过几年的艰苦奋斗，"调庄"初见成效，人们逐渐接受并尝到了甜头，尕布龙的心里这才踏实了！渐渐地，开始有农民来家里找他，向他表示感谢，有人拿来自家的粮食、鸡蛋登门道谢。

尕布龙感慨万千，心中洋溢着快乐："只要你们能过上舒心的日子，比让我吃什么好东西都高兴。粮食、鸡蛋得来不易，你们还是拿回家自己吃吧！"

1989 年，简顺生带着工作组去海西州回访，看望搬迁到那里的海东人。

返回时，行至日月山下已是黄昏，金色的阳光照在波光盈盈的草原上。守候在路边的尕布龙正在翘首遥望，整整一个下午他都在这里等候，他是希望能尽快了解"调庄"到海西州后的农民的生活，也是在用自己的行动，表彰简顺生、表彰海东工作组取得的优异成绩。

微雨静落，窗外的杨树叶仿佛也在凝神细听。近年，正是举国上下脱贫攻坚的最后几年，每个州，每个县、乡都有来自北京、上海、天津、浙江、山东的援青干部帮助指导当地扶贫脱贫，可早在 20 世纪七八十年代，尕布龙就已经在用自己的实际行动践行着这项庄严、神圣，富有创举的扶贫工作，并取得了卓越成效。

70 多岁的简顺生，高大魁梧，身体硬朗，和我聊了 5 个多小时，没觉得累。但是，他的腿，因为跟着尕布龙在山上种了近十年的树，也是不敢见一点风寒的。他站起来，给我添了水，活动着僵硬的双腿。

简顺生是从 20 世纪 50 年代拍摄的那部故事影片《金银滩》中，知道尕布龙这个人的。其实，还有一部影片《草原风暴》，是反映农村互助合作化的，里面的一些故事情节，也来自当时在海晏县工作的尕布龙。那部片子是 1960 年上海电影制片厂拍摄的，演员大部分用的是青海黄南藏族自治州文工团的演员。

简顺生认为，尕布龙是西北地区一个了不起的少数民族干部，而尕布龙一直信奉的"人民为上，人民为天"这一点绝不是挂在口头上的，而是一点一滴地落实在了他的行动上。他让来自最基层的农牧民住在家里，免费提供食宿，实际上也是他长年来不脱离群众，与群众保持密切联系，听取群众意见的一种工作方法。这是简顺生一再向我强调的，在尕布龙身边

some with grain and some with eggs.

Gabulong was full of emotion and said with joy, "I could not be happier as long as you are able to live a comfortable life, which is much better than any good food. Grain and eggs do not come easily, so you'd better take them home and eat them yourselves!"

In 1989, Jian Shunsheng took his working group to Haixi Prefecture to pay a return visit to see the Haidong people who had relocated there.

When they were on their way back, it was already dusk at the foot of Riyue Mountain, and the golden sunlight reflected on the shinning grassland. Gabulong, who had been waiting on the side of the road all afternoon, looked up from afar. He wanted first of all to learn about the life of farmers after "Transferring Villages" as soon as possible, and secondly, he wanted to commend the excellent achievements of Jian Shunsheng and the Haidong working group with his own actions.

The light rain fell silently, and the poplar leaves outside the window seemed to be listening attentively. In recent years, China's poverty alleviation had reached its final stage. Every state, county, and township had youth cadres from Beijing, Shanghai, Tianjin, Zhejiang, and Shandong to help guide local poverty alleviation. However, as early as the 1970s and 1980s Gabulong was already practicing this solemn, noble, and innovative work and had made great achievements.

Jian Shunsheng, who is in his 70s, is tall and burly, with a strong body. He chatted with me for more than five hours without feeling tired, but his legs, planting trees with Gabulong on the mountain for nearly ten years, couldn't stand the wind and cold. He stood up, filled my glass with water, and moved his stiff legs.

Jian Shunsheng knew Gabulong from the feature film Gold and Silver Beach filmed in the 1950s. Actually, some of the storylines in another film Grassland Storm, which reflects cooperative movements in rural areas, also tell the story of Gabulong working in Haiyan county at that time. The film was shot by Shanghai Film Studio in 1960, and most of the actors were from the Qinghai Huangnan Tibetan Autonomous Prefecture Cultural Troupe.

Jian Shunsheng believed that Gabulong was a great minority cadre in the northwestern areas, and Gabulong always believed in "the people are supreme, and the people are the heaven." His belief was not just verbal, but it was implemented in his actions bit by bit. He allowed farmers and herdsmen from the grassroots to live at

工作时，他深切的体会。

尕布龙带着简顺生去青海湖边调研，听说有个村民家里非常困难，就专程去看望。农民家里什么也没有，也不知道该怎样脱贫致富。他们和村子里几个干部在一起合计了一会儿，给这个村民出了个主意，由尕布龙亲自联系，给他买十几只羊来养，然后再慢慢扩大发展。

农民同意了，尕布龙就专门去刚察县，给他联系到了十几只很便宜的羊。

第二天，农民来刚察县拉羊。见到尕布龙，就一屁股坐在地上，把一个布口袋倒了个底朝天。

一堆揉得皱皱巴巴的钱撒了一地。大多是脏兮兮的毛毛钱和黑乎乎的硬币。尕布龙定定地看了一会儿农民，什么话也没说，就埋下头和那个农民认认真真地数了起来。数完了，他抬起头，看着这个老实巴交的庄稼汉，叹了一口气，显然，这些钱是不够的。尕布龙把钱重新塞进布口袋里，索性自己掏钱，给农民买了羊。

农民含着热泪，颤巍巍地从放在脚边的另一个口袋里拿出几个熟鸡蛋，一定要留给尕布龙。尕布龙好说歹说，让农民揣着鸡蛋回去了。

农民走远了，尕布龙的心里却恹恹的，他感到自己身上的责任很重，脚下的路还很长，什么时候，能够让我们的农牧民彻底摆脱贫困，过上好日子啊？！

为了帮助贫困的牧民，吃亏的事也有。20世纪70年代中期，有一次，尕布龙竟然哄着女儿召格力把自己家的50只羊和同村宫保家的50只羊，借给了海东的两户贫困户。想帮助那两户人家尽快脱贫致富。那两户人家的男主人给他做了保证，一定能把羊养好。

他说："过了年，产下了小羊羔，那户人家一定会把羊还给你。"召格力相信了父亲的话。

第二年的秋天，尕布龙好像忘了这件事。到了初冬，还是不提这件事。召格力

尕布龙在基层调研

Gabulong was investigating in grassroots communities

his place and provided free room and board. In fact, it was also a working method that he kept close contact with the masses and listened to their opinions for many years. This was what Jian Shunsheng had repeatedly emphasized to me, and it was what he experienced deeply when working with Gabulong.

Once Gabulong took Jian Shunsheng to Qinghai Lake for an investigation. Hearing that a villager's life was very difficult, he made a special trip to visit. The villager had nothing at all, and he didn't know how to get out of poverty. They discussed the situation with a few cadres in the village and came up with the idea that Gabulong himself contacts to buy a dozen sheep to raise and then gradually expanded the size of herd.

The villager agreed, and Gabulong went to Gangcha himself to arrange the purchase of more than a dozen sheep at a low price.

The next day, the villager came to Gangcha to draw away the sheep. When he saw Gabulong, he sat down on the ground and poured a cloth pocket upside down.

A pile of crumpled money was scattered all over the ground, and most of them were dirty dimes and black coins. Gabulong stared at the farmer for a while and then lowered his head and counted the money seriously with him without saying anything. After counting, he looked up at the honest and docile farmer and sighed. Obviously, the money was not enough. Gabulong put the money back into the cloth pocket and bought the sheep for the farmer.

The farmer tremblingly took out a few boiled eggs from another pocket at his feet with tears welling up in his eyes, and he insisted on leaving the eggs for Gabulong. However, Gabulong persuaded him to keep the eggs for himself.

The villager had gone far, but Gabulong still felt distressed. He felt that he had a huge responsibility and a long way to go to help farmers and herdsmen get out of poverty and live good lives. How long would it take to achieve this goal?

In order to help poor herdsmen, there were some losses. In the mid-1970s, Gabulong once coaxed his daughter Zhao Geli to loan fifty sheep from her own family and fifty sheep from the Gongbao family in the same village to two poor households in Haidong in a bid to help them alleviate poverty. Masters of the two families assured him that they would raise the sheep well.

Gabulong said to his daughter, " After Spring Festival when new lambs are born,

终于忍不住问父亲："小羊羔怕是都长大了，我的那些羊呢？"

尕布龙没法子推脱，就带上召格力去了一趟海东。这可是少有的事，召格力坐在父亲的车上，一路欣赏着窗外的风景，心里乐滋滋的。

到了村子下了车，父亲在前面走，召格力跟在父亲身后，没想到的是，尕布龙帮忙盖起的羊圈空空的，送来的 50 只羊，一只也没剩下。

问牧民："羊呢？"

牧民说："有些吃了，有些卖了。"

尕布龙苦笑着向女儿摊开双手，摇了摇头。

召格力吃惊地张大了嘴巴。

20 世纪 80 年代末，简顺生跟尕布龙与当时的省计委主任靳建华去玉树下乡，到了杂多县，谈完工作上的事，县上的领导邀请他们一行晚上看电影。

尕布龙很高兴。平日里他哪有空闲看电影，下乡时能和牧民群众一起看场电影，也是一件轻松愉快的事。

吃过晚饭，大家有说有笑地去看电影。

太阳已经落山，一抹淡淡的余晖照在静谧的街道上。在一截低矮的土墙前，大家站住了。土墙上挂着一块牌子，上面写着"电影院"三个大字。拐进墙里面才知道，杂多县电影院，其实就是一小块由四面土墙围起来的空场地。

银幕挂在前面的墙上，旁边是一个毡房，毡房里面是放映机，有一些牧民已经坐在银幕前的几张长条凳子上。

这场景显然有些意外，有些让人不知所措。

看见他们进来，牧民们站了起来。县上的同志也很热情，招呼大家坐下。牧民们看着尕布龙，尕布龙向牧民摆摆手。他裹紧身上的大衣，端端正正地坐下了，其他人也都找了凳子坐下。

电影开演了，那天晚上放映的是《地道战》。

杂多县电影院一共只有两部影片，一部是《地道战》一部是《天仙配》，长年轮换着放。从没有进过新片子，但也从未间断过放映，那天正好轮到放映《地道战》。

天色渐暗，由于昼夜温差极大，仲夏的杂多县，晚上气温骤降，像三月里的天。大家虽然有下乡的经验，都带着防寒的大衣，可谁也没想到会

the family will definitely return them to you." Zhao Geli believed her father's words.

When the next autumn came, Gabulong seemed to have forgotten about it. In early winter, he still did not mention it. Zhao Geli finally couldn't help asking her father, "I'm afraid that the lambs have grown up. Where are my sheep? "

Gabulong could not evade the issue any more, so he took Zhao Geli to Haidong. Sitting in her father's car, Zhao Geli was delighted and enjoying the scenery outside the window, which did not happen very often.

They got out of the car when they arrived, and Zhao Geli followed her father walking into the village. Unexpectedly, the sheepfold that was built under the help of Gabulong was empty, and of the fifty sheep, none were left.

They asked the herdsman, "Where are the sheep?"

The herdsman replied, "Some of them were eaten, and some were sold."

With a wry smile, Gabulong spread out his hands to his daughter and shook his head.

Zhao Geli opened her mouth in surprise.

In the late 1980s, Jian Shunsheng, Gabulong, and Jin Jianhua, the director of the Provincial Planning Commission, went to Yushu for investigation and arrived in Zaduo County. After talking about work, leaders of the county invited them to watch a movie in the evening.

Gabulong was very happy, because it was not easy for him to enjoy a movie in his daily life. It was a relaxing activity to watch a movie with the local herdsmen when he visited rural areas.

After dinner, everyone went to the cinema, chatting and laughing.

The sun had set, and a faint afterglow shed a light over the quiet street. Everyone stopped in front of a low cob wall on which there was a sign with the word "Cinema" on it. They turned into the wall and found out that the Zaduo Cinema was actually a small empty space surrounded by four cob walls.

The screen was hanging on the front wall and there was a projector in a yurt next to it. Some herdsmen were already sitting on a few long stools in front of the screen.

This scene was obviously unexpected, and they were a bit perplexed.

Seeing them come in, the herdsmen stood up. The comrades in the county were also very hospitable and asked everyone to sit down. The herdsmen looked at Gabulong,

在露天看电影。没过一会儿，大家身上的衣服便无法抵御夜晚的风寒了。

坐在前面的尕布龙一声不响，一动不动地坐着看完了那场电影。

看完电影的尕布龙毫无睡意，拉着快要冻僵的靳建华主任进了自己的房间。

"怎么样？"尕布龙恳切地望着低头不语的靳建华。"你们计委，想办法出点血吧！这么艰苦、边远的地方，海拔4200米，一年到头没有个暖和的时候。牧民群众不容易，又没有什么娱乐文化设施，就喜欢看个电影。"

靳建华主任深知尕布龙的为人，同时，也被眼前这个简陋得令人辛酸、惭愧的"电影院"所震撼。

他握着尕布龙的手，表了态："我回去后，一定向上级反映，尽快解决这个问题。"

尕布龙目不转睛地看着靳建华主任，满含期望。

回西宁后不久，就传来了好消息。青海省计委决定拨款，为玉树州杂多县修建一座小电影院。

尕布龙知道后，乐了好几天。见到简顺生，一把拉住他，脸上布满了笑容："这下好了，这下好了！你们再联系文化厅，给县上多送些电影片子。"

这同样是一件对一位省级领导来说，不足挂齿的事。可是，想想看，假如我们每一个领导干部，都能像尕布龙这样深入基层，了解基层人民的生活，并竭力帮助群众解决困难，基层的很多问题，不都可以被提前发现，提前解决了吗？而我们的老百姓又怎么能不信任我们的党和我们的政府呢？

在担任副省长主管农牧业工作那几年，尕布龙几乎走遍了全省所有乡镇，指导当地的经济发展和生态绿化建设。在针对民族宗教、解决草山纠纷等问题中，他始终坚持党性原则，同时，又尽可能耐心地用他熟练的藏语与蒙古语和群众沟通思想、交流感情、疏导情绪。他说："边界要安定，民族要和谐，民族团结是发展稳定的前提；经济发展，民族振兴进步，稳定是压倒一切的重中之重。"

由于他亲自指导，亲自做工作，许多矛盾纠纷在萌芽中得到化解，即使有了严重分歧，造成不良影响的，也被他很快解决，既维护了民族间的团结，又使人民生活安宁。而且，作为一名民族干部，他在解决问题中，毫无民族情绪和倾向性，坚持公平公正办事的工作作风也深深地感染着当

and Gabulong waved to them. He wrapped himself in a tight overcoat and sat down upright, and everyone else found a stool to sit down as well.

The movie started. Tunnel Warfare was screened that night.

There were only two films in Zaduo County Cinemas. One was Tunnel Warfare and the other was Tian Xianpei, which had been in rotation for many years. Although the cinema had never acquired a new film, the loop was never interrupted. That day, it was the turn of Tunnel Warfare.

It was getting dark. Due to the great temperature difference between day and night, the night temperature dropped sharply. Although it was midsummer, it felt like March. Everyone had experience in going to the countryside and had worn thick coats, but no one expected to watch a movie in the open air. After a while, everyone felt that they were not dressed warmly enough to withstand the cold of the night.

Sitting in front, Gabulong finished the movie without a move nor a word.

After the movie, Gabulong, who was still wide awake, pulled Director Jin Jianhua, who was about to freeze, into his room.

"How was it?" Gabulong looked earnestly at Jin Jianhua who lowered his head silently. "You are in charge of the Planning Committee. Try to find a way to give some financial support! Living in such a difficult and remote place at an altitude of 4200 meters, with cold temperatures all year round, is not easy for the herders. They do not have any entertainment facilities, and watching movies is their only recreation."

Jin Jianhua knew Gabulong very well, and he was also shocked by this dilapidated and pitiful "cinema" in front of him.

He held Gabulong's hands and said, "When I go back, I will report to my superiors and solve this problem as soon as possible."

Gabulong looked at Director Jin Jianhua intently, full of expectations.

Soon after he returned to Xining, good news came. The Qinghai Provincial Planning Commission decided to allocate funds to build a small cinema for Zaduo County, Yushu Prefecture.

Gabulong was in a good mood for several days after hearing the news. When he saw Jian Shunsheng, he held him with a smile on his face. "This is so good! You can contact the Department of Culture to send more movies to the county."

For a provincial leader, this might be seem like a trivial matter. However, if every

地干部。

在他担任河南县委副书记时，蒙古族和藏族群众因草场发生纠纷，蒙古族乡亲找到他，理所应当地认为，身为蒙古族的尕布龙一定会偏袒他们。结果，却遭到他的严厉批评，让那个乡亲回去后坚决按照原则处理问题。

尕布龙没有上过大学也没有上过党校，但是他谦虚好学、聪慧过人、思维活跃、记忆力超常。只要中央下发新的文件，他都要认真学习，请身边的同事为他读一遍，把不认识的字记下来，吃过晚饭后，在院子里一边散步，一边背诵，直到完全领会，吃透精神。他开会讲话的时候，基本脱稿，讲得逻辑分明、层次清楚，而且从不讲大话、套话，只用具体数字、具体事例说明问题。秘书为他撰写好的每一篇讲话材料，他都要亲自把关。有一回召开全省农牧区工作会议，因为秘书给他写的讲话稿和另一位领导的有些雷同，他便让简顺生连夜加班，重新修改完善，直到满意方才入睡。

简顺生和尕布龙共事多年，长年累月一起下乡，对他有着很深的感情。简顺生知道，尕布龙的妻子一直在老家瘫痪在床，他身边没人，生活过于简朴，常常于心不忍。逢年过节，总想给他带点好吃的东西，可是他每次都拒不接受。

尕布龙在作报告

Gabulong was making a report

leader and official could go to the grassroots level, understanding the lives of the people there and trying their best to help the people solve their difficulties, many problems at the grassroots level would be discovered and solved in advance. Then how can our people distrust our party and our government?

In the years when he was the vice governor in charge of agriculture and animal husbandry, Gabulong visited almost all villages and towns in the province to guide the local economic development and ecological afforestation. He always adhered to the principle of party consciousness in dealing with ethnic and religious issues and resolving disputes in the grasslands and mountains. At the same time, he used his proficiency in Tibetan and Mongolian to communicate ideas, exchange feelings, and ease emotions among the masses as much as possible. He said, "The border should be stable, and the nation should be harmonious. Unity among ethnic groups is the prerequisite for development and stability. Economic development and steady revitalization and progress are absolutely critical."

Because of his personal guidance and work, many conflicts and disputes were nipped in the bud. Even if there were serious differences which caused adverse effects, he would quickly solve them. This not only safeguarded the unity of the ethnic groups, but also helped people live in peace. Moreover, as an ethnic minority cadre, he had no national inclination and sentiment in solving problems, and his work style of adhering to fairness and justice deeply affected local cadres.

When he was the deputy secretary of the Henan County Party Committee, the Mongolian and Tibetan people had a dispute over the pasture. The Mongolian villagers came to him, and they believed that Gabulong, as a Mongolian, would stand on their side. However, the Mongolians were severely criticized by him and were told to resolutely deal with the problem in accordance with the principles.

Gabulong had never been to a university or a party school, but he was modest, studious, intelligent, active in thinking, and had an extraordinary memory. Whenever the Central Committee would issue new documents, he would study them carefully. First, he would ask his colleagues to read them for him and write down the words he didn't know. After dinner, he would walk around the yard while reciting the documents until he could fully understand their spirit. When he spoke at a meeting, he was basically out of manuscript with clear logic and structure. Instead of talking with big words or clichés,

有一年的农历八月十五中秋节，终于把简顺生给惹恼了。简顺生红着脸朝他吼道："在一起工作这么长时间了，跟您简直连朋友都没法做！"

尕布龙不生气，也不解释，定定地望着他，简顺生就气呼呼地把礼物拿回了家。想了想，终是放心不下，又让爱人蒸了两个又松又软的大月饼给他拿过去，他这才勉强收下，可还要拿出多一半价值的东西，让简顺生带回去。

最难忘的一次，是尕布龙家乡海晏的房子修好后。简顺生专门买了一块红色的地毯，请人画了一幅画，兴冲冲地去海晏看望他。简顺生想，长年上山搞绿化，尕布龙的腿疼得走不成路，铺个地毯可以防潮。

可是，尕布龙竟然当着众人的面把地毯退还给了简顺生。

这冷冰冰的举动，让简顺生非常难过，也非常尴尬。那时候，尕布龙已经退休多年，在简顺生心里，他就是一个老人，一个在一起共事多年的老朋友，可尕布龙还是要坚持原则。

好在，简顺生送去的那幅画上画着一朵荷花，一朵出淤泥而不染的荷花，尕布龙很喜欢，总算留下了，这才让简顺生心里稍稍有了一点安慰。

出了尕布龙家，简顺生把地毯送给了村里的一位乡亲。他怎么能再带回去呢，他希望至少能带给尕布龙的乡亲

会议中

in the meeting

哪怕一点点温暖，一点点安慰。

说起尕布龙，提起青海的经济建设，简顺生有说不完的心里话。虽然退休多年，但是，他的心里还是想着老百姓，牵挂着青海农牧业的经济发展。他很珍惜、很想念与尕布龙在一起工作的那些日子，尽管很累、很苦，没有高朋满座的宴席也没有迎来送往的场面。

尕布龙有一句常说的话："人民的期盼，就是共产党员的奋斗目标。

he used specific figures and examples to illustrate the problem. He would personally check over the speech material that his secretary had written for him. Once, there was a provincial conference of the agricultural and pastoral areas. Because he found the speech draft was similar to that of another leader, he asked Jian Shunsheng to work all night to revise and improve it. He did not sleep until he was satisfied.

Jian Shunsheng, working and traveling with Gabulong for many years, had a deep affection for him. He knew that Gabulong's wife was in their hometown, and she had been paralyzed in bed for many years, so there was no one by Gabulong's side. He couldn't bear to see how simple Gabulong's life was, so he always wanted to bring Gabulong some good food during the holidays, but Gabulong refused to accept it every time.

One year, while trying to give Gabulong a gift during the Mid-Autumn Festival, Jian Shunsheng had finally had enough. He yelled at Gabulong with a red face, " I have been working together with you for such a long time, but I can't even make friends with you!"

Gabulong did not get angry or explain anything, but simply gazed at him. Jian Shunsheng took the gift home angrily. After thinking about it, he was still unable to sit down, so he asked his wife to steam two large mooncakes for Gabulong. This time, Gabulong accepted them reluctantly, but he presented something of more than half of the value in return.

The most unforgettable experience was that once after Gabulong's house was completed in Haiyan, Jian Shunsheng bought a red carpet and asked someone to draw a picture for him. He took the gift and went to Haiyan excitedly. Jian Shunsheng thought that the carpet could prevent moisture to protect Gabulong's legs because his legs hurt so much he could not walk due to years of working in afforestation on the mountains.

However, Gabulong returned the carpet to Jian Shunsheng in front of everyone.

Jian Shunsheng was very sad and embarrassed by his cold reaction. At that time, Gabulong had been retired for many years. In Jian Shunsheng's mind, he was an old man and an old friend with whom he had worked for many years. However, Gabulong still stuck to his principles.

Fortunately, the painting depicting a lotus flower which had come up out of the mud was accepted by Gabulong, and he liked it very much, which gave Jian Shunsheng

不然，要我们这些党员干啥！"

他是这样说的，也是这样做的，没有一丝一毫的含糊。

尕布龙一生所做的事似乎很简单，没有惊天动地的大事，有很多都体现在日常生活的细微之处。但就是这样朴实的一言一行，长时间的坚守，才给人们留下了一笔无法用金钱衡量、无法用数字丈量的精神财富。尕布龙对党无比忠诚，对人民无比热爱，为了党、为了人民，他甘愿付出一切，这就是他生活和工作的信念。

给他开过车的郑师傅一直忘不了，毛主席去世后，他三天三夜没说话，三天三夜没吃饭。

几十年来，尕布龙身上洗得发白的蓝色中山装上，始终佩戴着一枚毛主席像章，每次洗衣服前，都要小心翼翼地摘下来，换上干净衣服后，又认认真真地把它佩戴在原来的位置，一直到他离开人世……

a little comfort.

After leaving Gabulong's house, Jian Shunsheng gave the carpet to a villager. How could he bring it back? He hoped to bring at least a little warmth and comfort to Gabulong's villagers.

Speaking of Gabulong and Qinghai's economic construction, Jian Shunsheng had a lot to say. Although he had been retired for many years, he was still thinking about the lives of villagers and the economic development of Qinghai's agriculture and animal husbandry. Although he had been very tired and bitter during the long days of working with Gabulong, with no banquets full of friends or scenes of visitors coming and going, Jian Shunsheng still cherished those memories and missed the old days very much.

Gabulong often said,"The expectations of the people are the goals of the Communist Party members. Otherwise, what should we party members do?"

That's what he said, and his actions followed his words without the slightest ambiguity.

The things Gabulong accomplished in his life seem to be very simple. There were no earth-shattering events, and many of them occurred in the subtleties of daily life. However, just such simple words and deeds with long-term persistence left people with a spiritual wealth that cannot be measured by money or numbers. Gabulong was extremely loyal to the party and extremely loving to the people. For the party and for the people, he was willing to give everything, which was his belief in life and work.

Mr. Zheng, who had worked as his driver, never forgot that Gabulong did not speak or eat for three days and nights after Chairman Mao passed away.

For decades, Gabulong had always worn a faded blue Chinese tunic suit with a badge of Chairman Mao on it. Every time he washed clothes, he would carefully take it off. After putting on clean clothes, he would pin it in the original position. He kept this routine until he passed away.

让田野开满鲜花

沿着高速公路往日月山走，太阳正挂在头顶。绿草绵延，山色淡然。前面就是倒淌河，海南州共和县倒淌河镇哈乙亥村就在公路边上。

1980年，时任青海省委常委、省畜牧局局长的尕布龙，来到哈乙亥村蹲点。村子的寂寥与萧瑟，牧民的贫困与无望，令他担忧。他知道，接下来的日子对他来说没有那么简单，救济扶贫在客观上存在一定的难度。他一连几天住在生活最困难的村民更藏家，仔细倾听意见，向村里的书记、干部了解情况，给村民反复讲解党的富民政策。他有些焦虑，恨不得让他眼前的牧民一夜间过上好日子。

哈乙亥村的草场面积达14万亩，有73户人家。村子里没电、没水，饮水要从1公里以外的地方运来，加上没有防疫措施，牲畜的死亡率很高。

尕布龙了解清楚村民的状况后，当即采取措施，并努力实践。他在短时间内协调电力单位，给村子里拉上了电。然后又联系省水利局局长李志刚，动用空军力量在哈乙亥村上空拍摄卫星云图，勘察村子所在位置的地质断层，按照卫星云图指示的方向，掘了13米深的井，找到了水源，解决了村子里最基本的饮水问题，让村民看到了希望。这希望在农牧民心头燃烧，在田野地头蔓延，很快便成为一种动力。

通电的那一天，村子里像过年一样，不，比过年还要热闹，还要开心。尕布龙充满深情地对欢呼雀跃的村民们说："点煤油灯、点蜡烛的生活已经成为历史。共产党之所以伟大，就因为它是给老百姓办实事的，是为了

Let the fields bloom with flowers

Driving along the highway towards Riyue Mountain, the sun is hanging overhead. The green grass extends to the color of the mountains. The Daotang River is in front. Ha Yihai Village, Daotanghe Town, Gonghe County, Hainan Prefecture is just beside the highway.

In 1980, Gabulong, then a member of the Standing Committee of the Qinghai Provincial Party and director of the Provincial Animal Husbandry Bureau, came to Ha Yihai Village to investigate. He was worried by the loneliness and depression of the village, the poverty and desperation of the herdsmen. He knew that the following days would not be easy, and there must be many objective difficulties in alleviating poverty. For several days, he lived in the Gengzang's home, the family in the most difficult situation, and listened carefully to their opinions, learned the conditions from the village secretaries and cadres, and repeatedly explained to the villagers the party's policy of enriching the people. He was so anxious that he could not wait to help the herdsmen in front of him live a good life overnight.

Ha Yihai Village had a grassland area of 140,000 mu (9333.33 hectares) and 73 households. There was no electricity or water in the village, and drinking water had to be transported from one kilometer away. In addition, there were no epidemic prevention measures, and the mortality rate of livestock was very high.

After Gabulong understood the situation of the villagers, he immediately adopted

拉夫旦讲述当年尕布龙在哈乙亥村扶贫蹲点的故事

Lafudan was talking about the story of Gabulong's investigation in Ha Yihai Village

让老百姓过上幸福的生活。你们要听党的话，要好好劳动，尽快脱贫致富。"

这番话，出自尕布龙心底，也是拉夫旦——当年的村支书、带头人，回忆当时的情景时，刻在心上的话。因为，从那一天起，哈乙亥村就在尕布龙的亲自指导、扶持和30多年来亲人般的关怀、呵护下，开始发展畜牧生态经济、市场经济、劳务经济、旅游经济，最终使哈乙亥村走上了富裕的新生活之路。

乡村是一首田园诗，美丽的哈乙亥草原芬芳如锦，但是，牧人的生活还需要党的关怀和指引。

第一次见到尕布龙时，拉夫旦心中是那样的胆怯。从小生活在农村，近40岁的拉夫旦连省城都没去过，哪里见过省上的领导，更别说是副省长了。但是，他发现，这个省长最喜欢到穷人家去聊天，最愿意和他们这些村干部推心置腹地交谈。这个省长没有官架子，也不盛气凌人，真心关怀和支持他们这个藏族村落的发展，亲切得有些像自己的兄长、自己的家人。慢慢地，他向这位省长敞开了心扉，向这位朴实、直爽，像普通牧人一样的领导说出了自己的心里话。他还发现，这位省长最不爱听的是谎话、虚话，最反对的行为是浪费，最讨厌的是不思进取、懒惰、虚伪的人。

此后，村子里的干部们私下商量，得尽快纠正村子里过去做得不那么

measures to help the village and made great efforts to carry them out. He contacted the electric power sector within a short time had connected electricity to the village. Then he contacted Li Zhigang, the director of the Provincial Water Resources Bureau, and used air force to take a satellite cloud map over Ha Yihai Village, surveying the geological faults at the location of the village.According to the direction indicated by the satellite cloud map, he dug a well thirteen meters deep and found the water source, which not only solved the most basic problem of providing the villagers access to drinking water but also gave them hope. This hope burned in the hearts of the farmers and herdsmen, spread through the fields, and became a driving force for success.

On that day when electricity came to the village, the atmosphere of the was as joyful as the Spring Festival. No, it was more bustling and happier than the Spring Festival. Gabulong spoke to the cheering villagers affectionately, "The time of lighting kerosene lamps and candles has become history. The reason why the Communist Party is great is that it does practical things for the people, so that the people can live a good life. You must listen to the party, work hard, and shake off poverty as soon as possible."

These words came from the bottom of Gabulong's heart, and they were also engraved in the heart of Lafudan, the leader and the village party secretary then, when he recalled the scene at the time. From that day on, under the personal guidance and support of Gabulong for more than thirty years, Ha Yihai Village began to develop animal husbandry ecological economy, market economy, labor economy, and tourism economy. Ha Yihai Village embarked on a new road of prosperity.

The countryside is like an idyllic poem, and the beautiful Ha Yihai grassland is fragrant, but the life of herdsmen still needs the care and guidance of the party.

When Lafudan first saw Gabulong, he was so timid. Although he was nearly forty years old, he had lived in the countryside since childhood and had never been to the provincial capital, so he had never seen a provincial leader, let alone the vice provincial governor. However, he found that what this governor most liked was visiting the poor people's homes and talking with village cadres heart-to-heart. The governor had no air of an official, and he was not domineering or overbearing. Instead, he sincerely cared for and supported the development of this Tibetan village. His kindness was like that of an older brother. Gradually, Lafudan opened his heart to Gabulong and spoke his mind to this simple, straightforward leader who was just like an ordinary shepherd. He also found that

正确、完善的事，要说实话，千万不能对这位省长说假话。

尕布龙对他们说，改变村子贫穷的面貌，最根本的问题是要让村民们接受教育，让村里的孩子上学、读书，培养有文化、有知识的人才，用知识、科学的头脑改变贫穷的生活。同时，让孩子们成为对国家、对社会有用的人。

1983 年，尕布龙亲自主持召开了村党支部扩大会议，由村委会提议，办起了自己的学校。村干部齐心协力，选校址、选校长，给每家每户做工作，由全村自筹资金，让孩子们到学校读书。

几个月后，3 顶帐篷、3 位老师、7 名学生的帐篷学校落成。尕布龙

哈乙亥村的远景规划
Future planning of Ha Yihai Village

副省长担任了学校的名誉校长。又过了几个月，学生增加到 24 名。其中，最大的 16 岁，最小的 7 岁。一年后，拉夫旦担任了该校的名誉校长。

1984 年的六一儿童节。村里雇了湟源车队的一辆公共汽车，带着学生、村干部和还没有入学的儿童 50 多人来到了省城西宁。除了在省畜牧厅招待所订了两间房供大家打地铺外，其余 30 多人全挤在了尕布龙副省长的家。尕布龙家本来就住着来西宁看病的牧人，这下可真是乱了套。

what the governor least liked to hear was lies and empty words, what he most opposed was waste, and what he most hated was lazy and hypocritical people.

After that, the cadres in the village discussed in private that they had to correct the problems of the village as soon as possible and that they could never lie to Gabulong.

Gabulong told them that the most fundamental ways to lift the village out of poverty are to help the villagers receive education, support the children to go to school for study, cultivate educated and knowledgeable talents, and to change the impoverished life through knowledge and scientific approaches. At the same time, children should be encouraged to become useful members of society and the country.

In 1983, Gabulong presided over a meeting to enlarge the village party branch. The village committee proposed to set up their own school, and then under the joint efforts, the village cadres chose the school site and the principal. They raised funds from the whole village and visited every household to persuade them send their children to school.

A few months later, a tent school with three tents, three teachers, and seven students was completed. Vice Governor Gabulong served as the honorary principal of the school. After a few months, the number of students increased to twenty-four. The oldest was sixteen years old, and the youngest was seven years old. A year later, Lafudan served as the honorary principal.

On Children's Day in 1984, the village hired a bus from Huangyuan and brought more than fifty people, including students, village officials, and preschool children, to the provincial capital of Xining. Besides the two rooms reserved at the guest house of the Provincial Animal Husbandry Department for everyone to make beds on the floor, the remaining thirty people were all crowded into the house of Vice Governor Gabulong, which was also housing herdsman who had come to the city for doctor visits. As a result, the house was in chaos.

However, Gabulong was happy. The village where he stayed had opened a school, and the children had a place to learn. The pure and innocent children finally left their homes and came to the city, seeing the world, which made him very gratified and indescribably happy.

At night, Gabulong's house was crammed full of people. Six children slept in his bed, and he himself slept in his neighbor Bu Wei's house.

During the three days in Xining, the children visited the airport, railway station,

但是，尕布龙高兴啊，自己蹲点的村子办起了学校，孩子们有了读书的地方。纯洁、天真的孩子们终于走出自己的家门，来到了城市，见了世面，他的心里乐滋滋的，别提有多开心了。

到了晚上，尕布龙的家里挤满了人。他的床上睡了6个孩子，他自己则睡在了邻居布伟家。

在西宁玩了3天，孩子们参观了飞机场、火车站，去了人民公园、儿童公园和百货商场。

孩子们兴奋得晚上睡不着觉，白天不觉得累。

3天后，孩子们回去了，村里报名上学的孩子又增加了几名。

而尕布龙的家里，很长时间都留存着孩子们的欢笑声。

数年后，过去只有一个小学文化程度干部的哈乙亥村，有了大学本科生32人、留学生5人、博士生1人、国家干部26人。

那几年，尕布龙隔三岔五来到哈乙亥村，每次来了，他都会不厌其烦地教导村里的干部："致富的基础是扶贫，扶贫的目的是缩小差距，促进公平。缩小了教育的差距后，接下来，你们的任务就是要缩小生活的差距了。"

村子里有了阅览室

The library in the village

People's Park, Children's Park, and a department store.

The children were so excited that they couldn't sleep at night and didn't feel tired during the day.

Three days later, the children returned home, and the number of children in the village who enrolled in school increased.

And in Gabulong's house, the laughter of the children lingered for a long time.

Years later, Ha Yihai village, which used to have only one official with primary school education, cultivated thirty-two undergraduate students, five international students, one doctoral student, and twenty-six state cadres.

In those years, Gabulong visited Ha Yihai Village frequently, and every time he came, he would tirelessly tell the village cadres, "The foundation of getting rich is to alleviate poverty, and the purpose of poverty alleviation is to narrow the gap and promote fairness. Now the gap in education has been narrowed, so your next task is to narrow the gap in life."

Gabulong did not say this casually. He bought sixty sheep with his salary, thirty-five of them were distributed to the low-income household Kaxiujia, and twenty-five were distributed to the household living below the poverty line, Danzeng. Gabulong not only supervised and encouraged Kaxiujia to pasture the sheep well, but also sent him to the county to learn the techniques of repairing cars, loaders, and excavators, which quickly improved the life of Kaxiujia's family.

More importantly, Gabulong opened the minds of cadres and herdsmen in Ha Yihai Village. They realized their natural conditions, living environment, and favorable factors that they could make use of. Apart from that, he also helped people in Ha Yihai Village become aware of the importance of knowledge, broadening their horizons, and understanding science and ecological protection.

At that time, Gabulong had already realized the reality of overloaded grazing on the grassland and the rapid deterioration of the ecology. Ha Yihai Village was one of the most prominent pastoral villages in the Qinghai Lake Basin where a clash between human life, livestock, and the grassland existed. He knew the best that a grassland full of wild flowers was a sign of grassland degradation. He began to guide the people of Ha Yihai Village to reinforce the improvement of livestock species, plant oats in the deserted beach, promote artificial grass planting in order to provide forage for cattle and sheep, and

尕布龙这话，可不是随便说的。他用自己的工资买了60只羊，35只分给了低保户卡秀加，25只给了贫困户旦增。不但监督和鼓励卡秀加放好这些羊，还送卡秀加到县上学习维修汽车、装载机、挖掘机的技术，很快使卡秀加家的生活得到了很大改善。

更重要的是，尕布龙改变了哈乙亥村干部和牧民群众的观念。让哈乙亥村的农牧民认识到自己生存的自然条件、生活环境和可以利用的有利因素。不仅如此，他还让哈乙亥村的人懂得了知识的重要性，开阔了眼界，理解了什么是科学、什么是生态保护。

那时，尕布龙早已经意识到草原上超载放牧、生态急剧恶化的现实，而哈乙亥村，便是环青海湖流域人畜草畜矛盾最为突出的牧业村之一。他最清楚，野花烂漫的草场是草原退化的标志，他开始引导哈乙亥村的人加大畜种改良力度，在荒滩种植燕麦、推广人工种草，为牛羊提供草料，减轻冬季草场压力。他让拉夫旦组织村民大力实施划区轮牧，回填草皮，对已沙化的草场实行禁牧，加强草原基础设施建设，使草原得以休养生息。

环青海湖流域的倒淌河地区，纳滩有草场3万多亩，其中哈乙亥村拥有2万多亩。过去，这片草原上的牲畜瘦弱，因为严重的肝吸虫病死亡率很高，尕布龙就请来专家，对纳滩草滩采取封闭围栏措施，实施夏秋季禁牧，冬季轮牧，趋利避害，使草滩恢复生机。

几年后，哈乙亥村人的生活终于有了起色，牛羊发展到了2万多只。

青海有大片不可多得的良好牧场，发展畜牧经济，发展养殖业，发展生态农业，前景广阔。尕布龙从小在草原上长大，是牧民的儿子，他熟悉青海的每一片草场，也知道如何发展牧区的生产。青海的土种羊大多是藏系羊，藏系羊最大能长到40多斤，产毛量也低，只有2斤左右，且夹杂着许多干细毛，不容易上色。

尕布龙担任畜牧局局长后，他首先考虑到的就是绵羊的改良问题。他想办法从我国新疆，澳大利亚引进细毛羊，把青海的本土藏系羊成功地改良成了毛肉兼用的半细毛羊，并在全省范围内推广，进而研发深加工产品，为青海的轻工业建设做出了贡献。改良后的半细毛羊不仅个头大，肉质鲜美，体重增加到了50斤左右、产毛量提高到了5斤左右，绵羊的改良还让原本就具有一定弹性、密度，适合编织地毯的藏系羊毛，变得更加鲜亮、容易上色，改良的藏系羊被世界公认为地毯最佳原料的新品种。

reduce the pressure on the pasture in winter. He asked Lafudan to organize villagers to implement zoning rotational grazing, backfill turf, ban grazing on desertified pastures, and strengthen infrastructure construction on the grassland, which could enable the grassland to recuperate.

In the Daotang River area of the Qinghai Lake basin, Natan had more than 30,000 mu (2,000 hectares) of grassland, of which Ha Yihai Village had more than 20,000 mu (1,333.33 hectares). In the past, the livestock on this grassland were thin and weak because of the high mortality rate from severe liver fluke disease. Gabulong invited experts to adopt closed fence measures on the Natan grassland, implementing grazing prohibition in summer and autumn, and allowing rotational grazing in winter. These measures successfully revitalized the grassland.

A few years later, the lives of Ha Yixuan villagers finally improved, and the number of cattle and sheep had grown more than 20,000.

Qinghai has a large area of rare and good pastures, so the development of animal husbandry economy, breeding industry, and ecological agriculture has broad prospects. As Gabulong was the son of a herdsman and grew up on the grasslands, he was familiar with every pasture in Qinghai and also knew how to develop production in pastoral areas. Most of the native sheep in Qinghai were Tibetan sheep which could grow up to more than twenty kilograms with low wool yield , only about one kilogram each. The wool were mixed with many dry and fine hairs which were difficult to dye.

After Gabulong became the director of the Animal Husbandry Bureau, the first thing he considered was the improvement of sheep. He tried to introduce fine-wool sheep from Xinjiang in China and Australia, and successfully improved the native Tibetan sheep into semi-fine-wool sheep so that both wool and meat could be utilized. The sheep were promoted throughout the province, and deep processing products were developed, which made a great contribution to the light industry in Qinghai.

The improved semi-fine wool sheep were not only large in size, but also made for delicious in meat. Their weight increased to about twenty-five kilograms, and wool production increased to about two and a half kilograms. In addition, the Tibetan wool which originally had a certain elasticity and density that was suitable for weaving carpets become brighter and easier to color. After joint efforts, the Tibetan wool was recognized as a new type of raw material that was best for carpets in the world.

改良初期，由于人们认识不到新品种的优势，没有人愿意带头。尕布龙只好把 30 只远道而来的种公羊，送到家乡永丰村，让大哥才布腾试验。

才布腾是村子里的劳动模范，干活踏实，坚决支持弟弟的工作，像照顾自己的孩子一样伺候起了这 30 只负有特殊使命的羊。

每天清晨，才布腾一睁开眼睛，就先到羊圈里放出那 30 只种公羊，赶着它们在草原上撒欢，增强它们的体质，提高配种能力。吃饭的时候，他都要给每只羊喂两个自己都不舍得吃的鸡蛋，隔日在草料里拌上盐巴让它们吃。重要的是，还把过去秋配冬产的老传统，改成了现在的冬配春产，让小羊羔在春天逐渐温暖的季节长大，提高了成活率。

两年多后，改良后的青海半细毛羊数量增加到 200 多只，永丰村成了草原上第一个育有新品种半细毛羊的"配种站"，并源源不断地向周边牧区输送。又过了几年，哈勒景草原上白云般浮动的一群群羊，全都是改良

尕布龙带着畜牧局的干部职工到草原上考察改良后的半细毛羊

Gabulong took the cadres and staff of the Animal Husbandry Bureau to the grassland to

inspect the improved semi-fine-wool sheep

In the early stages of improvement, no one was willing to take the lead because people did not recognize the advantages of the new variety. Gabulong had to send the thirty breeding rams from afar to his hometown of Yongfeng Village so that his older brother, Caibuteng, could experiment first.

Caibuteng was a model worker in the village. He worked hard and firmly supported his brother's work. He began to take care of these thirty sheep with a special mission like his own children.

Every morning, as soon as Caibuteng opened his eyes, he first released the thirty breeding rams from the sheepfold and drove them to run around on the grassland to enhance their physical fitness and improve their breeding capacity. During meals, he would feed each sheep two eggs that he begrudged to eat and mixed forage with salt for them to eat the next day. More importantly, he changed the old tradition of breeding in autumn and bearing in winter to breeding in winter and bearing in spring, allowing the lambs to grow up in the warmer spring season, which increased the survival rate.

More than two years later, the improved Qinghai semi-fine-wool sheep expanded to more than 200, and Yongfeng Village became the first "breeding station" on the grassland, continuously transporting the sheep to the surrounding pastoral areas. After a few more years, the flocks of sheep floating like white clouds on the Halejing grassland were the all the improved new breed of semi-fine wool sheep. Later, more pastoral areas became breeding stations for the promotion and delivery of semi-fine-wool sheep to pastoral areas across the province, such as Tianjun County in Haixi Prefecture, Qilian County in Haibei Prefecture, and Gonghe County in Hainan Prefecture.The meat processing and textile industries of semi-fine wool had gradually emerged in Qinghai.

Ha Yihai Village was where Gabulong worked to help with poverty alleviation, and it naturally become a new base for semi-fine-wool sheep production. He instructed the cadres in the village to focus on the main industry of animal husbandry economy and carry out a wide variety of food processing around yaks and semi-fine wool sheep, so that the economic income of Ha Yihai village began to take the lead.

Li Zhigang, then the director of the Qinghai Provincial Light Textile Department, gave great support and help in the process of promoting and developing wool products. During that period, the wool textile factory in Qinghai, using the high-quality wool of semi-fine-wool sheep, produced a series of woolen products like gabardine, serge,

后的新品种半细毛羊。再往后，海西州的天峻县、海北州的祁连县、海南州的共和县等牧区都成了向全省牧区推广和输送半细毛羊的配种基地，与半细毛羊研发相关的肉类加工和毛纺织业在青海逐渐兴起。

哈乙亥村是尕布龙蹲点扶持的乡村，这里也自然成为半细毛羊生产的新基地。他指导村里的干部抓住畜牧经济这个主业，围绕牦牛肉和半细毛羊开展了各类食品的加工，使哈乙亥村的经济收入走在了前列。

在推广和发展羊毛产品的过程中，时任青海省轻纺厅厅长的李志刚给予了很大的支持和帮助。也就是在那段时期，青海的毛纺织厂利用半细毛羊的优质毛，在短时期内生产出了当时曾经轰动全国、远销国内外市场的毛华达、毛哔叽，双虎牌毛毯、毛线等毛纺织品，带动和发展了青海的轻工业生产。

但多年后，青海牧区又渐渐恢复了放养藏细羊的习惯，半细毛羊品种越来越少。原因是，改良后的半细毛羊，虽然非常适应青海高原的气候，肉和羊毛兼用。但因为半细毛羊这个品种性格较为孤僻，喜欢独行或者三五只在一起，放养起来使牧民感到有压力、有风险，大多牧民在疏于督促的情况下又渐渐放弃了。而同时，青海各地的毛纺织工业，因产品陈旧，纷纷破产、夭折。但是，在当时，由尕布龙提出建议，主张改良的半细毛羊，的确为青海的畜产品开发、轻工业生产指明了方向，它的开发和利用价值，至今仍然值得深入思考研究。

74岁的拉夫旦身体还那么结实，像一头壮牦牛。他是在尕布龙亲自培养下，在青海牧区成长起来的第一个个体户、第一个董事长，第一个走向市场的人，也是最了解尕布龙的人。

说起哈乙亥村的发展，说起自己的事业，拉夫旦很激动。但是，我让他谈谈他跟尕布龙私人之间的友情，他却不想说太多的话。听尕布龙的孙女达什姐莉说过，尕布龙和拉夫旦很谈得来，他是尕布龙生前十分要好的朋友。

拉夫旦亲自给我拌了一碗酥油糌粑，看着我吃。他说："尕布龙省长是我的恩人，也是我们哈乙亥村的大恩人。自从他来到我们这个贫困村，村子里的生活渐渐好了，日子过得越来越红火。"尕布龙对哈乙亥村感情也很深，他没有过多的时间关心家人，对亲人、身边的工作人员要求严格，从来不搞特殊，甚至连一般的照顾都谈不上。可是，对哈乙亥村的人却关

blankets, and yarn in a short time, which were sold to both domestic and foreign markets and became a sensation in China. Consequently, Qinghai's light industry was encouraged and developed quickly.

Unfortunately, many years later, the Qinghai pastoral area gradually resumed the tradition of stocking Tibetan fine sheep, and there were fewer and fewer semi-fine wool sheep. The reason was that the improved semi-fine-wool sheep were very adaptable to the climate of the Qinghai Plateau, and both of their meat and wool could be utilized, but they were relatively withdrawn and liked to walk alone or in groups of three to five, which gave the herdsmen a lot of pressure and risks to herd. As a result, many herdsmen gradually gave up with loose supervision. At the same time, the wool textile industries all over Qinghai went bankrupt and died due to obsolete products. However, at that time, Gabulong's proposition of the improvement of semi-fine-wool sheep indeed pointed out the direction for Qinghai's livestock product development and light industry production. Its development and value is still worthy of consideration today.

At 74 years old, Lafudan is still as strong as a bull. Under the personal training of Gabulong, he was the first self-employed person, the first chairman, and the first person to go to the market in the Qinghai pastoral area. He is also the person who knew Gabulong best.

Speaking of the development of Ha Yihai Village and his own career, Lafudan was very excited. However, when I asked him to talk about the personal friendship between him and Gabulong, he didn't want to say too much. I heard from Gabulong's granddaughter, Dashijieli, that Gabulong and Lafudan had talked a lot and they were very good friends during his lifetime.

Lafudan made me a bowl of tsamba (a traditional Tibetan food) himself and watched me eat it. He said, "Gabulong is my benefactor and the great benefactor of our Ha Yihai Village. Since he came to our poor village, life in the village has gradually improved, and our lives have become more prosperous." Gabulong also had a deep affection for Ha Yihai Village. He did not have much time to care about his family, and he was very strict with his relatives and the staff around him. He never gave them privileges or even general care. However, he was very concerned about the people in Ha Yihai Village, not only in the development of production and the formulation of measures, but also to provide specific guidance and help to solve practical difficulties. Moreover, every Children's

怀备至，不仅在发展生产、制定措施方面具体指导帮助，解决实际困难。每逢儿童节、教师节、春节和元旦，他都要亲自来村里，给老师和学生送来用自己的工资买的糖果、米、面和学习用品。多年来，从未间断，直到他重病在身，再也不能下乡。每一次来，他都不厌其烦地教诲村里的干部，不断对他们提出更高的要求。他说，日子好过了，人口增加了，就会出现草畜、人畜的矛盾。今后，要以抓牧业经济为本，利用科学技术，加强基础设施的建设。即使今后，牧业生产发展了，也不能无节制地加大对资源的开发，要保护生态，科学养畜，发展生态经济。

这么多年了，拉夫旦和他领导的村民认认真真地履行尕布龙的谆谆教诲，在发展生态畜牧、科学养畜的道路上越走越远，越走越宽，逐步实现了规模化、产业化、市场化，做到了"人人有事做，事事有人做"。

在一起时间长了，尕布龙和拉夫旦像亲兄弟一样。有一年，拉夫旦的腰受了伤，得了和尕布龙的妻子一样的病——腰椎结核。尕布龙亲自派人把拉夫旦接到青海大学附属医院，找名医、拍片子、抓中药，从外地医院买药吃。因为治疗及时，拉夫旦的腰病痊愈了，还能干重活。

拉夫旦一边说，一边伸了伸胳膊，活动了一下腰。

我定定地望着他，心里想，他怎么这么有福气。当年，尕布龙的妻子华毛的腰受伤后，没有现在的医疗条件，尕布龙又远在河南县工作，没有照顾好妻子，让妻子在炕上躺了半辈子，让自己孤单寂寞了一辈子，想到这里，我的心里有了一丝淡淡的惆怅……

尕布龙是一个心胸宽广的人，他容得下千山万壑，忍得下千般万般的苦，他的心里又是怎样想的呢？我不得而知。可他健硕的体内，难道就没有丝毫儿女情长，没有对爱的渴望？

工作中，他的思路更广，从不因循守旧。

和拉夫旦一起去西宁的路上，路过日月山时，尕布龙对拉夫旦说："日月山是汉藏友好的象征，见证着1300多年前的文化历史，年轻美貌的大唐文成公主远嫁吐蕃，从此经过。咱村子就在日月山附近，应该发展具有民族特色，突出传统文化的旅游经济。"为此，他建议旅游部门，在日月山修建了日月亭。

聪明机智的拉夫旦，马上领会了尕布龙的意思，在村子里修建了唐蕃和韵如意塔、文成公主观海亭，让翻越日月山的人，可远观美丽的青海湖，

Day, Teacher's Day, Spring Festival, and New Year's Day, he would personally visit Hai Yihai to bring the teachers and students sweets, rice, noodles, and school supplies bought with his own salary. There was no interruption over the years until he became seriously ill and could no longer go to the countryside. Every time he came, he would tirelessly teach the cadres in the village and put forward higher requirements for them. He said that when life became better and the population increased, there would be conflicts between the grasslands and livestock, and humans and livestock. In the future, we must focus on the animal husbandry economy and strengthen infrastructure construction with science and technology. Even if animal husbandry production develops in the future, we cannot uncontrollably exploit resources. Instead, we must protect the ecology, raise livestock scientifically, and develop the ecological economy.

For so many years, Lafudan and the villagers under his leadership have conscientiously carried out the instruction of Gabulong and have gone further and broader on the road of developing ecological animal husbandry and scientific livestock breeding. They have gradually achieved large-scale market industrialization and realized "Everyone has something to do, and everything has someone to do".

Gabulong and Lafudan were like brothers after working together for a long time. One year, Lafudan's waist was injured, and he suffered from the same disease as Gabulong's wife — lumbar vertebral tuberculosis. Gabulong sent someone to take Lafudan to the Qinghai University Affiliated Hospital, to find a famous doctor, get X-rays, and buy Chinese medicine, as well as medicine from a hospital outside the city. Because of the timely treatment, Lafudan's waist disease was cured, and he was able to do heavy work .

Lafudan talked about the past while he stretched out his arms and moved his waist.

I looked at him fixedly and thought to myself, how could he be so lucky? In those years, after Gabulong's wife Hua Mao's waist was injured, current medical services were not available. Gabulong worked far away in Henan County and did not take care of her. He let his wife lie on a bed for half of her life, leaving him lonely for a lifetime. Thinking of this, a faint sense of melancholy arose in my heart.

Gabulong was a broad-minded person who could endure all kinds of hardships throughout the mountains and valleys of his life. I don't know what was in his heart. But in his strong body, was there no desire for love?

At In his work, he had broader ideas and never followed the old ways.

感受到汉藏融合中那悠远绵长、博大精深的民族文化。

拉夫旦感慨地说："尕省长没有来哈乙亥村之前，村子里每个人的月均收入只有105元，现在已经到了每月9000元。村子里有了钱，首先给贫困户修建住房，接着又给富裕户修建，如今75%的人都住上了新房。修房的费用，每户只拿出4400元，其余由村子里支出，这在以前真是想都

尕布龙一家和拉夫旦

The Gabulong family and Lafudan

杨杰带笔者去拉夫旦家采访

Yang Jie took the author to Lafudan's house for an interview

Once on the way to Xining with Lafudan, when they were passing Riyue Mountain, Gabulong said to Lafudan, "Riyue Mountain is a symbol of Han-Tibetan friendship, having witnessed more than 1,300 years of cultural history, from the time when the young and beautiful Princess Wencheng of the Tang Dynasty married Tubo up until the present day. Since our village is near Riyue Mountain, tourism with ethnic characteristics and traditional culture should be developed." For this reason, he proposed to the tourism department to build a the Riyue Pavilion at Riyue Mountain.

The clever and resourceful Lafudan immediately understood Gabulong's meaning and built the Ruyi Pagoda of Tang and Tibetan Harmony and the Princess Wencheng Lakeview Pavilion in the village. This allowed people crossing Riyue Mountain to view the beautiful Qinghai Lake from a distance and experience the long and profound culture resulting from the integration of Han and Tibetan ethnicities.

Lafunda said with emotion, "Before the governor came to Ha Yihai Village, the average monthly income was only 105 yuan, but now it has reached 9,000 yuan. Since the village started becoming prosperous, they prioritized building housing for poor households and then for the wealthy. Currently, 75% of the villagers live in new houses. In terms of cost, each household only spent 4,400 yuan, with the rest subsidized by the village, which was truly unthinkable in the past."

Back then, Lafudan, pulling a handcart, was a salesman in a supply and marketing agency. He would be very happy if he could earn three yuan a day. But now, he is a national model worker and chairman who owns many companies and factories.

In December 1986, Lafudan participated in the First National Congress of Self-employed Workers and was elected as the executive director; in the second session, he was elected as the vice president.

Three years ago, Lafudan, who had served as the village party secretary for thirty-seven years, retired and handed over the company he founded to his eldest daughter. Lafudan is a successful entrepreneur on the grasslands of Qinghai, and every step he has taken in his growth is inseparable from the hard work of Gabulong.

The accountants and school principals in the village are not as fluent in Chinese as Lafudan, but they are very sincere, and they also hold deep gratitude for Gabulong in their hearts.

Actually, the poverty-stricken villages and families that Gabulong had supported in

不敢想的事。"

当年，拉夫旦拉着架子车给供销社当代销员，一天能挣上 3 元钱都高兴得合不拢嘴。现在，他已经是拥有多家公司、工厂的全国劳模、董事长。

1986 年 12 月，拉夫旦参加了全国第一届个体劳动者第一次代表大会，当选为常务理事；第二届又当选为副会长。

3 年前，担任了 37 年村支书的拉夫旦退休了，把一手创办起来的公司也交给了大女儿。拉夫旦是青海草原上成功的企业家，他成长道路上走过的每一步，都离不开尕布龙的心血。

村子里的会计、学校校长，汉语说得不如拉夫旦流利。但是，他们很朴实，内心里同样深藏着对尕布龙的一片感激之情。

其实，尕布龙一生中，扶持过的贫困村、贫困户又何止哈乙亥一个村、拉夫旦一个人。在青海 72 万平方公里的很多地方、村落，都留下过尕布龙风尘仆仆、不辞辛劳的身影。他到过无数个村庄、无数个牧业点。每到一个地方，牵挂的都是老百姓的生活、老百姓的冷暖。他这一辈子，心里装的全都是老百姓的疾苦、老百姓的安危，这成了他这一生不变的工作作风。这样的人，难道不值得我们敬重、学习，不值得我们赞美、称颂吗？

在他担任省人大常委会副主任期间，海东市民和县的满坪乡被确定为省人大常委会的定点扶贫对象，他便主动分管了此项工作，经常到那里检查指导。每次去，他都不去乡上，而是直接去村里。他总在半路上下车，然后绕道步行，并叮咛驾驶员崔生满在他身后行驶，不得在他到达之前先到。他不摆领导的架子和派头，身边不允许有前拥后簇的陪同人员，完全像一个走亲戚的老农一样轻轻走进一户户贫穷的院落，静静坐在每一张散发着麦草气息的土炕上，向那些温饱无着的乡亲们嘘寒问暖。每一次攀谈，他的心里都会涌起一股温暖的热浪；每一碗捧在他手心里滚烫的热茶，都会让他内心怀有羞愧和酸楚。他感动的是老百姓的宽厚和善良，愧对的是老百姓对党和政府的信任。

那年，走进满坪乡河口村一扇低矮的柴门时，尕布龙的心被刺痛了。当他进到屋内，握住陈老汉那双如干柴般皲裂的大手时，眼前的一切使他泪如泉涌。只见老人家的屋内空空荡荡，一贫如洗，土炕上的毛毡七零八落，卷在墙根儿的那堆破被子，已经旧得辨不清是什么物件。尕布龙在屋子里站了很久、很久，悲悯之情在他的心中翻腾。

his life were not limited to just one village, Ha Yihai, and one family, Lafudan. Gabulong tirelessly traveled and worked hard in many places and villages across Qinghai, covering an area of 720,000 square kilometers. He visited countless villages and pastoral sites, always prioritizing the well-being and happiness of the people. Throughout his entire life, his heart was dedicated to the safety and welfare of the people, reflecting his unwavering work ethic and unique personal charisma. Such a person is truly worthy of our respect and admiration, as well as our praise and commendation.

During his tenure as deputy director of the Standing Committee of the Provincial People's Congress, Manping Township in Minhe County, Haidong City, was identified as the poverty alleviation target by the Standing Committee of the Provincial People's Congress. Gabulong took the initiative to lead this effort and frequently visited for inspection and guidance. Every time he went, he did not go to the town, but went directly to the village. He always got out of the car halfway, walked a detour, and instructed the driver, Cui Shengman, to drive behind him without arriving before him. He did not want to put on official airs, and he did not want escorts around him. He was like an old farmer visiting relatives as he entered the impoverished courtyards, sitting quietly on brick beds amidst the scent of straw, engaging in conversations with the villagers who were struggling to meet their basic needs. Every exchange stirred warmth in his heart, and each cup of hot tea in his hands held a tinge of guilt and sorrow. What touched him the most was the generosity and kindness of the people, while he felt ashamed of the people's unwavering trust in the party and government.

That year, Gabulong felt a sharp pain in his heart as he entered a low wooden gate in Hekou village, Manping township. The sight of the house brought tears to his eyes as he grasped the hands of the owner, an old man named Chen, whose hands were as wrinkled as dry wood. The house was basically empty and impoverished. The felt on the brick bed was threadbare, and a pile of quilts were rolled up against the wall, too warn to discern their original state. Gabulong stood in the house for a long time, the feeling of compassion constricting his chest and stirring in his heart.

After so many years of liberation, how did the farmers live like this? While talking to himself, he walked out of the simple courtyard in tears. He couldn't bear to witness this situation.

Back in Xining, he lay in bed, unable to fall asleep. As soon as he closed his eyes, the

这么多年了，农民的日子怎么会过成这样？他一边自言自语，一边流着泪走出了那个简陋的院落，他不忍目睹此情此景。

回到西宁，他躺在床上，怎么也睡不着。一闭上眼睛，陈老汉家土炕上那一堆破烂的被子就像一块石头压在他的心上。

第二天一大早，他就把何巴拉了起来。他说："你把家里新一点的那6床被子全装到小崔的车上，我今天要去满坪乡看望那个老人。"

昨晚听说了那老人的事，何巴的心里也很不好受，尤其看到尕布龙连吃晚饭的心思都没了时，更加心神不安。

但他还是没忍住："你把家里新一点的被子全拿走，家里来的这些人盖什么？"

尕布龙看了他一眼，斩钉截铁地说："先凑合几天，我们的困难总会比那老人的好解决得多。"

说着话，立即装好被褥，又拉了一些别的生活用品向满坪乡驶去。

这样的事做得多了，每当有人询问他为什么要这样时，他总是说："没有那么多为什么！我们口口声声说自己是人民的公仆，这么点事都不愿意做，还算得上是共产党员吗？"

有人说，尕布龙倾毕生心血为百姓操劳，什么也不图；也有人说，也许就图个好名声吧——可是，有了这样的好名声又能如何呢？

他自己是这样说的："我从没想过做一点点小事就图个啥。如果一个人，每做一件事都想着要图个啥，那他还会有心思静下来认认真真地做事吗？我只是凭着天地良心生活和工作而已，这难道不应该吗？还需要解释吗？"

尕布龙在哈乙亥村蹲点5年，目睹了农牧民在生活和观念上发生的巨大变化，他为此心满意足。尕布龙的80岁生日是在哈乙亥村过的。从来不接受礼物的尕布龙，穿上了拉夫旦为他定做的一件蒙古族寿服。

那是一个值得怀念的日子，也是尕布龙感到非常幸福的日子。不为别的，只因为他多年的辛勤操劳，他对群众的拳拳之心，在曾经贫瘠荒凉的土地上、干涸的田野里，开出了一朵又一朵鲜艳美丽的花朵。

image of the pile of tattered quilts on Chen's brick bed weighed heavily on his heart.

Early the next morning, he woke up Heba and said, "Take all six relatively new quilts from our home and load them onto Cui's car. Today I am going to Manping township to visit that old man."

When he heard about the old man the night before, Heba was also very uncomfortable, especially when he saw that Gabulong had no intention of having dinner.

Even so, he couldn't help but ask, "If you give away all of the new quilts, what will be left for the people living here?"

Gabulong gave him a look and said firmly, "Let's manage with what we have for a few days. Our difficulties will always be much easier to solve than the old man's."

After saying this, he immediately loaded the car with bedding and other daily necessities and drove to Manping township.

He did many things like this. When people asked him the reason, he always said, "There aren't so many 'whys'! We keep saying that we are public servants of the people. If we are reluctant to do such things, how could we be regarded as Communist Party members?"

Some people said that Gabulong had worked hard for the people all his life, and he did not want anything for himself. Others said that maybe he just wanted a good reputation. However, what could a good reputation bring him?

He himself said, "I never thought about doing something to gain something in return. If a person acts with ulterior motives, how can they sincerely dedicate themselves to their work? I simply live and work according to my conscience. Shouldn't that be enough? Do I still need to explain?"

Gabulong stayed in Ha Yihai Village for five years and witnessed the tremendous changes in the lives and ways of thinking of farmers and herdsmen, which greatly satisfied him. Gabulong celebrated his 80th birthday in Ha Yihai Village. He had never accepted gifts before, but this time he wore a Mongolian birthday suit customized for him by Lafudan.

It was a memorable and joyous day for Gabulong, because after years of hard work and sincerity for the people, flowers now bloomed everywhere in the once barren and desolate land and in the dry fields.

风雪中的挚爱

　　深秋，高寒地带的玉树草原风景如画。牧民们有赶着牛羊从夏秋草场往冬春草场搬迁的，有已经搬进冬窝子安顿好了的，还有依然在夏秋草场上悠闲放牧准备动身的。

　　1985 年 10 月 16 日凌晨，大雪突然降临，飘了三天三夜，丝毫没有停下来的意思。一切和昨日不一样了，早上起来的牧人，突然就找不到羊圈里的羊了，仔细看时，才发现羊全部被大雪覆盖，活着的，只剩下两个出

1985 年尕布龙带领工作组赴玉树曲麻莱开展抗雪救灾工作

In 1985, Ga Bulong led a working group to Qumarlêb County, Yushu, to combat the snow disaster.

Love in the Snowstorm

It's late autumn, and Yushu Grassland, nestled in the alpine, is adorned with picturesque scenery. Herdsmen are busy driving their cattle and sheep from summer and autumn pastures to winter and spring ones. Some have already relocated to their "winter nests" and settled down, while others are still leisurely grazing on the summer and autumn pastures and are preparing to depart.

In the early morning of October 16, 1985, a heavy snow began and continued for three days and three nights with no sign of stopping, blanketing the entire county. Everything changed overnight. When the shepherds arose in the morning, they found nothing but snow as far as the eye could see. Looking carefully, they discovered that all the sheep were buried under the heavy snow. Those still alive were barely breathing.

The sky way gloomy and gray, and snowflakes fell silently, but with such force that one could hardly breathe. The four townships of Qumahe, Maduo, Yage and Qiuzhi in the northwest were seriously affected----blanketed by up to 3-4 meters of snowfall, with temperatures plummeting to minus 37-40 degrees Celsius. Herdsmen lacked the food and fuel necessary to keep out the cold, and livestock died in large numbers from cold and hunger. All roads leading to the counties and villages were blocked. Lost cattle and sheep fell into the Tongtian River and drowned. Hungry animals even began to eat herdsmen's tents to appease their hunger. Little birds, stubborn Tibetan antelopes, wild donkeys, wild yaks, and other animals wandered along the highway in search of food.

气的鼻孔微微翕动着。

天灰沉沉的，洋洋洒洒的雪片不声不响，然而又是那么有力地落在地上，逼得人透不过气。西北部的曲麻河、玛多、叶格、秋智四个乡灾情严重，局部地区积雪厚达三四米，气温降至零下 37～40 摄氏度。牧民群众缺乏食物和御寒的燃料，牲畜也因寒冷和饥饿大量死亡。通往县乡村的道路全部被封死，道路不通、信息不畅。迷失方向的牛羊，掉到通天河里全被淹死了；饥饿难耐的牛羊竟然开始啃食牧民的帐篷来充饥。无力的小鸟和倔强的藏羚羊、藏野驴、野牦牛等野生动物无法觅食，在公路沿线徘徊。处在寒冷、饥饿和死亡边缘的牧民们，深陷困境。

时任副省长的尕布龙，接受了省委省政府交付的重任，亲临一线，赶赴灾区，开始带领干部职工紧急组织人员、物资救灾。

这次抗雪救灾的任务与1975年尕布龙在果洛指挥抗雪救灾的情形完全不同。那年，省委省政府提出的是"抗灾保畜"，而这次，提出的是"抗灾救人"，可见这次雪灾的严重程度。

青海省畜牧局草原总站保护科的全体人员被调去参加抗雪救灾工作，科长星智担任尕布龙的生活秘书，一直跟随在他身边。

当时，指挥部完全可以设在格尔木，坐镇指挥。但尕布龙不同意，他坚决要求到一线去。尕布龙说："这次雪灾非比寻常，我们要尽快上去了解情况，一分一秒不得耽误。"没办法，大家只好跟着尕布龙，把指挥部设在了海拔4675米的五道梁。

五道梁被世人称为"生命禁区"。高海拔，含汞量较高的土壤，使此地空气不畅，极度缺氧，植被难以生长。一般人经过时，会有明显的高原反应，被认为是青藏线上最难经过的路段。

五道梁属曲麻莱县管辖，选择五道梁作为抗雪救灾总指挥部，仍然是尕布龙一贯的作风。他认为只有身临其境，离重灾区最近，才能更迅速更及时地解决牧民群众目前出现的问题，住在市区招待所，能睡得着觉、吃得下饭吗？

在青海湖自然保护处工作的星智是我的同事，他从湟源牧校毕业，刚参加工作时在青海省畜牧局，曾经跟随尕布龙赴果洛参加过抗雪救灾工作，他能够理解尕布龙的心情。

沿路，当尕布龙看到进藏的几位新兵冻得在大卡车上挤作一团，心里

Cold and hungry, the herdsmen were on the verge of death.

Gabulong, then vice governor, accepting the important mission assigned by the provincial party committee and government, rushed to the snow-stricken area and led all the cadres and workers in disaster relief efforts.

This anti-snow disaster relief mission differed significantly from the one Gabulong had led in Golog in 1975. That year, the provincial government tasked relief workers with "disaster resistance and livestock protection." However, this time, the objective was "disaster resistance and rescue," highlighting the severity of the snow disaster.

All the staff of the Grassland Protection Department of the Qinghai Animal Husbandry Bureau were transferred to take part in the snow relief work. The department head, Xing Zhi, served as Gabulong's life secretary and accompanied him at all times.

The headquarters could have been set in Golmud with Gabulong sitting and commanding. However, Gabulong disagreed and insisted on going to the frontline. He said, "This snowstorm is a rare occurrence. We need to get to the frontline as soon as possible to get a full picture of the situation. There's no time to waste." The staff had no choice but to follow his instructions and set up the headquarters at Wudaoliang, situated at an altitude of 4,675 meters.

Wudaoliang is known as the "Forbidden Zone of Life." Due to the high altitude and the high mercury content of the soil, the air is not freely breathable, extremely oxygen-deficient, and vegetation struggles to grow. When passing through, the average person will experience a noticeable reaction to the altitude. It is considered to be the most challenging section of the Qinghai-Xizang route.

Wudaoliang is under the jurisdiction of Qumalai. Setting up the headquarters for snow disaster relief in Wudaoliang was just Gabulong's way of doing things. He believed that only by being personally present and closest to the hardest-hit areas, they could they address the most urgent problems for the herdsmen. He knew that by staying in a urban hostel, he wouldn't be able to eat or sleep thinking about the people affected by the disaster.

Xing Zhi, my former colleague who now works in Qinghai Lake Nature Conservation Department, first served in the Animal Husbandry Bureau of Qinghai Province upon graduation from the Huangyuan Animal Husbandry School. He once accompanied Gabulong to Golog for for the snow disaster relief, so he could empathize

非常难受，把随身带的熟牛肉和饼干全都留给了战士。星智记得，那次他们还在途中遇到了青海省交通厅一位姓张的厅长，陕西人，能够背诵毛泽东选集四卷本。尕布龙为此赞叹良久，教育他们，要向张厅长学习。

风雪
Snowstorm

一路上，眼见茫茫大雪铺天盖地，牛头羊头睁着一双眼睛，直瞪瞪地望着天空，冻死的藏羚羊在楚玛尔河边直挺挺地站着，像冰雕一样。气温低到了人们难以想象的程度。那些把孩子装在褡裢里，想走出雪地的牧民，走了一会后，回头一看，发现孩子已经冻僵。

看到这一切，尕布龙心急如焚，眼睛里充着血，嘴上全是燎泡。

他抢过别人手里的铁锹，钻进雪地里和救援人员一道铲雪，疏通道路。可那时，铁锹无济于事，厚厚的积雪纹丝不动，他更急了。

按照省委省政府指示，一切工作围绕救人展开。指挥部人员一到位，尕布龙就立即组织突击队，调用推土机，抢修道路，抢运救灾物资。10月

with Gabulong's perspective.

When Gabulong saw several recruits entering Xizang huddled in a big truck due to the cold along the road, he felt very sad and left all the cooked beef and biscuits he had with him for the soldiers. Xing Zhi remembered that on the way, they also met the director of Qinghai Provincial Communications Department, surnamed Zhang, a Shaanxi native who could recite four volumes of the Selected Works of Mao Zedong. Gabulong admired him for a while and encouraged them to learn from Director Zhang.

Along the way, they were met with snowfall blanketing everything, cows and sheep staring at the sky, and frozen Tibetan antelope standing upright by by the Chumar River like ice sculptures. The temperature was unbelievably low. A herdsman put his child in the pouch on his back and tried to get out of the snow. After walking for a while, he looked back and found that the child had frozen stiff.

Seeing all this, Gabulong's heart was torn with anxiety. His eyes were bloodshot and his mouth was filled with blisters.

He grabbed a shovel from someone's hands and got into the snow with the rescue workers, attempting to clear the road. However, the shovel proved useless. The thick snow was as motionless as a statue, leaving him even more anxious.

According to the instructions of the provincial government, the priority for all the relief efforts should be saving people's lives. As soon as personnel from the headquarters arrived, Gabulong immediately developed plans to organize a commando team, deploy bulldozers, repair roads, and transport relief supplies. From October 23rd to 29th, the military coordinated planes and helicopters to air-drop coal and grain several times, alleviating the situation for ground rescue teams. Meanwhile, he organized working groups and medical teams to go from door-to-door to deal with frostbite and snow blindness in a timely manner. He also led the masses towards highways and the western part of the region to evacuate the snow disaster area as quickly as possible.

The snow continued falling for more than ten days. Gabulong ran along the Chumar River, with his mouth open, nose bleeding, and gasping for breath. The river was blanketed by snow, reflecting strong sunlight and experiencing severe ultraviolet radiation. He visited Ulan Moron, which was more than 5,000 meters about sea level, along with the other most severely affected areas to assess the situation, address difficulties, and personally determine the airdrop locations. Day after day, he caught a

23日至29日，协调军方集中空运，启动运输机和直升机多次空投煤块、粮食，缓解了地面救援的问题。同时，组织工作组、医疗队深入帐房，及时处理冻伤、雪盲，又带领群众向公路、向西大滩方向转移，尽快脱离雪灾重灾区。

大雪整整下了十几天，尕布龙张着嘴，流着鼻血，大口大口喘着气，

家园

Homeland

嘶哑着嗓子，奔跑在风雪弥漫、日光反射强烈、紫外线辐射严重的楚玛尔河畔和海拔5000多米的沱沱河，到灾情最严重的地方检查灾情、解决困难，亲自确定空投区域。连日下来，他患了感冒，糖尿病也加重了，夜里无法入睡。

有常识的人都知道，在高原生活，一场严重的感冒有可能夺去一个人的生命。可是，救灾正处在关键阶段，他还不能下山，他瞒着别人，随便吃了点药对付了一下。结果，感冒加重，呼吸极度困难，加重的肺心病差点要了他的命。就是这样，他还是不听劝阻，不肯下山。

他说："这个时候，我不能走，等群众都安全了，我再走！"

无奈，身边的人只好看着他一边输液、吸氧，一边指挥抗灾救灾工作。

那一年，尕布龙59岁。

身边的年轻人，被他深深感动，抢着用双手给他端着洗脸盆让他洗脸，端洗脚水给他烫脚。

cold, and his diabetes worsened. As a result, he could hardly sleep at night.

Anyone with common sense knows that on the plateau, a serious cold may take a person's life. However, the disaster relief was still at a critical stage, so he could not go down the mountain yet. He kept it a secret and took some medicine. As a result, the cold worsened. It was extremely difficult to breathe, and aggravated pulmonary heart disease almost killed him. Even so, he refused to go down the mountain.

He said, "I just can't leave at this critical moment. I'll go when all the people here are safe!" The people around him could do nothing but watch him direct the disaster relief work while being put on a drip and oxygenated.

That year, Gabulong was 59 years old.

The young people beside him were deeply moved by him and rushed to carry some water for him to wash his face and feet.

One herdsman even burned the poles of his tent and cooked him some mutton as there was a tremendous lack of firewood at that time. However, by the time it reached Gabulong, it had frozen solid. The gesture deeply touched Gabulong. Only then did he know that many shepherds had burned their tent poles, felt, and saddles. He immediately instructed the air force to prioritize dropping red willow branches to address the fuel shortage and prevent people from freezing to death.

In this way, Gabulong directed the deployment of relief work for fifteen days in Wudaoliang, which experiences cold temperatures year-round, often reaching close to minus 40 degrees Celsius.

These fifteen days of extraordinary hardship left a deep impression on Xing Zhi for the rest of his life, enabling him to fully understand the value of a person's life and the meaning of existence. He was deeply grateful to Gabulong, an outstanding cadre, from whom he witnessed undaunted spirit and loyalty to the people and the country.

Boasting a vast territory, China experiences a wide range of natural conditions, with disasters occurring frequently, often leading to serious consequences without timely relief efforts. In the face of the disaster, Gabulong never thought about his own gains and losses. His primary concerns were the safety of the herdsmen and how to minimize the losses caused by this irresistible disaster.

A'wang Jiancuo, who took part in the relief work together with Gabulong and served as the director of the Agricultural and Pastoral Bureau of Qumalai County,

当时，牧民们最缺的是柴火，有个牧民竟然把自己的帐房杆子烧了给他煮了一点羊肉。可是等送来时，已经冻成了冰疙瘩。尕布龙很感动，这才知道，很多牧人家里都已经把帐房杆、毡子和马鞍烧完了。他马上通知部队，让空军先空投红柳树枝，首先解决燃料问题，不至于把人冻死。

就这样，尕布龙在终年寒冷，气温接近零下40摄氏度的五道梁，指挥部署抗雪救灾工作15天。

这异常艰苦的15天，让星智终生难忘，也让他真正懂得了一个人生命的价值、存在的意义。他在内心深处深深地感激尕布龙这位优秀的领导干部，从他身上，他看到了一个人的大无畏精神和对人民、对国家赤胆忠心的高尚品格。

中国地域辽阔，各地自然条件相差悬殊，灾害发生频繁，如果不能及时救助，很可能会产生严重后果。在灾难面前，尕布龙从来没想过自己的得失，他只担心牧民群众的安危，只想着用怎样的方法来减轻这场无法抵挡的灾难带来的损失。

担任过曲麻莱县农牧局局长的阿旺尖错无法忘记和尕布龙一起参加抗雪救灾的经历，那是一次前所未有的雪灾，带来的破坏几乎是毁灭性的。如果不是青海省委省政府采取的措施得力，如果不是副省长尕布龙指挥有方，如果没有武警海西支队、广大救援队伍夜以继日地拼死努力，损失将无法估量。

还有一件让星智至今都无法释怀的事。

当时，很多乡村干部，骑着马到指挥部给尕布龙汇报灾情和救援情况，又立即返回乡里组织救援。他们来时脸冻得铁青，走时，马蹄子被冰碴子磨得血淋淋的，可那些乡村干部，在抗雪救灾取得胜利后，连姓名都没有留下来，而星智却无比荣耀地站在省政府的大院里戴上了大红花，接受了省委省政府的表彰。这是让星智至今想起来都觉得十分内疚的事。

星智知道，还有一件事、一个人重重地压在尕布龙心上，让他隐隐作痛。那个人，是玉树军分区的一位军官，抗雪救灾前线的英雄。

当时，指挥部接到消息，数百名牧民被大雪围困，生死未卜。

尕布龙要求那位军官带领救灾突击队的官兵搜寻营救。

军官有些犹豫："这么大的风雪，会不会迷路？"

尕布龙一听急了："那牧民群众的死活谁来管呢？"

would never forget that unprecedented, devastating snow disaster. Without the effective measures taken by the Qinghai Provincial Party Committee and the provincial government, without the competent leadership of Vice Governor Gabulong, and without the desperate efforts of the Haixi Detachment of the Armed Police Force and the vast rescue team, the vast number of rescue teams hard work day and night, the losses would have been incalculable.

There is another thing that Xing Zhi cannot forget.

At that time, many village cadres rode horses to the headquarters to report the disaster and rescue situation to Gabulong, and then immediately returned to the village to lead the rescue operation. When they came, their faces were nearly frozen, and when they left, their horses' hooves were bloodied by ice debris. However, those rural cadres, after the victory of the disaster relief, did not even leave their names, while Xing Zhi stood gloriously in the courtyard of the provincial government and was commended by the provincial leaders with a large red flower. Xing Zhi feels guilty just thinking about it.

Xing Zhi knew that there was another man who weighed heavily on Gabulong's heart, causing him a dull pain. The man was an officer in Yushu Military Division and a hero in the frontline of the disaster relief.

The headquarters received news that hundreds of herdsmen were besieged by heavy snow, and their lives were in jeopardy.

Gabulong then asked that officer to lead a disaster relief commando in the search and rescue efforts.

The officer hesitated and asked, "Will we get lost in such a big snowstorm?"

Hearing this, Gabulong was furious. "Then who's supposed to take care of the lives of the herdsmen?"

The officer did not say another word and led the commando to set off immediately. In a short time, he disappeared into the vast snow-blanketed field.

Unfortunately, the officer was unable to get out of the field alive.

At the moment of seeing the hero's body, Gabulong stood there, motionless. A few seconds later, tears gushed from his burning eyes. With a cry of agony, he fell to the snow.

It turned out that after receiving the rescue order, the officer and several soldiers

军官没再吭声，立刻带领部队出发，不一会儿便消失在茫茫雪野中。

但是，很遗憾，那位军官没能活着走出那片雪野。

见到英雄遗体的一刹那，尕布龙呆立在那里。几秒钟之后，从他那双熬得通红的眼睛里喷出了眼泪，他撕心裂肺地呼唤着，倒在雪地上。

原来，接到营救的命令，那名军官就带着几名战士乘车扑向了雪野。

天空中秃鹫盘旋。这来自上天的使者，灵敏地叼啄着堆成小山般的羊的尸体。洁净的雪原一片狼藉，小羊温柔的双眸悲哀地望着苍天。

车身下积雪深厚，兵车犁过坚脆的冰层。

最后一户牧民家里，除了六张黝黑惊恐的面孔外，可烧可吃的东西荡然无存。晨光中的雪地放射出夺目的金针，战士的脸被灼伤，军官的眼睛辨不清方向，可这户牧民家里最小的儿子不堪饥寒，于夜里出门后至今未归。

为了找到这位藏族少年，军官带着两名战士驾车返回30里外的公路。等车回来时，只能看见站着的藏族少年，而军官已躺在战士怀里。是十几米高的冰槽，好似迷宫，让双眼一直流泪的军官栽在大雪坑里，等两位战士费尽气力把他拖上来时，军官的身体已经僵硬。

尕布龙赶到格尔木，茫然地目送军官，办完了后事，安慰着军官的家人。心里的疼痛、悔意，缺氧造成的心肺功能衰竭，让尕布龙本来患有糖尿病、肺心病的身体更加受损。从此以后，这个身强力壮、性格倔强的蒙古族汉子，落下了一身无法治愈的病痛，这困扰着他晚年的生活，给他带来了莫大痛苦。到了病重时，连他深深爱恋着的家乡海晏，深藏心中的那片草原他都不能去了，一到高海拔地区，他的肺心病就会发作，面临生命危险。

而他原本是打算把自己余下的日子交给家乡的，交给哈勒景大草原那清清的河水，烂漫的山花……

set off by car.

Vultures, the messengers from heaven, oscillated between hovering in the sky and sensitively pecking at the sheep carcasses piled up like hills. The snowfield was a mess, with the lambs' gentle eyes looking sadly at the sky.

The snow was deep beneath the vehicles, and the military vehicles plowed through the brittle ice.

In the last herdsman's home, except for six dark and frightened faces, there was nothing. The snow emitted dazzling light in the morning, blinding the soldiers' eyes, making it impossible for them distinguish the direction. However, the youngest son of the herdsman's family had ventured out during the night due to unbearable hunger and coldness and did not return.

In order to find the Tibetan teenager, the officer and two soldiers drove back to the highway thirty miles away. When the car returned, the Tibetan teenager was alive, while the officer was lying in the arms of a soldier. It was a maze-like ice trough, more than ten meters high, which made the officer, with tears in his eyes, fall into a snow pit. When the two soldiers pulled him up with difficulty, he was already stiff.

Gabulong arrived at Golmud to honor the officer. After finishing his funeral, he comforted the officer's family. The pain, regret, and heart-lung failure caused by lack of oxygen further deteriorated Gabulong's body, which was already afflicted by diabetes and pulmonary heart disease. Since then, this strong and stubborn Mongolian man. suffered from an incurable illness that plagued him in his later years and brought him great pain. When he was seriously ill, he couldn't even return to his beloved hometown of Haiyan, as once he reached a high altitude area, his pulmonary heart disease would attack his body, putting his life in danger.

Yet he had originally intended to live the rest of his life in his hometown, together with the clear river and the vibrant mountain flowers of Halejing Prairie...

承 诺

春天的早晨，尕布龙端着一杯用热水冲泡的山上的黑刺叶坐在地埂上，深邃的目光俯瞰着苍山大地，凝视着远方。这是年过六旬的他，最感惬意的事。

远方是高原湛蓝的天空、白色的云朵和与北山相望的南山，身后则是曾经荒芜、寂寞，如今变得枝繁叶茂、郁郁葱葱的层层绿林。

尕布龙深深地吸了一口清凉的空气，这熟悉的气息是从山林里传来的，有山鸡、野兔，青翠的小草、绚丽的花朵，有他亲手插栽的一棵棵嫩苗。他每天都要抚摸着拳头粗细的幼苗，细细端详着，给它们起名字，跟它们唠家常，就像看着自己的孙子孙女一样，希冀它们尽快粗壮起来，立在山洼里、坡地上，为他深深爱着的青海、为干涩的荒山撑起一片绿荫。

他摘下草帽，任徐徐微风吹拂他浸满汗水的额头。他有些累了，肢体的疲乏透支着他渐渐虚弱的身体，只有周身流淌着的热血，依旧如火焰般沸腾。

在他的瞳仁里，交替映现着南北山今日的雄壮与昔日的苍凉。数十年间，他像守卫者一样，用他坚韧而不乏柔情的目光，如期地镀亮了每一个黄昏和黎明。

这个世界上，还有什么比眼前披上绿装的这座大山，更让他动情的呢？

青海省是长江、黄河、澜沧江的发源地，独特的地理位置，使青海具

Commitment

On a spring morning, Gablong sat on the ridge with a cup of hot water brewed with black thorn leaves from the mountain. His deep eyes gazed down upon the land of Cangshan Mountain and into the distance. This was the most pleasant thing for him in his sixties.

In the distance stretched the blue sky and white clouds of the plateau, with South Mountain facing North Mountain. Lying beyond these mountains were lush layers of green forest, once desolate and lonely.

Gabulong took a deep breath of cool air, a familiar scent wafting form the forest, teeming with pheasants, hares, green grass, gorgeous flowers, as well as tender seedlings he himself had planted.

Every day, he stroked the thick seedlings, examining them closely, giving them names, and talking with them, treating them as his grandchildren. He hoped they would grow up healthy and strong to stand on the slopes and provide shade for the once dry, barren mountains of his beloved Qinghai.

He took off his straw hat, allowing the gentle breeze to cool his sweaty forehead. He was a little tired, and the fatigue of his limbs exhausted his gradually weakening body. Yet the blood coursing through his veins still burned with the fervor of a flame.

In his pupils, the majestic North and South Mountains of today, as well as the desolation of the past, were alternately reflected. For decades, like a vigilant guard, he illuminated every dusk and dawn as scheduled with his tenacious yet tender eyes.

尕布龙和老干部视察南北山时合影（前排中是马万里）

Gabulong and veteran cadres took a group photo when they were inspecting the South and North Mountains (Ma Wanli in the front row)

2007 年 6 月，尕布龙陪同马万里等老干部视察南北山绿化

In June 2007, Gabulong, Ma Wanli and other veteran cadres were inspecting the greening of the South and North Mountains

What else in the world could evoke more emotion in him than the greening mountains before him?

Qinghai is the birthplace of the Yangtze River, the Yellow River, and the Lancang River. Its unique geographic location grants Qinghai an irreplaceable ecological status. However, the ecological characteristics of the arid and fragile plateau have also posed significant challenges to its environmental protection and development.

Xining, the long-established provincial capital, is situated in the valley of the Huangshui River, surrounded by mountains on all sides. Despite the river flowing through the city, the semi-arid continental climate of the plateau, combined with long-standing unsustainable development and environmental degradation, had transformed the once densely wooded North and South Mountains, stretching for 200 square kilometers on both sides of the valley, into barren wastelands.

The environment continued to deteriorate with each passing day, leaving the dry mountains thirsty and cracked, particularly the towering North Mountain, characterized by steep slopes and relentless winds. With an annual rainfall of only 360mm, contrasted with evaporation rates reaching 1,783mm, the region faced formidable environmental challenges.

Spring was the most difficult season for people living in Xining. When the wind blew through the fields and hills, calcium-deficient and nutrient-free dust and sand rushed along the mountains with the wind, sweeping through the streets and alleys, bringing suffering to the people of Xining. Over the years, the Qinghai Provincial Party Committee and the provincial government mobilized units and manpower to plant trees year after year, aiming to cover the mountains with the roots of Caragana korshinskii and the sharp edges of black thorns. However, due to the adverse environment, insufficient financial resources, and lack of technical expertise, the results were meager. Newly planted trees soon died of thirst.

When the central leaders were inspecting Qinghai in July 1983, they pointed out that drought was the biggest problem of Qinghai and even the entire Northwest region of China that led to slow agricultural development and poverty. Developing animal husbandry by planting trees and growing grass is the fundamental way to cast off poverty, which was also a major strategic issue related to the overall development of Qinghai.

When central leaders inspected Qinghai in July 1983, they highlighted drought as the region's most significant issue, affecting agricultural development and contributing to poverty not only in Qinghai but also across the entire Northwest region of China. Developing animal husbandry through tree planting and grass cultivation emerged as the fundamental solution to alleviate

有了不可替代的生态地位。但干旱、脆弱的高原生态特征，也给当地的生态环境保护和建设带来了极大困难。历史悠久的省会西宁坐落在湟水谷地，四面环山，城中虽有湟水汩汩流过，可是，半干旱的高原大陆性气候、长期以来的不合理开发和破坏，使谷地两岸绵延百里的大山、近30万亩树林茂密的北山和南山，变成了寸草不生的荒野。环境日趋恶化，干燥的山地焦渴皲裂，特别是北山，山高、坡陡、风大，年降雨量只有360毫米，蒸发量却达到了1763毫米。

春天，是西宁人最难熬的季节。当狂风吹过原野，吹过一座座山丘，缺乏钙质、毫无营养的尘沙随风而起沿山奔突，横扫大街小巷，让西宁人饱受其苦、深受其害。多年来，青海省委、省政府一年又一年组织单位、人力上山植树，试图用柠条的根茎、黑刺的锋芒覆盖大山。然而，囿于环境恶劣，财力、技术经验不足，收效甚微。刚刚种下的树，很快焦渴致死。

1983年7月，中央领导在视察青海后指出：青海以至整个西北地区，农业发展迟缓、人民生活贫困的最大问题是干旱。唯有种草种树，发展牧业，才是改变青海面貌、治穷致富的根本大计，也是关系全局的重大战略问题。

在那次青海省委、省政府工作会上，尕布龙做了有关青海农牧业发展状况的工作汇报。会议结束后，中央领导紧紧握住身着蓝色中山装，挽着衣袖，神色坚毅，面目俊朗的常务副省长尕布龙粗糙、结实的大手，深情地说："尕省长，一看你，就知道你是一个实干家！"

数日后，中央考察团离开了西宁。

可主管农牧业的常务副省长尕布龙，内心却翻腾着无法平静的波澜。

之后，马万里、马元彪、汪福祥、尕布龙等许多老干部，以及有关部门负责人纷纷到南北两山上观察地形，四处张罗，向省委、省政府呼吁，写报告，建议成立专门机构绿化南北两山。

马万里同志在报告中说："植树造林，绿化祖国是党和国家的一项指令，是每个公民应尽的义务。在绿化南北山工作中，有难度，有困难，关键是提高认识，要使我们的思想尽快回到党中央、国务院关于开展全民义务植树运动上来。"他还说："有些同志对绿化南北山的工作有顾虑，有看法，可以到外面去学习，去看一看、走一走，兰州就有对口单位，问题是会解决的。"

1989年3月，青海省委、省政府正式成立了西宁市南北山绿化指挥部，

poverty, representing a crucial strategic concern for Qinghai's overall development.

At the conference of Qinghai Provincial Party Committee and Provincial Government, Gabulong reported on the development of Qinghai's agriculture and animal husbandry. When the conference was over, a central leader of China tightly clasped the rough and sturdy hands of Vice Governor Gabulong. He looked at this man dressed in a blue Chinese tunic suit, with rolled-up sleeves, appearing handsome yet resolute. The central leader said affectionately, "Governor Ga, from the moment I saw you, I knew you were a man of action!"

A few days later, the central delegation left Xining.

However, Gabulong, the vice governor in charge of agriculture and animal husbandry, was filled with uneasiness in his heart.

After that, many veteran cadres including Ma Wanli, Ma Yuanbiao, Wang Fuxiang, Gabulong, and the heads of relevant departments, conducted topographical observations in the North and South Mountains. They wrote reports and appealed to the party committee and government, recommending the establishment of a special institution for afforesting the two mountains.

Comrade Ma Wanli stated in the report, "Planting trees and greening the motherland is a directive of the party and our country, and it is the obligation of every citizen. There are obstacles in the work of reforesting the North and South Mountains. The key is to raise awareness and urge prompt action from the Party Central Committee and the State Council to carry out the national voluntary tree-planting campaign as soon as possible." He further remarked, "Some comrades have concerns about the work of greening the two mountains. They should go out and investigate for themselves. Lanzhou has a counterpart unit that can provide us with support. I believe there problems will be resolved in the end."

In March 1989, party committee and government of Qinghai formally established Xining North-South Mountain Reforesting Headquarters. Secretary of Qinghai Provincial Party Committee, Yin Kesheng, personally served as the General Director, and a grand plan was finally set out. Former leaders of the Provincial Party Committee, Ma Wanli, Ma Yuanbiao, and Wang Fuxiang, along with the then Deputy Director of the Standing Committee of Qinghai Provincial People's Congress, Gabulong, were invited as consultants.

In August of that year, Ma Wanli gave a report on titled Seminar about Reforesting Xining North and South Mountains to the Party Committee and Government of Qinghai. On the 18th, Yin Kesheng, then Secretary of the Provincial Party Committee, gave important instructions to Xining North-South Mountain Reforesting Headquarters.

由省委书记尹克升同志亲自担任总指挥，挂帅出征，立下宏图，并聘请省委原老领导马万里、马元彪、汪福祥和时任青海省人大常委会副主任的尕布龙等同志为顾问。

同年8月，马万里向省委省政府做了《关于绿化西宁南北两山研讨会的情况汇报》。18日，时任省委书记的尹克升对西宁市南北山绿化指挥部做出了重要批示。

那是1989年，中国改革开放初期，在全国许多地方，只顾及眼前利益，拼命抓经济建设，忽略生态环境保护的大背景下，青海省委、省政府就作出了"绿化西宁南北山、改善西宁生态环境"的重要决策，正式启动了功在当代、利在千秋的西宁南北山

尕布龙与民工在西宁南北山植树
Gabulong and migrant workers were planting trees in the South and North Mountains of Xining

绿化工程，而且在全年财政收入仅为6.69亿元的情况下，拿出1350万元，实施南北山绿化一期工程。

这在全国实属罕见。

这一令人欢欣鼓舞的消息，在全社会引起反响，新闻媒体争相宣传报道，广大市民翘首以盼。

尕布龙激动得一夜未眠。是因为青海省委、省政府领导的勇气和韬略，是为他们这些老同志的建议得到采纳，也是为南北山即将迎来的春天。

他积极响应省委号召，动员省人大带头划地500多亩，每逢节假日，便带干部上北山植树。仅仅两年多时间，便在省人大的绿化区修通了水、电、路，栽植了各种苗木两万株，成为南北山绿化先进单位。也许是把所有的心思都用在了绿化上。那段时间，他经常在山上走来走去，检查省人大的

In 1989, during the early stages of China's reform and opening up, many regions across the country focused solely on immediate economic interests, ignoring ecological and environmental protection. However, the party committee and government of Qinghai made a significant decision to prioritize "reforesting the North and South Mountains of Xining and improving its ecological environment". Xining North and South Mountains Greening Project was formally initiated, promising benefits for future generations. In that year, Xining had an annual fiscal revenue of only 669 million yuan, yet 13.5 million yuan was allocated for the first phrase of the project.

This rare and encouraging news evoked widespread interest among the public. The news media scrambled to publicize and report on it, and the general public eagerly awaited further developments.

Gabulong, filled with excitement, stayed up all night reflecting on the courage and strategy of the leaders of the Qinghai Provincial Party committee and Provincial Government. He also celebrated the adoption of proposals put forth by his old comrades and anticipated the upcoming spring of the North and South Mountains.

Gabulong actively responded to the call of the party committee. He mobilized the Provincial People's Congress to take a lead in being responsible for an area of more than 500 mu (33.3 hectares), and during each holiday, he took cadres to the North Mountain to plant trees. In less than three years, water and electricity were supplied, roads were built, and 20,000 seedlings were planted in the green area of the Provincial People's Congress, earning it the honor of being recognized as an Advanced Organization for Reforesting the North and South Mountains. Perhaps, it was because Gabulong put all his thoughts into greening. During that time, he often walked around the mountains to inspect the green area of the Provincial People's Congress. He cherished every plant in this land and could not tolerate even the slightest damage to the trees, let alone if turfs were dug and woods were spoiled. He would feel distressed if it really happened and would deal with it without hesitation.

When I returned from Haiyan, I found the two big mountains on both sides of the Huangshui River resembled flames, appearing different from the past. The dense forest in the sunset still graced the horizon, winding around the mountains like flowing water. Birds sang, flowering branches swayed among green leaves, and small paths of the mountains seemed to solemnly tell me stories about how Gabulong planted trees on the mountains.

At dawn after the rain, I set out from Tongren Road and walked to the foot of the North Mountain. As I got closer to the mountain, I noticed a dark green screen separating a noisy market

绿化区，万分珍惜着青海大地上的一草一木，容不得半点破坏林木的行为，见不得有人挖草皮、糟蹋树林。见了就心疼，见了就要管。

海晏归来，湟水河两岸的南北两座大山炽热如焰，与往日不同。那晚霞中密密的长林在天边静止着，流水般缠绕山间。每一片绿叶、每一条山间的小路里，都有鸟虫在鸣叫，都有花枝的影子，仿佛在向我庄严地诉说尕布龙在山上种树的事。

雨后的黎明，我从同仁路出发，一直走到北山脚下。山由远及近，伸手可触，一道深色的绿屏，隔开了与南北山绿化指挥部相邻的嘈杂市场。指挥部办公室主任张奎、副主任白前、行政处处长刘素梅、绿化处副处长朱洪杰、森林派出所民警崔德云等，都是和尕布龙共事过的人。我和他们

站在大寺沟的山坡上遥望

Looking into the distance on the hillside of Dasigou

246

from the North-South Mountain Reforesting Headquarters.

Zhang Kui, Director of the Headquarters Office, Bai Qian, Deputy Director, Liu Sumei, Chief of the Administrative Division, Zhu Hongjie, Deputy Chief of the Greening Division, and Cui Deyun, a police officer from the Forest Police Station, all worked with Gabulong at that time. We sat together, and I listened, visualized, and recorded their words. It was as if I could see how Gabulong overcame difficulties to build roads, divert water, and repair pumps for irrigation, as if I could see him working tirelessly from dawn until nightfall, sweating profusely, and forgetting to eat day after day.

The small building of the headquarters is very quiet, with many award-winning certificates displayed in the corridor. It's evident colleagues in the Headquarters Office hold deep affection for Gabulong. They respect the old comrade and leader from the depths of their hearts. They always follow him as an example and work together in unity. Over the years, they have won the honorary title of "Civil Servants to the Satisfaction of the People" by Organization Department of the CPC Central Committee and Publicity Department of the CPC Central Committee, been named as "Outstanding Contributor to the Construction of North-South Shelter Forest" by China Afforestation (Greening) Committee, and were also awarded as Advanced Unit of Qinghai South and North Mountains Greening Project Phase I & II and Advanced Primary-Level Party Organization. They have not fallen short of the expectations of Gabulong and the people of Xining.

Liu Sumei, Chief of the Headquarters Office Administrative Division, and Yang Haifeng, the secretary, took me to a mountain path lined with lush trees.

I felt both nervous and excited. I knew very well that only on this mountain can I experience Gabulong's enthusiasm and perseverance in a truer and closer manner; and can I observe that his lifelong longing and endeavor turned into a seed that can take root and sprout in the vast land of Qinghai, full of vitality and toughness. I also knew that only in this profound, incomprehensible, and silent mountain, can I truly feel all the dignity and strength of Gabulong, a shepherd and leader who grew up on the grassland, a true communist and cadre, and a man of indomitable spirit.

The sun was rising, the sky blue and clear, the willow leaves passed over heads and cheeks, and the fresh scent of pine, mixed with earthy smell, lingered in the mountain. The chimney-like high buildings lined the city in the valley of Huangshui River as far as I could see. People were living a better life in Xining. However, how many of them had paid attention to the changes in the North and South Mountains?

Leaves, whirling in the wind, blew against my face. Though I had imagined the appearance

坐在一起，倾听、想象、记录，似乎看到了尕布龙克服重重困难，劈山修路、引水上山、修泵灌溉的情景；看到了尕布龙起早贪黑、挥汗如雨、废寝忘食的一个又一个日日夜夜……

指挥部的小楼很肃静，走廊里展示着很多获奖证书。我能感受到指挥部办公室的同事对尕布龙的感情，他们是从心里尊重这位老同志、老领导的，也一直以他为榜样，团结奋进、努力工作。多年来，他们获得了中共中央组织部、宣传部授予的"人民满意的公务员集体"荣誉称号，被全国绿化委员会评为"南北防护林建设突出贡献单位"，成为青海省南北山一二期绿化先进单位、先进基层党组织，没有辜负尕布龙和这座城市对他们的殷切希望。

指挥部办公室行政处处长刘素梅和文秘杨海峰，带着我走上了一条绿树葱茏的山间小路。

我的心里有些忐忑和激动，我很清楚，只有在这座山上，我能更真、更近地体验到尕布龙痴痴不改的恒心、热情和执着，才能看到他一生的渴望，与他终身奋斗的理想在青海广阔的土地上，化为一颗能够生根发芽、充满灵性与泪水的种子时，散发出的勃勃生机。我也知道，也只有在这座深奥、难解、沉默不语的大山里，才能真正感受到，尕布龙作为一个草原上长大的牧人、领导，一名真正的共产党员、国家干部，一个顶天立地的男人的全部尊严与强大。

太阳冉冉升起，蓝色的天空澄碧透彻，柳叶划过头顶顺着面颊而过，清新的松香味夹杂着泥土的气息，在山间缭绕。放眼望去，湟水谷地中的西宁，烟囱般林立的高楼次第相间，人们的生活越来越好。但是，又有多少人关注过南北两山的变化。

婆娑的一片片叶子迎面拂来，虽然在心里无数次地想象过北山绿化区的阵容，但还是无法相信，眼前如此密集的青杨、圆柏、油松、柠条、沙枣和开满红色碎花的柽柳真的长在了北山上。

1993 年 2 月 25 日，省委书记尹克升在西宁市南北山绿化指挥部会议上，作了重要讲话。他说："我们的目的就是要搞绿色高原，改变生态环境。青海荒凉、艰苦，是客观存在，但并不可怕。尕布龙同志干劲大，省委决定由尕布龙同志任指挥部副总指挥，具体抓两山绿化工作。"

1993 年，66 岁的尕布龙，从青海省人大常委会副主任的位置上退休，

of the green area of the North Mountain countless times, I still couldn't believe that Cathayana, Sabina Chinensis, Chinese pine, Caragana korshinskii, Oleaster, and Floral Tamarix Chinensis grew so densely on the North Mountain.

On February 25, 1993, Yin Kesheng, Secretary of the Provincial Party Committee, delivered an important speech at a meeting of the Xining North-South Mountain Reforesting Headquarters. He said, "Our goal is to create a green plateau by changing its ecological environment. Qinghai is desolate and a difficult place to live. This is objective, but we shouldn't be afraid. Comrade Gabulong is motivated, so the provincial party committee has decided that Comrade Gabulong should be the Deputy General Director of the headquarters to undertake specific work of reforesting the two mountains."

In 1993, 66-year-old Gabulong retired from the position of Deputy Director of the Qinghai People's Congress Standing Committee. Instead of staying at home and enjoying the treatment of retired provincial leaders, he accepted a tough challenge and took the important task of being a full-time Executive Deputy General Director of the Xining North-South Mountain Reforesting Headquarters, with his continued selfless dedication to Qinghai and its people.

It was not an easy task to plant trees on the two mountains. Many years ago, I was moved by Yin Yuzhen, the well-known "Queen of Desertification Control" in Ordos. Over the past twenty years, this resilient woman planted 60,000 mu (4,000 hectares) of Salix, aspen, apple trees, and grapevines in the Maowusu Desert by herself. I have also heard that Yang Shanzhou, the former leader of tHebaoshan Prefectural Committee of Yunnan, took root in Daliang Mountain, and voluntarily planted trees. He donated a wood farm of 56,000 mu (3,733.33 hectares) in Daliang Mountain, worth more than 300 million yuan, to the country for free. How did Qinghai's Gabulong uphold the dedication and noble ideas advocated by mankind while planting young seedlings on the two large mountains under harsh weather conditions?

The burden was on his shoulders. He didn't have much time to think, and he didn't want to indulge in endless fantasies about how to proceed. Now that he had accepted it, he had to confront it and move forward courageously. For an upright Mongolian, an outstanding Communist, a tough man who had dedicated his life to the people, what did he have to be afraid of?

As early as May 29, 1981, at the forestry working conference of Qinghai, Gabulong made a speech on the importance and urgency of improving forestry construction in Qinghai. He stated, "Accelerating forestry construction is not only necessary for the planned and proportional development of the national economy and for maintaining ecological balance, but also essential for

他没有在家颐养天年，享受省级领导的待遇，而是接受了一项严峻挑战，怀着一颗继续为人民、为青海无私奉献的赤子之心，挑起了西宁市南北山绿化指挥部专职常务副总指挥的重任。

在南北两山上种树，可不是一件容易的事。多年前，我曾经被鄂尔多斯市家喻户晓的"治沙大王"殷玉珍感动。这位柔弱女子20年间，竟以一己之力，在毛乌素沙漠种下了6万亩沙柳、白杨、苹果、葡萄；也听说过，云南原宝山地委领导杨善洲扎根大凉山，义务种树，将5.6万亩、价值超过3亿元的大凉山林场，无偿交给国家的感人事迹。那么青海的尕布龙，又是怎样在两座气候恶劣的大山上种下一棵棵青苗，使人类所崇尚的奉献精神和高贵理念相接轨的呢？

重担压在他的肩上。他没有过多的时间思虑，也不想展开漫无边际的幻想。既然接受了，就得面对，就得勇往直前。对一个有血性的蒙古族人，一个优秀的共产党员，把终身交给了人民的硬汉子，有什么可以惧怕的呢。

早在1981年5月29日，在全省林业工作会议上，尕布龙就提高青海省林业建设的重要性和迫切性问题在会上作过重要发言，他说："加快林业建设，不仅是有计划按比例发展国民经济的需要，是保持生态平衡的需要，而且也是加速实现农业现代化的需要。现代农业发展趋势之一，就是农林牧结合，为农业的高产稳产创造条件。其中，森林植被分布状况是一个重要的因素。缺乏林业的农业，是一个很不完全的农业，从长远来说，也是没有保证的。农林、牧业都是土地利用的重要部门，在人口增长、耕地和草场有限的情况下，使用土地方面的矛盾将会日益突出。这就要求我们必须妥善地解决这些矛盾，从大农业的全局观点出发，准确处理三者之间的关系。"

这些观点至今看来，仍然对我们发展青海农牧业生产大有裨益。

他还说："林木对保护农田、草原免遭风沙侵袭的作用是很显著的。香日德农场坚持农田防护林带，已经收到了明显的增产效果。共和县沙珠玉公社过去的风沙对农业的危害是很严重的，他们从1976年开始，下决心苦干了5年，基本实现了农田林网化，控制沙区面积2800多亩，锁住大小沙丘46个，风沙灾害已有明显的缓和。从一定意义上讲造林就是造粮。"

发展林业是社队集体和社员尽快富裕起来的一个重要方面。湟源县小高陵大队的农业机械价值15万元，其中12万元是从林业收入中解决的。

expediting agricultural modernization. One of the trends of modern agricultural development is the integration of agriculture, forestry, and animal husbandry to create conditions for high and stable agricultural yields. Among these, the distribution of forest vegetation plays an important role. Agriculture without forestry is incomplete and unsustainable in the long run. Agriculture, forestry, and animal husbandry are all important sectors of land utilization. Under the circumstances of a growing population and limited arable land and grassland, conflicts concerning land utilization will become increasingly prominent. This requires us to properly resolve the conflicts and accurately handle their relationships from the overall perspective of large-scale agriculture."

These views are still of great benefit for Qinghai's agricultural and animal husbandry production to this day.

He also stated, "The role of forests in protecting farmland and grassland from wind and sand is significant. Xiangride Farm adheres to the construction of forest belts for farmland protection, having already received a significant increase in production. Wind and sand used to cause severe harm to the agriculture of Shazhuyu Commune in Gonghe County. From 1976, they worked hard for five years and basically realized a network of forests in farmlands. More than 2,800 mu (186.7 hectares) of sandy areas were brought under control, with forty-six dunes of various sizes stabilized, significantly alleviating wind and sand disasters. In a certain sense, afforestation equates to food production."

"The development of forestry is one important factor for the well-being of the community and its members. The agricultural machinery of Xiaogaoling Brigade of Huangyuan County is worth 150,000 yuan, of which 80% is paid by forestry income. By the end of last year, Yahe Brigade, Xishan Commune of Huzhu County had a total forestry income of more than 40,000 yuan, which provided the community with wood used in more than 390 houses, firewood of nearly 100 tons, as well as wood for various small farm tools. Therefore, planting trees and developing forestry beneficial to the country, communities, and individuals without any harm . Afforestation, especially in low mountains, is an effective way to alleviate poverty and produce wealth. It will yield results in ten or twenty years, as long as you persist in doing it."

After Gabulong retired, his persistence in developing the forestry economy by changing the appearance of two barren mountains in the north and south of Xining was his foresighted wisdom and his solemn commitment to the people of Qinghai.

Standing on the mountain and smelling its fragrance, I am full of curiosity about Gabulong's old age and the green life he created.

互助县西山公社牙合大队到去年年底林业总收入已达 4 万多元，为集体和社员解决了 390 多间房子的木料、近 100 吨烧柴和各种小农具的用材。所以，植树造林，发展林业，无论对国家、对集体、对个人，都有百利而无一害，特别是在浅山，植树造林更是治穷致富的好路子。只要坚持搞，十年、二十年就会见效。

可见，尕布龙退休后，立志改变南北两座荒山面貌，发展林业经济，是他深谋远虑的智慧，是他心中对青海人民的庄严承诺。

此时，我站在山上，闻着清香扑鼻的气息，充满好奇，对尕布龙晚年的生活，以及他所创造的绿色生命。

尕布龙在草原上长大，在担任河南县县委书记的艰苦岁月中，积累了丰富的经验，在省级领导岗位上 22 年间分管农牧，长期和牧场、牧人、草原打交道的经历，让他深知，在青海，只抓经济建设不搞好自然生态环境，是没有发展前途的，而南北两山的绿化，实际上，是他一直放在心上、渴望实现的梦。

南北两山，总面积 27.9 万亩。南山东起杨沟湾，西至阴山堂，南接总寨镇；北山东起小峡口，西至巴浪沟，北与湟中县、大通县、互助县接壤。山势地形条件不同，种树的规模、品种、方法也不同。如何使这两座光秃的大山充满活力，如何让这两座大山给西宁人的生活带来福音呢？长期深入基层调查研究的尕布龙对绿化，对自然生态的保护有自己的真知灼见。

他忘不了，早在 1986 年，他便用 5 万元钱雇用了一架飞机，在北山上撒了三天种子，其结果是没种活一丛草、一棵树。

他同样忘不了，三北防护林建设初期，由于自己没有经过实地调查，急于在湟源大风口佛海乡布置一道防护林造成的经济损失。

那一年，当地牧民种下的一大片树苗后因海拔过高、气候干旱，一棵树也没有活下来。

当时,他懊悔万分。他不回避问题，也不想原谅自己。他召开现场大会，向当地的干部群众做了检讨。

他恳切地说："我对不住大家，是我太急躁、瞎指挥，给大家造成了经济上的损失。是我错了，我在这里给大家道歉了！"

佛海乡的村民，哪里见到过大领导给他们道歉的场面。面对尕布龙的坦荡无私和满脸的内疚，在场的群众感动得流下了眼泪。佛海乡的人纷纷

Gabulong grew up on the grassland, and he accumulated rich experience during his arduous years working as secretary of the Henan County Party Committee. He spent twenty-two years in provincial leadership positions, overseeing agriculture and animal husbandry, and gaining long-term experience in managing pastures, herders, and grasslands. He was aware that in Qinghai, there was no future for development if only focusing on economic construction without also maintaining the natural ecological environment. In fact, the greening of the North and South Mountains was a dream that he cared about and longed to realize.

The two mountains in the north and south have a total area of 279 thousand mu (18.6 hectares). The South Mountain starts from Yanggouwan in the east, borders Zongzhai Town in the south, and stretches to Yinshantang in the west. The North Mountain starts from Xiaoxiakou in the east, borders Huangzhong County, Datong County, and Huzhu County in the north, and extends to Balanggou in the west. Due to different topography, the scale, varieties, and methods used in planting trees also vary. How could they create vitality in these two barren mountains and let them bring better lives to people of Xining? Based on deep and extensive investigation and study, Gabulong gained insights into the greening and protection of nature and ecology.

He could not forget that, as early as 1986, he hired an airplane for 50,000 yuan to sow seeds on North Mountain for three days. The effort was a failure, as not a single tree or blade of grass survived.

He also couldn't forget that, due to his eagerness to deploy a shelter forest in a wind gap of Fohai Township in Huangyuan during the initial stage of constructing the Three-North Afforestation program, economic loss was incurred without proper fieldwork.

That year, a large number of saplings planted by local herders did not survive due to the high altitude and drought.

At that time, he was very regretful. He did not evade the problem, nor did he want to forgive himself. He held an on-site meeting and conducted a self-review with local officials and the public.

He said earnestly, "I need to apologize to all of you, because I was too impatient and commanding, which caused everyone financial losses. I was wrong, and I apologize to everyone here!"

The villagers of Fohai Township had never seen such a high-ranking leader like Gabulong apologize to them. Gabulong's selflessness and guilt moved the crowd. Fellow villagers in Fohai said, "Governor Ga, don't blame yourself. Let's start again and think of better ways to plant the mountains with grass and trees. As long as we work together, there are no difficulties that cannot

绿化前的北山

North Mountain before afforestation

表示："尕省长，您别太自责了，让我们重新来，让我们一起想更好的法子封山育林、封山育草。只要人在，就没有克服不了的困难。"

尕布龙感动得满脸泪水，他为村民们骄傲，为村民宽厚仁慈的胸怀感动。

那几年是尕布龙最难的时候，资金捉襟见肘，人力又少，对荒山的了解、认识，对绿化的科学分析都有待探讨。他首先进行了调查研究，针对南北两山绿化区多而分散，地处青藏高原和黄土高原过渡带的干旱条件，以及面对资金不足、经验不足等问题，提出了一系列开创性的举措，使西宁南北山绿化工程在宏观把握、微观调配上有了行之有效的方向和具体步骤。

be overcome."

Gabulong was moved to tears. He felt proud of what the villagers had done and was greatly touched by their generosity and kindness.

Those years were the most difficult time for Gabulong. Funds were stretched, and manpower was scarce. More discussions were needed to understand tHebarren mountains and scientifically analyze afforestation. After investigation and research, Gabulong put forward a series of groundbreaking measures in response to problems such as the drought conditions of the massive and scattered green areas of the two mountains in the transitional zone between the Qinghai-Tibet Plateau and the Loess Plateau, insufficient funds, and lack of experience. As a result, there was a clear direction for grasping the Xining North-South Mountain Reforesting project at the macro level and effective measures to deploy it at the micro level.

He rushed around the mountain ridges every day, seeking guidance from experts in the forestry department, humbly learning from forestry, agriculture, and water conservancy technicians, listening to opinions from experts, and collaborating with specialists. After that, based on the conditions of Qinghai, he finally concluded a greening pattern that primarily selects native tree species, which then develop shrub as cover, broad-leaved forests as skeleton, and coniferous mixed forest. Adopting the method of scientific afforestation, law-based forest governance, and a combination of engineering, biology, and technology, each green area was able to grow and supply seedlings independently.

To meet the actual needs of greening the North and South Mountains of Xining, he requested "to green two mountains, water conservancy shall be first" in each green area. Focusing on the construction of water conservancy and water diversion has always been a priority. Despite extreme difficulties in raising funds for afforestation, most of the funds were invested in water conservancy construction to ensure irrigation. At the same time, close attention was also paid to building roads. Gravel tracks, trunk roads, and paths in woodland were constructed.

He sent people to Lanzhou, Gansu, to learn from the afforestation experience of neighboring provinces. He put forward the idea of contracting greening responsibility areas by different departments and industries, and implemented contract responsibility system by clarifying responsibilities and asking unit leaders to directly take charge of them. He allowed individuals in Xining to personally contract green areas, sign a contract with the headquarters office, and then be under the unified leadership of the headquarters, with hierarchical responsibility. Under this system, they cooperated well.

已经不担任副总指挥的尕布龙依然坚持上山

Gabulong, who was no longer Deputy General Director, still insisted on going up the mountains

　　他天天奔波在每一道山梁，请林业部门的专家指导，虚心向林业、农业、水利技术人员学习，听取专家意见，同专业人员一起，结合青海省省情，总结出以优选乡土树种为主，进而发展灌木覆盖、阔叶林为骨架、针叶林混交的绿化格局。采用科学造林、依法治林，工程、生物、技术相结合的方法，让各绿化区自行育苗，自给自足。

　　为了适应西宁南北山绿化的实际需求，他要求各绿化区"绿化两山、水利先行"。坚持把兴修水利、引水上山作为重点，在当时绿化资金极为困难的情况下，拿出大部分资金投入水利建设，保障灌溉。同时，狠抓道路建设，建设砂石主干道、林间道路。

　　他派人到甘肃兰州学习邻省绿化经验。提出了由各部门、各行业划片承包绿化责任区的思路，明确责任，让单位领导亲自负责，实行承包责任制。他允许西宁个人承包绿化区，与指挥部办公室签订承包合同，再由指挥部统一领导，分级负责，条块结合。

In order to emphasize the importance to of greening across all units, he took the lead in proposing that the annual greening target amount should be included in the indicators for the year-end assessment of each unit. Green areas under the authority of the Provincial Department of Commerce, the Provincial Water Resources Department, the Provincial People's Congress Standing Committee, the Provincial Electric Power Bureau, and the municipal organs were set as examples for each unit to visit, learn from, and communicate with others. He also promptly granted honors and rewards to advanced units and individuals contributing to the greening of the two mountains.

Having lived and worked on the grassland since an early age, he knew the hardship and value of labor and therefore mobilized farmers who planted trees to stay on the mountains for long-term management. He recommended that departments and bureaus of the province retain skilled and responsible migrant workers as much as possible in their green areas. He cared about migrant workers and mobilized their families to move with them so they could stay on mountains and feel secure in engaging in long-term greening and management work. Throughout the year, people were stationed on duty in the mountains to prevent fires and other disasters. A unified model of voluntary afforestation by units and the masses, alongside full-time afforestation by professional teams, was formed. A new management model of "planting trees by professional teams; managing and protecting trees by specialized personnel" was explored. He tried every means to stimulate the enthusiasm of migrant workers, encouraging more of them to devote themselves to the labor of afforestation and pushing them to become experts in forest protection and development.

In the early stages, many people, including some leaders, were skeptical about greening the North and South Mountains. These two barren and undulating mountains, with altitudes of close to 2,800 meters, had separated ridges, rugged terrain, exposed rocks, and infertile soil. They had an average temperature of only six degrees Celsius, and the frost-free period was only 140 days. When the wind blew, the dusk obscured the sky, and sunlight was scattered. Technically speaking, these two mountains, especially the front slope of the North Mountain, were fundamentally unsuitable for forest land.

However, Deputy General Director Gabulong was not resigned. He aimed to turn the decision of the provincial party committee and government a into reality. He sought to change people's ideas with his own hands. His determination and will were as solid as the rocks of the mountain.

In order to reassure leaders of the provincial party committee and government, to help people in Xining realize the importance and urgency of greening the North and South Mountains,

为了让各单位重视绿化，他率先提出，把每年的绿化目标量纳入各单位年终考核的指标，在两山绿化区树立省商业厅、省水利厅、省人大常委会、省电力局、省环保局、市直机关等几种不同类型的绿化先进榜样，经常组织各绿化区相互观摩、学习、交流，并对两山绿化先进单位和个人及时进行表彰奖励。

他从小在草原上生活劳动，知道劳动的艰辛、可贵，他动员会种树的庄稼人，长期上山驻点管护。建议全省各大厅局绿化区，尽可能地留住一部分有技术、责任心强的民工。他关心民工们的生活，动员他们的家属随迁，使他们能够安心留在山上，长期从事绿化和各项管理工作。保障一年四季有人在山上值班，做到防火、防灾，形成单位、群众义务植树，专业队专职植树造林的统一模式。探索出了一条"专业队植树，专门人员管护"的管理新模式。他想尽各种办法，激发农民工的热情，让更多的农民工投身到植树造林的劳动中来，让更多的农民工成为护林、养林专家。

造林初期，许多人，包括一些领导，对南北山绿化持怀疑态度。两座海拔接近2800米的荒山，山势起伏、沟岭相隔、地形破碎、岩石裸露、土壤贫瘠，平均气温6摄氏度，无霜期只有140多天。吹起风来，黄土遮天蔽日混沌无光，尤其是北山的前坡面，从专业角度讲，根本就属于非宜林地。

可担任了副总指挥的尕布龙不甘心，他要让省委、省政府的决策成为现实，他要用自己的双手，彻底改变人们的观念，他的决心和意志比山上的石头还要坚硬。

为了让省委、省政府的领导放心，为了让全市人民意识到南北两山绿化的重要性、迫切性，调动大家的积极性，更为了向人们证明南北两山绿化的可能性。他毫不犹豫地选择了北山坡度最陡、土质条件最差、水土流失最严重、绿化难度最大的大寺沟，作为南北山绿化的突破口，并亲自上阵，带着办公室全体干部和他组织来的民工上了山。

当时的大寺沟，寸草不生，崖深无路，只能找块较平坦的坡地，勉强扎下一顶小帐篷。

白天，尕布龙带着民工干活。晚上，年轻的农民工段国禄独自一人住在帐篷里。

段国禄是湟中县维新乡新庄村人，父亲是新庄村的支书。本来，他可

to mobilize their enthusiasm, and to demonstrate the possibility of greening the two mountains, he resolutely chose Dasigou. Dasigou had the steepest slope, the worst soil conditions, the most serious soil erosion, and presented the most challenging task of greening the North Mountain. He led the work by himself, bringing all of the office cadres and the migrant workers he had organized to the mountain.

At that time, there was no grass on Dasigou. The cliff was deep, and there was no way out. He could only find a flat slope, on which a small tent was pitched.

During the day, Gabulong and the migrant workers worked together. At night, Duan Guolu, a young migrant worker, lived alone in the tent.

Duan Guolu is from Xinzhuang Village, Weixin Township, Huangzhong County, and his father is the secretary of the village. He could have lived an easy life if he had married a girl from a neighboring village, forming a family in the village and doing farm work with his brothers. However, because of an unexpected encounter between his father and Gabulong, his fate was changed. Duan Guolu has lived on this mountain for nearly thirty years since he followed Gabulong to plant trees. Now, he is already a fifty-year-old middle-aged man.

His father was a stubborn old man who was busy with village affairs all day and rarely spent time with his family. Once, the vice governor Gabulong came to the village for an investigation. In the secretary's home, they talked and became good friends due to their similar personalities.

In 1991, Gabulong, who was the Deputy Director of the Standing Committee of the Provincial People's Congress, thought of Duan Guolu, the son of his old friend, to help him build the green area of the Provincial People's Congress.

When the village secretary heard this, the old man sent his son to the mountain without hesitation.

At that time, Duan Guolu was too young to understand what means planting trees on the mountain entailed. He went to the mountain and came to the green area of the Provincial People's Congress.

At that time, the Provincial People's Congress had slightly better conditions in its green area, as it provided houses to live in. Every morning, Gabulong and Liu Zhiping, director of the Provincial People's Congress Office, would be driven by Zhao Zhonghai to the mountain, and they would start to dig pits, plant trees, and water them. When it was time for lunch, they only ate steamed buns soaked in hot water and pickles with the migrant workers. In the evening, Duan Guolu, who lived on the mountain, would light a candle to read a book Gabulong had given

以娶个邻村的姑娘在村子里成家，和弟兄一起种地，过小日子。可是父亲与尕布龙一次意外的相逢，却改变了他的命运。自从跟随尕布龙上山种树，段国禄已经在这座大山上住了近30年，如今，他已是快50岁的中年人了。

段国禄的父亲是一个倔老头，一天到晚为村子里的事奔忙，很少操心家里的事。有一回，来到湟中县维新乡新庄村调研的副省长尕布龙，来到他们家，一说话，两人性格相投，竟处成了好朋友。

1991年，担任省人大常委会副主任的尕布龙，为了建设省人大的绿化区，想到了他这个老朋友的儿子段国禄。

给村支书一说，老汉二话不说，就把儿子送到了山上。

那时候，段国禄太年轻，根本就不知道在山上种树是怎么一回事。他糊里糊涂地上了山，来到了省人大绿化区。

当时，省人大绿化区条件稍好，有房子住。每天早上，驾驶员赵忠海就准时把尕布龙和人大常委办公室的刘志平主任送到山上，和民工一起挖坑、种树、浇水，一起吃开水泡馍馍就咸菜。晚上，住在山上的段国禄，点着蜡烛读尕布龙送给他的一本写雷锋的书；这本书还是尕布龙叫驾驶员崔生满领了当年的书报费，费了好长时间才买到的。第二天，尕布龙一边干活一边还要询问，检查段国禄学了没有。那一年，段国禄20岁。

担任南北山绿化办公室的专职副总指挥后，尕布龙又把段国禄带到了大寺沟。

大寺沟山高坡陡，地形复杂，土质盐碱大、红土多，全是没有一点营养的大白土。平时硬得像铁，雨后又像失了筋骨的散沙流淌不止，绿化难度非常大，挖坑要用钢钎打，坑挖好后，要用有营养的土填上，再把树种下去。

这还不是最难的。在这两座山上种树，最艰难的要算浇水。

尕布龙就让段国禄承担了这个重任。

我见到段国禄时，他正守护在金融系统绿化区。

长相端正、体格精瘦的段国禄，面色黝黑。长期待在山上的他沉默寡言，有一个机灵调皮的小儿子。这个绿化区原来属于指挥部办公室，不但树木茂盛，规划整齐，办公楼前还种了一大片蔬菜。

段国禄一家三口住在一楼，小儿子放暑假也来到了山上。段国禄的妻子很年轻，长着高挺的鼻梁，大大的眼睛。

him about Lei Feng. Gabulong spent a long time buying the book after he asked his driver, Cui Shengman, to draw fees for purchasing books that year. The next day, Gabulong would check whether Duan Guolu had learned it or not while working. That year, Duan Guolu was twenty years old.

When he served as the full-time Deputy Commander of Xining North-South Mountain Reforesting Headquarters, Gabulong brought Duan Guolu to Dasigou.

It was a mountain with high and steep slopes, complex topography, saline-alkaline soil, plenty of red soil, which contained fewer nutrients. The soil was usually as hard as iron. However, after a rain, it became loose sand, as if a person without bones and muscles. It was difficult to plant trees on this kind of soil. Drilling steel was needed to dig pits. After the pit was dug, nutritious soil must be filled, and trees were then planted.

This was not the hardest job. To plant trees on the two mountains, watering is the most challenging part.

Gabulong asked Duan Guolu to take on this important task.

When I met Duan, he was guarding the green area of the Financial System.

Duan Guolu, well-featured and lean, has a dark complexion. Staying on the mountain for a long time, he is a man of few words and has a clever and mischievous little son. The green area originally belonged to the headquarters office. It has lush trees, neat arrangement, and even a large area of vegetables planted in front of the office building.

Duan Guolu's family of three lived on the first floor. His youngest son also came to the mountain during summer vacation. His wife is young, with a tall nose and big eyes.

I was sitting on a simple sofa. Under the glass of the tea table, there was a photo of Duan Guolu and Gabulong. Gabulong looked very serious in the photo, wearing a dark blue clothing and a light gray hat. He appeared a bit tired and haggard. Liu Sumei said enviously, "I worked with Director Ga for many years. How come I never took a single photo with him?"

I looked at Liu Sumei and also felt regretful for her.

After Gabulong took Duan Guolu to the mountain, Duan has been living on it, and his wife has also been staying together with him on the mountain.

Initially, his wife didn't want to come, but changed her mind after Gabulong's repeated persuasion. Now, she is used to it.

Gabulong knew very well that a single person, no matter who, could not stay long on the mountain. As long as their small families were placed on the mountain, they could steadily follow

我坐在一个简易的沙发上，茶几的玻璃下面，有一张段国禄和尕布龙的合影。照片上的尕布龙很严肃，穿着一件深蓝色的衣服，戴着一顶浅灰色的礼帽，看上去有些疲倦、憔悴。刘素梅羡慕地说："我跟尕主任在一起共事那么多年，怎么连一张与他合影的照片都没留下来！"

我望着刘素梅，也替她遗憾。

尕布龙把段国禄带上山后，段国禄就一直在这座大山上生活，媳妇也娶到了山上。

媳妇原本是不想来的，可禁不住尕布龙反复做工作，现在，她也已经习惯了。

尕布龙非常清楚，无论是谁，一个人在山上都坚持不了多长时间。只有把他们的小家安置在山上，他们才能踏踏实实跟着他种树。

每天，段国禄都要从大寺沟的山顶沿着管道线下到沟底，开阀门，把水抽到三岔岭的山顶，然后再原路返回。大寺沟沟深崖险，一趟十几公里，一天跑三趟，才能给树苗浇足水。

在大寺沟种树的日子，是尕布龙最辛苦、最操劳的几年。

每天早上 7 点，头戴草帽、身穿蓝大褂、脚穿黄胶鞋的他就准时到了山上，等民工们到齐时，他已经在山上四处勘察，拄着棍子跑了两个小时了。中午，尕布龙和民工一起用工地上支起的大锅，熬茯茶，吃馍馍。

一天从早干到晚，实在太累了。有一回尕布龙竟靠在苗圃的地埂上睡着了。山上的风，又硬又冷，发现他时，他的身上、脸上、耳朵、鼻孔里全是土。

晚上，本来就有些感冒的他，病情更加严重了。何巴劝他："明天别上山了，吃点药，在家休息一天。"可他不愿意："那怎么行，我死了是一个人的事，山上的树死了是大家的事。"

早晨起来，他坚持上了山，到了傍晚时分，才直起腰，用沙哑的嗓子喊了声："大家收工，回家吧！"自己却扔下铁锹一屁股瘫坐在地上。歇了一会儿，准备起身，可腰部一阵酸痛，已经无力撑起他高大的身躯，司机和几个民工只好把他抬到车上。

车灯亮了，一束白色的光伸向大山深处，他直起身子，望着一株株栽植整齐的树苗，忘记了劳累，心里充满了欢乐。

尕布龙白天劳动，夜里惦记着浇水的事，每天都要对段国禄千叮咛万

his plan to plant trees.

Every day, Duan Guolu has to walk along the pipeline from the top to the bottom of Dasigou, opens the valve to pump water to the top of Sancha Ridge, and returns along the same path. Dasigou has deep and dangerous cliffs. It takes more than three trips a day, walking more than ten kilometers per trip, to draw enough water for the saplings.

The days of planting trees in Dasigou were Gabulong's most difficult and tiring years.

At 7 o'clock every morning, he would put on a straw hat, blue coat, and yellow rubber overshoes, arriving on the mountain promptly. By the time the migrant workers arrived, he had already spent two hours walking with a stick, surveying the mountain. At noon, Gabulong and the migrant workers set up a cauldron on the construction site to boil Fuzhuan tea and eat steamed buns.

It was truly exhausting to work from morning to night. Once, Gabulong leaned on the ridge of the nursery and fell asleep. The wind on the mountain was harsh and cold. When he was found, his body, face, ears, and nostrils were covered with dirt.

At night, already suffering from a cold, his condition worsened. Heba persuaded him, "Don't go to the mountain tomorrow, take some medicine, and rest at home for a day." But he was unwilling. "How could do that? If I die, it is only a matter of one person. If the trees on the mountain die, it is everyone's business."

In the morning, he got up and insisted on going up the mountain. In the evening, he straightened his back and called in a hoarse voice, "Stop working. Let's go home!" However, his shovel dropped, and his body flopped over the ground. After a break, he was about to get up, but unable to support himself because of the soreness in his waist. His driver and a few migrant workers had to lift him into the car.

The car headlights cast a beam of white light into the depths of the mountain. He stood up and looked into saplings neatly planted, feeling no fatigue and full of joy in his mind.

During the day, Gabulong worked diligently, and at night, he worried about watering. He urged Duan Guolu again and again every day, and went to the ditch from time to time to check if the trees were adequately watered. One day, it snowed at the East Ditch. Gabulong insisted on going to the ditch. He went down and didn't go up right away. When he finished cutting tamarisk twigs at the bottom of the trench with others, his legs were so sore that he couldn't move. As a result, he had to be carried up by several workers.

Spring was the busiest season for tree planting. Gabulong lived on the mountain for more

嘱咐，还要不时地下到沟底检查水浇透了没有。有一天，东沟下雪，尕布龙不听劝硬是要下去。下去了，又不马上上来，等到和大家一起在沟底插完了红柳，腿疼得不能动了，几个民工只好把他背了上来。

春季，是植树最繁忙的日子，尕布龙一连40多天吃住在山上，和农民工一起干活。每天清晨，是他叫醒民工；每天晚上，他还盯着民工给每一棵树苗浇足水。白天，还要拄着棍子，满山满坡地跑，查看验收水利工程，检查道路建设。

又是一天，早上6点他去二十里铺拉云杉苗子，本想中午赶回家吃午饭，可因修路堵车，过了吃中午饭的时候苗木还没装好，患严重糖尿病的尕布龙身体出现不适，跑到一个老乡家里想要点洋芋充饥。可能是他满身泥土的样子令人生疑，竟被这位老乡没好气地给赶了出来。事后，那个老乡得知，来他家讨饭的就是那个在山上植树的副省长尕布龙，后悔得捶胸顿足。

1994年夏天，大寺沟发了洪水，尕布龙怕把民工冲走，把苗子冲没了，一大早就来到山上，摔得满脸满身都是泥。这也促使他痛下决心，动员大家到河里挖石头，垫到沟里，修好沟底的路。

修路的过程十分艰辛，让民工们费了不少力。尕布龙心疼大家，见几个身强力壮的人经过沟底，喊住他们让他们帮着搬几块石头垫到路上。其中一个人非但不搬，还要出手打尕布龙，段国禄气得冲上去拧住了那个人的胳膊，那个人反手抓住段国禄，就要出手。随后跟上来的人，小声对那个人说尕布龙就是那个在山上种树的大领导，那个人才跑了。

大寺沟沟底的路终于修好了，那是尕布龙难得露出笑意的一天。

当时，他已经不大吸烟了，可是那天，他却蹲在路边，给段国禄递了一支烟，高兴地说："来，让我们抽一支胜利烟。"

那是段国禄唯一一次见到他老人家笑。他的笑容太金贵了。

由于大寺沟的环境太差，遇到了很多难题。尕布龙请来西山林场的场长刘万祥当技术顾问。

可是，刘万祥的眼睛高度近视，听力也不好。

尕布龙就让刘万祥教段国禄如何看水准仪，教段国禄植树方面的知识，逼得段国禄在刘万祥那里学到了很多技术。现在的段国禄不仅可以解决种树的许多技术问题，还学会了记账，算成本。可以自己埋水管子、接水管子、换阀门，只要是山上的事情，什么都难不住他。

than forty days to work alongside the migrant workers. He woke the migrant workers early in the morning and urged them to water the saplings each night. During the day, he would walk the hills and slopes, holding a stick to inspect and approve water conservancy projects and to check road construction.

One day, at 6 o'clock in the morning, he went to Ershilipu to haul spruce seedlings. He wanted to go home for lunch at noon, but the seedlings were not yet loaded due to a traffic jam. Gabulong, who suffered from diabetes, felt uncomfortable and ran to a fellow villager's home for some potatoes to ease his hunger. However, the villager drove him away because he looked suspicious and was covered in mud. Afterwards, the villager regretted his actions when he learned that the man was Gabulong, the Deputy Governor who was responsible for planting trees on the mountain.

In the summer of 1994, there was a flood in Dasigou. Gabulong was afraid that the flood would wash away both the migrant workers and the seedlings. He came to the mountain early in the morning, but fell down, covering himself with mud. This prompted him to decide to build a road for the ditch. He mobilized people to dig stones from the river and lay them in the ditch.

The process of road construction was extremely difficult, requiring hard work from the migrant workers. Gabulong felt sorry for them. When he saw a few strong people passing through the ditch, he called them to help move a few stones to the road. One of them not only refused to move, but also threatened to beat Gabulong. Duan Guolu was so angry that he rushed up and twisted the person's arm. However, the person retaliated and attempted to strike back. Another person intervened, whispered to the aggressor, and told him Gabulong was the provincial leader responsible for planting trees on the mountain. Hearing this news, the man ran away.

The road under Dasigou was finally built. It was a rare day for Ga Bulong to smile.

At that time, he didn't smoke much, but that day, he squatted on the side of he road, handed a cigarette to Duan Guolu, and said happily, "Let's smoke a cigarette in celebration of our victory."

It was the only time Duan Guolu saw him smiling. His smile was precious.

Due to the poor environment of Dasigou, they encountered a lot of problems. Gabulong invited Liu Wanxiang, head of the West Mountain Forest Farm, as a technical consultant.

However, Liu Wanxiang was severely nearsighted and his hearing was not good.

Gabulong asked Liu Wanxiang to teach Duan Guolu how to read the level and acquire knowledge about planting trees. This forced Duan Guolu to learn a lot of technical information from Liu Wanxiang. Now, Duan Guolu can not only solve technical problems related to planting

到最后，连春季的造林计划、冬季的工作总结，都由尕布龙口述，段国禄写，写完了，读给尕布龙听，再修改。

年轻的段国禄成了尕布龙的好帮手，种树的土专家。尕布龙很喜欢这个实实在在、聪明好学的小伙子，把他当成了自己的儿子。当然，也因为对段国禄格外亲近的原因，尕布龙对这个小伙子要求十分严格，从来不会因为他们之间密切的关系，而对段国禄有所照顾。别的民工上山后申请一个煤炉子，尕布龙会马上解决，可轮到段国禄时，尕布龙犹豫再三，最后，竟然把自己家的煤炉子搬上山给了段国禄。一段时间后，段国禄理解了尕布龙，尕布龙感到很欣慰，段国禄成亲的时候，尕布龙按照蒙古人尊贵的礼节，给段国禄的妻子送了一块漂亮华丽的缎子，一只吃过饭的碗，祝福小两口一生美满幸福，更希望他们能一直留在山上，植树、育苗，看管他们一起种下的树苗长大成材。

4年的苦战是异常艰辛的，旁观的、看笑话的大有人在。可谁也想不到，尕布龙和20多个农民工，竟然在林业专家认定最不宜植树的大寺沟种下了1000亩树，成活率达到了80%。43万株成活的小树尽管瘦弱，却无比坚强地屹立在了光秃秃的山顶上、沟底里，不仅提前完成了绿化任务，还通过了林业专家的验收。

终于，在这条披上绿装，深不见底的沟壑面前，人们沉默了，看笑话的人也惭愧地低下了头。

南北山绿化指挥部的文秘杨海峰一路拍照，他在积累绿化区的图片资料。我继续向上攀登，觉得难以置信。

大山还在沉睡，静寂无声，植物的味道直入心肺，令我心神荡漾。眼前的一切完全来自我脚下，来自北山干枯的土壤。

植树的那些年里，尕布龙很少在办公室待着，因为只有了解不同海拔、不同地区的具体实际情况，才能够准确地提出具有前瞻性的关于南北山植树造林、生物多样化的思路，摸索出一整套适合南北两山自然条件的新方法，比如种植和管理相结合；种树和种草相结合；让草木共生，竞相成长；群众植树与专业管理相结合；巩固与发展相结合，这条新路子奠定了青海生态建设发展的基础。

1992年，根据尕布龙提出的四条意见，南北山绿化指挥部成立了两山林业派出所，加强两山管理，维护林区安全，使两山绿化工作杜绝了偷盗

trees but also handle bookkeeping and calculating costs. He can bury water pipes, connect them, and change valves by himself. As long as it is a matter on the mountain, nothing is too difficult for him.

In the end, he even wrote an afforestation plan for the spring and a work report of the winter based on what was dictated by Gabulong. After writing, he read it to Gabulong and then revised it.

The young Duan Guolu became a good helper for Gabulong and a local expert in planting trees. Gabulong appreciated the honest, smart, and hardworking young man very much and regarded him as his son. Of course, because of his closeness to Duan Guolu, Gabulong was very strict with this young man and never gave special care to him because of their closeness. When other migrant workers applied for coal stoves to use on the mountain, Gabulong would solve it right away. However, when it was Duan Guolu's turn, Gabulong hesitated and finally moved his own coal stove to the mountain and gave it to Duan Guolu. After some time, Duan Guolu understood Gabluong, who was then pleased. When Duan Guolu got married, Gabulong gave Duan's wife a beautiful satin, as well as a bowl that had been used, in accordance with the noble etiquette of the Mongolians. He wished the young couple a happy life, and what's more, hoped them stay on the mountain to plant trees, grow seedlings, and look after their efforts for a long time.

The four-year arduous struggle was exceptionally difficult, with many people watching and laughing from the sidelines. However, people would never have expected that Gabulong, along with two dozen migrant workers, planted 1,000 mu (66.667 hectares) of trees in Dasigou, on which forestry specialists regarded the most unsuitable soil for planting trees. However, their survival rate reached 80%. Despite being thin, 430,000 saplings stood firmly on top of tHebare mountain and in the yard of the ditch. They not only completed the greening task ahead of time, but they also passed the acceptance of forestry specialists.

When people saw the bottomless ditch in green clothes, they were finally silent, and those who had laughed at them lowered their heads in shame.

Yang Haifeng, secretary of Xining North-South Mountain Reforesting Headquarters, took photos all the way, collecting pictures of green areas. I continued to climb the mountain, feeling that everything was beyond belief.

The mountain was sleeping in silence, and the fragrance of the plants was refreshing, filling me with joy. The scene before my eyes was grew from the dry soil of the North Mountain beneath my feet.

和火情，走上了依法管理的轨道。随后，他又将两山绿化纳入省绿化规划，协调有关部门，降低了山上的水电费用，解决了病虫害问题。

更让人欣喜的是尕布龙组织农民工成立的绿化专业队。

这是一支特殊的队伍，由尕布龙亲自带队，也是一支人员年龄偏大，十分吃苦耐劳的专业队。

他对民工要求严格，重视对他们的管理和教育，随时给他们讲解爱林、护林、安全的道理。同时，又体恤着他们的处境和生活，他要求各绿化区给农民工创造必要的工作和生活条件，消除他们的后顾之忧。每到一个绿化区，都要检查他们的生活。逢年过节，他一定要用自己的工资，给他们购置鞋、烟、茶叶、食品、药品，力所能及地解决他们家里的实际困难，让他们感受到指挥部对他们的关心与爱护。

那时候，农民工的工资待遇不是很高，年轻力壮的又都不愿意跑到山上吃苦，可许多农民工在山上一干就是几年，甚至一二十年。这些农民工之所以能够坚持上山种树，并在山上驻守、管护，主要原因是尕布龙，是尕布龙尽心尽力、无私忘我的精神激励着他们，是尕布龙亲人般的关怀温暖着他们。

段国禄一家

Duan Guolu's family

During the years of planting trees, Gabulong seldom stayed in the office. He frequently went to the field, allowing him to understand the real conditions at different altitudes and regions. Only then could he accurately provide forward-looking insights about the afforestation and biological diversity of the North and South Mountains, and therefore develop new methods suitable for the natural conditions of the two mountains. These methods included the integration of planting and management, combining the plantation of trees and grass, promoting the symbiosis of vegetation and growth, advocating for the combination of planting trees by the masses and professional management, and pioneering the new road of consolidation and development. These methods laid a foundation for Qinghai's ecological construction and development.

In 1992, based on four suggestions proposed by Gabulong, Xining North-South Mountain Reforesting Headquarters established the forestry police station for the two mountains to strengthen management and maintain the safety of the forest. Theft and fire were put to an end in the greening project of the two mountains, and management was brought in line with the law. Subsequently, the greening of the two mountains was included in the greening plan of Qinghai Province, which helped to coordinate concerned departments to reduce the cost of water and electricity on the mountain and solve problems such as plant diseases and insect pests.

What's more, Gabulong pushed forward the formation of a professional team for afforestation.

This professional team, led by Gabulong, primarily consisted of old but hardworking migrant workers.

He was strict with the migrant workers, attaching great importance to their management and education. He taught them principles of forest protection and the importance of safety. At the same time, he was sympathetic to their situations and lives, so he required units responsible for the green areas to create necessary working and living conditions for them and eliminate their concerns. Every time he visited a green area, he would check their living conditions. During holidays, he would use his salary to buy shoes, cigarettes, tea, food, and medicine for them, solving practical difficulties of their families as much as possible, so that they can feel the care and love of the headquarters.

At that time, the wages of migrant workers were not high. Unable to endure hardship, young and strong workers were unwilling to stay on the mountains. However, many migrant workers stayed on the mountains for many years, and some even ten or twenty years. It was mainly because of Gabulong that these migrant workers could stay there to plant, guard, and protect the trees. It was Gabulong's dedication and selflessness that inspired them. It was Gabulong's care, as if they

在农民工眼里，尕布龙不是高高在上的领导，只是一位退休的老人，一位把整个身心扑在两山绿化上的种树人。他无怨无悔，像一棵饱经风霜的参天大树，呵护着他们、鼓励着他们。

1994年8月26日，西宁南北山各绿化区指挥长会议召开，尕布龙再次强调秋季整地、春季造林的优势，他说："秋季整地土质松、水分好、气候暖，整地质量高、劳动效率高，还可以起到保墒作用，要大力提倡秋季整地、春季造林的方法，以提高树木成活率。"

如今，尕布龙总结的变春季整地为秋季整地的这一灵活措施，不仅在南北两山绿化中得到普遍推广，还得到了林业专家的认可。

1995年2月28日，尕布龙负责在北山召开了西宁南北山绿化区负责人会议。在会上，他回顾了1994年南北两山绿化工作的成绩，明确了1995年的任务和要求，强调了绿化工作需要注意的问题：思想认识到位；造林前准备工作到位；树木灌水到位；协调、配合工作到位；补栽工作到位；落实工作到位。确保了绿化的全面性和实效性，把两山绿化推向了新的征程。

担任西宁市南北山绿化副总指挥期间，尕布龙在这座荒凉的大山上义务植树已经10年。退休后，他又往山上跑了6年。张奎、白前、韩强、刘素梅、刘霞、张有福等许许多多在指挥部工作过的人，见证着尕布龙为这座荒凉的大山付出心力、劳累的每一天，也和他一道为这座大山付出了心血和劳动。直到今天，他们仍然想念和尕布龙在一起植树的日子，怀念着和他在一起度过的艰苦而充实的日子。

我继续向上攀登，那原本荒凉的山梁上，浓浓的绿色随山势起伏泼向半空，每一片树林里，都有一对朴实的乡下夫妻驻山管理，每一个人，都传颂着尕布龙在这两座山上留下的美名。

韵家口小寨村北山、三岔岭一间简陋的平房里，住着一对平凡的夫妻。他们来自乡下，在山上植树、护树20多年。另一座山头大墩岭，还有一对年轻的夫妻，他们也来自乡下，在山上种树20年。

我尽可能多地与他们交谈，迫切地希望了解有关尕布龙，有关这两座山更多的故事。

我们来到尕布龙当年精心培育的苗圃基地，他在北山上的"家"。

这片绿地，原是南北山绿化指挥部办公室亲自经营的苗圃，是尕布龙

were his family, that warmed their hearts.

In the eyes of migrant workers, Gabulong was not a superior leader, but just a retired old man, a person who planted trees and committed himself to the greening of the two mountains. He had no regrets, caring and encouraging them like a towering, weather-worn tree.

On August 26, 1994, Gabulong reiterated the advantages of soil preparation in autumn and afforestation in spring during a meeting of commanders from each green area in the North and South Mountains of Xining. He said, "Soil preparation should be performed in autumn because of its loose and moist soil, warm climate, and high labor efficiency. Additionally, it can play a role in preserving soil moisture. We must vigorously promote the method of soil preparation in autumn and afforestation in spring to increase the survival rate of trees."

Today, Gabulong's flexible measure of changing soil preparation in spring to autumn has been not only widely used in greening the two mountains, but also recognized by forestry specialists.

On February 28, 1995, Gabulong was in charge of convening a meeting of leaders of the Xining North and South Mountains green areas in the North Mountain. At the meeting, he reviewed achievements of greening the two mountains in 1994, clarified tasks and requirements to be achieved in 1995, and emphasized issues that needed to be focused on in afforestation. These included: ensuring well ideological recognition, thorough preparations before afforestation, proper irrigation, effective coordination, adequate supplementary planting, and precise implementation of work. This ensured the comprehensiveness and effectiveness of greening efforts and pushed the greening of the two mountains to a new journey.

Gabulong had been voluntarily planting trees on this desolate mountain for ten years during his tenure as the Deputy General Director of the Xining North-South Mountain Reforesting. After retiring, he was busy running about the mountain for another six years. Zhang Kui, Bai Qian, Han Qiang, Liu Sumei, Liu Xia, Zhang Youfu, and many others who had worked in the headquarters witnessed Gabulong's mental and physical efforts for this desolate mountain, and, together, they devoted themselves to the big mountain. To this day, they still reminisce about the days that they planted trees together with Gabulong, cherishing the hard but fulfilling days spent with him.

I continued to climb the mountain. The originally desolate ridge was now covered in thick green, decorating a rolling and lush sky. In each forest, there is a modest couple from rural areas who stay in the mountains to look after the trees. The deeds of Gabulong on these two mountains are always on their lips.

An ordinary couple lives in a simple single-storey house in Sancha Ridge, North Mountain,

和他雇来的农民工用一身土、一身汗换来的。

他的"家"有个小院子，坐北朝南的几间房住着王凤梅两口子，院子的东头有一排简易的房舍，是仓库。

以前，太累了，天又黑，尕布龙就住在东头那一排房舍中间的那间房子里，后来没人住了，那里就变成了仓库。

我走过去，想透过窗户看看，可里面黑乎乎的什么也看不见。

这么破的房子，尕布龙当年是怎么住的，夜里会不会很冷？

那排房间左边，朝着山下的地方，是一个用砖砌起来的小园子，里面种着花、种着菜。

王凤梅夫妇是尕布龙从湟中县大元乡请来的农民，是最早和尕布龙一起在这里培育苗圃的人。他们听从尕布龙的教诲，一直住在山上，守着这片苗圃。

见到熟悉的刘素梅，王凤梅紧走几步迎上前，又匆匆忙忙地拿出几个

老汪和王凤梅、刘素梅在交谈

Lao Wang was talking with Wang Fengmei and Liu Sumei

小凳子，抬出一张三条腿的小方桌，摆在屋檐下。

这就是那几年尕布龙经常坐的地方，这张小方桌就是他喝茶吃午饭的桌子。吃完了饭，或者身体不舒服，累得动不了，他就坐在这里，吩咐农

Xiaozhai Village of Yunjiakou. They originally lived in the countryside, and they have planted and taken care of trees on the mountain for more than twenty years. On the other hill, Dadun Ridge, there is a young couple who also came from the countryside and have been planting trees on the mountain for twenty years.

I talked to them as much as possible, eager to learn more stories about Gabulong as well as these two mountains.

We came to the nursery base carefully nurtured by Gabulong at that time, which was Gabulong's "home" on North Mountain.

The green area was originally a nursery operated by the North-South Mountain Reforesting Headquarters Office. It was built by Gabulong and migrant workers he hired, after much hard work and sweat.

There is a small yard in his "home". Wang Fengmei's family lives in the rooms facing south. At the east end of the yard is a row of rough warehouses.

When it got dark out and Gabulong felt to tired to continue, he would stay in the middle house at the eastern end, which later became a warehouse after no one lived in it.

I walked by and looked into the window, but I was unable to see anything because it was so dark inside.

How did Gabulong live in such a shabby house? Wouldn't he feel cold at night?

On the left side of the row of rooms, there is a small garden down the hill, built of bricks, where flowers and vegetables grow.

Wang Fengmei and her husband were farmers that Gabulong invited from Dayuan Township, Huangzhong County. They were the first to live here with Gabulong to cultivate the nursery. They listened to the words of Gabulong, lived on the mountain, and guarded the nursery.

Seeing her old friend Liu Sumei, Wang Fengmei walked a few steps forward to greet her. She then hurriedly took a few small stools, carried out a three-legged little square table, and placed it under the eaves.

This is where Gabulong sat in those years. On the small table, he used to have tea and lunch. He would sit here to instruct the labor of migrant workers if he finished lunch or felt sick and too tired to move. Looking at the green saplings, his mind was wandering. Sometimes, he fell asleep with his head leaning against the wall.

Wang Fengmei brought us steamed buns and boiled tea. The three-legged table was so unstable that Yang Haifeng found a wooden stick to support it.

民工干活，看着绿油油的树苗出神。有时候，他头一靠在墙上就睡着了。

王凤梅为我们端来自己做的馍馍、熬好的茶水，三条腿的桌子实在不稳当，杨海峰找来一根木棍撑住。

一只黑色的大狗狂吠一阵后，安静了。

尕布龙很喜欢吃王凤梅做的馍馍、喝她熬的茶，晚上回不去了，就吃一碗面。

刚来的时候，指挥部给他们每人一天发8元钱，他们嫌低不干。尕布龙就说："你们不要嫌工资低，你们要是躺在家里，一分钱都挣不上，在这里种树还能行善积德呢！"

王凤梅笑了笑说："我们几次想回老家，可尕布龙死活不让回。没办法，我和老伴犟不过他，就留在这里和他一起种树了。现在我们两人的头发都白了。"

"你们刚来的时候，这里是什么样子？"

王凤梅搓了搓手说："我不会说呀，等老伴来了再给你说。"

我不答应："他来了说他的，你先说。"

王凤梅迟疑了一下，坐在凳子上。她说："刚来的时候，这里啥也没有，只有推土机推出的土印子。"

我们都笑了。

说得多好，多形象啊！的确什么也没有，只有土，只有干沙一般的黄土啊！一滴水、一棵草都没有。

这些朴实的乡民，把自己的一辈子扔在了大山上，他们是应该被青海人记住的呀。

坐在尕布龙"家"的房檐下，我的心里有些愧疚。

"家"虽然简陋，但是，坐在这里，很踏实，能看得很远很远。

太阳晒在身上很暖和，仿佛和尕布龙的心贴近了。

王凤梅听我夸她说得好，开心地笑着。

同他们夫妇一起来的农民有十几个，刚来的时候，只有推土机推过的地。尕布龙就带着他们，在推土机推过的地上平整地、浇水，盖了这四间平房。水是从泵站抽出来的，泵站的水是从湟水河里引上来的。

解决浇水问题的同时，尕布龙从老家哈勒景乡永丰村，拉来了几卡车的羊粪。沤肥、上肥，做充分的准备。

After a big black dog barked for a while, it became quiet.

Gabulong liked to eat Wang Fengmei's steamed buns and drink her tea. If he couldn't go back at night, he just ate a bowl of noodles.

When they first arrived, the headquarters gave them eight yuan a day, but they thought the wage was too low. Gabulong said, "Don't think that way. If you lie at home, you won't be able to earn even a penny. However, if you plant trees here, you can take pleasure in doing good!"

Wang Fengmei smiled and said, "We wanted to go back to our hometown for several times, but Gabulong was so obstinate and wouldn't allow it. My spouse and I couldn't change his mind, so we stayed here and planted trees with him. Now we both have gray hair."

"When you first came, what was it like here?"

Wang Fengmei rubbed her hands together and said, "I can't describe it. Let's wait for my spouse."

I disagreed, "He will talk later, and you can share first."

Wang Fengmei hesitated for a moment and sat on the stool. She continued, "When I first came, there was nothing here, only prints left by bulldozers."

We all laughed. What a good and vivid description! There was indeed nothing but soil, not a drop of water or a blade of grass, only loess like dry sand!

These humble villagers, who have devoted their lives to the mountain. They should be remembered by the people of Qinghai.

Sitting under the eaves of Gabulong's "home", I felt a little guilty.

Although the "home" was simple, it was comforting to sit here because one could see far.

The warmth of the sun touched my body, as if feeling the warmth of Gabulong's heart.

Wang Fengmei smiled happily when I complimented her on what she had said.

There were more than a dozen farmers who came together with the couple. When they first came, only the imprints left by bulldozers could be seen. Gabulong led them and built these four bungalows after leveling and watering the ground pushed by the bulldozer. The water was drawn from the pump station, which was uphill from the Huangshui River. While addressing the watering problem, Gabulong pulled a few truckloads of sheep manure from his hometown, Yongfeng Village, Halejing Township, to fertilize and prepare the soil for planting trees.

In the spring of the following year, it was finally time to plant the trees. Everyone was full of ardent hope.

While talking and laughing, they were busy with the work in their hands.

来年春天，终于能够种树了，大家的心里抱着热烈的希望。

他们热热闹闹地说笑着，手里不停地干着活。

最先种的是黑刺、柠条，长大一点后，把树苗分配到其他绿化区。然后，再扦插红柳，接着又播种油松、圆柏。

尕布龙经常带着指挥部办公室的同志们和二十几个农民一起扦插红柳。扦插红柳时，他不让大家用铁锨，怕伤到苗子，一边解释，一边让大家用手将红柳苗一点点往里按，就连深度都要一株一株地测量。按上一天，每个人的手掌都磨出了血泡，疼得钻心不敢碰。

刘素梅瞧着自己的一双手说："尕主任，你真是心疼苗子不心疼人啊！"

尕布龙头都不抬："人没那么娇气，你还得好好干。"

刘素梅说，那阵子，尕主任一叫指挥部的同志上山，大家的头皮都发麻。他不仅亲自干，还要监督大家，不许大家偷懒。山上的风又大又硬，吹得脸上结了一层皮，山上的温度忽高忽低，手上冻得满是伤。

刘素梅被借调到指挥部办公室时，以为指挥部是临时单位，谁知一干就是20多年。那时候，哪有这么好的路，哪有汽车，瘦小单薄的她不仅得扛着水平仪，跟着尕布龙徒步上山测量，检查种树的效果，还得在尕布龙的带领下，挖树坑、插苗、浇水、种土豆、挖土豆。有一次，尕布龙见她一铁锨把土豆挖成了两半，毫不留情地批评了她。

"你为什么不往深里挖，为什么不使点劲，把土豆挖烂了多可惜啊。"

尕布龙还常常嫌她娇气，实在看不惯了，会沉下脸来训斥她，随后一个劲地冲着大家吆喝："在这里种树，坑得挖深挖大，树要栽直栽稳，地埂要踩实，水要往透里浇，不要马马虎虎地糊弄人。"

尕布龙自己则穿着蓝大褂，戴着白帽子，和农民工一起浇水、插苗，一会儿也闲不住，一点也没有领导的样子。

干完活，下了山，大家的肚子饿得咕咕叫，他也不请大家吃顿像样的饭。指挥部办公室的张奎主任，看到尕布龙疲惫的样子，不忍心就这样让他饿着回去。他说："尕主任，今天我请客，咱们吃一碗炒面片、要一份糊羊肉，您看行不行？"

其实，尕布龙早就饿得没劲了，患有糖尿病的他不按时吃饭就头晕目眩。

他眯着眼看着张奎："真的是你自己请客？"张奎点点头。"那行，那

The first plants they cultivated were black thorns and Caragana korshinskii. Once they had grown a bit, their saplings were distributed to other green areas. After that, tamarisk was cultivated by cuttage, and then Chinese pine and sabina chinensis were sown.

Gabulong often took staff of the headquarters office, as well as two dozen other farmers, for tamarisk cuttage. When they were cutting the tamarisk, he did not allow them to use shovels for fear of hurting the seedlings. As he explained, he asked everyone to press in the seedlings with their hands little by little and measure their depth one by one. After a day, blood blisters were on everyone's palms, which were too painful to touch.

Liu Sumei looked at her hands and said, "Director Ga, you care seedlings more than us!"

Gabulong didn't look up. "People are not as delicate as seedlings. You have to work hard."

Liu Sumei said that at that time, every time when Director Gabulong called them to go to the mountain, their blood would freeze. He not only worked by himself but also supervised others, not allowing them to be lazy. The wind on the mountain was strong and harsh, and the temperature fluctuated, which caused peeling in their faces and frostbite in their hands.

When Liu Sumei was seconded to the headquarters office, she thought that it was a temporary assignment, never imagining it would last for more than twenty years. At that time, there was no well-built road, let alone cars. Despite being a small woman, she not only had to follow Gabulong to hike up the mountain to measure and check the effects of planting trees, but she also had to dig pits, plant seedlings, water the ground, grow potatoes, and dig the potatoes up. Once, when Gabulong saw her cut a potato in half while digging with a shovel, he criticizer her mercilessly.

"Why don't you dig deeper? Why don't you work harder? It's a pity to make damage the potatoes like that."

Gabulong often disliked her being squeamish. He would frown and reprimand her when he couldn't bear the sight, shouting at everyone, "If you plant trees here, you need to dig wide and deep pits, plant trees steadily, stomp down the ridges solidly, and water them thoroughly. No one should be careless or fool around."

Wearing a blue coat and a white hat, Gabulong was watering and cutting seedlings with migrant workers. He was busy all the time and didn't seem like a leader at all.

When they finished a day's work and left the mountain, everyone's stomach was growling, but he didn't invite them to have a good meal. Director Zhang of the headquarters office, seeing Gabulong's tired appearance, couldn't bear to see him go home hungry like this. He said, "Director Ga, let's have fried noodles and stewed mutton, my treat. What do you think?"

我们就去吃，明天我来请。"

王凤梅的茶很浓，馍馍有点硬，但是很香，我慢慢地嚼着有劲道的馍馍，听他们说着那些印象深刻的事。

王凤梅的丈夫老汪回来吃午饭，我们坐在一起继续聊着。

尕布龙在全省召开的绿化工作会议上讲话

Gabulong delivers a speech at a conference of greening work held in Qinghai

金秋的北山美景

The beauty of North Mountain in golden autumn

In fact, Gabulong had been hungry for a long time. Because of his diabetes, he would feel dizzy if he didn't eat on time.

He squinted at Zhang Kui and asked, "Is it really your treat?" Zhang Kui nodded. "Then, we'll eat. I'll treat you tomorrow."

Wang Fengmei's tea was very strong and the steamed buns were a bit hard, but they were very delicious. I slowly chewed the steamed buns and listened to them talking about the things that had impressed on them.

Wang Fengmei's husband, Lao Wang, came back for lunch. We sat together and continued our talk.

In the morning, Lao Wang walked around the mountain. It rained a lot these two days, and saplings were growing high.

Lao Wang said, "When planting trees on the mountain, what we look forward most is rain. Watering is always worse than raining as it is always uneven. A rain can satisfy the saplings and make people who plant trees on the mountain smile from ear to ear."

Lao Wang is a down-to-earth and capable person. Having planted trees with Gabulong for many years, he is a reassuring person for Ga. They all know that water is the life of man, the life of the Trea, and the life of the mountain.

Gabulong knew that they had a hard time planting trees on the mountain. Every Spring Festival and Dragon Boat Festival, he would spend his money to buy delicious food for the couple, as well as for the couples guarding in North Mountain, Sancha Ridge, and Dadun Ridge of Xiaozhai Village, Yunjiakou. If they encountered difficulties and needed to borrow money from him, he would lend it to them without hesitation.

I once saw a bookkeeping notebook, which recorded the time and amount of money borrowed by migrant workers. Every autumn, he would spend money inviting the hired migrant workers and staff of the headquarters office to have a meal in the little yard. He was grateful to everyone for cooperating with him in the work of planting trees throughout the year. He also sincerely wanted to reward the migrant workers with mutton from his hometown to make them happy. The work was not easy for the migrant workers, especially planting on the North Mountain, because the steep slopes made it hard to dig trenches and plant trees. Water preservation and moisture were also difficult, and each year they had endless tasks, such as watering for seven times in summer and ensuring winter irrigation at the end of the year. Gabulong was also afraid of disappointing them. He feared that if they were disappointed, no one would go to the mountain to plant trees with him

上午，老汪在山上转了一大圈，这两天雨多，树苗一个劲地往上蹿。

老汪说："在山上种树，最盼的是下雨，浇水浇得再多也不均匀，总不如一场雨。一场雨，能让树苗喝个饱；一场雨，能让山上种树的人好几天乐得合不拢嘴。"

老汪是一个踏实能干的人，和尕布龙一起种了这么多年树，是让尕布龙放心的人。他们都知道，水是人的命，也是树的命，山的命。

尕布龙知道他们在山上种树很辛苦。每年春节、端午，都会用自己的钱给王凤梅夫妇，给守候在韵家口小寨村北山、三岔岭、大墩岭的夫妇买好吃的送来。有的人家里生活困难，向他借钱，他总是毫不犹豫地答应。我见过一个记账的小本子，上面记满了民工借钱的数额和时间。每年秋天，他都要自己掏钱，请雇来的农民工和办公室的同志们，在这个小院子里吃一顿饭。他感激大家一年来配合自己的植树工作，也是真心想慰劳农民工，请他们饱餐一顿自家的羊肉，让农民工高兴。农民工不容易，在北山上植树更不容易，山大坡陡，挖沟、栽树不易，保水保墒困难，夏天浇七遍水，年底还要保证冬灌，一年四季干不完的活。他也怕怠慢了他们，冷了他们的心，第二年没人再上山和他一起种树。

请客的羊是从女儿召格力的羊圈里拉来的，羊肉他要亲自煮，不让别人碰，怕别人把沫子撇去没了营养。肉肠、血肠他也要自己亲手灌，做好了还要挨个给大家端上。他自己则什么也不吃，就坐在房檐下，靠着墙，看着大家伙吃。他觉得这才是真正的请客，才能表达他对大家的一份诚心。

可平时，他对农民工是有要求的。晚上也不让他们闲着，给他们开会、读报纸，讲植树护林的知识。

他甚至想为他们在山上成立个党支部。无奈，因为只有老汪一个人是党员才作罢。他就只好给老汪一个人上党课，让他学党章。提起这事，老汪忍不住笑出声来。

几年后，这里变成了山上的第一个苗圃基地，源源不断地向各绿化区提供树苗。各单位也纷纷向尕布龙学习，在自己的绿化区开辟苗圃基地，人们对绿化更有信心了。

吃过喝过尕布龙在山上经常吃的馍馍和茶水，和王凤梅夫妇道了别。他们夫妇有些舍不得刘素梅走，在一起建苗圃的日子，让他们有了感情。

离开苗圃，离开尕布龙在山上的"家"，我继续向山顶走。

in the following year.

The sheep for the meal were taken from his daughter Zhao Geli's sheep pen. He cooked the mutton himself, not allowing others to do the job, for fear that they would skim the froth and lose the nutrients of the mutton. He also poured the meat and blood sausages with his own hands. When they were ready, he would serve them to everyone one by one. He didn't eat anything himself, instead, he would just sit under the eaves and lean against the wall to watch the others eating. He felt that this was the way to express his sincerity to everyone.

However, he had requirements for the migrant workers. In the evenings, they were not allowed to be idle. They would have meetings, read newspapers, and discuss tree planting and forest protection.

Gabulong even wanted to set up a party branch on the mountain for them. He had to give up the idea because only Lao Wang was a party member. He gave one-on-one party lessons to Lao Wang and let him learn the party constitution. When it was mentioned, Lao Wang couldn't help but laugh.

A few years later, this place became the first nursery base on the mountain, continuously supplying saplings to the green areas. Other units also learned from Gabulong and opened up nursery bases in their green areas. They became more confident in greening the mountains.

After having the steamed buns and tea that Gabulong used to eat on the mountain, I said goodbye to Wang Fengmei and her husband. The couple did not want Liu Sumei to leave as they had grown very close during the days of building the nursery together.

Leaving the nursery, Gabulong's "home" on the mountain, I continued to walk towards the top of the mountain.

The fertile green leaves of poplars covered the path, and a few rural women, wrapped in colorful headscarves, sat by the side of the road. They took a rest here after finishing their work in the morning. I took out my camera and wanted to take photos of them. They laughed happily and leaned in front of me to see the photos I had taken for them. After that, they talked with cheerful voices and left with shovels on their shoulders. They were from Huzhu County, working on the mountain during the day and returning home at night. Looking at the view of their backs, I sighed inwardly. If Gabulong could plant trees and work with them now, would he laugh as happily as they did? Gabulong's voice and expression seemed to appear on the horizon from time to time. Everything was in the past, and time couldn't be reversed. What remained here was only the green color stained on the once desolate mountain.

杨树肥嫩的绿叶遮蔽了小路，路旁坐着几位裹着彩色头巾的农村妇女，她们这是干完了活在这里歇晌呢。我拿出相机想为她们拍几张照片，她们快活地大笑着，不但非常乐意，还凑到我跟前，看了我给她们拍的照片，才说着话又嘻嘻哈哈地扛着铁锨走了。她们是从互助来的，每天到山上干活，晚上回家。看着她们的背影，我心中感叹，如果尕布龙现在能和她们在一起种树、收工，会不会也像她们一样发出开心的笑声呢？尕布龙的音容笑貌仿佛在天边时隐时现。一切都成为过去，时光不能倒流，只有荒芜的山丘染上了绿色。

　　可是，大家都说尕布龙是个不爱笑的人，表情比较严肃。

　　在省政府司机班工作过的一位师傅罗海林对我说，有一回，尕布龙的司机有事，让他顶替了两天。

　　头一天，把尕布龙送到山上后，他就想下山。

　　尕布龙双眼一瞪，塞给他一把铁锨："你这小伙子，年纪轻轻的，不在山上干活跑什么？"

　　年轻的师傅罗海林也是农村出身，从小在地里干过农活的，拿起铁锨下了地。可是，才干了一会，就累得直不起腰来了。北山上的土，硬得像

尕布龙介绍南北山绿化情况

Gabulong introduces greening of the South and North Mountains

However, they all said that Gabulong was a serious person who didn't like to smile.

Luo Hailin used to be a driver for the provincial government. He told me that once Gabulong's driver asked for a leave, so he replaced him for two days.

On the first day, he wanted to go back after dropping Gabulong off at the mountain.

Gabulong glared at him and gave him a shovel, saying, "Young man, why don't you work here?"

The young driver Luo Hailin, who came from the rural area, had worked in the fields at a young age. He picked up a shovel and went to the field, but after a while, he was too tired to stand straight. The soil on North Mountain was as hard as iron lumps.

However, when he saw Gabulong was working without saying a word, he had to persevere. When it was noon, Gabulong remained silent. After 12 o'clock, Luo Hailin's stomach was growling with hunger, but Gabulong still didn't stop. When it was 12:30, Gabulong finally said, "Okay, let's have lunch!" Luo Hailin was stunned.

Wasn't this old man going to back home for lunch?

Seeing Luo standing there, Gabulong said to him, "Go get my cloth bag and thermos from the car!"

Luo Hailin ran to take out the cloth bag and couldn't help but open it and took a look. It was around Tomb-Sweeping Day at that time. Inside, there was only a chunk of guokui and a box of pickled Chinese cabbage that had not been eaten during the winter.

Gabulong pointed to a ridge and said, "Master Luo, sit down and eat with us."

Luo Hailin walked over and sat down. He saw the food was already placed on the ground. Most of the food brought by the migrant workers was the same as Gabulong's, the best of which was a few soft steamed twisted rolls, one or two boxes of fried potato shreds, and pickled Chinese cabbage with vermicelli. Gabulong chatted with everyone and ate happily.

The next day, Luo Hailin needed to send Gabulong to the mountain again. He asked his wife to get up early in the morning and bake several fried oil cakes for him. However, at noon, he saw that Gabulong still brought a piece of guokui and pickled Chinese cabbage. Looking at the migrant workers who were sitting on the ground eating dry buns and drinking boiling water, he hesitated and suddenly didn't have the courage to take out the yellow fried oil cakes. He had to make an excuse of going around the mountain so that he could eat the oil cakes secretly.

Luo Hailin said to me, "What had the old man suffered to grow the seedlings on the two mountains! People who don't plant trees on the mountain can't experience it." Luo Hailin shook

铁疙瘩。

但是，尕布龙却不言不语不停地干着，罗海林也只好坚持着。好不容易挨到中午，尕布龙不吭气。12点过了，罗海林肚子饿得咕咕叫，还不见他停下来。终于熬到12点半了，尕布龙才说："好，吃中午饭！"罗海林一愣。

难道，这个老头不打算回家吃午饭？

见他傻站着，尕布龙对他说："去，到车上把我的布口袋和暖瓶拿来！"

罗海林跑过去拿出布口袋，忍不住打开看了看。那时，正是清明时节，布口袋里放着一大块锅盔、一饭盒冬天没有吃完的腌酸菜。

尕布龙指着一块隆起的地埂："罗师傅，坐下来，和我们大家一起吃。"

罗海林走过去坐下，见地上已经摆好了吃的，农民工带来的饭大多和尕布龙的一样，最好的是几个比较松软的花卷，一两盒炒好的土豆丝和酸菜粉条。尕布龙和大家聊着，开心地吃着。

第二天，罗海林又要送尕布龙上山，他让媳妇一大早起来烙了几张油饼带着。但是，到了中午，看见尕布龙带上来的依然是一块锅盔、腌酸菜，迟疑了一下，看了看坐在地上吃着干馍、喝着开水的农民工，他突然没有勇气把炸得黄澄澄的油饼拿出来了，只好借口到山上转转，偷着把油饼吃了。

罗海林对我说："为了这两座山上的棵棵绿苗，他老人家吃了多大的

绿化后的北山一角

A corner of North Mountain after afforestation

his head and was buried in thought, filled with guilt.

Passing Sancha Ridge, I saw hilltops extending northward without end. The vegetation on their tops was green, dense, fresh, and pleasant.

Next to the hardened road, a silver main water pipe circled up the road to the top of the mountain. Only with water could trees survive and grow. This was common sense that everyone knew. However, it was indeed a miracle to lead water to such a high mountain. Building reservoirs one after another on such a mountain was beyond imagination, which was also a result of the hard work and sweat of Gabulong, as well as the builders he led.

At this time, I was in a daze. This is the "Chengji Green Area" of North Mountain, Yunjiakou. Li Chengji, the owner of this green area, is actually standing beside me.

Li Chengji was an advanced representative who responded to Gabulong's call for individual contracting of the green areas. He was formerly a deputy director of the Qinghai Provincial Taxation Service Office, who was responsible for the greening work of the unit. Because the leaders of the Qinghai Provincial Taxation Service thought highly of the work, the green area that Li Chengji was responsible for was quite successful, which was highly praised by Gabulong due to its outstanding achievements.

Li Chengji said, "In the past few years, in front of a leader like Gabulong, I had no courage to complain and no time to slack off, only to work hard."

In 1997, Li Chengji was about to retire. When Gabulong heard about it, he encouraged Li Chengji to contract a large area of wasteland left by Qinghai Wool Textile Company.

Over the past few years, although Li Chengji learned forestry knowledge and accumulated experience in planting trees while he was in charge of the green area, he was still unsure if he could do the job well due to lack of funds and water.

For half a year, Li Chengji avoided Gabulong. He dared not readily agree to his suggestion. He understood that if he did, it meant a desperate fight to do the work well. Otherwise, he couldn't explain it to Gabulong.

One morning, half a year later, Gabulong asked his driver Cui Shengman to took take Li Chengji to the north slope of Yunjiakou.

He pointed to a large, uneven, and dry slope and said, "Lao Li, this is the land. I can only rest assured if you contract this barren slope!"

Li Chengji looked at Gabulong, not knowing what to say. The hills in front of him were compacted with loess and covered with sand and rocks. There were also two huge dumps and a

苦啊！不上山亲自种树的人，是体会不到的。"罗海林摇摇头，内疚地沉思着。

过了三岔岭，看见一座又一座山头向北延伸，没有尽头。山顶上的植被苍翠、茂密、新鲜可人。

硬化结实的道路旁边，一根银色的主水管道和这条路一起盘旋而上，一直到山顶。有了水，树才能成活，才能长大。这是谁都知道的常识。可是，能把水引到这么高的山上，简直就是奇迹。能把一个又一个蓄水池建在山上，更是使尕布龙和他带领的建设者们，付出了常人无法想象的心血和汗水。

此时，我有些恍惚，这就是北山韵家口的"成基绿化区"，而这个绿化区的主人李成基就站在我身边。

李成基是当年响应尕布龙号召个人承包绿化区的一位先进代表。他原是省国税局办公室的副主任，负责本单位的绿化工作。因为国税局领导的高度重视，李成基负责的绿化区搞得风生水起，成绩突出，得到了尕布龙的高度赞誉。

李成基说："这几年，在尕布龙这样的领导面前，我没有发牢骚，也没有埋怨的勇气，更没有懈怠的条件，只能踏踏实实努力干。"

1997年，李成基要退休了。尕布龙听说后，鼓励他承包青海省毛纺公司扔下的一大片荒地。

几年来，虽然李成基在负责国税局绿化区的工作中学到了丰富的林业知识，积累了植树经验，可是真让他自己干，心里还是没有底，最关键的是缺资金、缺水。

有半年时间，李成基躲着不见尕布龙。他不敢轻易答应他。他明白，如果答应了，就得拼上命，就得干好，不然，没法给尕布龙交代。

半年后的一天上午，尕布龙让司机崔生满开车，把李成基带到了韵家口北坡。

80多岁的李成基在绿化基地

Eighty-year-old Li Chengji at the green base

rock pit next to them. It was tough to put green clothes on such a place.

Gabulong was staring at Li Chengji, with trust and inspiration in his eyes.

Seeing Gabulong's gaunt face exposed to the harsh weather of the mountain and his faded blue coat, Li Chengji was moved and nodded his head.

He couldn't refuse such a leader, an old man who carried shovel, lived on the mountain, worked from dawn to night, and devoted everything to the greening of the North and South Mountains, a former vice governor and deputy director of the Standing Committee of the Qinghai Provincial People's Congress.

In August 1998, Li Chengji officially retired and went to North Mountain, just as Gabulong had done.

Every day, he carried a shovel, steamed buns, and a military kettle with him, hiking up the mountain with the hired migrant workers before dawn, and returning home exhausted only when the sky was full of stars.

Besides the 1,000 yuan he set aside for his wife's daily expenses, Li Chengji used all of his salary to purchase saplings, water pipes, and tools. At that time, due to insufficient funds and a lack of construction machinery, Li Chengji had to rely on migrant workers to dig and carry materials by hand. They leveled more than 80 mu (5.33 hectares) of nursery land from a total of 300 mu (20 hectares) spread across six hilltops. Additionally, they dug horizontal ditches and fish-scale pits on a 200 mu (13.3 hectares) barren slope to implement the strategy of "mud staying in the mountain and water flowing within the ditch".

Soon, working in the cold wind and under the scorching sun turned Li Chengji into a gray-headed old farmer. It didn't bother him; his biggest headache was a lack of money. Li Chengji knew that drought was the biggest factor affecting the survival rate of trees in Qinghai. Planting trees without adequate investment would inevitably lead to failure. Li Chengji did not smoke or drink. All his savings, salary, and the 500,000 yuan borrowed from others were spent on the mountain. First of all, the construction of water supply facilities accounted for most of the expenses. Only by wrapping water pipes around the mountain like a blood vessel, could water be continuously pumped to this barren mountain, as blood to human beings, and therefore ensure the survival of the saplings. However, it took a considerable amount of money to build reservoirs, lay irrigation pipes, build vacant houses with valves, dig inspection wells, buy seedlings and fertilizers, build houses for management and protection, mend roads, or to hire workers. In order to build reservoirs and management and protection houses, Li Chengji would collect old bricks from

他指着一大片高低不平、干涸的坡地说："老李，就是这块地，只有把这片荒坡交给你老李，我才放心！"

李成基望着尕布龙，不知说什么好。

眼前的座座山丘黄土板结、沙石遍布，旁边还有两个巨大的垃圾场，一处乱石坑，要让这样的地方披上绿装谈何容易。

尕布龙则目不转睛地盯着李成基，眼睛里流露出的是信任和鼓励。

看着尕布龙在山上风吹日晒日渐憔悴的脸、穿在身上褪了色的蓝大褂，李成基感动地点点头。

他无法拒绝这样一位领导，一位扛着铁锨，吃住在山上，起早贪黑，为南北山绿化付出一切的老人，曾经的副省长，省人大常委会副主任。

1998年8月，李成基正式退休上了北山。

和尕布龙一样。他每天天没亮就扛着铁锨，揣着馍馍，背着军用水壶，和雇来的农民工一起上山，直到天上挤满星星的时候才拖着疲惫的身子下山。

除留下1000元给老伴用于日常生活外，他每月的工资全部用来购买树苗、水管子、各种工具。当时，没有充裕的资金，缺乏施工机械，李成基只好带着农民工靠手挖肩扛，硬是在6座山头300多亩的山地上，平整出了80多亩苗圃地，还在200多亩荒山坡上挖出了一道道水平沟、鱼鳞坑，为的是"泥不下山，水不出沟"。

很快，冷风、烈日下的劳作，把李成基变成了一个灰头土脸的老农。可这不算什么，最让他头疼的是缺钱。李成基深知干旱是影响青海树木成活率的最大因素，靠天种树只能失败，必须舍得投入。李成基不抽烟不喝酒，把自己的全部积蓄、工资，东挪西借的50万元全都贴补到了山上。首先，建设供水配套设施就占了绝大部分资金，因为只有这如同血管般缠绕在大山上的水管，才能给这座贫瘠干旱的大山不断输送血液，保证树苗成活。但是修建蓄水池、铺设灌溉管道、盖阀门控制房、挖检查井、买苗购肥、盖管护房、修路、雇工，哪一样都得用钱。没办法，为了修建蓄水池和管护用房，李成基曾天天跑到建筑工地上捡旧砖头，也曾四处赔着笑脸讨要水泥；为了修绿化区的简易道路，他又跑了好几家单位拉来炉渣……

眼看李成基劳累奔波，家里人心疼不已，可又劝不住，就由着他去折腾。有一次，老伴实在放心不下，悄悄跑到山上，远远看见几个干活的人，根

construction sites every day and beg for cement with a smile. In order to repair the simple road in the green area, he ran several units to pull the slag…

Seeing Li Chengji's weariness, his family felt distressed but couldn't stop him, so they had to let him go to the mountain. Once, his wife was so worried that she went to the mountain secretly. She saw a few people working from a distance but couldn't tell which was her husband. Were it not for Lao Li's bright white teeth and his tired but piercing eyes, she might not have recognized him. His face was covered in dirt, hands stained with frozen blood, and mouth blistered. Her heart tightened, and her throat constricted. The following day, she quickly went to the mountain to cook meals for everyone. From then on, Li Chengji and the migrant workers could have good meals, instead of just eating tasteless dough sheet with only potato lumps. When his children found that their father was almost obsessed with planting trees, they stopped trying to dissuade him and went to the mountain on weekends to help him dig tree pits and lift rocks.

Three years later, Chinese pine, spruce, and Qilian juniper were planted on 210 mu (14 hectares) of land, which was leveled and flat. However, water was urgently needed for these trees. Due to the lack of funds at that time, water conservancy facilities could not be constructed immediately. Li Chengji found Gabulong for help, and Ga was burning with anxiety.

The problem could only be solved by first pumping water from the pump station of Yunjiakou. Gabulong immediately asked the driver Cui Shengman to buy rock candy, cigarettes, liquor, and Fuzhuan tea with his own money. He went to the home of the villager who managed the pump station to convey how urgent the situation was and ask for his favor. Fortunately, the villager who managed the pump station agreed.

210 mu (14 hectares) of saplings could be irrigated, which gave greater motivation to Li Chengji.

On the morning of the day Li Chennai went to Yunjiakou, the rain had stopped shortly before his arrival. Walking through the beautiful green canopy of the spruce trees, he enjoyed the fragrance.

His face beamed with pleasure. "We have better conditions in those years. The provincial authorities supported the greening campaign enthusiastically. But during the years Gabulong planted trees, the province suffered from economic hardship."

Li Chengji told me, "Due to Qinghai's weak economic foundations, the distribution of some funds on the greening campaign was truly praiseworthy but simultaneously rare. Therefore, most of the time, it was Vice Governor Gabulong who thought of ways to raise money. Because of the

本分不清哪个是老李，哪个是雇来的农民工。若不是老李那一口亮白的牙齿，疲惫而依然有神的眼睛，老伴都不敢认眼前这位满头满脸土、两手布满冻裂血口子、嘴皮子上全是血泡的人为自己的丈夫。老伴心里一紧，喉头哽咽，第二天就抱着被子上了山，给大伙做上了饭。从此，李成基和农民工们才吃上了像样的饭，不用每天只吃加了洋芋疙瘩、清汤寡水的面片了。看到父亲植树几近痴迷，儿女们也不再相劝，一到周末就上山，帮着父亲挖树坑，抬石头。

3年后，210亩平整过的土地，宽阔平坦，栽下的油松、云杉、祁连圆柏急需浇灌。可是，水跟不上。由于当时资金紧张，水利设施建设不能马上到位。李成基找到尕布龙，尕布龙心急如焚。

只能先抽韵家口村泵站的水解决困难了，尕布龙马上让司机崔生满用尕布龙自己的工资买上冰糖、烟酒、茯茶，亲自到管理泵站的村民家里求情，说明情况。还好，管理泵站的村民答应了。

210亩小树苗喝上了水，李成基的干劲更足了。

去韵家口的那天上午，小雨才停了不久。走在树冠秀丽的云杉丛中，植物的味道好闻极了。

李成基的脸上洋溢着幸福的笑容："这几年的条件好多了。省上对绿化的支持力度很大，可尕布龙种树那几年，经济上非常困难。"

李成基告诉我："青海的经济基础本来就弱，省上能拿出部分资金搞绿化已是难能可贵，很多时候，都得靠尕布龙副省长四处化缘，想办法。一开始，因为缺钱，我们只能栽种便宜的树种。红柳，3分钱一株；沙棘、黑刺1分钱一株；榆树2分钱一株。到了2002年，卖出了第一批树苗后，我们才有了改良树种的条件，种上了圆柏、云杉、油松。"

经过多年的实践经验，李成基和尕布龙一样也成了植树育林的行家。到了造林后期，水利设施的布点安装、工程要求，他都懂，都要一一过问，彻底搞清楚。若发现地下输水管道渗漏，有山体滑坡的可能，就马上要求以最快的速度进行检查维修、排除故障。他还经常对水利设备逐个进行质量检查，教育管护人员加强管护、爱惜设备，防止事故发生。检查中，发现平整土地、栽植树苗、林木灌溉不符合规范要求，一律命令返工重来，绝不姑息。为保证造林质量，他又提出整地要平、地埂要实、树要栽直栽实的要求，并且边栽边浇水，每年浇透五到七遍，最后再来一次冬灌，在

lack of money, we could only purchase cheap saplings of tree species, like rose willow, which cost 3 cents each, sea buckthorn and blackthorn, 1 cent each, and elm, 2 cents. In 2002, after we sold the first bale of saplings, we could finally afford to plant Sabina chinensis, spruces, and pines."

Li Chengji, like Gabulong, has become an expert at planting and afforesting through many years of practical experience. In the later stages of afforestation, he asked the workers how they had laid out and installed water conservancy facilities since he knew these things and project requirements. If he found out there were risks of underground pipeline leakage, water seepage, and landslides, he would demand to inspect the pipes and fix the problems as quickly as possible. Moreover, he often carried out quality inspections of water conservancy facilities one by one and instructed the workers to better maintain all the equipment to prevent accidents. During the inspection, as long as he saw that the land, saplings, or water irrigation failed to meet the standards, he would order them to start all over again with zero tolerance. In order to guarantee the forests' quality, he required that the land must be flat, banks must be solid, and trees must be planted straight and deep. Besides, he asked to water the trees as soon as they were planted and also requested watering five to seven times a year, ending with irrigation in winter. Regarding saplings selection, he demanded choosing good and robust ones, enhancing inspections of plant diseases and pests, as well as pre-plant management.

Gabulong was pretty satisfied with Li Chengji's achievements, which assured him that he had been right about Li. After retirement, Gabulong chose to devote himself to voluntary tree planting on tHebarren mountains. He was a man of boldness, wisdom, and courage. He had no ulterior motives or selfish interests, giving priority to fulfilling the obligation of the provincial government's decision about the North & South Mountains Greening Campaign. He was driven to cover tHebarren mountains with trees, sincerely serving the people wholeheartedly. He feared nothing, neither divergent opinions nor diverse comments. He courageously and successfully marched forward without regard to his aging body and ailing health, without even caring about red tape associated with policies and regulations.

Planting trees on mountains often entailed purchase of a lot of equipment and tools. Gabulong completely ignored financial systems; he bought cheap and good-quality items he needed in stores regardless of whether there was an invoice or not. At the same time, he was a very careful person. He asked Duan Guolu to keep detailed accounts of all the purchases, leaving nothing, even the purchase of a small nail, unlisted.

At the end of the year, the papers, on which written the prices and items, properly passed

树苗的选择上，要求选优苗壮苗，加强病虫害检疫、栽前管理。

对李成基取得的成绩，尕布龙非常满意，他觉得自己没看错人。退休后，在荒山上义务植树，是尕布龙自己的选择。尕布龙是一位不缺乏胆量，更不缺乏智慧和勇气的人，他的心底坦坦荡荡，没有一丁点私心杂念，只有把省委、省政府绿化南北两山的决策付诸现实的责任、只有让荒山披上绿装的坚定信念、只有甘为人民服务的担当和意识。他无所畏惧，他不怕众说评议，他不顾自己年迈多病的身躯，他甚至不顾及政策的条条框框，他勇往直前，他所向披靡。

在山上种树，经常要买很多设备工具，尕布龙不管什么财务制度，哪家的东西既便宜又好用就买哪家的，从来不管有没有发票。但同时，他也是一个非常细心的人，买任何东西，哪怕是一颗钉子，也要让段国禄记在小本子上。

年终，审计部门清点东西后认为没有问题，可驾驶员崔生满拿着一大把白条子去财务报账时，遇到了麻烦。

谁都知道，财务是不认白条子的。满腹委屈的崔生满生气地给尕布龙发牢骚："这活没法干了！白条子报不了账，您老人家不能为了省钱不开发票，违反规定啊。"

尕布龙也很生气，"开什么发票，简直就是浪费！"他认为，为了单纯开发票就买贵东西，是乱花国家的钱。

晚上，尕布龙就把他原来的秘书杨牧飞叫到家里，给当时的省长打了一份报告。第二天，尕布龙一大早赶到省长家门口，亲自把报告递给省长。省长立即拿起电话，给时任西宁市委书记的赵乐际同志打了电话。

赵乐际是这样说的："审计是财务制度，应该严格执行，但是所有的规章制度，都是用来监督的。对于尕老汉来说，别说乱花钱，只要是共产党的钱，一分一厘他都会省！"随即指示审计局，想办法解决这个问题。

2003年，时任青海省省长的赵乐际，亲自参加了春季植树造林动员大会。在那次会上，李成基向赵乐际提交了一封请求政府帮助解决植树造林中节水灌溉、人畜饮水资金和苗木出路问题的信函。

时间过去了两个月，就在李成基以为这封信一定是石沉大海的时候。有一天，时任省长的赵乐际同志竟然带着省林业部门，省水利厅、计委、财政厅的一把手来到了他承包的绿化区。

the check of the auditing department, but failed to receive reimbursement when the driver Cui Shengman rendered them at the office that dealt with finance.

Everyone knows that the funding can only be reimbursed by invoices. Cui Shengman, brimming with grievance, complained bitterly to Gabulong, "The job cannot be done! Those pieces of paper are not invoices, and they won't reimburse us. You cannot dismiss invoices just for saving money. It goes against regulations."

Gabulong was angry too, "What's the use of invoices? It's such a waste!" In his opinion, to buy expensive things only for getting invoices was the equivalent of squandering taxpayers' money.

In the evening, Gabulong called his previous secretary, Yang Mufei, and asked him to write a report to the governor at that time. The next day, Gabulong arrived at the door of the governor early in the morning and personally presented the report. The governor picked up the phone and called Zhao Leji, then secretary of the CPC Xining Municipal Committee.

Zhao Leji replied, "Auditing is the financial system and ought to be strictly followed. But all the rules and regulations are for supervision. The elderly man, Gabulong, has exerted himself to save every cent that belongs to the Communist Party." Thereupon, he gave directions to the auditing agency to figure out a way to solve the problem.

In 2003, Zhao Leji, then Governor of Qinghai Province, personally attended the mobilization meeting of the spring tree-planting activity. At this meeting, Li Chengji presented a letter to Zhao Leji, in which he asked for government's help in settling three problems encountered in afforestation: to implement water saving irrigation, to solve the lack of funds for safe drinking water, and the sales of seedlings.

Two months passed, and Li Chengji thought his requests must have fallen on deaf ears. But one day, the governor Zhao Leji came to the Green District contracted by Li Chengjir, accompanied by the heads of the Provincial Forestry Bureau, Provincial Department of Water Resources, Provincial Planning Commission, and the Department of Finance.

Under the blue sky embellished with some white clouds, one, getting an eyeful of green saplings and flattened land of the North Mountain, couldn't help being overwhelmed with the refreshing air of the early summer.

Zhao Leji stayed on the mountains for a long time, joyfully climbing one after another. He said to Li Chengji, "Planting trees on mountains is a good deed. Future generations will benefit from it. In the past, Zuo Zongtang planted trees along the road on his way to Xinjiang. Even now,

那天，初夏的北山弥漫着沁人心脾的空气。天上飘着淡淡云彩的北山山坡上，满眼是绿油油的树苗、平整过的土地。

时任青海省省长的赵乐际同志在山上待了很久，从一座山头登上另一座山头，非常高兴。他对李成基说："你在山上植树是好事，是造福千秋的大业。想当年，左宗棠远赴新疆，一路走一路种树，甘肃河西走廊至今还生长着他种下的左公柳呢！"

从山上下来时，他对身边的市林业局局长说："今年，你们可以从这个绿化区里买树苗了。"转而又笑着对李成基说："你可要按市场价要钱哦！"李成基心里乐开了花，眼睛笑成了一条缝。

自从尹克升亲自挂帅南北山绿化指挥部的总指挥，协调南北山绿化工作后，指挥部部长都由历届省长或书记亲自担任，在资金上给予最大限度的支持，省上的领导、各单位的领导节假日都喜欢到北山上走走、转转。

时任青海省省长的赵乐际同志在担任省商业厅厅长、省财政厅厅长、西宁市委书记时，都十分关心和支持南北山绿化。1994年，担任省财政厅厅长的赵乐际，对本单位的造林工作做了周密部署，及时解决了种苗、水灌、技术标准、管理责任四落实的问题，不失时机地种下了云杉、青杨、榆树、油松、红柳等7万株树苗，使财政厅率先完成了全年造林任务，苗木成活率达到94%，同各单位承包的绿化区相比，形成了栽植认真、浇水充足、普遍施肥、适当密植的特点。

2001年6月6日，时任青海省省长的赵乐际在视察了南北山绿化工作后，提出了在总结南北山一期工程经验基础上，进行二期规划以及指挥部、办公室组成机构报省政府的要求。2014年，时任青海省省长的郝鹏在北京开会时，已经担任中央政治局委员、中央书记处书

李成基绿化基地——绿化后的山梁

The Green Base of Li Chengji — hills being planted with trees

there are willows planted by him along Hexi corridor in Gansu province. The willows were named after him, called Zuo Gongliu (willows planted by Zuo Zongtang and his subordinates).

When they were going down the mountain, Zhao Leji said to the director of the Provincial Forestry Bureau next to him, "This year, you can purchase saplings from the Green District." Then, he turned to Li Chengji, smiling, "You can set the price according to the market." Li Chengji had a broad grin on his face, his eyes narrowing into a line.

Ever since Yin Shengke became the chief commander of the North-South Mountain Reforesting Headquarters and took over all the jobs related to afforesting, successive governors or secretaries of Qinghai province were in charge of the headquarters, granting the biggest financial support. Provincial leaders and officials loved to take a walk on North Mountain during holidays.

Zhao Leji, who was the governor of Qinghai province at the time showed great concern for the North and South Mountains Greening Campaign and supported it greatly when he was appointed to the head of the Commercial Department, Financial Department of Qinghai Province, and to the Secretary of Xining Municipal Party Committee. In 1994, when he was the director of the Provincial Department of Finance, he thoroughly prepared and planned the departmental share of the afforestation campaign. He promptly finalized the planting, irrigation, technological standards and administrative responsibilities. They took the opportunity to plant 70,000 trees such as spruces, populus cathayana, elms, pines, rose willows, and the survival rate reached 94%. Compared with green districts contracted by other departments, the area overseen by the financial department stood out for its careful planting, sufficient irrigation, widespread fertilization, and proper density of trees.

On June 6, 2001, having inspected the South and North Mountains Greening Work, Zhao Leji, then Governor of Qinghai Province, proposed, based on the experience derived from the first–stage project of North and South Mountains Greening Campaign, to report to the provincial government to start the second–stage program. He also recommended that they set up an institution composed of the headquarters and the general office.

In 2014, Zhao Leji, as a member of the Political Bureau of the CPC Central Committee, the general secretary of the Secretariat of the CPC Central Committee, and the minister of the Organization Department of the CPC, continued to show concern for Qinghai's afforestation. He asked Hao Peng, then governor of Qinghai province, about the North and South Mountains Greening Project of Xining.

After seventeen years, the 211 mu (hectares) of barren mountains contracted by Li Chengji

记、中央组织部部长的赵乐际同志，依然关切地询问西宁南北山绿化的情况，牵挂着青海的绿化事业。

尕布龙陪同时任省委记的赵乐际视察北山绿化工作

Gabulong accompanies Zhao Leji, the then Secretary of the CPC Qinghai Provincial Committee, to inspect the North Mountain Greening Work

17年后，由李成基承包的211亩荒山成了油松、青杨满坡，圆柏挺立、沙枣飘香的盈盈绿地，这成了他从心底里，向他敬重爱戴的副总指挥尕布龙递上的一份最为满意的答卷，一种出自尕布龙对他的品质和能力充分肯定与信任的报答。

70多岁的李成基和当年的尕布龙一样，每天一早让自己的孙子李金潇开车把他送上山，太阳落山后，再由孙子接他下山，几乎天天在山上忙碌。他说："是尕布龙给了我无穷的力量，使我实现了自己的人生理想，让我的晚年生活在健康幸福、辉煌灿烂中度过。"

在尕布龙正直、无私、伟大的人格面前，李成基无法退缩、无法停止，也无法放弃每一株蓬勃向上的绿色的希望。

一只鸟正从空中掠过，成片成片的树林像山地里的麦田，沿山势一行行排列，从山顶到沟底，从这座山到那座山，连绵中构成的是最简单、朴实的风景，然而这又是最美的风景。山下的人流像平日一样来往穿梭，也许对山上的变化浑然不觉，但是，我有一种强烈的感觉，仿佛在山上种树

became a green land filled with upright Sabina chinensis, fragrant oleaster, and slopes full of pines and spruces. Li Chengji thought that this gratifying outcome would be a great way to express gratitude to the Vice Chief Commander Gabulong, whom he highly respected and admired, for the trust and faith that Gabulong bestowed on his character and personality.

Li Chengji, who was is in his 70s and just like Gabulong, was driven by his grandson Li Jinxiao onto the mountain every morning and picked up after sunset, spending almost everyday on the mountains engaging in land greening. He told me, "It is Gabulong who has bestowed on me infinite power. He helped me realize my dream and spend my remaining years in happiness, healthiness, and glory.

In the face of Gabulong's upright, selfless, and noble example, Li Chengji could not retreat or abandon the sprouting hope given by each sapling.

A bird was flying over the sky, under which thousands and thousands of trees, much resembling wheat fields among mountains, lined along the terrain, from the top to the bottom, from this mountain to that mountain, altogether rendering the simplest but also the most beautiful view. People, coming and going as usual under the foot of the mountain, were probably totally unaware of any changes that had occurred on the mountains. However, a strong feeling overpowered me, and two pictures of Gabulong planting trees appeared. One image was him approaching us wearing a blue overcoat, straw hat, and Chinese Jiefang shoes, and taking a spade on his shoulder. Another was the portrait of him making inspection tours expectantly around the mountains with a frown and a stick in his hand for support.

These are the clearest images that Gabulong left in the minds of his colleagues of at the general offices of the North-South Mountain Reforesting Headquarters, and also are what he imprinted on my heart forever.

Some people said that without Gabulong, it would have been impossible to plant so many trees in such a short time. Even if it were possible, it would have been difficult to achieve such a high survival rate. This heartfelt sentiment speaks the truth. More importantly, through four years of painstaking practice, Gabulong enabled the people of Xining to witness the existing hope and prospect of the South and North Mountains Greening Campaign and the practical program that included site preparation, planning, adaptation to local contexts, construction of a nursery base, and the "first-green-then-beautify" method. Gabulong and his team built water conservancy projects with pipeline networks, water-saving irrigation facilities, prevented water erosion and soil loss, and managed to "keep mud in valleys." By means of zone-based control and focusing on actual

的尕布龙，正身穿蓝大褂、头戴草帽、脚穿胶鞋，扛着一把铁锹，带着一身泥土向我们走来，又仿佛挂着棍子，紧锁眉头、满眼期望地在山上四处巡查。

这是尕布龙留在南北山绿化指挥部办公室同事们心中最清晰的画面，也是他印在我脑海里挥之不去的身影。

有人说，假如没有尕布龙，就不可能在这么短的时间里种下这么多的

武警青海总队的战士在樟脑山植苗

Solders of Qinghai Armed Police Corps were planting seedlings on Zhangnao Mountain

树；就是能种下这么多树，也绝难达到这么高的成活率。这的确是一句发自肺腑的大实话，更重要的是，通过4年的艰苦实践，尕布龙让西宁人验证了南北山绿化的希望、前景，一套整地、规划，因地制宜、自建苗圃，先绿化再美化的具体方案。实现了水利建设管道网络化、节水灌溉、防治水土流失的格局，做到了"泥不出沟"，从低层次向高层次过渡，分片治理，注重实效，逐步实现"山连山、沟连沟，满山满坡绿如画"的真实图景。

不仅如此，尕布龙还注重绿化项目的实施、论证、总结，重视长远规划、阶段性成果和一年的总结。他和指挥部的同志达成共识后亲自把关、斟字

effectiveness, they gradually transformed the vision of "mountains joining mountains, valleys connecting valleys, green trees covering the whole mountains" into reality.

Moreover, Gabulong attached great importance to the implementation, verification, and generalization of afforestation projects. He emphasized the long-term plan, the summary of periodic and annual achievements. The consensus with the comrades of the headquarters permitted Gabulong to personally check every word of the work summary and deliberate on the use of particular words repeatedly in order to draw lessons from practices and have future generations make fewer mistakes. He also, by taking the chance of attending meetings in Beijing, reported the situation of the North and South Mountains Greening Campaign to the Forestry Department and Water Conservancy Administration Departments to settle some problems.

During the span of the time, Gabulong turned into a prominent expert on forestry from an administrative leader.

In October 2000, Feng Quanzhong, the famous female entrepreneur of Qinghai Province and chairman of Jiesen Cor., responded to the call of the provincial government to return farmland to forests and contracted 3,900 mu (260 hectare) of wasteland around Zhangnaowan, South Mountain.

In that year, Feng Quanzhong had undergone an operation on her leg in Beijing. But, in the spring of the next year, she was already impatient; holding onto a pair of crutches, she climbed onto Zhangnao Mountain with her still-recovering leg.

There was neither water nor path nor irrigation facilities on the mountain. The irrigation condition was extremely poor. Besides, the land she contracted skirted Zhangnaowan and was completely barren and much worse than she had imagined. Nevertheless, she has already signed the "Agreement to Transform Barren Mountains by Returning Farmland to Forestry and Grass in Zhangnaowan" with Shenjiazhai Village. She had to grit her teeth and move forward.

At that time, before the government's funds to support the conversion of farmland to forests were in place, Feng Quanzhong personally went to Yanglin, Shaanxi Province, and purchased 20 thousand saplings of spruce with her 4 million yuan. A local expert, an elderly man with the surname Wang, instructed her the technique of planting trees in arid areas after seeing she was on crutches—covering pits with a piece of plastic, digging a hold in the middle of the plastic, and letting the saplings grow out through the holes. He advised keeping the plastic covering even after the saplings survived, as it could help preserve warmth and retain a certain amount of water.

After returning to Xining, Feng Quanzhong mobilized students from the Xining Armed Police Force Academy through the Qinghai Armed Police Corps and contacted students from Qinghai

杰森集团董事长冯全忠女士（右一）

Feng Quanzhong, the chairman of Jiesen Cor. (the first on the right)

酌句、反复考量，为的是总结经验，为的是吸取教训，让后来人少走弯路，并利用在北京开两会的机会，向林业部、水利部汇报两山绿化情况，解决困难。

这时的尕布龙同志，俨然由一位行政领导，变成了一位出众的林业行家。

2000 年 10 月，青海有名的女企业家、杰森集团董事长冯全忠响应省政府退耕还林的号召，承包了南山樟脑湾一带的 3900 亩荒地。

那一年，冯全忠刚刚在北京做了腿部手术，第二年春天，心急的她便拄着双拐，拖着还没有完全康复的腿，登上了樟脑山。

山上没有水，没有路，没有一点灌溉条件和设施，而且她承包的这块地还是樟脑湾最偏僻的地方，举目望去，一片荒凉，环境比她想象的还要差好几倍。可是，与沈家寨村的"樟脑湾退耕还林（草）治理荒山承包责任书"已经签了，她只能硬着头皮朝前走。

当时，政府扶持退耕还林的资金还没有到位，冯全忠便亲自赴陕西杨陵，拿出近 400 万资金购进了 20 万棵云杉树苗。当时，杨陵有一位土专家王老汉，见到拄着双拐的冯全忠后，给她教了一个在干旱地区种树的窍门——在挖好的树坑上铺一块塑料布，塑料布的中间挖一个洞，让树苗从

Nationalities University to help the company plant seedlings with the above-mentioned method. As a result, more than half of the saplings survived that year.

The next spring, Feng Quanzhong, with all the company staff and solders from the Armed Police Corps, climbed the mountain again to plant trees. However, the condition of the roads they had built last year was terrible, and certain roads were not concrete any more. One afternoon, a bulldozer was halfway up the mountain when it was discovered that half of its wheels were hanging in the air. It was so frightening that the driver dared not to move in the cockpit. Having known the accident, Feng Quanzhong couldn't fall asleep. She watched the clock tick past five in the morning, then she asked for help from the provincial fire corps, which managed to drag the bulldozer out with the help of fire trucks.

It was in this year that 1.5 million yuan allocated by the Qinghai Provincial Development and Commission to support reforestation became available. Feng Quanzhong embarked on the construction of basic infrastructure, and the road construction was almost completed. But, Zhangnao Mountain was far away from water resources, so irrigation was still a huge problem. Up until then, water could only be diverted to Zhangnaowan from the foot of Laji Mountain, which was 35 kilometers away.

In the third year, Feng Quanzhong met the Vice Chief Commander Gabulong via the North-South Mountain Reforesting Headquarters.

Upon seeing Feng Quanzhong, Gabulong, without a word, led her directly to the area of Zhangnaowan she had contracted.

Gabulong said, "Forty bulldozers will be designated to flatten the area and create terraced fields with ridges, then you can plant trees."

For several days, Gabulong personally gave directions on Zhangnao Mountain. Through days of hard work, 200 mu (13.33 hectares) was flattened. Having seen the view in front of her and the leader who embodied simplicity just as farmers do, Feng Quanzhong, who was on crutches, was moved to tears.

Subsequently, Feng Quanzhong went to Zaozhuang, Shandong Provence, bought a batch of seedlings of cherry and nectarine, and planted on the 200 mu (13.33 hectares) land. All the seedlings survived, but due to the high altitude, they couldn't bear any fruits. So, Feng Quangzhong gave all of them to the citizens of Haidong and the county's Animal Husbandry Department.

But in that year, Feng Quanzhong's leg, owing to overwork and excessive fatigue, suffered a relapse and underwent another operation.

洞里穿出来，成活后，也不把塑料布拿掉，这样既可以保温，还可以保持一定的水分。

回到西宁后，冯全忠通过青海武警总队，动员西宁武警指挥学校的学员，又联系到青海民族大学的学生，帮助公司照此办法种树，20万棵树苗当年就成活了一大半。

第二年春天，冯全忠和公司员工、武警战士又上山种树了。可是，头一年在山上修的路，路况很糟，有些地方的土是虚的。有一天下午，推土机行至半山腰时，突然发现半边的轮子悬空着，十分骇人。司机在驾驶室里吓得动都不敢动。冯全忠知道后，一夜没合眼，好不容易挨到5点钟后请求省消防总队支援，借助消防车拖出了推土机。

就在这一年，省发改委拨下来的150万扶助资金到位，冯全忠开始了基础设施的建设，路修得差不多了。可是，由于樟脑山离水源地遥远，灌溉依旧是一个大问题，当地至今无法通水灌溉，只能从35公里外的拉脊山下引水到樟脑湾。

第三年，通过南北山指挥部，冯全忠见到了副总指挥尕布龙。

一见到她，尕布龙啥话也不说，带着她就走，一直来到了她承包的樟脑湾。

尕布龙说："我先给你调40辆推土机，把地推平，让这里成为梯田，打上塄坎，然后你再种！"

那几天，尕布龙亲自上樟脑山指挥。经过几天的日夜苦干，200亩地推平了。看着眼前的情景，看着这位像农民工一样朴实的老领导，挂着双拐的冯全忠流下了感动的热泪。

随后，冯全忠又跑到山东枣庄，进了一批樱桃、油桃的苗子种在200亩土地上。树苗是活了，但由于海拔太高，不能结果实，冯全忠便把这些成活的苗子全部送给了海东市民和县农牧局。

可那一年，因为劳累过度，冯全忠的腿病复发，做了第二次手术。

术后不久，冯全忠又挂着双拐上了樟脑山。尕布龙看见她说："你的腿不好就别上山了，指挥部给你把山推平了你再上来！"可冯全忠怎么能忍心让这位老人总往她的承包地上跑呢。

她就带着自己5岁的女儿梦恬一起在山上待着，干不了活就给种树的员工们做午饭。尕布龙来了，她要给他煮肉，可尕布龙不要，说给他做一

Soon after the operation, Feng Quanzhong again limped onto Zhangnao Mountain on crutches. Gabulong saw her and said, "It's better if you don't climb the mountain with your poor leg. You can come after the area has been flattened by the headquarters." But, Feng Quanzhong didn't have the heart to leave the elderly man all the work that belonged to her.

She climbed the mountain with her five-year-old daughter and stayed there the whole day. She couldn't do much labor, so she cooked lunch for the workers. She wanted to cook meat for Gabulong, but he refused, saying that a pot of potatoes would be wonderful.

At that time, Feng Quanzhong often felt depressed. She encountered many unimaginable difficulties since she had contracted the area. In spring, it's hard to plant due to the red soil of Zhangnao Mountain. On rainy days, the soil turned to red clay soil, while in sunny days, it became so heavy that it had to be shattered by bombs. In winter, irrigation was the biggest headache. She had tried to plant many species of Chinese medicinal plants on the mountain, such as liquorice, astragalus, bupleurum, Radix Isatidis, only to find that they grew with little yield and had little medicinal value. The large amount of money invested in the undertaking yielded no returns. She told Gabulong through tears that she couldn't carry on any longer.

Gabulong, looking at the female entrepreneur in her grievance, said, " Don't be sad. Where there is a will, there is a way. You go on with your work, and plant whatever you think should be planted. What you are doing is a good thing, a great thing. What you leave for offspring will be shades of green trees, which will accumulate extraordinary merits in the future."

After several years, having seen each small sapling grow into a 15-centimeter thick tree, Feng Quanzhong felt the years of efforts had paid off. Probably, these trees could only serve the roles of ecological and environmental protection at most, rather than generating any economic benefits in a short time. Nevertheless, she didn't forget Gabulong's words. It was he who helped her understand that one was bound to look retrospectively on life and discover, despite how much one had achieved, only what's left for posterity matters.

Liu Weidong, Feng Quanzhong's husband, was an expert on grass. He introduced a type of perennial grass seed named "alfalfa" from the United States and sent two bags to Gabulong's hometown Halejing. He told the people to try to plant the seeds 15 centimeters between apart. As a result, alfalfa grew magnificently well on Halejing prairie. Liu Weidong called Gabulong and told him that alfalfa over 10-centimeter-high could be mowed for livestock and they would grew better after mowing.

Gabulong gave the couple a Tibetan mastiff as a reward for their contribution.

锅土豆就好。

那时候，冯全忠常常会觉得十分沮丧。自从承包了这块地后，她遇到了许多无法想象的困难。春天种树难，樟脑山的土是红土，下了雨是红胶泥，干燥时，得用炮炸，冬天最担心的是浇水。她曾经在这片山上尝试种植了许多中药品种，比如甘草、黄芪、柴胡、板蓝根，但基本上没有任何效益，长出来的几乎没有什么药用价值，投入的大量资金没有回报。她含着眼泪

绿树成荫
Shade of green trees

对尕布龙说，自己快撑不下去了。

尕布龙看着这位受了委屈的女企业家说："你别难过，老天爷不负有心人，你该种啥还种啥。你做的是好事、干的是大事，给子孙后世留下的是一片片绿荫，积了大德啊！"

时隔多年后，眼见一棵棵小树苗长成了15厘米粗的树，冯全忠这才觉得自己这几年的付出是值得的。也许这些树不可能在短时间内产生经济效益，最多只能起到绿化作用，但是，她没有忘记尕布龙对她说过的话。是尕布龙让她知道了，一个人活在这个世界上，不论干了多少事，迟早有一天你会回头看一看的，看完你会明白，给后人留点什么才是最重要的。

冯全忠的丈夫刘卫东是种草的专家，他从美国引进了一种多年生的草

Through fifteen years of strenuous and arduous efforts, Qinghai Jiesen Corp., represented by Feng Quanzhong, reforested 3,915 mu (261 hectares) of wasteland with cumulative investments amounting to 60 million yuan. Additionally, 1,000 mu (66.67 hectare) of cultivated land had been reforested by devising slopes to terraced fields, resulting in a greening rate of over 90%. With the completion of digging a 163-meter underground tunnel in the water diversion project, constructing an 8000-meter rubble-and-mortar irrigation canal, and a 5000-meter iron pipe channeling water from the canal to each field, the former wasteland transformed into irrigated land, covering more than 3,000 mu (200 hectares) of terraces and slopes with trees.

In 2002, Gabulong resigned from the position of commander.

Gabulong had planted trees for ten years, working for 3,520 days with no pay. From the first to the third day of every Chinese Lunar New Year, he replaced rural migrant workers and stayed on the mountain without any pay in order to have the workers go home and celebrate the festival with their families.

Over ten years, the two barren mountains became green. More than forty green districts began to take shape. Countless young saplings personally planted by Gabulong have already grown into towering trees on the wasteland.

But then, he was unable to carry a spade, unable to measure every itch of land with his feet.

Severe pulmonary heart disease, high blood pressure, and diabetes condemned him to a life of fatigue and exhaustion. Nevertheless, he cared so much for the newly planted saplings that he still, bringing food for himself, climbed the mountain and traversed valleys, patrolling for irrigation in scorching hot days and for flood control on rainy days. He inspected forest fire prevention in winter and forest protection in autumn. When he couldn't conduct any inspections, he served the workers with boiled tea and roasted steamed buns.

Many people said to him, "Old governor, you are elderly now, you'd better not go onto the mountains. Let the young do the job!"

He responded, "I am unable to do any work now, but I can still watch and protect the trees. Even if I climb the mountain and sit there without doing anything, just looking at the green seedlings and talking to them makes me feel comfortable."

When Zhang Qingyong, who was then director of the Research Institute of Culture and Arts and lived opposite the family court of the Provincial Government where Gabulong dwelled, went to work early in the morning, he would see him in a blue overcoat and yellow Jiefang Shoes, waiting in front of the court gate for the driver to take him to the mountains, holding a thermos

籽"紫花苜蓿"，拿了两袋送到尕布龙老家哈勒景，让尕布龙家乡的人采用 15 厘米点种的方法试种。结果，紫花苜蓿在哈勒景草原长势极好。刘卫东打电话告诉尕布龙，长到 10 厘米以上就可以割下来让牲畜吃，割完以后，它们会长得更好。

为此，尕布龙还给他们两口子送了一只纯种藏獒，以示奖励。

经过艰苦努力，15 年间，冯全忠代表的青海杰森集团累计投入近6000 万元，完成荒山治理面积 3915 亩。其中坡改梯退耕还林 1000 亩，绿化率 90% 以上，开挖引水隧道工程 163 米，浆砌石支渠约 8000 米，铁管斗渠约 5000 米，昔日的不毛之地变成了水浇地，3000 多亩梯田和坡地披上了绿装。

2002 年，尕布龙从专职副总指挥的位置上退了下来。

尕布龙种树的 10 年间，没拿过一分钱报酬；10 年中，劳动日达 3520 天，每年大年初一至初三，都要给住在绿化区的农民工放假，让他们回家过年，他自己却驻守在山上，从不间断。

10 年来，两座荒山一点点变绿，40 多个绿化区初具规模。无数棵他亲手栽植的小树苗葱郁成林，覆盖着脚下的层层荒丘。

可此时的他，已无力拿起铁锹，无法用双脚丈量山上的每一寸土地。

严重的肺心病、高血压和糖尿病使他心力疲惫，可他还是放心不下山上刚刚栽下的树苗，每天依旧自带干粮，上山看护林木，在一道道沟沟梁梁上奔波。天旱了察看浇水情况，下雨了看防洪措施。冬天防火，秋天管护。干不动了，就给农民工烧茶水、烤馍馍。

有很多人劝他，"老省长，你年龄大了，就不要再上山了，让年轻人去干吧！"

他说："我是干不动了，可是，我还能看护林木，还能做点力所能及的事！哪怕就是什么也不干地坐在山上，看着那些绿苗苗，跟它们说说话，也让我觉得踏实！"

时任文化艺术研究所所长的张青勇家住省政府家属院对面，每天早上上班时都会在家属院门口看见站在路边的尕布龙，身着蓝色大褂，脚穿黄胶鞋，一手提暖壶，一手提着布口袋，等司机送他上山。

张青勇眼睁睁看着日渐衰老的尕布龙渐渐消瘦，心里难过，可也只能在远处看看。

flask in one hand and a cloth bag in the other.

Zhang Qingyong felt sad seeing Gabulong's gradual decline, but he could only watch him from afar.

In this way, Gabulong persisted in his work for another six years.

He thought that it was the party that raised him from a boy who herded sheep to a leader. The trust of the party organizations drove him to perform well in afforestation and leave lush mountains to the future generations.

It made no difference for him whether or not he had an official position, and he had never cared about that.

In the autumn of 2008, Gabulong climbed onto the mountain for the last time.

Gabulong, sitting on the top of the mountain and gasping for air, looked pretty haggard. The blue veins and blood vessels on tHeback of his hands protruded out, and calluses blanketed his palms. He looked up, inviting soft willows to stroke his face at their will.

Magpies warbled pleasantly. The sunlight slanted through the trees from the sky, painting a picture of shades just like Chinese dark ink splashed splendidly onto every corner of the mountain. His heart throbbed quickly, and his eyes filled with tears. Thinking that he had neither strength nor chance to come here again, he felt disappointed. He's really too old to do anything.

It is the same mountain, only greener now.

It is the same wind sweeping through the valleys and fields, only now it has became gentler.

I imagined the dark-red face of elderly Gabulong when he strolled the alley with trees on both sides between the two mountains, leisurely enjoying the wonderful landscape on the highland and breathing the humid air.

In this world, how many people can beam a pleasant smile at others' heartwarming behaviors and be grateful? How many people are busy pursuing fame and fortune? How many people know that it was Gabulong who pioneered reforestation on the two mountains, a modern-day "foolish old man," the elderly man past seventy who had been a provincial leader for twenty-two years and had been awarded the first "Mother River Protection Award"? And how many people know that he donated all the prize money (20,000 yuan) from the award to buy more saplings? He worked hard and lived frugally his whole life. When counting his possessions, people only found two sets of overcoats and underclothes to alternate between washing, a pair of leather shoes, cloth shoes, Chinese Jiefang shoes, galoshes, a garment, a straw hat, a bed made of hardboard, a quilt, a mattress, a pillow, and a toiletry case.

就这样，尕布龙又硬撑着干了6年。

他认为，是党把他从一个"放羊娃"培养成领导干部，党组织信任他，他就要把两山绿化好，为子孙后代留下一片青山。

担任不担任职务，对他来说一个样，他从不在乎这些。

2008年秋天，尕布龙最后一次上山。

坐在山顶上的他，喘着粗气，面容憔悴，手背上青筋、血管突起，手掌上布满了老茧。他仰起头，任温柔的柳丝抚摸着他粗糙的脸膛。

喜鹊欢叫着，太阳的光线渐渐从高空斜照下来，树影如一抹黛色的香墨，泼洒在大山的角落里。他的心一阵悸动，眼里噙满了泪水。再也没有力气、没有机会上山了，他感到有些怅然若失。自己真的老了，干不动了。

大山还是那座大山，却青绿了许多。

山风还是那阵山风，却温柔了许多。

我心中想着年迈的尕布龙黑红的脸膛，漫步于两山的绿荫小道，轻松地享受着这片高地上难得的生态景观，呼吸着湿润的空气。

这个世界上，有多少人能够在怀抱温暖时唇齿开花、心生感恩；有多少人在为追逐名利四处奔波，又有多少人知道，率先在这两座山上植树造林的尕布龙，是曾经担任了22年省级干部的领导、接受了首届"母亲河奖"的古稀老人、"两山老愚公"，又有多少人知道他把2001年荣获首届"母亲河奖"的两万元奖金全部捐出来买了树苗。他一生勤俭节约，清点家产时，只有两套换洗的外衣、内衣，一双皮鞋，一双布鞋，一双胶鞋，一双雨靴，一件大褂，一顶草帽，一张硬板床，一套被褥，一个枕头，一套洗漱用具。

更叫人不忍回想的是，那么多年，那么多个鞭炮齐鸣、礼花漫天的年三十晚上，家家户户围坐在餐桌前把酒言欢，享受天伦之乐时，这位老人，却嚼着干馍馍，喝着黑刺叶冲泡的水，守护着寂寞无声的山林，为山下古城西宁星星点点的万家灯火，勾画着美丽的蓝图。

我不敢想，又常在想……

他这一生为什么要这样做？

这一切，有多少人能够理解，又有多少人能够做到？

有一种人的生命，有一种人的精神就是这样，要求自己最大限度地造福人类，最小限度地向社会索取。

哲人说，在孤寂里，生命往往能更有效地体现生命自身和世界。尕布

What I couldn't bear to think is that Gabulong, over so many years, spent every Chinese New Year's Eve on the mountain. He chewed dry bread and drank tea made of blackthorn leaves, guarding the silent forest. He outlined a blueprint for every family under the foot of the mountain in the ancient city of Xining. Meanwhile, people were drinking alcohol and talking merrily around a dinner table as a family union in the festive atmosphere created by setting off firecrackers and displaying spectacular fireworks.

I dare not to think, but I can't help thinking...

Why did he devote his whole life to this?

How many people can appreciate what he did? How many people can do what he accomplished?

There is a type of people destined to dedicate their lives and spirits to the creation of more benefits to society with their utmost effort while asking for as little as they can in return.

Philosophers say that in loneliness, life can often more effectively reflect itself and the world. Had not Gabulong endeavored to infinitely spread and magnify his effort and hard work in this world, from prairie to rivers, from fields to valleys?

Who said Gabulong was in his twilight years? He had already uplifted his ordinary life to a magnificent degree! Who would dare to say that his name will be forgotten? His spirit will be passed down from generation to generation; his generosity and altruistic deeds will be a model for the world for centuries to come!

My heart as well as the pen in my hand became unusually heavy, so heavy that I couldn't bear it, couldn't drag myself from it.

Human beings are born equal. They are survivors and creators of this universe, and just like flowers and trees, are basking in the generosity of nature and relishing the air and sunshine. But how they can be so different?

It confirmed an old Chinese saying, "It takes ten years to grow a tree, while a hundred years to bring up a generation of good men." Gabulong's rock-solid faith of and the Foolish Old Man's spirit have infected countless people and stimulated Qinghai people to carry on "The Two-Mountain Spirits" embodied by Gabulong from generation to generation, to face up with difficulties and explore a new model of afforestation in arid areas of the plateau region.

Several years ago, lush trees sang in choir through the wind, proving to people that the North and South mountains could be greened. 430,000 trees on more than 1,000 mu (66.67 hectares) of land resembled green flags, awakening people's confidence in afforestation and strengthening

龙不就是在努力地让自己的付出和努力在这个世界上无限扩展，无限放大，从草原到河流，从原野到山脉吗？

谁说他已是垂暮之年？他已将平凡的灵魂升华得这般绚烂夺目！谁又敢说他的名字会被人遗忘？他的精神将代代相传，他的感人事迹将流芳百世！

我的心，我手中的笔变得异常沉重，沉重得难以忍受、难以自拔。

人是平等的。在天地万物中，人是生存者、创造者，和花草树木一样饱受大自然恩泽、享受空气和阳光，然而人为什么又是这样的不同。

一切都应验了中国一句老话："十年树木，百年树人。"尕布龙百折不挠的坚强信念和愚公移山的精神感染了无数的人，也激励着一代又一代青海人发扬尕布龙留下来的"两山精神"，迎难而上，探索出高原干旱地区造林绿化的新模式。

多年前，阵阵风吹过那苍翠浓郁的林木，树林"呼啦啦"拍手吟诵，向人们证明南北两山是可以绿化的事实；那1000多亩土地上的43万株树木，像一面面绿色的旗帜，唤醒了人们心中对绿色的信心，也更加坚定了青海省委、省政府绿化南北两山的决心。南北两山的生态工程，不仅成就了青海人集体劳动、集体创造的壮举。同时，也庄严地宣告了青海省委、省政府作出"绿化西宁南北山、改善西宁生态环境"重大决策的正确性。

更多的人自愿上山种树了，更多的责任单位、行业和个人争先恐后承包了绿化区，实现了省委省政府当初下决心搞绿化，是为了让全民参与南北山植树造林，以此推动和发展青海生态文明建设步伐，护佑"中华水塔"，保护高原生态的最初梦想。几年后，绿化承包责任区增加到了100多块，200多个单位和个人划片承包，与指挥部签订了绿化合同。省财政、发改委、农业、水利、交通、电力、环保、林业、科技等部门，把南北山绿化的基础设施建设、植树造林和科技推广项目纳入了本部门的总体规划，省市近千万人次参与南北两山绿化，省市领导亲自担任总指挥，下定了向荒山要绿色，创造生态建设成果的决心。

四季更替，春来秋往，青海省委、省政府的领导在变，可治理南北山、绿化南北山的计划、决心、信心和热情没有变。省委、省政府历届主要领导，尹克升、赵乐际、杨传堂、宋秀岩、骆惠宁、郝鹏都在任职期间亲自担任南北山绿化指挥部总指挥的职务，以协调解决重大问题，推进南北山绿化

the Qinghai Provincial Government's determination to further implement the North and South Mountains Greening Campaign. The ecological project of greening the North and South mountains not only represented the magnificent accomplishment of the collective and joint work of the people of Qinghai, but also made a solemn announcement that the Qinghai Provincial Government's major decision on "Greening North and South Mountains in Xining, Improving Ecological Environment of Xining" has been accurate.

More and more people voluntarily took part in tree-planting activities, and organizations, trades, and individuals competitively scrambled to contract green districts. The provincial government's initial dream, which aimed to have all citizens participate in the North and South Mountains Greening Project, to accelerate the construction of ecological civilization, and to protect China's "water tower" and plateau ecology, had been realized. Several years later, more than 200 organizations and individuals had signed the greening contract with the headquarters, increasing the number of contracted districts to over 100. The provincial financial department, the development and commission, the provincial agriculture department, the provincial water resources department, the provincial transport department, the provincial electricity department, the provincial enviro nmental protection department., the provincial forestry department, the provincial science and technology department and other departments have taken infrastructure projects, afforestation projects, science and technology projects of the North and South Mountains Greening Campaign into their overall plans. Nearly 10 million people joined in the campaign, with provincial and municipal leaders personally serving as commanders. People were determined to plant trees on wasteland and make significant achievements in ecological construction.

With the lapse of time, the governors of Qinghai province have changed, but the plan, determination, faith, and enthusiasm of reforesting the North and South Mountains have not altered. All the previous governors, Yin Kesheng, Zhao Leji, Yang Chuantang, Song Xiuyan, Luo Huining, and Hao Peng, had acted as commanders of the North-South Mountain Reforesting Headquarters to facilitate coordination in resolving major problems and to push the development of the Mountain Greening Campaign.

Having completed the first stage of reforesting 45,000 mu (3,000 hectares) of land in 2002, the provincial government launched the second stage of the North and South Mountains Greening Project as well as the South Mountain Green Barrier Construction Project.

The vast mountain boiled, and the entire city seemed to be aflame with greenness.

Through 25 years of hard work, Xining, up to 2014, had completed the project on time by

进程。

2002年，在完成了4.5万亩绿化一期工程的任务后，省委、省政府又启动了南北山绿化二期工程和大南山绿色屏障建设工程。

茫茫大山沸腾了。整座城市仿佛被绿色的火光点燃。

经过25年的艰苦鏖战，截至2014年，西宁市南北两山完成造林20.93万亩，栽植苗木2000余万株，造林成活率85%以上，工程规划完成率达100%。其中，林地10.23万亩，占总数的48.9%；灌木林地10.70万亩，占总数的51.1%。2006年以后，森林覆盖率达75%。建成泵站62座，各种管道1159千米，蓄水池378座，总容量4.25万立方米，可控灌溉面积21万亩。修筑通向各绿化区的硬化道路252千米，通向各山头地块的简易道路507千米，瞭望台、检查站、管护房128处。

这是一组枯燥的数字，不够柔软、轻灵，缺乏文学性，但对于这片广阔而深厚的土地，对于生活在这片土地上的人民，我认为，再没有比这组数字更优美、更温柔、更动人的语言了。

黄昏临近，我再次登上这座每天都在发生变化的大山。一条条嵌着金边的绿化带，似河水汩汩流淌，绿叶上的光斑盈盈闪烁。如今，南山、北山、西山已经成了西宁人休闲的最佳去处。春季柳丝鲜绿，沙枣花香；夏季八瓣梅、紫丁香、蜀葵竞相吐艳；秋季火红的沙棘果挂满枝头。即使在冬季漫长的日子里，也有那挺拔的松树、圆柏在风中沙沙作响。不知有多少次，我打着雨伞在细雨霏霏的山中漫步，听水滴落在肥嫩的树叶上发出的动人声音，不禁热泪盈眶。

西宁古城的景色美了，风沙少了，雨水多了，空气湿润了，水土流失得到了控制，大气环境质量有了改善。南北两山相继开放了湟水森林公园、红叶谷、植物园、动物园、南山公园，还增添了意蕴丰厚，异彩纷呈的丁香山、文峰耸翠、北山烟雨等景点。当人们在此徜徉流连时，感受到的又何止是人们化苍凉为蓬勃，化贫瘠为神奇的力量。

不知道，绿化这两座荒山的工程还将持续多久，还会衍生出多少值得这片森林永远铭记的故事。我走着，在布满林荫的山间小路上，在种满葵花、丁香的山坡上，体会着每一棵树、每一朵鲜花怀念尕布龙的心情，享受着作为生活在这座古城里的人所有的甘甜与幸福。

2015年11月24日，由国家林业局、全国政协人口资源委员会、安徽

planting more than 2 million saplings and afforesting 2.093 million mu (13,953.3 hectares) of land, (1.023 million mu (6,820 hectares) of forest, and 1.07 million mu (7,133.3 hectares) of grassland on the two mountains. The survival rate was over 85%. After 2006, forest coverage had risen to 75%. Sixty-seven water pumps had been installed, along with various pipelines totaling 1159 km in length. 378 reservoirs with a total water storage capacity of 425,000 cubic meters had been built, increasing irrigation areas to 210,000 mu (14 thousand hectares). Moreover, a 252 km long road leading to all the green districts, a 507 km long path reaching to hills and mountains, as well as 128 watchtowers, checkpoints, and rooms for tools had been constructed.

These numbers may seem boring, neither soft nor literary. But to the large expanse of land and people who live there, no language is gentler, more beautiful, and touching than this numerical data.

As dusk approached, I again climbed onto the mountains which were changing every day. The green belts edged with the color of gold resembled gurgling rivers. The dew gathered on the leaves glittered and shined. Now, the North, South, and West Mountains have become the best resorts for the people of Xining. In spring, the willows are bright green, oleaster is fragrant. In summer, plums, lilacs, and hollyhock are competitively blossoming. In autumn, the red fruits of oleaster are all over the branches. Even in the long winter days, there are pines and cypresses rustling in the wind. I don't know how many times I have rambled on the mountain on rainy days, but each time when I heard the wonderful sound of rain dripping on green leaves, tears welled up in my eyes.

With less sand, more rain, humid air, the control of water and soil erosion, and the improvement of the atmospheric environment, the ancient city of Xining became more beautiful. Huangshui Forest Park, Hongye Valley, Botanical Garden, Zoological Garden, Nanshan Park, one after another, opened on the North and South Mountains. Besides, scenic spots like Dingxiang Mountain, Wenfengsongcui (a scenic spot in the North Mountain), have been added to the North Mountain. When people are strolling and lingering, what they felt was more than the power of turning wasteland to forest, transforming barrenness with magic.

I have no idea how long the North and South Mountains Greening Campaign will last, or how many stories worthy of being remembered by the forest will come from it. I wandered on the path shaded by trees on two sides and roamed on the slopes covered with sunflowers and lilacs, experiencing the feeling that each tree and each bright flower missed Gabulong, and enjoyed all the sweetness and happiness of people living in this ancient city.

On November 24, 2015, a symposium, co-hosted by the State Forestry Administration,

省人民政府、经济日报社联合主办的"2015中国城市森林建设座谈会"在安徽宣城召开，会上对青海西宁、安徽宣城等21个2015年"国家森林城市"进行了命名授牌。西宁市由此成为西北地区第一个获此殊荣的省会城市，也是西北地区唯一获得"国家园林城市"和"国家森林城市"双荣誉的省会城市。

这让我不得不再次想起尕布龙紧蹙眉头，一身布衣，手握铁锹，奔波劳累的身影……

森林生态系统是陆地生态系统的主体，山林向城市渗透，是人类赖以生存的基础。城市森林是建设宜居城市、美丽中国的象征。西宁南北山绿化的成功实施，是人类敬畏自然、尊重生命、绿色发展思想的体现；是西宁人征服荒漠、改造生态，在高寒干旱地区超前绿色发展的创举；是提前践行党的十八大提出的建设生态文明的成功实践；是尕布龙坚韧不拔、矢志不渝、亲力亲为、无私奉献精神的传承；是尕布龙勇气、智慧、韬略与才能的体现；是个人的魅力，是群体的力量，是发生在现实生活中的神话。

我身临其境，周身的细胞都在急速地跳跃，只叹自己笔下乏力，千思万虑出的好词都不够确切、精美。

2020年春，我又一次登上北山山顶，来到大寺沟，来到段国禄日夜坚守的金融系统绿化地。

杏树还未发芽，段国禄和他的妻子，还有几个务林人员正在为这片杏树林修剪枝丫。天还是那么蓝，云还是那么白，空气还是那么清新，透彻心肺，可尕布龙已经离开我们9年了。段国禄的眼睛里噙着泪水，心里沉甸甸的。他无时无刻不在怀念与追思中度过，无时无刻不铭记着尕布龙对他的殷殷重托。想当年，20岁的段国禄跟随尕布龙来到大寺沟，在艰难的日子里创造了人工造林的奇迹。如今，他更是离不开，舍不下，这座苍苍莽莽的大山上印着尕布龙的足迹，渗透着尕布龙的心血和汗水。他没有别的能耐，他只会施肥、挖坑、种树、浇水、护树，剪枝修叶，只会望着每一棵长大的树出神地发呆。他能去哪儿呢？哪个地方能收留他，又有哪个地方，能让他的日子过得这般踏实、舒心？

刚上山的时候，尕布龙曾经代表西宁南北山绿化指挥部和段国禄签过一张40年的用工合同。尕布龙说："你要答应我，在山上种40年树，一直到60岁干不动为止。"他又说："你一定要安下心、扎下根。你放心，

CPPCC Population Resources Committee, Anhui Provincial Government, and Economic Daily, and titled "2015 Construction of State-level Forest Cities," was held in Xuancheng in East China's Anhui Province. At the symposium, 21 "State-level Forest Cities" of 2015, including Xining in Qinghai Province and Xuancheng in Anhui Province had been named and awarded. Xining became the first among provincial capitals in Northwest China that won the name, and Xining has been the only city in the Northwest region that has obtained both "National Garden City" and "State-level Forest City".

This made me think of Gabulong climbing from one hill to another in cloth garments, with a deep frown on his face and a spade in his hand.

The forest ecosystem is the main body of the terrestrial ecosystem. Integrating mountains and forests into cities is fundamental for modern living. A forest city is the symbol of building livable cities and a beautiful China. The successful implementation of the North and South Mountains Greening Campaign showcases the essence of the idea for revering nature, respecting the laws of nature and green development. It represents the achievements that the people of Xining accomplished by conquering the desert, promoting ecosystem preservation, and calling for green development in arid, alpine plateau regions. It has practiced in advance the eco-civilization construction proposed by the 18th National Congress of the Communist Party of China (CPC), and has carried on the tenacious and altruistic spirit of Gabulong. It also symbolizes the courage, wisdom, strategy, and capability embodied by Gabulong, and reflects individual charisma and collective power. It is a magic that happened in reality.

I am totally immersed in the scene, every cell in my body is leaping quickly. I lament the wonderful words garnered by racking my brain are not accurate or elegant enough to convey my thoughts and feelings.

In the spring of 2020, I climbed onto the top of the North Mountain again. I went to Dasigou and the green area that Duan Guolu has been holding fast to.

The apricot trees have not yet blossomed. Duan Guolu, along with his wife and some other forestry workers, was pruning the trees. The sky was still so blue, the clouds still so white, and the air so refreshing, but Gabulong had already left us for nine years. Duan Guolu's eyes filled with tears; his heart was full of sadness. He reminisced about the old days every day, remembering the great trust that Gabulong had for him. In retrospect, 20-year-old Duan Guolu came to Dasigou with Gabulong and created afforestation magic in hard times. Now, he doesn't want to leave the mountains imprinted with the footprints and embodying the devotion and perspiration of

你个人的问题，迟早会得到解决。"现在，那张合同早已丢失，可尕布龙的话却一直放在段国禄的心上，从未失去它原有的分量，也让他别无选择。他和以前一样，每年正月十六开始运肥、修剪树枝、检修输水管道、试水。清明前后栽种、补种、浇水、施肥、喷药，完成林分改造任务。夏天，天晴浇水，阴天挖坑、修筑隔离带。冬天管护、防火、冬灌，从未有过一天的懈怠。每逢下雪，为避免上下山的人和车辆发生危险，段国禄带头扫除山路上的积雪，从绿化区一直扫到山下。如今，这项工作已经成为各绿化区管护人员习以为常的事。

还记得那位经尕布龙作工作，承包了青海省毛纺公司绿化区的李成基吗？今年，他已是82岁高龄的老人，却依然在他承包的绿化区忙忙碌碌。由于长年在山上劳动，李成基的身体非常健康，看上去比同龄人至少年轻10岁。经过多年努力，450余亩荒山，已然被层层绿色覆盖，种植类型由过去的阔叶林新疆杨、青海杨、柳树、榆树，增加到常绿乔木油松、云杉、落叶松、樟子松、祁连圆柏，走上了林分结构平稳，高质量发展的路子。2009年，李成基荣获"全国离退休干部先进个人"的表彰，更让人欣慰的是，李成基的孙子李金潇，不仅负责送爷爷上山植树的任务，还依照国家和青海省有关林地建设的相关优惠政策，积极从事社会公益和生态活动，鼓励更多的人上山植树，创造更多的生态价值和社会价值。

今年，爷孙俩又向指挥部申请管护预计面积600～1000亩的荒山，打算在绿化区多种些丁香、探春、红刺玫、黄刺玫、碧桃、干柴牡丹、天山月季，不仅让南北两山添上绿色，还要让它变得更美，更艳。

尕布龙种下的树已经长大成材，尕布龙对这两座大山的承诺绵延不绝，回响在大山深处。

尕布龙走后，西宁市南北山绿化指挥部启动了南北山绿化三期工程，到2018年底，累计绿化荒山面积51.6万亩；栽植青海云杉、祁连圆柏、油松、青杨、柽柳、柠条等20余种优良乡土树种4470余万株；治理沟道36条，修建提灌站93座，总容量14.7万立方米，建成了覆盖整个林区的节水灌溉管道系统；修筑贯通各个绿化区的绿化道路500千米，形成了比较完善的路网系统；建成管护房111处，保障了各绿化单位管护人员的生活用水、用电，初步建起了服务林木资源建设与保护的基础设施系统；形成了"水、土、路、树、技、管"六字绿化方针，探索出了高寒干旱地区大规模国土

Gabulong. He doesn't have other talents or skills, except to fertilize, dig holes, plant, water, protect and prune trees, and to watch these growing trees in a trance. Where can he go? Which place will take and offer him a job? And which place can make him live in such a comfortable and down-to-earth way?

When Duan Guolu first worked on the mountains, Gabulong, on behalf of the North-South Mountain Reforesting Headquarters, signed an employment contract with him that asked for him to work forty years. Gabulong said to him, "You have to promise me that you will plant trees on the mountains for forty years until you cannot work any more." He also told him, "You have to settle down here. Don't worry about your personal problems, we will get them figured out sooner or later." Now, Duan Guolu has lost that contract long ago, but he always remembers what Gabulong said to him. These words still carry the same weight and left him with no other choice. As usual, from the sixteenth day of the first Chinese lunar month, he began to transport fertilizer, prune trees, inspect water pipes, and test water. Around Tomb-Sweeping Day, he started planting and replanting trees, irrigating, fertilizing the fields, and spraying pesticides, all to complete the task of improving the forest stand. On sunny summer days, he irrigated, while on rainy days, he dug holes and mended isolation strips. In winter, he was responsible for tree protection, fire prevention, and winter irrigation. He never slacked off in his work for a single day. Whenever it snowed, Duan Guolu initiated to sweep thick snow away on roads from the green districts to the foot of the mountain, so people and vehicles could safely pass. Now, the task has become a habitual routine to the forest workers in each green district.

Do you still remember Li Chengji, who was persuaded by Gabulong to contract the green district of Maofang Company in Qinghai Province? This year, he is eighty-two years old, but he has been busy with the contracted districts. Owing to the works he did on the mountains for many years, he has been very healthy and looks ten years younger than his peers. Through years of hard work, over 450 mu (30 hectares) of wasteland had been transformed into fields covered with plants and trees, adding evergreen arbor species like pine, spruce, larch, Pinus sylvestris, Qilian sabina chinensis to the previous types of trees, like broad-leaved Xinjiang aspen, Qinghai aspen, willow, elm, and the province embarked onto the road of "steady forest stand structure, high-quality development". In 2009, Li Chengji won the award "Advanced Individuals of National Retired Cadres". What's more gratifying is that Li Jinxiao, the grandson of Li Chengji, not only still drives his grandpa to the mountains to complete the afforestation task, is also, in line with China's and Qinghai Province's favorable policies in forest restoration, enthusiastically engaged in social

绿化建设的成功模式。

不仅如此，尕布龙在艰苦磨砺中铸就的不屈不挠的奋斗精神、奉献精神，在南北两山同样得到了巨大传承。历届省委、省政府的大力支持和倾情关注，奠定了青海造林事业发展进步的基础；"无私奉献、艰苦奋斗、锲而不舍"的南北两山精神，成了西宁南北两山这两道绿色屏障的灵魂；扎根在山上的段国禄夫妇、老汪夫妇，还有许许多多我不知姓名、不曾见过面的，把毕生精力献给这两座大山的普通农民，是这两座大山持有无限生机的希望。

benefit and ecological activities, encouraging more people to join in afforestation and creating more ecological as well as social value.

This year, the grandfather and grandson applied to the headquarters to plant and protect, predicatively, 600 mu (40 hectares) to 1000 mu (66.67 hectares) of wasteland. They plan to plant lilacs, Jasminum floridum, red roses, yellow roses, peaches, peonies, and Chinese roses. These plants will not only make the two mountains greener, but also make them look more beautiful and colorful.

The saplings planted by Gabulong have grown to towering trees. The promise that he made to the mountains stretched afar and reverberated in the mountains.

After Gabulong left, the North-South Mountain Reforesting Headquarters in Xining started the third phase of the project. By the end of 2018, a total area of 516 thousand mu (34 thousand and 4 hundred hectares) of wasteland had been greened, on which more than 44.7 million trees of over 20 species like Qinghai spruce, Qilian sabina chinensis, Chinese pine, cathay poplar, willow and Caragana were planted. The project enabled the regulation of 36 valleys to prevent further erosion, set up 93 irrigation stations, totaling capacity to 1.47 million cubic meters of water and covering the whole forest with water-saving irrigation systems. Additionally, it built 500 kilometers of green roads that reach all the green districts, shaping a relatively complete road network, and constructed 111 houses to ensure water and electricity supply for forest rangers. Thereby, establishing a six-word reforestation policy that focused on "water, land, road, tree, technology, pipeline" and basically constructing infrastructure that served for reforestation and forest protection. The success in reforesting the two mountains has pioneered a new model for planting a large number of trees in arid, alpine plateau regions.

Moreover, Gabulong's perseverance, devotion, and efforts in confronting hardships have equally been carried forward on the North and South Mountains. All the previous provincial governments' great support, care, and concern laid a foundation for the development and advancement of Qinghai's afforestation campaign. "Devotion, hard working, perseverance," which is the spirit of the two mountains, has become their soul. People like Duan Guolu and his wife and Lao Wang and his wife, who rooted their lives on the mountains, along with many other ordinary farmers whose names I do not know and whose faces I have never seen, devoted their whole life to the mountains, contributing to the vitality and vigor of the two mountains.

永生的精神高地

　　高原的夕阳是猛烈的，伴着落日的余晖，追着树影、洒在葵花金色的面庞上。进入林中，我的体内仿佛也有了一片树林。体内叶脉的呼吸，来自山上飞鸟的鸣叫、大山的低语、百姓的呼声，来自尕布龙刚强、伟岸的身躯。

　　离开大山后的最后两年，尕布龙几乎是在医院里度过的。

　　他什么也吃不下，喝不下。心里念念不忘、牵肠挂肚，能触动他，让

第一届"母亲河奖"

The First "Mother River Protection Award"

Eternal Spirit of the Highland

The sunset on the plateau is dazzling, accompanied by the afterglow, and glimmering on the trees and on the golden land. A forest, it seemed, appeared in my body when I walked in the forest, into which life was bestowed by the tweets of birds flying up high, the whisper of the mountains, the voice of the people and Gabulong's big and tall body.

After leaving the mountains, Gabulong spent most of his last two years in the hospital.

He couldn't eat or drink. What he bore in mind were the mountains and the green land, into which he instilled his life, and only they could make his eyes glow and his heart throb.

When his family members, secretaries, drivers and colleagues from the headquarters came to see him, he would ask all about the mountains.

As soon as he saw Duan Guolu enter the ward, he removed his breathing tubes, sat up straight, and inquired about the rose willows and pines. Each time, he told Duan Guolu, "You mustn't leave the North Mountain after I die. If you go, the seedlings of rose willows will die. They are like little children that we raised together."

Duan Guolu dissolved into tears and couldn't speak.

Reaching the last moment, he was unconscious and unable to to speak. However, as long as Duan Guolu came in, Gabulong would, though motionless, stare at him

他的眼睛发出光泽，让他的心为之震颤的，还是那座高山和那些他用心血浇灌出的绿色的希望。

家人、指挥部的同事、秘书、司机来看他，他问的全是山上的事。

一看见段国禄走进病房，他就拔掉氧气管直起身，问红柳、油松。每一次，都要对段国禄说："我死后，你千万不要离开北山啊。你要是走了，那些红柳苗苗就死了。那可是我们俩像带"月娃娃"一样带大的孩子啊！"

段国禄泣不成声。

到了最后的时刻，他已经神志不清，不能说话。但是，只要段国禄去了，他就会一动不动，直勾勾地望着他，似有千言万语哽在心头、万般嘱托需要交代。

多年来，尕布龙被糖尿病、高血压、肺心病、肺气肿、前列腺肥大等各种疾病困扰。他很清楚自己的身体，他知道，一生所剩的日子不是很多了。他想回到海北海晏，因为那里是他的家，再不回去，他就永远回不去了。他想念故土，想念女儿，想念他的外孙。他想起他回家偶尔带给孙女达什姐莉、孙媳妇几枚彩色的小发卡时，她们快乐的样子；想起过年时，他给孩子们带去小炮仗，看见男孩们躲在一边抢来抢去，他就会猫着腰，朝大外孙东珠招招手，示意聪明的东珠，爷爷给他悄悄藏了几个的情景。

奖牌和奖状

Medal and certificates

想起这些，他毫不犹豫地退掉了省政府分给他的那套楼房。

当时，省政府考虑到他年事已高，身体有病，不让他退房，可他不同意，省政府又让他在新修建的家属楼中选一套小点的住房，他也不答应。

fixedly, just like thousands of words welled up in his heart and millions of instructions needed to be explained.

For years, Gabulong suffered from diabetes, high blood pressure, pulmonary heart disease, emphysema, prostrate hypertrophy, and other diseases. He was aware of his physical situation and knew that there was not much time left. He wanted to return to his home in Haiyan, Haibei, in Qinghai Province. He felt that he would never be able to go there if he didn't head back there now. He missed his homeland, missed his daughter, and his grandson. He recalled the happy faces of Dashijieli and his granddaughter-in-law when he came back home occasionally with colorful hairpins for them. He remembered how he stooped to beckon his grandson Dongzhu, indicating to the clever boy that he had hidden some without telling anybody after watched children grabbing fireworks in a corner given by Gabulong.

Thinking about these memories, he returned to the house given to him by the provincial government without hesitation.

At that time, taking into account his age and illness, the provincial government decided to not allow him to check out. However, he disagreed. They asked him to select a smaller house in the newly built residential quarters, but he did not answer.

Gabulong insisted on returning to the prairie, to be an ordinary and down-to-earth herdsman.

He, for the first time, reported to the party for personal affairs.

Due to his resolution and adamancy, the provincial government decided to allocate him 400,000 yuan as a setting-in allowance to help him build some rooms in his homeland. Having learned this, he paced around the house as if he had done something wrong, not knowing what to do.

"I haven't done many things for the party, but the party has bestowed on me so much money. I can't help feeling guilty!"

He returned home apologetically and spent 230,000 yuan building a courtyard and five rooms.

He had been expecting to go back to his homeland, listening to the songs of skylarks, calls of cattle and sheep, and smelling the fragrance of milk and flowers in his precious old age.

It's the prairie that sits far from cities, toward which he has been affectionate and

他执意要回到草原，做一个普普通通、实实在在的牧人。

他第一次为自己的事向组织上做了汇报。

因他态度坚决，省政府决定给他发40万元安家费，让他在老家盖几间平房。他知道后，像做错了事似的在屋里踱来踱去，不知该如何是好。

"我这一辈子没为党做几件事，可是，党却给了我这么多钱，我惭愧啊！"

他心怀歉意地回到家乡，花了23万元请人给他盖了一个小院、五间平房。

他盼望着能回到家乡，在弥足珍贵的晚年时光，聆听百灵鸟的歌唱、牛羊的欢叫，嗅闻飘香的奶茶、花香。

那是他充满情思的草原，远离城市，坦坦荡荡一如神灵的胸怀。

那是令他沉醉的家乡，洁净、纯粹，一如泥土的清香。

他还在心里制定了一个计划，在哈勒景草原上搞一个牛羊育肥示范项目，修建畜棚，购买牛羊，还要在房前屋后、道路两旁栽满绿树……

房子落成后，与他共事多年的马万里、李志刚、简顺生，从西宁赶来给他贺房。那天，他高兴极了，难得地绽开了笑脸，可也是只收下了一幅字、一幅画，权作纪念。

在她女儿召格力的家里，我看到了青海省著名的书法家李海观先生专门为他写的那幅字：

> 房间福地风亦暖
> 身居乐土苦也甜

然而，这样一点点甜也没有让他享受上。

在自己新盖的房子里住了一段时间后，尕布龙积劳成疾的肺气肿再度复发，而且越来越严重，晚上睡觉呼吸困难。一开始他还扛着，后来扛不住了，才到西宁检查治疗。

医生诊断，他再也不能回老家永丰村，再也回不到草原上去了。

他只能在梦里、在回忆中，骑着骏马，挥舞羊鞭，

盖好的小院又捐给了永丰村

The newly-built house was donated to Yongfeng village

324

which, in turn, symbolized his divine-like spirit.

It's the homeland that mesmerized him: pure, clean, exuding the faint scent of mud.

He even made a plan in his mind, considering constructing pens and purchasing cattle and sheep to start a demonstration project to breed and fatten cattle and sheep on Halejing Prairie. Additionally, he thought about planting trees around the courtyard and alongside the road.

After the completion of the construction of the house, Ma Wanli, Li Zhigang, and Jian Shunsheng, who worked with him for many years, came from Xining to congratulate him on moving into the new home. On that day, he was overjoyed and, rarely, showed his smiling face. However, he only accepted a piece of calligraphy and a painting in commemoration.

At his daughter Zhao Geli's home, I saw the calligraphy dedicated to Gabulong by Li Haiguan, the famous calligrapher of Qinghai Province.

Home built on happy land,

Warm is the wind through it blows;

Man lives on happy land,

Sweetness replaces sorrow.

Nonetheless, Gabulong did not even taste a tinge of such sweetness.

After living in the newly built house for only a short time, Gabulong relapsed into emphysema caused by constant overwork. His condition worsened to the point that he had difficulty breathing. At first he held up, enduring the agony alone, but later it became intolerable, and he went to Xining to receive treatment.

According to the diagnosis, he could neither return to his hometown Yongfeng village nor the prairie.

Only in his dreams and memories could he ride his horse, crack the whip, and wander on the prairie covered with Potentilla fruticosa shrubs.

However, he had already returned the house allocated to him in Xining. Where could he live now? The Qinghai Provincial People's Congress accommodated him with a small house to have him live in temporarily. Miao Fahai and Bsod Nams Tshe Ring, the two elderly men from Gabulong's hometown, took care of him. They cooked him simple meals and had him drink a bottle of yogurt occasionally.

新房建好后朋友们从西宁赶来给他道贺

After completing the construction of the house, friends from Xining came to congratulate Gabulong for moving into the new home

徜徉在开满金露梅的草原上。

可是，房子已经退了，他能住哪儿呢？省人大给他找了一小套普通的住房让他借住，家乡的苗发海和索南才让两位老人照顾他的起居，给他做一些他能吃的简单食物，偶尔尕布龙也喝一瓶酸奶。

两年后，知道自己不可能再回去了，他彻底失望，又把盖好的小院送给了家乡人民，办起了哈勒景金银滩农牧民合作医疗室。

在海北州工作的作家原上草曾经陪我去过那个小院，照壁上的一行红字"宅焕春光，恩泽铭记"即是沉淀在他内心对党、对养育了他的父老乡亲的一片感恩之情。

自此，两袖清风、廉洁奉公的尕布龙，什么也没有了，只剩下劳累辛苦了一辈子的病弱身躯。

永丰村原来的村支书尕巴含着眼泪说："尕布龙就是草原上的牦牛。双肩担着的是国事民情，怀里装的是家乡父老，容天纳地啊！"

2008 年 3 月，青海省政府授予尕布龙同志"西宁南北山绿化工程突出贡献奖"，那是他最后一次，在公开场合露面。

那幅照片上，身着中山装，戴着大红花的尕布龙白发苍苍，看上去有些虚弱、浮肿，但棱角分明的面庞上，依然无法抹去任何环境下都不能使

After two years of treatment, he was helpless and completely disappointed to learn that he could never go back his home. He then donated the newly-built house to people in his homeland, transforming it to Halejing Jinyintan Cooperative Medical Office for Farmers and Herdsmen.

Yuan Shangcao, a writer working in Haibei Tibetan autonomous prefecture, accompanied me to the courtyard. A line of red words, reading "Residence brimmed with spring scenery, gratitude remembered permanently," on the wall directly facing the gate of the house, fully conveyed how Gabulong felt indebted in the deep recesses of his mind to the party and the people of his homeland.

Henceforth, Gabulong, who remained uncorrupted and worked dutifully in the interest of the public during his tenure, left nothing but a frail body resulting from a lifetime of hard work.

Gaba, the previous village secretary of Yongfeng, said in tears, "Gabulong is the yak of the prairie, shouldering the affairs of the nation and the feelings of the public, remembering rural folk in his mind. He was a great blessing."

In March 2008, Qinghai Provincial People's Government honored Gabulong with an award for his outstanding contribution to the North and South Mountains Greening Campaign. It was his final public appearance.

In that picture, gray-haired Gabulong, wearing a big red flower on his Zhongshan suit, seemed frail and swollen, but on his angular face still displayed a determination and persistence that could not be wiped out under any circumstances.

Seeing him in the picture, I wanted to ask: How could you serve in a high position and stay uncorrupted? How could you hold power and extend kindness to all people, yet not grant any special treatment to your own family? How could you live in a small house but happily invite strange herdsmen to lodge? How could you reject all the pomp and ceremony and avoid being companied by a full entourage when you were on business? How could you spend all your wages on others but be reluctant to use any on yourself? why, as a high officer with an imposing physique do you lack the personal and familial affections like ordinary people? How could you only cherish the common people, loyalty to the party, and implicit faith in the noble ideals of communism, giving little thought to yourself? Why did you choose to plant trees on the mountains instead of living an easy life in retirement? Why did you prefer to live in solitude and keep

他改变的坚毅与执着。

面对照片上的他，我特别想问
问：您这一辈子为何身居高位，却
冰清玉洁、纤尘不染？为何手握
重权、恩惠四方，却不给家人半
点殊遇？为何独居小屋，却不厌其
烦地让家里住满了陌生的牧民？为
何下乡时绝不让人前呼后拥、深居
简出？又为何舍不得给自己花一分
钱，情愿把所有的工资用在别人身
上？为何身为高官，高大魁梧的身
躯，竟无平凡人的儿女私情？为何
心中只有百姓、只有对党的无比忠
诚，对共产主义理想信念的笃信追
求，唯独没有自己？而退休后，为
何不颐养天年还亲自上山种树？又
是为了什么，宁愿一生孤独、两袖
清风，却也要初心不改、使命不忘？

尕布龙不会写诗，不会吟诵，
甚至不会歌唱，他更没有用他自己
的名字，在荒丘之上刻下浸透着他
对这片山水情深意长的丝毫印记。
他长眠在南山脚下一处不甚耀眼
的地方，默默地凝望着深邃辽阔的
天空。

可在我心里，他是一位真正的
诗人，浪漫而多彩的诗人，地上的
王者！

也许有人认为，这样的指认对
他并不合适。可是，难道把一片不
毛之地变为苍翠绿地的梦想还不

2008年3月，青海省政府授予尕布龙"西宁南北山绿化工程突出贡献奖"

In March 2008, Qinghai Provincial People's Government honored Gabulong
with award for his outstanding contribution to the South and North Mountains
Greening Campaign

unsoiled in order to remain true to the original aspiration and keep the mission firmly in mind?

Gabulong could neither write poems nor recite them; he could not even sing. He did not carve his name on tHebarren land, impressing the world with his everlasting love to the land. He slept his long sleep in an inconspicuous area at the foot of the South Mountain, silently watching the expansive and deep sky.

Nonetheless, in my heart, he was a genuine poet, the king on the earth, infused with romanticism and richness.

Some people may think that such recognition is inappropriate. However, wasn't the dream of turning barren land into green romantic enough? Wasn't the act of welcoming people from the homeland into his home warm enough? Wasn't the feeling of drenching every fiber in nostalgia passionate enough? Wasn't the individual, undeterred by ice or snow, sandstorms or hardships, who brought hope to others, strong enough? Isn't he the person who prioritized the party's cause and the organization's trust, bringing human wisdom and collective thoughts into reality? Wasn't he the one with lofty ideals, humanistic sentiments, and a noble heart?"

If the mind obsessed with helping strangers and entrusting others with faith does not belong to poets and the bravery, then imitative poems, symbolic poems, abstract poems, and scam poets who build flowery words don't merit anything.

In Gabulong's life, simplicity and integrity were never a character pursuit, but natural qualities that could not be altered under any circumstances. It was not that he did not face the temptation of money. When he was in charge of husbandry, he had access to tens of millions of yuan in agricultural support funds every year. The ultimate decision in how to use the funds certainly lay with him, so a flood of people came and bribed him to sign on "papers." Gabulong rejected various temptations.

During the fifty years of his political career and among which he spent twenty-two years as a provincial leader, Gabulong never forgot that he was the son of herdsmen, never had any doubts in the party, and had never forsook the pursuit of cause and faith. He believed in communism. He promoted the unity of ethnic groups. He paid back the cultivation, protection, and trust that the party bestowed upon him.

What he created in his life was not a myth, what he accomplished in his life were not a series of events. Instead, he dedicated his whole life to improving people's

够浪漫吗？难道把一批批陌生的穷乡亲接到家里，视为亲人的举动还不够温暖？难道让自己的每一寸肌肤都浸满乡愁的情怀还不够火热？难道在冰雪中、在风沙中、在困苦中给人带来希望的人还不够强大？难道把党的事业、组织的重托，看得比天高、比命重，把人类的智慧、集体的思想靠自己单薄的力量付诸现实的人，不是一个最富有远大理想、人文情怀、王者之心的人？

如果在生活的岸边，用痴心浇灌陌生人的浓情，用实际行动把信念和希望交付于他人的这颗痴心，不是一位诗人的心、勇者的心。那么，那些模仿的诗，那些象征的诗，那些抽象的诗，以及用言语堆砌断句的伪诗人，便会显得一文不值。

在他的生活中，简朴和廉洁从来就不是一种追求的品格，而是一种自然而然的天生品质，一种任何环境都无法改变的本色。在他面前，不是没有过金钱的诱惑。他主抓农牧业时，每年有上千万元青海支农资金，如何使用，他当然有决定权。找他"批条子"的人络绎不绝，但无论什么样的诱惑，统统被他拒之门外……

他从政50年、在省级领导岗位上任职22年，从未忘记过自己是牧民的儿子，从未对党有过一丝一毫的怀疑，从未放弃过对事业对信念的追求。他信仰共产主义，他心中没有民族界限，他的胸怀宽广无比，他用生命报答了党对他的培养、爱护和信任。

他一生缔造的不是人间神话，也不是一瞬间翩然而至的一系列碎片，他是在用自己的行动帮助人类，如何直接而真实地抵达人生目标，做一个有道德的人。

一个真正有理想、有道德、有信念的人，是不图回报、没有诉求的，一个修养极深、无私坦荡的人是完美的。他认为，只有把自己全部的力量和精神致力于伟大的、为人民服务的事业当中，献身于人民、献身于社会，倾其所有无私奉献，才能显示出他生命所有的意义。

他创造了一个奇迹，人间的奇迹。

他坚守了一个高度，精神的高度。

他守护了一方净土，心灵的净土。

不管时代的潮流与风尚如何纷纭变化，他总是凭着自己身性的高洁，自律与操行，严格要求自己，不被世俗诱惑。

awareness of the eternal verity and truth of life, to strengthening moral integrity, and instructing people on how to reach the goal of life straightforwardly.

A man with ideals, morals, and faith is one that asks for nothing in return. A cultured gentleman is the embodiment of perfection. In Gabulong's opinion, only devoting oneself to the great cause of serving people and society wholeheartedly, both physically and spiritually, could one showcase the significance of life.

He created a myth, the myth of humans.

He held fast a height, the height of the spirit.

He preserved a pure land, the pure land of the soul.

No matter how the trends and customs change, Gabulong exercised strict self-discipline and rejected worldly temptations by relying on his noble and pure character.

It's not difficult for a person to a good deed, but it is another thing to consistently do good throughout one's life. He had been unintentionally guarding his natural purity and kindness, which formed his innermost core. For decades, he insisted on having famers and herdsmen live in his house so that they could have better access to medical care. He was not only offering them spiritual and material assistance, but more importantly, he forged closer connections with grassroots communities from pastoral areas and was able to understand their needs through this down-to-earth approach. Every year during Spring Festival, he took cadres to herd sheep for the villagers in order to remind himself not to lose the nature of the herdsmen, not to isolate himself from the people, not to forget that he was and always would be an ordinary working person. He, owing to his broad mind and kindness, generously forgave the young man who had whipped him, and even let him live in his house to help him solve problems in life. Gabulong, as an intelligent leader, had already understood the real meaning of poverty alleviation when he was in Henan County, Qinghai Province. He then conducted extensive research in pastoral areas and embarked on the poverty alleviation campaign by better learning the situations of the villagers, establishing schools, dealing with the supply of water and electricity, and facilitating transportation. During the annual two sessions, Gabulong, as the deputy director of the Standing Committee of the Qinghai Provincial People's Congress, served tea for the attending members, which was not to play the role of a servant, but to allow members from grassroots levels to relax and speak up for themselves. The National People's Congress should better represent the

一个人一辈子做一件好事并不难，难的是一辈子做好事。他天性里的那种纯洁、善良，始终被他无意地坚守着，那是他意识深处最顽强最坚固的核。他几十年如一日，坚持让农牧民住在家里，给他们求医看病创造条件，不是单纯为他们提供精神和物质关怀，而是通过这种紧接地气的方式，接触来自基层的群众，了解基层的信息，与农牧民保持亲密的关系。他每年春节带着村干部替村民放羊，是为了时刻提醒自己，不要失去牧民本色、不要脱离群众、不要忘记自己始终是一个劳动者。他宽厚地接纳了曾经用皮鞭抽打过他的那个人，让他住在自己家里，为他解决生活困难，表现出的是他宽阔的胸怀、仁慈的心。他长期深入农牧区调查研究、了解情况，采用"调庄"，办学校，解决水电、交通等问题让贫困地区脱贫致富，是因为这位朴实聪慧的蒙古族领导干部在河南县任职时，就已悟出扶贫工

2016年，尕布龙被中宣部追授"时代楷模"荣誉称号

In 2016, Gabulong posthumously awarded Role Model of the Age by the Publicity Department of the Central Committee of the CPC

public, accept supervision from the people, become the principal channel to reflect society and public opinions, and mobilize all positive factors to boost the development and stability of the nation.

Gabulong was a kind, broad-minded, and honest man, who actively spread the tolerance and strength of character of the Chinese nation. I could neither experiment with his working methods nor achieve what he had accomplished. However, we can at least educate a great number of party members and cadres about the life and deeds of Gabulong, enabling them to be inspired by his story.

The mud underneath the feet is groaning, a groan touched by Gabulong.

The birds in the sky are chirping, a chirp singing for his deeds.

He was like a flower blooming on a rock, though weathered by wind and rain, is still flourishing.

He was like a weather-beaten sculpture, setting up a monument that symbolized uprightness, selflessness, and purity.

His commendable spirit, represented by a standing megalith, is eternal.

He was a serious man who did not like to talk big or practice falsification. He was as simple as farmers, herdsmen, and migrant workers. He had committed himself to all the sheep, fields, trees and the whole prairie, gratified with the merriment of farmers and herdsmen.

There are many things that do not make sense, but in the unseen world, there must be resurrection of spirit.

Gabulong was unrepeatable, and we could not do what he had done. But, that will not hinder us to learn his spirit, celebrate his qualities, and explore the thought-provoking essence of his soul.

Gabulong has left us, however, his spiritual wealth, strong personality and every little thing he has conducted indelibly imprinted on the brains of the common people.

The Chinese people's approach to deal with the paradox of morality originates from the idea of the essential goodness of human nature. To be a good individual is fundamental, but to be a man with morality is not easy. To cope with the matters of morality entails the settlement of the issues of pre-morality, the reasons why to be a good man. Authentically, a man with morality does not search for fame and fortune, and he does not ask for anything in return.

作的真实含义。每年召开两会期间，作为省人大常委会副主任的他，亲自为参会人员送茶倒水，不是充当服务员的角色，而是让来自基层的人大代表放松心情，掏出心里的话。使人大更好地代表人民，接受人民的监督，成为联系群众、反映民意、解决矛盾的主要渠道，并调动一切积极因素，促进国家的稳定和发展。

他胸怀博大，忠诚耿直，用一颗仁慈、宽厚的心紧贴着大地，散播着中华民族的气度和风骨。这样的实践，这样的工作方法，我们无法体验、无法做到，但至少可以警醒广大的党员干部，至少可以让人们从中受到启发和教育。

脚下的泥土在呻吟，那是为他感动流泪！

天上的鸟儿在啁啾，那是为他抒情歌唱！

他像一块岩石上的花朵，任凭风吹雨打，依然兀自开放。

他像一尊饱经风霜的雕塑，立起了一座正直、无私、纯粹的丰碑。

他可贵的精神不朽，这不朽之碑是一块站起来的巨石。

他不苟言笑，不说大话，不讲虚套。朴实得像农民、牧人、民工。他一辈子为农牧民的欢笑而欣慰，为这块大地上的每一只羔羊、每一块农田、每一片草原、每一棵树苗倾注心血。

人生有许多说不透的事，但冥冥世界里，必有精神的复活。

尕布龙是不可复制的，我们也无法做到他能做到的。但是，这并不妨碍我们学习他的精神，传颂他的品质，探知他灵魂深处令人深思的精髓。

尕布龙同志离开了我们，然而，他留下的精神财富，坚守着的人格力量，做出的点点滴滴，都深深地烙在了老百姓的心坎上。

中国人解决道德的悖论，源于人性本善。做一个好人，是一个人的基本，但做一个有道德的人却非易事。道德的问题首先是要解决前道德的问题，为什么要做一个好人的问题。一个真正有道德的人是没有任何功利心的，是不图回报的。

有人曾经问尕布龙："你为什么要这样做，难道仅仅是因为一个好名声？"

他说："我要那个好名声干吗？我什么都不需要。"

这个什么都不要的人，就是一个有道德的人。

面对各种欲望，他把人类自身的尊严放到了第一位，以修身养性建立

Someone once asked Gabulong, "Why did you do all these things, just for a better reputation?"

He replied, "What could I do with better reputation? I ask for nothing."

This type of man who does not ask for anything is a man with morality.

Confronting with all kinds of temptations and desires, he placed dignity on the top of the list. He sought the spirit of benevolence by means of self-cultivation and held fast to the height of human spirit. This type of person is noble, pure, morally upright, dedicated to serving others, and has separated himself from vulgar interests. There are not many such people, but they surely exist. It's like the inability to become saints does not deny the existence of them.

He was in high office, but he maintained his morality and personality in this materialistic society. He was a fairly impartial, generously benevolent, and morally upright man, who dedicated his life in the service of the public and who dutifully and bravely performed official responsibilities. He was the symbolism of living stately in this time. People have the impression that there seems to be a distance between the ordinary and people like Gabulong, but I think such a distance should be named reverence.

As natives of Qinghai, and as Chinese, we should thank him.

As men with humanistic feelings in this world and on this earth, we should venerate him.

His personal charisma was irresistible, and his noble qualities will be remembered forever. His bravery, honesty, tenacity, intelligence, and his lifelong search into the ultimate significance and nature of the human spirit showcased that he was a man who highly esteemed life, felt empathy towards people, and had a keen sense of social responsibility. His worldviews and values convey distinct and distinguished meanings to modern people.

He deserves to be remembered and commended by every party member and every Chinese.

He made us believe that life resembled the echo, sending back what one gave.

Since then, Gabulong intermittently received treatment from the hospital.

Then, he was hospitalized.

The town fellows, Miao Fahai and Suonancairang, were with him all the time.

了作为人性的善念，坚守着人类精神的高度。这样的人就是一个高尚的人、一个纯粹的人、一个有道德的人、一个脱离了低级趣味的人、一个有益于人民的人。这样的人不多，但确实存在。就像我们虽然不能够成为圣人，但绝不能否认圣人的存在一样。

他手握重权，却能够在物欲横流的当代社会保持道德完美、人格独立。他廉洁奉公、勇于担当、乐于奉献，是一个内心饱满有力、公正无私、仁慈宽厚的人。在人们的印象中，普通人与这样的人似乎会产生距离，但我认为，这种距离应该叫崇敬。

作为青海人，作为中国人，我们得感谢他。

作为这个世界上，这个地球上拥有人文情怀的人，我们得敬仰他。

他的人格魅力无法抵挡，他的崇高品质光照千秋。他勇敢坦诚、光明磊落，乐观坚韧、智慧善良，他用一生寻求着生命的终极意义和人类精神的本质，他是一位敬重自己生命意义，对他人真正富有同情之感，对社会有责任心的人，他的世界观和价值立场在当下有着独特而鲜明的意义。

他值得每一个共产党员，每一个中国人铭记和赞美。

他让我们相信生命是一种回声，你释放什么，就能收获什么。

这之后，尕布龙时断时续地去医院治疗。

再后来，就住在了医院里。

一直守候在他身边的还是他的乡亲苗发海和索南才让。那时候，尕布龙的病越来越严重，已经没有能力照顾来自牧区的人，家里来的人也渐渐少了。中午吃过饭，尕布龙就拉着苗发海的手到街上散步。一边走，还一边说："让我拉着你的手，别把你丢了。"看见商店里卖酸奶的碗上写着"尕龙碗"，他会难得地露出浅浅的微笑，对身边的苗发海说："你看，现在人们吃的都是我的碗，龙碗！"苗发海和索南才让了解尕布龙，从心里敬重他。可是，他从不对他们倾诉他富有传奇色彩的往事，从不炫耀自己身居高位时的权力与风光，更不谈及自己的家人，自己心里的事。

他能说什么呢？是痛在心里早逝的儿子，半辈子患病在床的妻子华毛，下一辈侄女华毛措，女儿召格力，还是倒在身边的战友……

妻子华毛去世后，尕布龙一下子显得衰老了。他虽然一心扑在工作上，没有把妻子接到城里居住，平日里对妻子照顾得很少，可是有妻子的老家毕竟是温暖的，有妻子的家才是他真正的家。每次回到家里，他都会坐在

Gabulong got worse, unable to take care of people from pastoral areas, so fewer and fewer people came in. After lunch, Gabulong led Miao Fahai by the hand and took a walk on the streets. As they were strolling, Gabulong said, "Let me take your hand, or you might lose your way." Having seen the bowl in shops served yogurt named "Galong Bowl," he showed his rare smile, and said to Miao Fahai, "Look, now people are eating from my bowl, Long Bowl." Miao Fahai and Suonancairang knew Gabulong and held him in high regard from the bottom of their hearts. But, Gabulong had neither boasted about his legendary past nor paraded his power and prime time; he had never talked about his family or his thoughts.

What could he talk about? The bitterness of the early death of his son, of his bedridden wife who suffered diseases for most of her life, or his niece Huamaocuo, daughter Zhao Geli, or the comrades-in-arms who had left him forever...

After the death of his wife Huamao, Gabulong aged a lot. Although he had been preoccupied with his work, hadn't had his wife live in the city, and normally had cared little about her, the home with the wife is, after all, warm and where he truly belonged. Each time he went home, he would sit at the edge of the bed and talk with her. Even if there was not much to say, he would sit there silently for a while. Sometimes, his wife got mad at him. Instead of yelling back, he would listen and then take a walk outside. He knew the pain and trouble his wife had been suffering. After his wife passed away, Gabulong increasingly felt guilty and spoke even less.

Many years have passed; he could not bear to think about the hurts deep in his heart. On countless lonely nights, during innumerable exhausting, heartrending moments of darkness, he condensed his thoughts and feelings, and the tide of enthusiasm for the party, the people, and the lofty cause he believed in rushed through his veins. He understood that the years marched on relentlessly, and the whole world is in a state of flux, but he, as a party member, tenaciously persevered in assuming the overall responsibilities, just like his personality, upright and determined.

He kept quiet, enduring his illness with stoicism, enduring the eclipse of the body.

When he was seriously ill, many people wanted to pay him a visit and talk to him.

His nephew Nima Tshe Ring has been with him. His daughter Zhao Geli lived on the prairie and came to look after him weekly with bean flower and highland barley fried noodles. He could only eat these things.

炕沿上，陪着妻子说说话，即使没多少话，也会静静地坐一会儿。有时，妻子华毛朝他发脾气，他也只是沉默着，去院子外面走走，从不大声对妻子发火。他体谅妻子的苦楚。妻子去世后，他负疚的心情越来越沉重，话更少了。

许多年过去了，烙在他心头的这些伤痛，让他不敢想，也不忍想。在无数个寂寞的夜晚，无数个身心交瘁、痛不欲生的黑夜里，他把他的情、他的思，以及他血管里如激烈潮汐般滚烫的豪情，全都浓缩为对党、对人民的挚爱，全都献给了他所崇敬和信仰的党的事业。他知道世事变迁、岁月无情，也知道大千世界的种种变故。但是，他仍然顽强、坚定地履行着一个共产党员应该践行的责任。

他沉默着，一声不响地忍受着病痛的折磨，忍受着体力慢慢散去的夕阳。

重病期间，很多人想来看望他，跟他说说话。

侄子尼玛才仁守护在他身旁，女儿召格力住在草原上，一周来一趟，给他带来家乡的豆面和青稞炒面。他只能吃这些东西了。

可除了组织上和家里人，杨杰、杨牧飞和崔生满，南北山指挥部的同事们外，他谢绝所有探望，尤其谢绝带钱带物的人来探望。他说，那会使他不清净，他想静静地度过最后的时光。

医院的 202 病房，可以从后窗看见大寺沟。大寺沟的清晨和黄昏，还有沉浸在阳光、雨雾、冬雪里的道道山梁，陪伴了他两年。

即使神志不清，即使说不出一句话，他也一眼不眨地望着那重重山脊之上隐隐约约的树影，一直到永远闭上那双曾经那么明亮、那么执着的眼睛。

轻风拂过，树叶的清香让我想起尼采赞誉歌德的诗行：

　　做地上的王者——
　　这也是我和一切诗人的事业。

仰望天空，俯瞰大地。

为人民而努力工作，为人民付出一切，这就是尕布龙，这个真正的共产党员、真正的创造者。

Except his family members and people from the organization, like Yang Jie, Yang Mufei, Cui Shengman and collogues from the headquarters, he declined all the visits, particularly those that brought money and gifts. He said that would disturb him, and he wished to spend his last days in tranquility.

From the rear window of the ward 202, Dasigou could be seen. Its early mornings, sunsets, and ridges steeped in sunshine, mist and snow accompanied him for two years.

Even if he was unconscious, even if he was unable to speak, he stared without a blink at the vague outline of trees on the mountain until he eventually closed the eyes, eyes that had once been luminous and determined.

As the wind blew, the scent of leaves reminded me of the lines Nietzsche used to commend Goethe:

To be the king of the earth----
That is also my and all the poets' cause

Look up to the sky, look down upon the land.

Gabulong defined the real meaning of a party member and a creator by working hard for the interest of the people and by sacrificing everything for the people.

Just think about it: faced with such a selfless and fearless Mongolian man, can we not derive some inspiration on humanity, on the verity of life, and on the wonderful experiences of human life from his miraculous qualities and behaviors?

A writer said that breathtaking beauty is always new. However, the man and all the things the man did in this age are not new to me. In front of his lofty image, I was awed by his nobility of human nature. His story might be ordinary and trivial, but, how many people can really do what he did? And how many people can stick to and keep doing what he did?

Some people say that Gabulong as a provincial leader did not make much contribution. Others say that it went against the grain that he had invited total strangers into his home while ignoring his wife and his relatives. Some even say that he was playacting by leading a thrifty and frugal life, putting on a show by serving tea to members from grassroots levels during the two sessions, a role not fitting for the leadership position he should have been taking. His real contribution was the voluntary

想想看，在这样一位如此无私无畏的蒙古族汉子面前，是否能够让我们带着对人性的思考，对人类生存的真实性与人类生活中那些美好的经验，对他令人惊叹的品质与行为有所感悟呢？

惊心动魄的美总是陌生的。这是一位作家的话。但是，发生在我们这个时代的这件事、这个人，他所做的一切，对于我却没有丝毫的陌生感。他让我在他高大的形象面前，产生了一种令人屏息的惊叹，对于高贵的人性的叹息。他的故事可能平凡、琐碎，但是，又有多少人能够做到？又有多少人能够坚守？

有人说，作为省级领导，他没有做出太大的贡献；有人说，他把跟自己毫无瓜葛的人请到家里，却忽略了自己身边的亲属、自己的爱人，有些超乎常情；有些人说，他一生节约、艰苦朴素是做给别人看的，是在作秀；召开两会期间，他为来自基层的人大代表端茶倒水，完全不是一个省级领导应有的风范。要说他真正的贡献，其实就是他退休后义务植树，为西宁两座大山留下的层层绿林。

难道，他是一个现代社会的独行侠士，孤军奋战的堂吉诃德？

难道，他的所作所为不值得人们缅怀、铭记？

这些说法，有没有道理呢？在我们这样的时代，像尕布龙这样的人，究竟给了我们一种什么样的启示、什么样的思考？我们究竟应该学习他的什么精神？我们有没有理由可以相信，尕布龙无限忠诚的政治品格、敢于担当的责任意识、清正廉洁的公仆本色、无私奉献的崇高品质，一定会成为共产党员干部唯一的精神追求、价值理念、自觉行动，一定会在青海高原这片神圣的高天厚土传承下去呢？

野花还在盛开，哈勒景的河水欢畅无比愈加明亮清澈。新时代如此喧哗、如此壮阔，就让我们在静静地聆听中接受，在尕布龙承载着中华民族绵厚深沉、包含浓情的人性的力量中引发共鸣，在他朴实而又伟大的光辉中勇敢地向前走吧！

我坚信，这是人类可贵的品质，是中国人生生不息的力量！

尕布龙去世前一个星期，女儿召格力喂土豆给他吃。他用筷子夹起一片，手抖着，送到女儿嘴里断断续续地说："你回家，明后天，我也回老家去……"这是他说的最后一句话。

2011 年 10 月 8 日，曾任中共青海省委常委，青海省副省长，省第七

tree-planting activity in his retirement, transforming barren mountains into green.

Was he the lone ranger of the modern society, like Quixote fighting by himself alone?

Do his deeds not merit to be remembered forever?

Do these statements make any sense? In this age, what enlightenments and reflections could people like Gabulong drive us to obtain? What should we learn from his spirit? Whether or not we have reasons to believe that his loyal service, great sense of duty, devotion, selfless dedication, and upright character will become the only spirit pursued, valued and consciously acted upon by the whole party, and whether it will be passed down to from generation to generation on the extensive land of Qinghai Plateau.

Wildflowers are still in full bloom, and rivers running merrily through Halejing prairie are crystal clear. Let's accept the roaring and splendid age through proper listening; let's strike a chord with Gabulong who embodied the strength of humanity typical of the Chinese nation; let's strive forward under his shining example of simplicity and greatness.

This, I firmly believe, is humanity's commendable quality, and it is the power accountable for the flourishing of the Chinese.

One week prior to Gabulong's death, his daughter Zhao Geli fed him potatoes. He, with a trembling hand, picked one up with chopsticks, brought it to his daughter's mouth, and told her stutteringly, "You go home, and I will come tomorrow or the day after tomorrow..." These were his last words.

On October 8, 2011, Gabulong, who had been a member of the Standing Committee of the Qinghai Provincial Committee, and served as vice governor of Qinghai province, deputy director of the standing Committee of the 7th Qinghai Provincial People's Congress, vice chief commander of the North-South Mountain Reforesting Headquarters, a deputy to the 12th National Congress of the Communist Party of China, a member of the National Committee of the Chinese People's Political Consultative Conference, a deputy to the 5th and 7th Qinghai Provincial People's Congress, left us forever with profound attachment to his town people, his saplings, and Halejing prairie, which he could not look back any more.

This is the end of the story of Gabulong.

届人大常委会副主任，西宁市南北山绿化指挥部专职常务副总指挥，中共十二大代表，第八届全国政协委员，青海省第五届、第七届人大代表的尕布龙同志怀着对他的乡亲、他的树苗和他再也无法回望的哈勒景草原深深的眷恋离开了人世……

尕布龙的故事讲完了。

也许，再过几年，他的故事会成为一个传说、一个神话，遥不可及。

也许，人们不会再想起他。

但是，不管你信不信，他都是一个活生生存在过的人。不管你承认不承认，他都是青海高地上的一盏明灯，会努力冲破重重漠视他英魂的心房，照亮华夏大地！

早春的阳光照在高大的油松上，它们曾经是尕布龙亲手栽下的幼苗。此时，它们正紧紧相依相偎簇拥在他身旁。

这里是他培育起来的，南北山指挥部的第一个苗圃基地，也是他长眠的地方。不知何时，青海省林业部门把他的墓迁到了北山上。这里松柏苍翠，小鸟啾鸣，林中唯一一棵光滑、挺秀的白桦树静静地陪伴着他。

墓冢简单、朴素，一如他生前的质朴、严肃，又好似草原上的蒙古包，将在许多个白天、黑夜，与太阳、星星一起守护着他心心念念，变绿、变美的大山。

我和指挥部的白前主任、驾驶员应成红，在尕布龙墓前深深地鞠躬默悼，从心里感受着他那只属于高天厚土的英雄之气、磅礴胸怀，他那醇厚、亲切、永恒的爱。

这是一件多么值得庆幸的事。尕布龙的故事，尕布龙蓬勃而辽远的意志和情怀，终于在他晚年所钟情的南北两山上，留下了深刻而永远的印痕。

地球生命的化身是林地，超越世俗功利的，与生俱来的生之悲悯、爱之真诚催人奋进。在宁静而柔和的气氛中，高原古风之苍劲遗韵在不断延伸，这郁郁葱葱的青山绿水，生命之树，难道不值得一代人，甚至几代人耕耘播种？

尕布龙，当您在山林的怀抱中，瞩目远方，呼吸着山野甜美的气息。您可知，经过30年的奋战，西宁周边荒山的森林覆盖率已经从1989年的7.2%提高到了79%。2014年，根据北京中林联林业规划设计研究院有限

After several years, his story might become a legend and a myth, unreachable to people.

People may not remember him any more.

However, believe it or not, Gabulong was a man who truly lived in this earthly world. Whether one admits it or not, he will always be a beacon on the highlands of Qinghai, breaking through all disregard for the soul and illuminating the vast land of China.

The sunshine of the early spring shone on the tall pines, which were young saplings planted by Gabulong personally. Now, they snuggled together around him.

This is the place that he had cultivated, the first nursery garden of the North-South Mountain Reforesting Headquarters, and it is where he slept his long sleep. The Forestry Department of Qinghai Province had, on an unknown date, relocated his grave to the North Mountain, where green pines and cypress are abundant and birds are chirping happily. The only silver birch, smooth, tall, and green, keeps his company.

The grave is simple and plain, just like his lifestyle. In shape, it resembles the Mongolian yurt on a prairie. With each passing day and night, under the sun and stars in the sky, it will guard the mountains, which have been turning green and beautiful, and to which Gabulong had been deeply attached.

Bai Qian, the director of the headquarters, Ying Chenghong, the driver, and I stood in silent tribute and bowed in front of Gabulong's grave, feeling his heroism, his great mind, his sincere, amiable, and everlasting love from the bottom of the heart.

It is so fortunate that his story, will, and mind have left a lasting imprint on the North and South Mountains, the two that he fell in love with in his old age.

The forest is the personification of life on the earth. The inherent compassion for life and sincere love are beyond secularism, and they drive people forward. In the tranquil and gentle atmosphere, the spirit of Gabulong has been spreading. The lush mountains and green trees, symbols of life, are worthy of the dedication of one generation, even several generations, aren't they?

Gabulong, when you are in the embrace of the mountains and trees, looking far into the distance and breathing in the sweetness of the mountains, do you know that after thirty years of campaign, the forest coverage of barren mountains around Xining has risen to 79% from 7.2% in 1989. According to the estimation of Zhonglin Union

公司的评估，近年来，西宁山地形成的森林生态系统中，森林的水源涵养、固碳、滞尘等能力显著增强，生态价值不断体现。沟壑相连的南北两山与山下的湟水森林公园、大墩岭公园、石峡清风接壤，像孩子般急切地奔走在湟水河畔，吟唱着人间最生动的情歌。

大山沉默，崇高必将横扫一切雾霾风暴。

行者的精神不败，肉体不衰。一条银河的界限，即使不曾让人顿悟，也可从荒原踏来的足音中领略思想，得到启示。

如此看来，尕布龙没有走远，也不会成为远古神话。

你看那春雨在微风中展翅，绿叶在晴空下又一次复活。劳动者的想象力和植物神一般的生命力，使青海大地的春天更加动人。

Forestry Planning and Design Institute Limited Company in 2014, the mountainous region in Xining has successfully formed a forest ecosystem, which remarkably strengthened the capabilities like water conservation, carbon sequestration, and dust retention. Forest ecosystem has been gradually demonstrating its value. The North and South Mountains, full of ravines and gullies, border with Huangshui Forestry Park, Dadunlin Park and Shixiaqingfeng. They are like children running along tHebank of Huangshui, singing the most beautiful love song on the earth.

The mountain is silent; loftiness will finally sweep away smog and storm.

Gabulong's spirit is eternal, his body immortal. If the distance between the earth and galaxy had not thrown some light, we can derive certain enlightenment from the footsteps of tHebarren mountains.

In this case, Gabulong has not gone far, and he will not become an ancient myth someday.

The spring rain falls gently in the wind, green leaves reborn with life. The imagination of workers and the divine vitality of trees contribute to the beautiful spring of Qinghai.

尕布龙同志简历

1926年，尕布龙出生在青海省海北藏族自治州海晏县哈勒景蒙古族乡永丰村。

1950年，尕布龙被送到西北革命干部培训班学习。

1950年7月，分配到海晏县工作，先后担任了民政科副科长、县委统战部副部长。

1952年，随解放军一军，王震统帅的部队进驻西藏，当翻译。

1952年6月，加入中国共产党，投身到海晏县新牧区建设中。

1954年10月，被派往黄南藏族自治州河南县任县委书记处第一副书记、副县长。

1959年11月，被任命为河南县县委书记。

1960年6月，被任命为黄南州委副书记，河南县县委书记，并兼任河南县政协主席、县人民武装部政委。

1963年，当选为青海省委候补委员。

1965年12月，当选为青海贫下中农协会副主席。"文革"中受到冲击停止工作，回到家乡养病。

1968年2月，回到河南县，在黄南州革委会生产指挥部工作。

1970年7月，任青海省畜牧兽医总站革委会主任。

1971年2月，当选青海省委常委，兼畜牧局局长。

1977年12月，任青海省委常委、省革委会副主任。

Brief Timeline of Gabulong's Life

In 1926, Gabulong was born in Yongfeng Village, Halejing Mongolian Township, Haiyan County, Haibei Tibetan Autonomous Prefecture, Qinghai Province.

In 1950, he was sent to the Northwest Revolutionary Cadre Training Class to study.

In July, 1950, he was assigned to work in Haiyan County, and successively served as deputy section chief of the Civil Affairs Department and deputy director of the United Front Work Department of Haiyan County Party Committee.

In 1952, he went to Xizang as a translator and interpreter with the First Army of the People's Liberation Army, commander Wang Zhen's troops.

In June, 1952, he joined CPC and devoted himself to the construction of new pastoral areas in Haiyan County.

In October, 1954, he was dispatched to Henan County, Huangnan Tibetan Autonomous Prefecture, as the first deputy secretary and deputy county magistrate of the Secretariat of the County Party Committee.

In November, 1959, he was appointed as the secretary of Henan County Party Committee.

In June, 1960, he was appointed as deputy secretary of the Huangnan Prefecture Party Committee, secretary of the Henan County Party Committee, and concurrently served as the chairman of the Henan County Political Consultative Conference and the political commissar of the County People's Armed Forces Department.

1979 年 8 月，任青海省委常委、副省长。

1983 年 2 月，任青海省副省长。

1988 年 1 月，任第七届青海省人民代表大会委员会副主任、党组副书记。

1992 年，不再担任省人大常委会副主任职务。

1993 年，担任西宁市南北山绿化指挥部专职常务副总指挥。

2001 年 7 月，不再担任西宁市南北山绿化指挥部专职常务副总指挥。

2011 年 10 月 8 日，在西宁因病去世。

In 1963, he was elected as an alternate member of Qinghai Provincial Party Committee.

In December, 1965, he was elected as the vice chairman of Qinghai Association of Poor and Lower Middle Peasants. During the "Cultural Revolution", he was forced to stop working and returned to his hometown to recuperate.

In February, 1968, he went to Henan County to work in the production headquarters of the Revolutionary Committee of Huangnan Tibetan Autonomous Prefecture.

In July, 1970, he served as the director of the Revolutionary Committee of Qinghai General Station of Animal Husbandry and Veterinary.

In February, 1971, he was elected as a Standing Committee member of Qinghai Provincial Party Committee and director of Animal Husbandry Bureau.

In December, 1977, he served as Standing Committee member of Qinghai Provincial Party Committee and deputy director of Provincial Revolutionary Committee.

In August, 1979, he served as Standing Committee member and Vice Governor of Qinghai Province.

In February, 1983, he served as Vice Governor of Qinghai Province.

In January, 1988, he served as deputy director and deputy secretary of the Party Group of the Seventh Qinghai Provincial People's Congress.

In 1992, he retired from deputy director of the Standing Committee of the Provincial People's Congress.

In 1993, he served as the full-time executive deputy commander of Xining Nanshan Mountain and Beishan Mountain Greening Command.

In July, 2001, he retired from full-time executive deputy commander of Xining Nanshan Mountain and Beishan Mountain Greening Command.

On October 8th, 2011, he died of illness in Xining.

后　记

写下最后一段文字的时候，已是 2020 年的春天。

阳光和煦，我的心温润恬静。文字犹如春天的花叶，阳光弥漫的夏日，经历过黏稠、浓郁的日子后，在温暖斑驳的落英间，被慢慢清洗、梳理、打磨，最终成为描述尕布龙一生不同于寻常人的付出、幸福与美好的记录。

尕布龙是一位值得永远尊重和怀念的人。他一生朴实无华，淳朴得像牧民、农民；他心地善良，用一颗透明的金子般敞亮的心，体味着百姓的疾苦和冷暖；他心灵纯洁，没有任何私心杂念可以让他低下高贵的头颅；他精神高洁，没有什么贪欲可以让他放弃作为人的尊严。他不炫耀、不摆谱、不说大话，甚至不愿意以身份、官衔自居；他细心观察、深入实践，实实在在地为百姓办事，为青海的经济发展，人民的生活安康呕心沥血；他热情豁达、宽厚仁慈，用宽阔的胸怀拥抱着这个世界。

采访中，我天天在学习，天天在受教育。当我一次次寻觅他生活的足迹、他资助过的农舍乡亲，站在南北两山上，望着蓝天下那绿树缠绵的层层绿地时，心中总是激荡着对他充满疑惑、惊奇，同时又充满感激和难以表达的缅怀之情。有时，会情不自禁地流下热泪。

如果说作为一个党的高级领导干部，对于青海农牧业发展、生态经济建设做出一定贡献，上千次地深入农村牧区调查研究，为农牧民的温饱想方设法是义不容辞的责任；如果说在暴风雪肆虐，海拔接近 5000 米的五

Postscript

When I wrote the last paragraph, it was the spring of 2020.

With warm sunshine, my heart is full of warmth as well as quietness. Words are like the flowers and leaves in spring, and, after experiencing thick and rich days in sunny summer, they are slowly cleaned, combed, and polished, and finally become a record describing the efforts, happiness, and beauty of Gabulong, whose life is different from ordinary people.

Gabulong is a person who deserves to be respected and remembered forever. His life is simple and unpretentious, like a herder and a peasant. He was so kind and perceiving the suffering and warmth of the people. His soul was pure, and there is was no selfish distraction that could make him lower his noble head. His spirit was noble and pure, and no greed could make him throw away his dignity. He didn't show off or speak big words, and he even ignored his official status and titles. He carefully observed and practiced in depth so that he could work hard for the people and for the economic development of Qinghai Province. He was enthusiastic, open-minded, generous, and kind, and he was always embracing the world with a broad mind.

During the interview, I was studying and being educated every day. When I searched for the footprints of his life and visited the farmhouses he sponsored, and stood on the top of the North and South Mountains, looking at the green land under the blue sky, my heart was always filled with questions and surprises, gratitude and memories. Sometimes, I could not help tearing up.

As a senior leading cadre of the CPC, it was his responsibility to have farmers and herders sufficiently fed and clothed, make thousands of investigations and studies in rural and pastoral areas, and contribute to the development of Qinghai's agriculture, animal husbandry, and ecological

道梁指挥抗雪救灾取得的成绩,是他和日夜奋战在高山雪岭的英雄们共同创造的奇迹。那么,30年来他为农牧民免费提供食宿,把自己的小家变成大家,变成农牧民来省城求医看病的驿站、接触基层生活的工作方法,并从中倾听群众声音;退休之后,不贪图省级干部待遇,用16年时间义务植树,只剩下病弱身躯、抱憾而终的时候,又有哪一个人不为之心生感喟、唏嘘不已。

在深切的感受中,我常常眺望着近在眼前的茫茫大山出神。

2015年底,西宁市成为西北地区第一个获得"国家园林城市"和"国家森林城市"双荣誉的省会城市,这怎能不让人想起尕布龙手握铁锹,一身布衣,奔波在一道道山梁上的身影。

2019年,当南北山绿化指挥部完成南北山绿化工程空间数据,信息管理平台建设项目,初步实现空、天、地一体的绿化区资源数据的动态监测和管理,在2020年即将推进南北山多样性树种栽植,高质量发展的今天,又怎能不让人饮水思源,为曾经在这座山麓之上献出聪明才智,洒下过辛勤汗水的尕布龙心怀敬意?

这个世界上,每一个人都有追求幸福与快乐的权利,而每一个人对幸福与价值观的理解又是这样的不同。尕布龙神圣的情感、思想和创造力,血液和骨髓中苦苦撑持的理想,究竟对增进当下人们的思想、道德和利益,对人类的生存进步有多大意义?我们是否能够确定,一个人只有把全部的力量和精神致力于某一事业,将身心完全融入,为他人的幸福而快乐,达到忘我境界,才是一个对生命有喜悦感,有人性,继而有神性,活着有庄严感的人。

尕布龙是一位需要人们慢慢体会、细细琢磨、潜心学习的人。也许他一生所为并非惊天动地,但是,他于细微中见真情、于平凡中见伟大,连茶叶都舍不得喝却把工资省下来帮扶别人的点点滴滴。对家人亲属、工作人员严格要求,希望他们勤勉努力,靠劳动生活的教诲和言行,难道不值得每一个共产党员、每一个人扪心自问吗?

我是一位青海土生土长的作家。作为青海人,我有一颗热忱的心;作为一名写作者,我有责任,用我朴实的文字、细腻的感觉,表达我对他的尊敬和爱戴。以不取悦任何人的心理,以文学的方式,还原一个真实、朴素、感人的尕布龙。让更多的人相信,在我们的党员干部中,确实存在过这样

economy. In Wudaoliang Town, where the blizzard was raging, and the altitude is about 5,000 meters, he successfully directed the anti-snow work, which was a miracle created by the heroes who struggled day and night in the snowy mountains. However, over the course of thirty years, he had provided free food and lodging for farmers and herdsmen, opened his small house as a hotel to everyone who was going to see a doctor in the provincial capital, and listened to suggestions from people. After retiring, he did not covet the good treatment of provincial cadres, but spent sixteen years voluntarily planting trees. When he was seriously sick and died with regrets, who would not feel sorry for him?

In deep feeling, I often appreciate the vast mountains in front of me in a daze.

At the end of 2015, Xining City became the first provincial capital city in Northwest of China to win the double honors of "National Garden-like City" and "National Forest City." How can this not be reminiscent of Gabulong, a figure who is was dressed in coarse cloth, holding a spade in his hands and working hard on the mountain ridges?

In 2019, the North-South Mountain Reforesting Headquarters completed the spatial data of the greening project and established an informative management system, initially realizing the dynamic monitor and management of the resource data of the space, sky, and ground in the greening areas. In 2020, there will be diverse tree species planted on the North and South Mountains. Today, with the high-quality development, how can we not memorize Gabulong, who left his talents and sweat on this mountain?

In this world, everyone has the right to pursue happiness, and everyone's understanding of happiness is so different. Gabulong's emotions, thoughts, creativity, and ideals in his mind never fade. How important are they to the improvement of people's thinking, morals, and interests? And how valuable are they to the survival and progress of mankind? We are not sure that only a person who devotes all his strength and spirit to his career, fully integrates his body and mind to be happy for the happiness of others, and reaches the state of selflessness, can be regarded as one who has a sense of joy, humanity, divinity and solemnity in his life.

Gabulong is a person who needs to be slowly experienced, carefully pondered, and absorbed in learning. Perhaps what he did in his life was not world-shaking, but he could see the truth in the subtle and the great in the ordinary. He was even reluctant to buy some tea for himself, but he often saved his wages to help others. He was strict with his family, relatives and staff, hoping that they would work hard and live diligently. Isn't his story worthy of inspiring self-reflection?

I am a writer born and raised in Qinghai Province. As a native of Qinghai, I have so passionate a heart that I have the responsibility to express my respect and love for him with my simple words and

一位视"百姓为天、百姓为地"的领导干部。

他不是独行侠堂吉诃德，也不是孤立无依的苦行僧。实际上，辽阔的青海大地上，不知有多少默默奉献、缺氧不缺精神；缺优越条件、不缺坚强意志，把为人民分忧解难视为天职的基层干部、普通党员、先进人物。但令人揪心的是，现如今，不少人诚信缺失，不少官员贪污腐化，冲击道德底线，和尕布龙相比，真乃天上地下。

感谢原青海省委宣传部副部长杨自沿先生，时任青海省海北州委组织部部长、现任海北州政协主席的马丽雯女士对本书的创作曾经给予的帮助；感谢作家张守仁、王宗仁，我的挚友、亲人对我的勉励和支持。特别要提到的是，2016年几乎同一时间，百花文艺出版社总编辑汪惠仁老师，希望全力出版《尕布龙的高地》一书，实在是让我感到又高兴又遗憾。感谢《人民文学》杂志社施战军主编、宁小龄副主编对这部书稿给予的肯定；感谢青海人民出版社为此书的进一步修订和出版付出的努力，还要感谢尕布龙的亲属，以及往日和尕布龙共事过的同事、朋友在我采访中提供给我的无私帮助。书中的图片由尕布龙的女儿召格力、西宁市南北山绿化办公室，摄影家樊大新、刘建平、王凤博、周俊、李金潇等提供，在此一并致谢！

尕布龙是不可复制的，我们无法做到他做到的。但是，这并不妨碍我们学习和传播他的精神、探知他灵魂深处令人深思的精髓。期望读到这本书的读者，熟悉他的领导、朋友对书中存在的疏漏之处，提出宝贵意见，以便修订。

祈愿文学的力量，能使尕布龙强大的人格魅力和惊人操守，绵长流传。祈愿他的离去，他思想的光芒和生存的意义在把人类引向美好的同时，能给我们留下更多耐人寻味的东西！

辛 茜

2020 年 2 月 24 日

exquisite feelings. In a literary way, I tell a true, simple, and touching story of Gabulong objectively, letting more people believe that in our party, there was indeed such a leading cadre who regarded people as everything.

He is not the Lone Ranger Don Quixote, nor is he an isolated ascetic. In fact, there are many grassroots cadres, ordinary CPC members, and advanced figures on the vast land of Qinghai Province, who are devoting themselves to serve people silently. But what is worrying is that nowadays, some people lack integrity, and some officials are corrupt and have impinged on the bottom line of morality. Compared with Gabulong, it is really a world of difference.

I would like to take this chance to thank Mr. Yang Ziyan, former deputy director of Publicity Department of Qinghai Provincial Party Committee, and Ma Liwen, then head of Organization Department of Haibei Tibetan Autonomous Prefecture Committee of Qinghai Province, and now chairman of CPPCC of Haibei Tibetan Autonomous Prefecture, for their help when I was writing this book. Thank you to the two writers, Zhang Shouren and Wang Zongren. Thank you to my close friends and relatives for their encouragement and support. Thank you to Mr. Wang Huiren, the editor-in-chief of Baihua Literature and Art Publishing House, who in 2016, wanted to publish The Highlands of the Gabulong, which really made me feel pleased and sorry. Thanks also go to Shi Zhanjun, editor-in-chief and Ning Xiaoling, deputy editor-in-chief of People's Literature magazine, for their affirmation for this manuscript. Thank you to Qinghai People's Publishing House for its your efforts to revise and publish this book. I would also like to thank the relatives, colleagues, and friends of Gabulong for their selfless help in my interviews. The pictures in this book are provided by Gabulong's daughter Zhao Geli, Xining North-South Mountain Reforesting Headquarters, photographers Fan Daxin, Liu Jianping, Wang Fengbo, Zhou Jun, Li Jinxiao, etc. I would like to thank all of them!

Gagulong is unique. We can't redo what he did. However, this does not prevent us from learning and spreading his spirit and exploring the thought-provoking essence in his soul. It is expected that readers, including Gabulong's leaders and friends, can put forward valuable opinions and suggestions after reading this book for future revision.

Hopefully, the power of literature can spread Gabulong's charming personality and amazing ethics. May the brilliance of his thoughts and the meaning of his life could lead mankind to the better, leaving us more intriguing things!

Xin Qian

2020/02/24